SNAPSHOT

By
Samuel Kalliman

An Aspirations Media Publication

An Aspirations Media™ Publication
www.aspirationsmediainc.com

Copyright © 2006 by Samuel Kalliman
Cover by Dave Palumbo
Layout by Jennifer Rowell
Design: Jennifer Rowell and Samuel Kalliman

LIBRARY OF CONGRESS CONTROL NUMBER: 2006910487

IBSN: 978-09776043-4-0

MANUFACTURED IN THE UNITED STATES

First Printing December 2006

To Deborah, who always believed in it.
It stands as testimony to the power of your encouragement.

Acknowledgements

It's a long road from first draft to final published work—a very long road—and several individuals have been kind enough (and brutal enough, thankfully) to offer their editorial guidance along the way, without letting ties of family or friendship interfere with their objectivity. I offer my sincere thanks to Polly Nimmer, Thea Curtis, Sharron Kalliman—and, of course, my lovely wife Caroline, who read the manuscript through without complaint each time I edited it, offering helpful suggestions every time—and there were many, many edits.

My gratitude goes as well to Patricia Stively and E.D. Easley, of Creative Editing Solutions; and to Lee Corrie and the entire team at Aspirations Media, Inc., without whom my dream of a published novel would still be only that—a dream.

Wo viel Licht is, ist starker Schatten.
Where there is much light, there is deep shadow.

– *Johann Wolfgang von Goethe*

PROLOGUE

Joseph Running Bear knew instantly that something was wrong. Pushing through his front door, the middle-aged Blackfoot Indian stopped mid-stride, all senses alert. The room was pitch-black, as he had left it when he'd gone out. Running Bear stepped fully inside and pushed the door closed behind him. His hand trembled as he struck a match, touching it to the wick of a small oil lamp on a table by the door. The blazing lick flared upward, and he turned the knob on the lamp's base to trim the flame down to a dancing inch of light. He placed a sooty glass chimney over the flame, and the shadowy details of the room emerged, stark and pallid.

His meager furnishings appeared unchanged. The same dishes and the same unfinished pot of stew he had left sitting on the counter were still there. The same fire-spitting, maddeningly lovable woman was still gone. The cabinet doors were closed. Running Bear looked over the table and two chairs, then across to the closed closet behind them on the right—this was everything in the main room, and everything was just as it should be.

He looked again. Had one of the chairs been shifted? He couldn't remember—checking the seating arrangement had been the furthest thing from his thoughts when he'd left for the bar three hours ago.

1

Running Bear shifted his eyes to the door on the left, careful not to move his head. The door was open, as always, and the bedroom beyond was dark. He listened intently, hearing nothing. His brain struggled to process any aberration in the signals reaching it. He sniffed the air. Was there just a trace of unnatural scent? He sniffed again.

Yes—that was it. He couldn't put his finger on the scent, but there was something new in the nose, something that had never been there before. As if in confirmation, the faintest sound whispered in his ears, a momentary rustle. It came from the other room and it left no doubt. Something, or someone, was inside with him.

Running Bear wiped his hand over his mouth. If it was an animal, he could get it. But this was no animal; some primitive instinct told him that.

He stepped forward heavily. Not drunk—he was never drunk—but he was tipsy, as he was every evening about this time when he returned home with six whiskeys in his belly. His nightly campaign at the tavern was the one luxury he allowed himself in life, his compensation for a dirt-poor existence. Running Bear did not know his father, though he could trace his lineage back through his mother and grandmother to several Blackfoot chiefs. From them, his mother had told him often enough when he was young, he was descended from Napi himself, Old Man, the creator of the universe. Running Bear had never questioned this genealogy, but his circumstances left it apparent to him that his august heredity had failed—or, perhaps, been filtered over the generations through too many women—for the scant contents of his home were all he possessed in the world. Opportunities to lift himself out of his destitution had been less common than feathers on a bison, and the one true joy he had ever known had been cruelly snatched from him six months ago.

So it was that every evening he drove into town to anesthetize his mind against his poverty in general, and his sorrow for a dead wife specifically—and it was there at the bar, drowning in a swirl of memories, heartache, and recriminations, that he had failed to notice a silent figure sitting on each of three successive nights at three different tables, always in the shadows, a gaunt form whose departure from the bar had, every evening without exception, immediately followed Running Bear's own.

Running Bear's hands were wet with excitement and nervousness. The alcohol had dulled his fear, and he felt the thrill of the hunt, which he had not known for some time. His lips twisted into a smile, baring his yellowed teeth. Don't let him suspect that you know, he told himself. Walking into the center of the room, he set the oil lamp on the table with great care to its position, though with an air of nonchalance. He placed one hand on the lapel of his coat as if to remove it and went past the table to the closet door. Its handle turned easily in his grasp.

He wrenched the door open like lightning. His hand plunged inside and seized the double-barreled shotgun he kept loaded in the corner. Running Bear spun around and dropped to one knee behind the table, lashing out with the gun's muzzle. The oil lamp flew off the table, through the air and into the next room. It crashed to the floor and erupted in a puddle of flame, casting that room's visible interior into incandescent motion. Running Bear's shotgun continued forward and its barrel lined up on the entrance.

His mind was exuberant and his breath whistled fast through his teeth. "Come out," he called, smiling grimly. "Show me your hands. I won't shoot." A lie, but it sounded reassuring.

Moments went by, and no one emerged. Running Bear felt the perspiration on his brow. He said urgently, "You'll burn to death if you don't come out. I can fix the place easily before winter. You're trapped. Admit it. I swear I'll let you live."

Come out, sly one, he thought angrily. He didn't want to spend the summer rebuilding his bedroom, sleeping outside under a blanket every night. "I know you're there," he shouted. "Come out!"

There was a rustle. The little fire vanished, plunging the whole interior into absolute, smoky darkness. Running Bear realized the blanket from his bed had been thrown over the blaze and he tensed, raising himself a fraction of an inch. He sighted down the length of the gun in the darkness.

A powerful light snapped on in the doorway. Running Bear was temporarily blinded, but he knew his barrel was dead on. He drew a hasty gasp of air, clenched his teeth, and pulled the trigger.

Click.

His heart turned to lead in his throat. He cocked both hammers back, and pulled the trigger again. *Click, click.*

A rasping chuckle touched his ears.

"Excellently done my friend. Better than expected." The voice was a low, lightly accented snarl, with just a trace of humor sounding like it could vanish in a heartbeat.

Running Bear could barely get his own words out. "Who— who are you?"

"A hunter, like you," the voice said conversationally. "One ought not drink before killing. Sober, you might have understood by its weight that I had unloaded your weapon. I have watched you for several days."

"Me?" the Indian said nervously. "Why?" His mind was clearing as his eyes adjusted to the strong light. He remembered the gun's shells, and inched his rear foot back toward the closet, toward the heavy cardboard box on the floor.

The voice answered him. "Why? Because there is no man to miss you. No man would think to look for you for weeks—" there was a soft laugh, "—should you chance to disappear."

Running Bear's foot felt and hooked onto the box. His heart thumped very fast. Were his movements shielded by the table? Did the man even have a weapon?

Now Running Bear could just make out a very tall, thin silhouette framed in the doorway. The searchlight was waist-high in the man's left hand. Running Bear said hoarsely, "You have followed me to kill me?"

"Of course," the man's voice replied. It paused, and took on an almost kindly tone. "Be brave, and proud, my friend. Your death will be the most important event of your life. Momentous things will transpire because of it."

"What things?" Running Bear had the box almost beneath him. The fingers of his right hand groped for the lid and gently lifted it. His fingertip touched one of the shells.

The voice chuckled again, and Running Bear heard the smile in it. "A fighter to the last," it said. "You possess a rare single-mindedness which I admire. Do not be concerned with the future. It is enough you have fulfilled the purpose for which you were born." The man's right hand came up. It held some object, but all details were obscured behind the intense blazing eye of the light. The shadowy hand reached the man's face.

Running Bear threw himself hard to the side, breaking open the shotgun's action. His hand flew to the chamber and the shell slid home as he rolled over and came up, snapping the gun shut and sighting frantically down the barrel.

He heard a faint, distant *click*. That was all.

Instantly, agonizingly, a ferocious pain blossomed inside his skull and lanced outward. Running Bear screamed and doubled over, the force of a jackhammer pulsing in his head. His face burned excruciatingly. He reached up to touch his temple, and astonishment cut through his torment as he felt the left half of his skull fluctuate, and one large cavity bulged roundly outwards. It was the last sensation of his life. His body convulsed once, and his world exploded before him in a blaze of light and pain.

Crimson spattered against the wall. The shotgun clattered to the floor as the corpse sprawled downward, arms and legs askew. A little viscous pool trickled out from under the motionless head.

The tall man in the doorway walked forward until he stood over the body. *"The just man is taken away from before the face of evil,"* he quoted. "Though in truth I would not say you were exceedingly just."

He rolled the corpse over and regarded the messy remnants of what had been the back of the Indian's head. Dark fragments were scattered between the body and the wall.

The man's grating voice said, "Thank you, my friend." He rose, reaching a long hand down. Without effort, he dragged the limp body into the closet. Then he drew an additional shell from the box on the floor and kicked the remainder in beside the corpse. In a moment the shotgun was reloaded. The man set it in the corner of the closet where it had stood before, and closed the door.

He walked into the bedroom, checked to make sure the fire was indeed out, then shoved the remains of the oil lamp and the smoke-ridden blanket against the far wall. Returning to the main room, he turned his mind fully to the week ahead, anticipating, planning—big things, the culmination of all he had worked toward—but there was much work yet to be done.

Undaunted by the prospect of the windswept walk to the clearing a quarter-mile up the road where he had left his car, the man went to the front door and opened it, pausing for a last glance around. Satisfied, he extinguished his flashlight and stepped out into the cold, starry night.

CHAPTER 1

"Full house!"

Tom Connor's eyes narrowed as Nick Brenner slapped his cards onto the tabletop. *Thump.* Nick's face was alight with the cunning enthusiasm of a cat that had cornered not one, but two plump canaries.

Seated beside Tom and across from Nick in the lounge car of the swaying train, Percy Norton gave a snort of disapproval and waved a large hand at Nick. "Why is it that he never has to bluff?" Tom looked at his fair-haired friend. "Always a good hand, and always better than mine, when I have a good one."

Percy, a devoted eater who had never met a morsel he didn't like, and who had, in consequence, attained nearly the shape of the average bowling ball—or the average bowler, for that matter—dropped his cards in disgust and reached for the section of newspaper on his voluminous lap. His other hand closed on the remaining quarter of a cold roast-beef sandwich, his third of the evening. The sandwich, pale and soggy, had long ago given up the battle for freshness, but Percy took no notice and dispatched it in two bites.

Turning back to the table as his friend ate, Tom watched Nick rub his hands together and rake the dozen red, white, and blue chips into the heaping pile before him. Tom said thoughtfully, in answer to Percy's question, "Could be he's luckier than we are." He paused. "Or, could be he cheats." The innocent twinkle in his dark brown eyes and the easiness in his voice belied the incisive mind behind them that scrutinized every detail of Nick's reaction.

Nick's green eyes flinched, and the smile above his pointed jaw flickered out. His thin lips twisted and he brushed a hand through light brown hair. "You don't need to cheat when you're lucky," he said. "What's wrong, Tom? They don't teach poker at Stanford?"

"They must have dropped it from the curriculum," Tom said. "Who teaches it at Berkeley?"

"Me. In night school, among other things." Nick began to rock gently back and forth as his veneer of confidence returned. "You're just jealous, Tom; all those muscles and straight-A grades, but you can't win a hand of poker to save your life." He shook his head and looked from Tom to Percy. "Come on, both of you, quit belly-aching. It's only chips."

True, Tom thought, and I don't care enough about a lousy stack of chips to make a scene. But you dealt yourself two off the bottom last hand, and I've watched you do it all night.

The lounge car, situated squarely in the center of the Empire Builder to provide equal access to passengers on both ends of the long cross-country train, was almost deserted. The reflection of the soft interior lights on the windows, and the little brown curtains swinging back and forth on either side of those windows, obscured the dark contours speeding by, mile after mile of slumbering blackness, an emptiness broken only occasionally by the lights of some brief, anonymous town.

Tom yawned. The monotonous day of travel had begun so early that morning. Now the hypnotic rhythm of the wheels drumming along the tracks and the gentle motion of the car conspired together to weight his eyelids and dull his thoughts. A couple more hands, he decided, lose the rest of his dwindled pile to Nick, then off to bed. Ordinarily he would not have relished the thought of the tiny bunks in the sleeping cabin they had pooled their money to reserve, but he was so tired he no longer cared. Tomorrow they would reach the mountains—that was what mattered. His spirits lifted at the prospect.

Nick scooped up the cards. With a flourish, he reached over and opened his hand, letting them cascade to the table in front of Percy. "All right big guy, your deal. Make it a good one. You losers need to be put out of your misery." He drank deeply from a green bottle plucked unsteadily off the table before him, set it down again, and waited.

Percy ignored the cards. His eyes were on the newspaper folded in his corpulent hands. "Hey guys, listen to this—" He pointed at the page. "It says, and I quote, '*This Wednesday, after several grueling visits abroad and a series of hard-fought policy campaigns culminating in decisive victory over our current do-nothing Congress, the President of the United States will journey to Glacier National Park for a much-needed respite amidst the splendor of the Rocky Mountains. Asked about the risk of encountering grizzly bears or other predatory wildlife, the president replied that all beasts lurking in the wilds of Montana were entirely tame compared to their suit-wearing brethren in Washington—most of whom seemed to have snaked their way into the Legislature for the sole purpose of bogging the government down in endless partisan savagery.*'"

Percy looked up with a smile. "How about that? If we're lucky, we might get to see the president."

Tom grinned. "Nah. If he's lucky, he might get to see us."

"My mistake. Right you are." Percy let the paper fall. He reached for the cards, gave them a single shuffle, and dealt unhurriedly.

Tom picked up his hand. It could have been any one of twenty dealt to him that night. A two, a three, an eight, a jack, and a king. As indifferent as could be, and him left with not nearly enough chips to carry a successful bluff. He looked at the two faces staring back at him expectantly, and shrugged. "Pass."

Nick's smile was even broader now. "Bid fifty," he said, pushing five blue chips to the center.

Percy placed five blues of his own in the center. "I'm just about gone anyway."

Tom glanced sideways at Percy. There was a tinge of excitement in the large boy's voice, and the gleam in the bright blue eyes confirmed that his friend had drawn a strong hand. Tom looked up from his own weak cards to the center of the table—and what had abruptly become a large pot—and tossed them down. "I'm out," he said. He sat back against the hard bench seat and folded his arms.

"Ha! One down." Nick's head bobbed approval. "You're next, fatso."

Percy smiled bravely. "We'll see, big mouth. How many?"

"One." Nick flicked a single card off to the side of the table.

With a frown and slump of the shoulders suggesting new doubts about the strength of his hand, Percy dealt one card face down in front of Nick. He straightened again. "And I'll take one."

"You can't scare me like that," said Nick. "Fifty more."

Percy exhaled and tapped a finger against the tops of his cards. Tom expected the inevitable conclusion that it was better safe than sorry, but to his surprise, his friend smiled and pushed forward a stack of blues.

"Your fifty, and," Percy poked his remaining chips into the middle, "sixty more. That's everything."

Nick had ample reserves, though losing this round would dent them and might extend the game by several hands. Tom knew by his furrowed brow that he had not expected Percy to stay in, either.

Far ahead, the mournful wail of the Empire Builder's horn sounded, a solemn intonation from the soul of the long train in which swirled romance and tedium in equal parts. Tom had thought from the moment they'd boarded how it captured the essence of the journey perfectly.

"Another Podunk town," Nick said, sounding bored. He pointed out the window. Tom and Percy turned to look at the new cluster of lights, but in an instant Tom twisted back. He was too late for a good look; what had happened was already passed. Out of the periphery of his vision, he had seen, maybe just imagined, Nick's slender fingers darting to and from the sleeve above his left wrist. Quickly he counted the cards in Nick's hand. Only five, just what there should be. If Nick had executed a switch, he had done it well.

Percy faced the table again, and Nick said, "Call." He put in chips to match Percy's final raise. "I could just overbid and force you out, you know."

"Nice of you to give me a fighting chance," Percy said.

Sure it is, thought Tom. Still searching, his eyes went down to the table as Nick said, "So, show."

Then, too late, Tom knew. Over to the side, where they had all tossed their throwaways, eight cards sat in a loose pile. Tom added them up. His own worthless five, plus one from Nick and one from Percy made seven, leaving one extra—one Nick must have shunted away in the instant of replacing it with one from his sleeve.

"Hey...." Tom's face reddened in anger, but play was already progressing.

Percy, whose bet had been called, was first to display his cards. "Two pair—king high," he announced hopefully.

Nick drummed his thumbs on the table, finishing with a loud smack as he brought his entire hand down. "Boom! Three jacks!" He cackled at Percy's chagrined face, and swept up the pile of chips. "So long, tubby. You're done for the evening."

Percy muttered something unintelligible, and stood up, edging past Tom into the swaying aisle. "I think I'll grab an apple," he said.

"That's right. Always tastes better after the third one," Nick said, leering up at him. "Wait, that was sandwiches. Oh well, go on. Drown your sorrows in another round of food."

"You drown things in liquid, bonehead. Like you with your fourth bottle of beer." Percy shuffled stiffly toward a counter where a girl in a white button-down shirt dozed.

Nick turned to Tom. "Okay. We got rid of him. I'd like to say I was hunting big game now, but you haven't been dangerous all night. Your deal." Nick began to hum, shaking his head in time to the tune, drumming away with his fingers on the table.

Tom, incensed, pointed to the pile of exchanged cards, prepared to expose the ploy and demand a confession and apology.

Wait a minute, he thought. Perhaps there was a better way. His mind raced. Could it be done? A smile spread slowly over his face, and he leaned forward. Yes, he thought, much better to strike a searing blow—make him feel it. Give him a taste of what it's like, and maybe he'd be sorry for cheating and not just for being caught.

Tom gathered the cards lying face up in front of Nick's towers of chips, then Percy's losing hand, flipping them all over and mixing them before squaring them on top of the unused portion of the pack. He broke the deck and gave it two fast shuffles, setting it down as Percy returned. He leaned aside for his friend to clamber back into the long seat, and pointed at the napkin in Percy's hand. "Are you going to use that?"

"Apparently not," Percy said, and Tom took it. He pulled a pen from his trousers pocket, scribbled hastily on the napkin, then folded it up and replaced both items in the pocket.

Nick looked at his watch. "You planning to deal those cards tonight...?"

Tom said slowly, "You'll wish I hadn't dealt at all." He picked up the deck as Percy shot him a quizzical look.

Five cards flicked across the table, alternating with five into a stack before Tom. They picked up their hands. Tom studied his for a moment before looking up to see Nick's contemplative expression give way to a grin.

"Thirty," Nick said with conviction, pushing the chips into the center.

Tom waited, shaking his head, biting his lip—baiting the prey to the trap. He gave a barely audible sigh and said, "I'll stay in." With a hesitating motion, he put his own chips forward, and raised his eyebrows.

"Two cards," said Nick. He put his discards on the table as the train clattered over a junction. Tom dealt two off the top of the deck and pushed them across.

"Two for the dealer," he said evenly, drawing to restock his hand. "To you to bet."

They were interrupted by a soft, tired voice from the side of the table. The girl had walked over from behind her counter. She had black hair, a good figure, and a face that would have been pretty if it hadn't been ten o'clock at night and the end of a long shift. Smiling at Tom, she said, "Would you fellows like anything else? We're closing down soon."

"No, thank you," Tom said. Percy, mouth full of apple, shook his head.

Nick said, "No." He paused. "Not just now, anyway." His normally abrasive voice turned silky, and Tom watched his fingertips brush with faintest contact over the hand the girl had rested on the table. Nick asked, "Long day?"

She turned with a half smile. "Very long. Boring, but hey, it's a job. It lets me travel."

"I see what you mean," Nick said, nodding solemnly. "Nothing broadens the horizons like hours watching empty fields roll by on a dark night."

The girl drew herself up. "Listen, bozo—"

"I'm kidding," Nick winked at her disarmingly. "Do you get to change routes, stay at different cities between runs?"

She scoffed. "I wouldn't be here if I couldn't. The train is strictly routine after the first couple trips."

"Nothing but lots of work and confined spaces?" Nick's eyebrows arched.

"Mm-hmm. Work, sleep; quick meals when there's time. All day, looking after morons like you."

"Me? That doesn't sound boring at all."

The girl smiled, and Nick said, "Don't worry, we won't be long. I just have to finish trouncing this guy—" he pointed at Tom, "—and we'll be out of your hair." His mouth cocked in a wolfish grin. "And off to bed."

Tom shook his head and Percy rolled his eyes as Nick added, "Unless you'd let me buy you a drink when we're finished. Before you close, of course. We could sit upstairs in the observation car and talk a while."

"Before other things," Tom muttered. Nick fired an angry glance across at him, but the girl hadn't heard. She was smiling with her eyes more than her mouth when she said, "Maybe...."

Nick winked again and said, "I'll catch up with you in a few minutes, then."

She nodded slowly and moved away, and Tom saw her fingers touch Nick's. He wondered for the dozenth time what it was they all saw in Nick, why they never figured out this was just a variation on a routine, plied on every girl he met. They might think twice if they could hear him talk the next day.

Nick was talking now, in hushed tones. "You see that? She wants me—" he broke off, sneering. "Uh-oh, Tom, what's that I see in your eyes? Disapproval?" He laughed as Tom ground his teeth. "You're just mad 'cause you probably never got a girl in your life. Unlike me. You think it's all about true love, and honor, and all that crap." He glanced over his shoulder at the girl and leaned in close. "You're wrong, man. Don't be good—be bad. Be a rebel. Girls will jump in your lap if you just—"

"Oh, shut up," Tom said. His eyes blazed. "You know what I think, and I know what you think. You want them all, and I want just one. Stop blabbering and let's finish this hand."

Nick gestured expansively. "You have no clue how easy they all are. Good girls just take a few more daiquiris." He winked, then looked solemn. "World's passing you by, Tom. You're not bad looking. You could get some for yourself if you tried."

Tom's glare threatened, and Nick looked away and cleared his throat. "It was my bet, I believe." He counted the chips in Tom's stack and pushed forward seven blues. "The bell tolls for thee. Seventy. Come on, just throw 'em in. I've got things to do."

As Tom shoved his remaining chips into the middle, Nick moved to put his cards down.

"Hold it," Tom snapped, wanting more than anything, more than avenging the cheating or the endless taunts against Percy, to strike the leering expression off Nick's arrogant face, the glib words from his smirking mouth. "I'm going to raise you."

Nick laughed out loud. "You're out of chips, blind boy."

"Not chips. The real thing." Tom paused. His eyes riveted Nick's. "I'll raise you the cost of our dinners at the lodge. Loser buys the whole time. And that'll be you."

Fire burned in Nick's face; the thin mouth clenched, but he hesitated and glanced again at his hand.

Good, thought Tom. At last, he's the one who's sweating.

Then Tom wondered whether, at a budget of $15 per person for dinner each day, over eight days, he had pushed too hard.

Chips were one thing; money was another. Nick might simply fold.

Percy's hand stopped with the apple midway to his mouth. "Say, Tom, that's a lot. Do you know what you're doing?"

Tom nodded. His eyes didn't waver.

Nick shook his head. "I don't think..." his voice trailed off.

"What's the matter?" said Tom. "No guts?"

Nick's finger shot toward Percy's belly. He said angrily, "He's the one with guts. Something's not right—"

"You know what?" Tom said, leaning forward. "You've been talking all night about how good you are—how you're going to whip us all. Well, go ahead—now's your chance. Step up and call me, or else fold up and admit you can't win at this game except by cheating."

"Tom...." Percy's voice was strained, but suddenly Nick was also leaning in, focused, intent. He squinted at something behind Tom's shoulder and a puzzled expression crossed his face. Tom twisted away, caught himself, and turned back.

Nick's fingers, returning from his sleeve, settled to the table, and his cards were fluttering.

Oh, no, thought Tom, as Nick looked up, new confidence spreading across his face.

"All right, Tom," Nick said, straightening. "You're on. Dinners at the lodge. I'll call you. No—I'll raise you. Let's see..." he paused dramatically. "Breakfast, lunch, and dinner. Every meal, every day. Loser buys it all for everyone."

Now Tom's heart began to pound. A moment ago, he had been as sure of the outcome of the hand as he was that this train would never get anywhere on time. But now, if Nick had gotten him, had made a switch of some kind with the momentary distraction—had changed the rules Tom had already broken— perhaps he had better fold.

They had budgeted $30 per person, per day—more than $700 in all, real money to near-broke undergraduates. More than Tom could stand to lose, especially on something as worthless as a hand of poker. But dropping out after his angry stance and lashing words would be a heavy defeat. Even if he folded, he would still be responsible for the cost of the dinners, as initiator of the unconventional bet. His mind clouded with doubt.

Then he remembered what he had forgotten, and knew that unless Nick had somehow switched his entire hand in one go, it would be all right.

Staring back with all the cold steel he could put in his eyes, Tom said, "All right. I call." His voice was resolute. "Let's see them."

Nick's hand trembled a moment, then threw the cards down. "Three jacks." His voice could not mask his feverish tension. "Now show yours."

Tom kept his own expression in check as he drew one card from his hand and laid it slowly on the table.

"King." His eyes never left Nick's.

A second card. "Two kings." Tom paused for full impact. The rumble of the train seemed to have receded into the distance. Nick's eyes were glued to the rest of the cards in Tom's hand as Tom traced a finger over their tops. There were little beads of sweat on Nick's brow despite the cool air in the lounge car. Tom set the third card down and said softly, "Three kings."

Nick stared in frozen torture. His mouth moved soundlessly, then he shot to his feet with a sharp intake of air. "No! You— you're—"

The girl looked up from her counter, startled. Nick pointed at Tom, but Tom cut him off sharply. "Sit down. *Now.*"

Nick sat, face reddening as the full magnitude of his loss sank in.

Tom wiped moist palms on his trousers and reached into his pocket, pulling out the folded napkin. He tossed it across the table. "Read that."

Nick opened it, and his eyes darted over the scrawled text. Fury shone from his face as he looked up.

"Get the point?" Tom asked.

Nick rose, but did not answer. He rubbed the back of his neck and his eyes focused on Tom's. His breaths came and went in short bursts. Startling both Tom and Percy, he lunged around the table and seized Tom's collar between trembling white fingers. Percy jumped, and the girl behind the counter gasped and balled her hand before her mouth. Nick's face drew close to Tom's and he said, "Yes, Tom. I get the point. I won't forget this."

Tom's face was level. He said softly, "No, I don't think you will."

Nick's grip tightened, and his voice wavered. "You don't know me, Tom, not even a little. You don't want me for an enemy."

Tom reached up and felt for Nick's wrist. His fingers closed around it. "I don't want you for a friend," he said deliberately, as his fingertips bore in and Nick's eyes widened. Suddenly Tom clenched his fingers tight. Nick's pale hand slipped off the shirt, and Tom finished, "—unless you start acting like one." Slowly he pressed the captive wrist back toward Nick's chest. Nick strained with all his might, but he couldn't match Tom's strength and his hand curved back until it thumped against his own breastbone. Tom held it there motionless for three long seconds, and then released it.

Nick stepped back, massaging the flushed wrist as he glanced at the girl. Her surprise at the change in his demeanor was evident. He turned and glared at his traveling companions for a long, silent moment, then spun around, stalking through the aperture leading to the narrow stairway. They heard his angry tread rising upwards.

Percy exhaled, a drawn-out whoosh from between flared lips. He looked at Tom. "Did you have to make that bet? He doesn't take things like that too well."

"You're joking." Tom wiped a forearm over his face as his thumping heart began to calm.

Percy's face was pained. "I'm quite serious. What he said is true—you don't know him well. He has highs and lows, and they're both extreme. This loss is going to upset him, badly."

"Maybe it'll wake him up," Tom said.

"What do you mean?"

Tom pushed the crumpled napkin across the table. Percy picked it up, and his face fell further as he read the text scrawled across it.

"'Three kings beats three jacks. How do you like it?'" Percy looked up. "You knew what the hands would be?"

Tom nodded.

"You cheated? *You*, of all people?" Percy seemed genuinely shocked.

"To make a point. Only to make a point."

"But you *cheated*."

"Look," Tom said with exasperation. "A policeman drives through a red light when he's chasing a crook, doesn't he? Nick was cheating throughout the game. You yourself asked why he always got the good hands."

"I knew perfectly well how he got the good hands," Percy said. "He always cheats."

Tom looked at Percy in surprise. "It doesn't bother you?"

"Why should it? It's just a game. He's got some sort of compulsive drive in him to win at everything: cards, girls, even school exams. He hates to lose, more than anything, more than anyone. It doesn't matter to me whether he comes out ahead at those things—at least when he wins, he's up and not down." Percy tapped his skull, "I don't think his problems are all his own doing; more like some kind of psychological disorder;

bi-polarity or whatever they call it. He needs support, not corrections officers."

Tom shook his head. "He needs a kick in the rear end, and so do you, talking like that. He's sound enough to answer for his actions without hiding behind a lot of psychological mumbo-jumbo."

"He needs friends," Percy said earnestly. "He's always on edge, and you've just poked him in the eye to the tune of hundreds of dollars. He'll be fuming about that now, but later, when the girl doesn't show up and he decides you also wrecked his chances with her...." His voice turned moody. "It could mean trouble. Wouldn't be the first time. You're lucky, Tom, if all he does is get into a funk for a while. My advice is, watch out."

Tom started to reply, then shook his head.

They sat for a time listening to the clatter of the wheels on the tracks below. The girl walked by and asked them to leave. She didn't mention Nick, and they did not see her again that night.

CHAPTER
2

At the rim of Glacier National Park, just over the boundary dividing the park from the adjoining reservation of the Blackfoot tribe, sits East Glacier, a small village fronted by a line of shops, motels, and restaurants paralleling the railroad tracks. This row of buildings constitutes the town most visitors take home in their memories, as few ever venture beyond to the several square blocks of dirty white homes belonging to the town's 400 residents—and their many dogs, most of which are permitted to roam the streets at will, marking territory and searching for friendly hands and lobbed branches.

Across the train tracks, behind a low-slung railway station, an expanse of gardens, fields and woods sweeps up 100 yards to Glacier Park Lodge. Built in the same style as other early 20th century Park lodges, the lodge combines the American log cabin with the Swiss chalet on a grand scale. At the time of its construction, the Indians, duly impressed by the girth of the great Douglas firs used throughout, christened it the "big tree lodge," and this is still its most appropriate name today.

Behind the lodge, vast plains from the east rise up through deep green forests to meet the Rocky Mountains, whose peaks tower thousands of feet above the surrounding countryside. This wall of stone was once a nearly impenetrable barrier, shielding the westward lands from all but the hardiest of explorers. Civilization dauntlessly progresses, however; that wall has long been breached, its heights scaled, the lands it once guarded, settled.

Today, twice a day, the Empire Builder roars into the little East Glacier rail depot, arriving in the morning from the West and in the evening from the East, delivering its cargo of expensively-outfitted professional tourists, rag-clad backpackers, and harried parents struggling to restrain children exuberant at finally escaping the long train's confines. With hardly a pause, the train collects its load of wistful travelers bound for home and sounds its loud whistle as it picks up speed and roars out again.

The morning after the poker game, with only a fitful night's sleep behind him, Tom Connor stepped from the growling train to the concrete platform to stare up in delight at the panorama before him. For minutes he remained quite still, enthralled, until Percy jabbed him in the ribs. "Are you going to stand there all day?"

"I'll bet I could," Tom said, smiling as a gust of clean, cold air blew over the jumble of milling passengers. "Mountains are what we don't have enough of back home. They're beautiful."

"You've done enough betting for a while. Let's go, I'm freezing. I can't believe it's the end of June." Percy, unlike Tom and Nick who both wore torso-length backpacks, had brought a suitcase, and Tom guessed his warm clothes were buried at the bottom of it. Percy was never one for planning ahead.

They moved around the side of the station into view of Glacier Park Lodge. Nick was already fifty yards ahead of them, walking fast up the long path toward it.

Percy pointed. "He's still sore. Hardly said a word all morning."

"I noticed," Tom said. "Loudest silence I ever heard. I'm hoping he'll get over it once we're out there," he gestured toward the mountains. "In the meantime, the less he talks, the happier everyone else is."

22

They both chuckled, and Percy said, "I have to ask: how did you rig those cards last night?"

Tom wagged his index finger. "Sorry. You know a good magician never reveals his secrets."

"Someone did, to you, once upon a time."

"True," Tom smiled. "All right. If you remember back to the hand before my deal, you had ended up with two kings and two of something else. I had one king in my own hand, and Nick had three jacks. I just stacked the six cards together, jack, king, jack, king, jack, king—very quickly, of course. I had also been holding the fourth jack, so I put that on the bottom of the deck to make sure he couldn't draw it. He almost scared me into forgetting it, though. Anyway, when I shuffled, I made sure the top six cards stayed together on top, and that was that. I didn't offer the deck for a cut, so they didn't get buried. He didn't notice. I'd never seen him try it, so I didn't think he'd know it when I tried it."

Percy shook his head. "The things you come up with...." He clapped his friend on the shoulder. "Come on, it's cold out here. Last one to the lodge is a rotten egg." He tore away, across the intervening road, through a small turnstile, and up the path through the gardens, his suitcase flailing wildly.

Tom grinned and broke into a run. Even with his backpack he easily outpaced the lumbering Percy. Halfway along the path, Nick looked up, startled out of his melancholy by the passage of his two companions in their headlong dash.

Tom reached the lodge's arching entrance and stopped, panting. A giant, garishly-colored totem pole scowled down at him as if to disapprove of the unruly proceedings. Tom scowled back good-naturedly and turned, keeping the stern look on his face as Percy thundered up. Tom held up a hand. "Stop there, friend. No rotten eggs inside this lodge."

Percy looked past him with wide-eyed surprise on his face. "Will you look at that!" Tom turned, saw nothing, and looked back as Percy slipped behind him. *"The race is not to the swift,"* Percy quoted cheerily, disappearing through the door.

"Obviously not," Tom called back. Stamping his foot, he decided he must stop falling for that gambit.

Nick reached the entrance, and walked past Tom in silence.

Tom called to him, "Nick!"

Nick stopped, but did not turn.

"Look. About last night, it was just a game," said Tom. "I was pretty raw then, but it's done now. Forget the cards and the bet. I'll pay my own grocery bill."

"Sure," Nick said coldly. He continued forward, past a doorman's stand just inside the large doors, to join Percy at the front desk.

Tom shook his head and followed his companions out of the cool air into the warmth of the lodge. By the time he reached the long wooden service counter, Percy had finished checking in.

Percy held up a key. "One only." He grinned. "Room's in my name, but we can negotiate. Who gets it?"

Tom motioned to Nick, and Percy held out the key. Nick snatched it and turned away.

They walked into the lobby, a vast atrium surrounded above by two stories of balcony-fronted walkways, and capped at the top by a wide skylight. To the left, at ground level, several people sat in comfortable padded armchairs around a cavernous hearth and a cheery crackling fire. Behind them was an elegant but aged grand piano, and, farther back, discrete floor displays elaborating the history and construction of the lodge. More chairs and couches were arranged throughout the lobby, and on the far right two doors opened into a woodsy, sumptuously adorned, undoubtedly expensive restaurant.

Encased in a box of glass directly before them, a stuffed mountain goat with long curling horns gazed through unseeing black eyes out the open entrance.

"Must be the welcoming committee," smiled Percy.

"Probably the oldest resident in these parts," Tom said, "after that piano."

Each of the levels ringing the atrium's perimeter was set back from the one below. Standing in the center of it all, Tom felt like an ant at the bottom of a colossal square stairway, with steps going up on all four sides. Their room was on the second floor, and Tom led the trio past a long gift shop to a recessed staircase.

They climbed two flights of wooden stairs and emerged onto the second floor balcony. As they walked along, Tom looked at the various oil paintings in ornate frames depicting rushing streams, towering mountains, and different species of wildlife. Most were exquisitely detailed, and very beautiful.

They turned a corner, passed several doorways, and halted outside their room, almost directly opposite the large entranceway one floor down. Nick fitted the key to the lock, opened the door, and they entered.

The room was small and comfortable in a plain sort of way that seemed appropriate to the lodge's décor. The headboard of the single bed was pressed against one wall, and its blankets sported Blackfoot designs in orange and brown. Next to the bed, a brown shaded lamp stood on top of a squat bureau. Light streamed through open-shuttered windows, illuminating tan carpeting, and overhead pipes painted white to match the ceiling ran from the small bathroom out through the wall over the door to join the main lines somewhere beyond.

"Let's flip coins to see who takes the bed first," Tom said with a covert glance at Nick.

Nick didn't answer, but dug sullenly into his pocket. They all produced quarters and tossed them in the air. Percy caught his and held it out. Heads. Nick showed tails.

"Well, it isn't me," Tom said amiably. "Odd man wins." He hoped his coin would show heads. To his relief, it did.

A smile darted across Nick's face for the first time that day, and he laid his backpack on the bed. He unhooked his sleeping bag from clasps at the bottom of the pack, tossed it into the closet, and said, "So, what's the plan?"

Tom paused from unrolling his own bag out on the floor, and said, "I vote we explore the countryside. Can't see it at night, and we can give the lodge a real going-over when we get back."

The others agreed, and ten minutes later had their gear unpacked and their canteens filled from the sink.

They went downstairs. Tom picked up a trail map from the front desk and bought several turkey sandwiches from the shop behind the stuffed goat. They went out the main entrance and waited as Tom read the map. He pointed right. "There's a deep gorge with a creek running through it over there. You can see the railroad bridge crossing over it. Looks like a dead end." He jerked his head left. "Let's go this way."

They took the path down to the far end of the lodge and stopped at an imposing row of bright red buses with black canvas tops.

"I read about these," said Percy. "They're tour buses. People ride them over a road running through the mountains from one side of the park to the other, the Going-to-the-Sun Road. The buses got called 'jammers' because the drivers used to jam their gears going up and down the steep inclines. They have automatic transmissions now."

"I've heard of the road," said Tom. "It's supposed to be an incredible view, and a great engineering feat."

"Well, you'd know about that, being the engineer of the group," Percy said. "But the buses don't seem to be running much today."

"The road was just opened. Sixty feet of snow every winter, and it doesn't get cleared till now. They may not be touring yet."

As Tom spoke, a group of chattering tourists from the lodge rounded the corner and stopped at the first bus in the row.

"You were saying?" Nick gibed. A man, obviously the driver, wearing a brown jacket with dangling name badge, white shirt and dark tie, joined the group. Everyone clambered aboard. Each of the bus's five passenger's rows had an individual door nestled into the right-hand sidewall. The bench seats inside spanned the bus's width with no aisle dividing them. The engine fired smartly, and the vehicle lumbered off down the winding road. The people inside looked happy and snatches of singsong voices carried back in the breeze.

"I guess the buses could be touring," Tom said. They laughed, and turned down the trail leading away from the buildings. It wound through several holes of a golf course, and past a large enclosed area and a few lone houses. Then all vestiges of civilization disappeared, except the path itself, and they spent the rest of the morning roaming the wilderness with all the gusto of three college students unleashing a semester's pent-up energy on a long-awaited break. They covered several miles at a good pace, thrilled by the endless sea of trees, the calm blue lakes and briskly flowing streams, the little pink, orange, and violet wildflowers, and the soaring hills—stark and gray, foreboding and majestic—nature in its most awesome, rugged glory.

The day, having begun cool, quickly warmed. Within an hour all three had pulled off their jackets and overshirts. A little after noon, breathing hard with sweat dripping down their foreheads, they stopped by a quiet lake in the woods with a steep hill rising up the other side. White-capped mountains peered over the top of the hill, and they devoured their sandwiches at the shore of the lake with their bare feet dangling in its icy water. Tom doused his sandwich with plenty of mustard, washing it down afterward with a deep gulp from his canteen.

Lunch accomplished, strength restored, they packed their trash and prepared to leave. As they rose, Nick's foot lanced out at just the right moment to trip Percy, who fell squarely on top of Tom. Nick's protestations of innocence, proclaimed through wailing laughter, went unheeded, and the ensuing three-way wrestling match ended two minutes later with Tom on top of the pile and all three knee-deep in the lake and soaked through.

The water felt good under what was by now a very hot sun, and they began to work their way back down the trail toward the lodge, talking, laughing, dueling with branches picked off the ground, shoving each other back and forth, talking some more, as their clothes slowly dried and the sun sank toward the horizon.

The afternoon was fully spent when they walked up the paved path leading to the lodge's entrance. The sun, now orange, just touched the peak of the tallest mountain behind the dark forest.

Tom had fallen a few steps behind the others, slowing for a last look at the magnificent view. Twisted around, not watching the path ahead, he was startled as he collided with his two stationary companions outside the entrance. He looked to see what had brought them to a halt, and immediately his own movement ceased.

A lone figure was walking up the path from the opposite direction, a girl, perhaps twenty years old. She had a vigor in her stride, and a trim figure that suggested radiant health, but it was her face that stopped all three in their tracks. Deep blue eyes gazed at them, alive and intense, their cool blaze softened by a pretty mouth that curved into a smile as she saw their mild disarray. Her cheeks were pink in the brisk air, and her long fair hair, lifted gently by the wind, was burnished bronze in the dying light.

Out of their jumble, the three young men all managed to gesture gallantly at the door. With a hint of a curtsy and a small chuckle, the girl flitted past them into the lodge.

"Wow," said Nick as his eyes followed her inside. "I'd like to—"

"Quiet," said Tom. "Don't spoil the moment."

He wondered who the girl was, and where she was from—and then, as Nick licked his lips, how she might react to his traveling companion's ploys. Tom had felt a strong sense of character in the level appraisal of the girl's eyes, and in the firmness of her mouth before it had broken into what he had to admit was a beautiful smile. She would not be easily conquered—at least, he conceded, that was what he wanted to think.

They returned to their room long enough to deposit their gear from the hike and clean up. Nick hummed to himself as he combed his hair and brushed his teeth, as Tom and Percy tried not to laugh. Then they went down to the cheerful atrium and sat by the fireplace, remaining there for some time as they talked over the day. The girl was nowhere to be seen.

Nick stood up and excused himself. They watched him go, and Percy said, "He's really picked up again since we went out this morning."

"And another notch or two since running into *her*," Tom said.

"Can you blame him?"

"No," Tom shook his head. "I'm impressed myself. But watching Nick Brenner is like watching a panther stalk a gazelle. You want to warn the gazelle."

"Ha! Chivalry lives on. Why, Tom, a girl that turns your stubborn head?" Percy grinned. "Honestly, I'd like to join the hunt myself. But girls like that never go for fat guys like me." He pulled himself to his feet. "Want a beer?"

"No, thanks." Tom sat back in the soft padded chair as Percy ambled off. He stared into the fire, turning the last twenty-four hours over in his mind, willing himself to think of something, anything, besides the girl, and failing. Where had she gone? Would he see her again?

He blinked. It burst through his introspection as he looked up that, of all the crazy things, she was right there, behind the chairs on the other side of the fire—and she was looking across at him.

His heart leapt and his throat went dry. He was glad she was far enough away that he did not have to speak. Realizing his face was grim, he pulled his mouth into a smile. The girl flashed a warm smile in return and then looked away shyly.

Tom waited. Sure enough, her head tilted sideways and her eyes looked back at his. His brain cut through his excitement, prodding him to get moving. He started to get up, but at that moment Nick strolled into view. Nick walked right up to the girl, and his hand touched her arm. Her head turned. Nick's mouth opened with some kind of introductory remark, and she smiled. Then Nick was smiling too, and he gestured toward the restaurant. The girl shook her head, igniting momentary hope in Tom. Nick said something else and raised his hands, sweeping one of them in a circle that encompassed most of the lobby. The girl shrugged, glanced reluctantly back at Tom, and nodded. The two of them moved off, Nick's hand again reaching for her elbow.

Tom felt his face twist into a scowl as he began to seethe inside. Stop it, he thought angrily. Nick got there before you, that's all. Tom shook his head to clear it, and was glad when Percy reappeared and sat down.

"Percy, did you see that?" he asked.

"What? The giant bear fall on that guy in the gift shop? It was pretty good," Percy chuckled.

"No, numbskull—Nick."

"Oh. Uh-huh. I saw him. With her." Percy eyed Tom speculatively. "Doesn't let the grass grow under his feet, does he?"

Tom stood up suddenly, determined to shake himself out of it, right now, before it took hold. He looked around.

After a moment, he spied the old grand piano sitting in the shadows near the fireplace. Why not? It was years since he had played anything, but he knew a little about music, and had taken piano lessons for a couple of years, long ago.

Tom walked over to the stately object. Were guests allowed to play? He decided he didn't care, and sat down, fingering a C-chord. He pressed the keys lightly. The muscles in his stomach tightened as sound boomed out from beneath the heavy cover, echoing into the vast atrium. Several people looked up. Tom saw an elderly man nudge his wife. They folded the papers they had been reading and sat up expectantly.

Committed now, Tom knew he'd better play like he meant it, and he drew a deep breath and plunged headlong into a spirited rendition of Joplin's *Entertainer*. He had always preferred ragtime and had learned several songs of that vein fairly well, but now his fingers felt like lead and as fat as, well, Percy's. He cringed as he hit several sour notes in succession, but played through them and, risking a glance upward, was encouraged by several approving smiles. Here and there along the balconies ringing the atrium, people had ventured out of their rooms and were leaning on the rails, watching him.

By the time he neared the end of the song, Tom's pounding heart had subsided, and his fingers were flying more easily over the keys. Feeling good again, the gloom evaporating from his system with every joyful note, he wrung as much drama as he could from the ending, and finished strong and loud.

A hearty round of applause filled the air around him, and he could not stop the grin breaking out on his face. Someone cried "More!" from off to his right, and as he looked that way he heard another voice behind his left shoulder.

"That was wonderful."

Tom twisted his head around, and started.

It was her. The girl. Blond, beautiful, and her blue eyes were looking right into his.

Tom's mouth was dry again. "Thanks," he murmured.

"Seriously, you played that very well. Where did you learn?" Her voice was soft and interested.

Tom cleared his throat. "My parents made me take lessons when I was little. I hated it, mostly, but got to like ragtime. It's fun to play and fun to listen to. Since then, I've fiddled around with it on my own. Do you play?"

"A little."

"By ear?" Tom asked.

She nodded.

Impulsively, Tom gestured toward the right half of the bench. "Then sit down and help me play a few tunes."

The girl did not seem taken aback by the sudden offer, but smiled and walked around the bench to sit beside him. Tom caught a hint of sweet apple scent from the girl's hair, and then she asked, "What will we play? I'm afraid I don't know any duets."

"No?" Tom smiled.

She shook her head. "I never had anyone else to play with."

"Well, anything then. Something people have heard before. *Baby Face*, key of C. Here we go."

Without waiting for a reply, he gave a short lead-in, and to his surprise, the girl jumped in without missing a beat.

Tom played bass notes with his left hand and chords with his right, creating a generic folk-ragtime sound that formed a structure for the melody. From the corner of his eyes he watched the girl's quick hands next to his, dancing over the keys, bringing out the melody in clear, fluid notes that held a smoothness altogether lacking in his own playing. As they moved into a second verse, she added first one harmony part, then two, and as Tom listened to the skillful blends, he realized that knowing a little about music meant a lot more for this girl than it did for him.

He said softly, "*Take Me Out to the Ballgame,*" played a transition chord shifting the music to another key, and watched with admiration as the girl took it in stride.

The crowd around them was building as more and more people came to see where the happy, bouncing sound was coming from. Even the desk clerks were leaning forward, watching, drumming their fingers on their counter-tops.

A few people who knew the words started singing. Others joined in, and suddenly a hearty, off-key sing-along was under way. They blared through *Darktown Strutter's Ball, Home on the Range*, and several others, and Tom shook his head at what he had started. Everyone was having a great time, and it would not have happened if Nick hadn't walked off with a girl Tom had never even spoken to.

Tom still didn't know her name, but, impossibly, there she was, sitting next to him, very beautiful and apparently very talented.

Come to think of it, where was Nick? Tom's fingers kept going, mechanically, as his eyes swept the room. Percy was standing nearby, waving the bottle in his hands like a symphony conductor, singing loud and having fun with all the others.

Thirty seconds later, Tom saw Nick, standing way at the back. He wondered how it could have taken so long to find him: Nick's face bore the only scowl in the room.

Nick hated to lose—more than anything—more than anyone, Percy had said. And to Nick's way of thinking, Tom reflected, I've beaten him twice in two days.

Look out, Percy had said. A shiver moved down Tom's spine, but he shrugged it off and looked away.

He and the girl played song after song, until the big clock by the door read quarter past ten. At last, one of the attendants from behind the desk edged through the crowd until he reached Tom's side. He said apologetically, "I have to ask you to stop, so people can sleep."

Tom nodded and announced that the next song was the last one. Someone hollered, "*California, Here I Come*," and Tom and the girl leapt into a powerhouse rendition, as the gathered audience bellowed out the words so strongly that Tom could hardly hear the piano in front of him. He hit the keys so hard on the ending that his fingers stung, and as the last notes died away, everyone erupted into long cheers and applause. Tom felt himself being clapped on the back and thanked by people from every angle. A few hands reached down, and suddenly he was clutching a fistful of dollar bills.

The elderly couple he had noticed at the beginning walked up, arm in arm. The man smiled kindly at Tom, and the woman unhooked her arm from his and hobbled over. She was very old, and her hand wavered as she reached out and pressed a $5 bill into Tom's. He tried to decline, but she would not hear it.

"I didn't think people knew those songs anymore. I can't remember the last time I enjoyed an evening as much as this, and Walter agrees. Thank you, young man." She leaned forward and her voice lowered conspiratorially. "Buy something nice for your lady-friend." She smiled at them both, returned to her husband's arm, and the two of them moved off.

Tom turned to the girl and nodded. "I'm with her. That was a lot of fun. And you're a pro. How long have you been playing?"

"All my life."

"You must have had a good teacher."

The girl shook her head. "I never took lessons."

"You learned it all yourself?" Tom heard the incredulity in his voice.

"I had nothing but time on my hands."

Tom smiled, "Didn't you go to school?"

"Not in the usual sense. My parents schooled me at home, until they died. That was when I was still quite young." Her eyes focused elsewhere for a moment.

"Are you out here by yourself?"

"No. I'm visiting with my uncle and," the corners of her mouth dipped, "his associate. They're on a working vacation. My uncle became my guardian when my parents died. But he was never around much."

"Why not?" Tom asked.

"He was always busy with his work, running from one place to another. As my guardian, he took me with him, all over the world, but after we arrived at a particular destination, I wouldn't see much of him. He made a point of having a piano around, though." The girl's eyes softened. "I'm sure it was for my sake."

What an unusual background, thought Tom. He smiled at her and stood up. "After all that playing and singing, it's a little warm in here. How about a short walk?"

She considered, and said, "I'd like that."

The crowd had largely dispersed, and a sleepy late-evening stillness had replaced the cheerful noise of the sing-along. Tom and the girl stood up and walked toward the door. The fire in the hearth was dying out. Halfway across the atrium, the girl looked up and gave a little shudder. Tom followed her line of sight in time to see a door close, high up on the third floor.

"What's the matter?" he asked. "Who's that?"

"No one," she said quickly. "My uncle's friend. He's been watching us for half an hour." They continued toward the door, and the girl's face was still tense when they reached it.

Tom wondered what sort of man could make her react like this. "Hey," he said. "What is it?"

"Nothing." She sighed, and shook her head. "No, that's not true. That man's a snake. I don't like him at all. Uncle Stam shouldn't hang around him."

Tom raised an eyebrow. With a shrug, the girl answered his unspoken question. "I don't know why, exactly. But he has something evil burning inside. I feel it when he's near."

Tom felt a quick thrill of interest. "What's his name?" he asked.

She paused, and said softly, "Villerot." Then she shuddered again.

They walked outside onto the veranda where several people sat in a line of old wooden rocking chairs. The sky was dark, and the air crisp and smelling of pines. Tom looked at the girl and said easily, "You haven't told me your name yet."

The tension eased in the girl's face. "Well, you never asked. It's Katherine Lancaster." She stared at him expectantly.

He grinned. "Mine's Tom Connor."

She curtsied flawlessly. "Well, Mr. Connor, how do you do?"

Tom laughed at the prosaic phrase. "Very well, until I met you. Extremely well since then—although I'm going to fine you if you ever call me 'Mr. Connor' again."

Katherine stuck her tongue out at him. They walked across the curving driveway, past the towering flagpole and down the path leading to the gardens. Outside, under the stars, the girl's demeanor had relaxed considerably. She arched on a single foot, pirouetted once, and looked up. There was excitement in her voice. "It's beautiful. You never see skies like this in the city." She pointed. "See Regula up there? It's so brilliant."

Tom glanced at the sky, "Which constellation is that?"

She waved a finger in mock disapproval. "Regula is not a constellation. It's a star. In Leo, the lion."

"I see. And that bright star over there, Professor?"

The girl laughed and put her hands on her hips. "It's sad. You're another victim of American schools. That isn't a star at all. It's the planet Jupiter."

Tom said, "I can find the North Star for navigation. What else do I need to know about the night sky?"

Katherine shook her head. "It's not what you need to know, silly. It's what it adds to your life. Variety, depth, culture. You look up and say, 'I know that constellation. It's Perseus. He's saving Andromeda, there, from Draco the dragon, overhead.'" She sighed happily. "I learned them all when I was a little girl. I guess if you don't learn them young, you're not going to later on. But everyone is so lazy nowadays." She read the injured dignity on Tom's face and said, "If nothing else, it helps keep your Greek mythology straight."

"And what use is that?" Tom scoffed.

The girl made a gesture of slapping her forehead and laughed. "You're hopeless. What *do* you know about?"

Tom reflected. "Ragtime," he said.

"Okay. I'll grant that."

"Hunting and fishing," he offered.

"Oh, dear. You seemed like such a nice person, too."

"If it makes you feel any better, I eat what I take. Unless it's full of mercury or something."

The girl cocked her head. "All that lead you've shot into it makes no difference, of course."

"Don't be nasty," Tom said, amused.

"All right. I am glad you don't kill animals only for sport." Katherine's blue eyes opened in candid appeal. "I can't help it, I like them better when they're alive. And I don't care who says what, I don't like it when people get enjoyment out of killing things." She kicked at a stone. "But I suppose if the civilized world collapses and everyone has to go live in the jungle, you'll be one of the prepared ones."

Tom shrugged, and the girl said, "Do you camp, too?"

"Absolutely. All the time—backpacking, the whole works."

Katherine's eyes took on a challenging quality. "So what's a rugged outdoorsman like you doing, staying here in a big fancy lodge?"

Tom laughed. "I've always wanted to try it." He decided not to add that Percy would never hold up to a weeklong backpacking trip.

"Hmm." The girl's nose crinkled as she said unmercifully, "Well, I imagine you can always pitch your tent in your room."

"Now look—" Tom began.

Katherine raised a hand in mild retreat. "I'm only kidding. I'll try to be serious." Her face wasn't serious. "Assuming you actually graduated from high school, are you out of college yet?"

"Do I look that old?" Tom asked incredulously. "I'm studying Mechanical Engineering. Senior next year."

"Really?" Katherine's expression became more interested and she looked back at the lodge. "My uncle is a professor of Mechanical Engineering. Or was, at any rate. He's even written a few textbooks."

"What's his name?" Tom asked. "Stam something or other, you said."

"Stamford Zimmerlee."

"You're joking." Now Tom was interested. "I know that name. I used one of his books last year. *Applied Thermodynamics*, by Zimmerlee. He must be a real authority." Tom's shoulders fell in mock dismay. "I hope you know I'm broke because of that man. His book cost more than three weeks' worth of food. No wonder you can all afford to come out here."

"I don't believe you're hurting too badly," Katherine said thoughtfully. "You're out here, too."

Tom chuckled. "I'm sharing a single room with two other guys as poor as I am, each of us sleeping on the floor two nights out of three."

"Oh," Katherine's face clouded. "I didn't like your friend much."

"Nick?"

"He had only one thing on his mind, very transparently." Frustration entered the girl's voice. "I don't know why you guys always assume...."

She saw Tom's frown, and added hastily, "I don't really mean you. I'm sorry, I didn't mean to spout like that. I just have this outdated idea that women should be courted, not seduced."

"It's not outdated," said Tom. "Although I don't think most men are quite as flagrant as Nick." He thought for a moment. "Is that how it is with Villerot, why you don't like him? Does he make unwanted advances?"

"No." Katherine's face was troubled again, but her tone was softer. "I don't think romance, love, or even lust mean anything to Villerot. All I sense in him is malevolence. He's angry, hurting, something—all the time. Rarely says anything to anyone except Uncle Stam, and I'm sure he just thinks I'm a nuisance. He'd probably like to get rid of me."

"Well, I hope he doesn't," Tom said amicably. "It sounds like he has other things to do. But if he and your uncle are working all day, what do you do?"

The girl smiled. "Oh, slip away and pursue my own devices. I've spent every day since we came here just walking, morning to night. It hasn't been bad. I love it here. And I keep a journal. I've had loads to write about since we arrived."

"When was that?" Tom asked.

"About a week ago. We're staying two more days."

They had reached the end of the gardens. Crossing the drive, they walked up the short hill and around the darkened train station. Several wooden benches dotted the outer wall, facing the rails. They sat on one, and looked across the silent tracks to the lights of East Glacier.

Two days, thought Tom. I've only just met this extraordinary girl, talented and beautiful and smart; unique, with a freshness unlike any other girl I've ever known—and she's gone in two days. Two days....

He debated whether or not to take the plunge, and made up his mind instantly. He looked at the girl and said, "Katherine, how would you like to go out with me tomorrow? Hiking every day you must have gotten through most of the area around here." Inspiration struck him. "We can take a ride on those jammers, the red buses, up the Going-to-the-Sun Road and back. It's supposed to be an awesome trip. Give you something new for your journal."

She looked at him sideways. "Not wasting time, are you?"

"You're going away in two days," Tom said. "There is no time to waste. Meet you tomorrow at nine in the lobby. We'll grab a quick breakfast and then jump on the bus. What do you say?" He held his breath.

"I don't know." Katherine let him dangle for what seemed like an eternity. Then she grinned. "I don't suppose very much can happen on a bus full of people. Okay."

They rose, and Katherine looked up at Tom. She reached out and squeezed his forearm. "I enjoyed playing the piano and talking with you." Flashing a final soft gaze into his eyes, she added, "Thanks for not being too predatory. See you tomorrow."

With that, she slipped quietly away down the path, back through the gardens and up toward the lodge. Tom watched her go, his mind full and heart sailing, thinking about her and the day tomorrow for minutes before starting down the path himself. He looked up the hill to the lodge. Which room was hers? He counted up three stories, then followed the long row of windows down to the end of the protruding center section.

He froze.

Silhouetted against the last yellow square of light was a dark, narrow head. Tom was too far away to distinguish any features, but he knew subconsciously that the head was looking directly at him, still and quiet as death. Tom swallowed hard as the dark figure betrayed no reaction at being seen, and made no move to draw the room's curtains together. He began to walk again, toward the lodge, unable to tear his eyes from the silent watcher. The head, he saw as he drew closer, turned slowly, following him all the way along until he reached the veranda and the overhanging canopy blocked the window from view.

How long had the man been watching? Katherine had seen Villerot looking down at them from the balcony before they left the lodge. Had he then followed their progress from his vantage point at the window of the upper room the whole time they had been together?

Tom crossed the deserted atrium quickly, and ascended the staircase. He reached the door of his room and knocked with an urgency that surprised him. Looking over his shoulder, he glanced up one level and across to the opposite row of doors, and wished he hadn't. One door was partially open, and the same narrow head, on a long, angular body, was looking across the empty space at him.

The door in front of Tom swung open, and a sleepy Percy yawned at him from the other side. Tom entered the darkened room and closed the door. The deadbolt slammed home with a metallic click, and the chain on the wall gave a comforting rattle as he fastened it to the door. He half expected to see the dark face appear at their own window, and he crossed the room and drew the shutters.

Nick was breathing heavily in the bed to his right. Percy walked up and said softly, "Well, Casanova, how'd it go?"

"What...oh," Tom tried to shove the uneasiness from his mind. "She's something. We're going to take a ride on one of those jammers tomorrow."

"How did you manage that?" Percy said, folding his arms. "You...."

Tom wasn't listening. As he had finished his sentence, the slow, rhythmic exhalations rising from the bed had cut off. Now they were going again, carefully measured.

Tom frowned. It was just as well he would be away from Nick tomorrow.

Percy was looking at him with eyebrows raised.

"Sorry," Tom said. "What were you saying?"

"That's my pal. Meets a beautiful girl and stops paying attention to his old buddy."

Tom winked, "Assuming he was paying attention in the first place."

Percy grinned and made a slapping motion in front of Tom's face. "Okay then. Get some sleep. Have a good day tomorrow."

"Thanks."

"But if you wake me up in the morning 'cause you're singing or something," Percy poked a large finger at Tom, "I'll sit on you and you won't go anywhere."

"Good night." Tom took off his shoes and socks and walked into the bathroom. He washed his face, scrubbing harder than usual as if to clean away his sense of disquiet. Then he brushed his teeth with a stout toothpaste that left his gums tingling. He stripped off his shirt and trousers, pulled on a pair of shorts, and went back into the main room.

Percy had settled down into his sleeping bag and was snoring softly. Tom listened to Nick's even breathing. Was he awake or not?

"Hey, Nick," he said.

No reply.

"Nick."

Again, no response, but the rate of the breathing had increased.

"Nick!"

With startling rapidity, a single two-word phrase, snarled in unambiguous Anglo-Saxon, spat forth from the bed in the darkness.

Percy stirred, and said, "Tom, please just go to sleep."

Tom tried once more. "Nick?"

Nothing.

Two thoughts from earlier in the evening rang again in Tom's mind.

He hates to lose, more than anything, more than anyone.

I've beaten him twice in two days.

Tom sighed, and got down into his sleeping bag. Jumbled images—his companions, the train, mountains, Katherine— swirled through his brain. In front of them, he saw again the silhouetted head in the window, its silent actions following his own.

What could make a person spy on another with so little concern at being caught in the act, Tom wondered? It couldn't be just idle curiosity, could it? But there was no basis for anything more than curiosity. Tom didn't know the man, and the man didn't know him. Or did he? What would Tom find out tomorrow? Was there anything to find out tomorrow?

He pushed the shadowy questions away, but they returned, clinging to his thoughts with stubborn tenacity. He knew it would be a long time before he slept, but he closed his eyes and lay still, waiting for the dawn.

CHAPTER
3

Morning light streamed through the window of the little room, driving out the last murky shadows. The shutters had popped open during the night, and outside the forest-tops and eastern-exposed faces of the granite peaks were painted in luminous golden hues. Tom sat up in his sleeping bag and stretched expansively, feeling some of his apprehensions from the previous evening melt away.

He climbed out of the bag and more carefully and methodically stretched his sleepy muscles. He shook himself out and felt the blood rushing in his veins. Then he surveyed the room, deciding that the only unobstructed section of vertical surface was the door. He stepped over the dozing Percy, who rustled in his sleeping bag as Tom passed.

"Oh, no," Percy's muffled voice rumbled from somewhere deep inside his pillow. Tom ignored him and planted his hands on the floor, eight inches from the threshold. He kicked himself up into a handstand, wincing as his feet overshot and his heels slammed into the wooden door with a heavy clunk.

"Hoo-yah," Percy snickered, adding officiously, "Perfect ten. Yes, friends, after only a single one-credit course in tumbling, you too will leap and bound through the air with the greatest of ease before the eyes of an awe-struck world."

"Oh, be quiet. Nobody's graceful after one semester," Tom said, upside down, as he fought to quell a chuckle. His left arm shook and he tottered unevenly before his legs settled upright against the door again. "Stop making me laugh, before I fall over."

"Now that would be worth waking up to see." Percy thumbed his nose in Tom's direction and rolled over, pulling the flap of his sleeping bag over his head.

Tom lowered his vertical body slowly toward the floor until the tip of his nose brushed the carpet. Then, with effort, he pressed himself back up to his starting position. He repeated the action eleven times before swinging his feet back to the floor, his head pounding. When his heavy breathing had subsided, he got down onto the floor and did three sets of twenty push-ups, placing his hands at various widths to exercise his chest and arms more fully. Then he rolled onto his back and stretched his arms and legs to full extension. Seventy times he raised them, bringing all four limbs toward one another till they touched, high above his flat stomach. At last his abdominal muscles burned, and he let his body sprawl across the floor.

"Nice workout." Percy had turned toward him again. "We're on vacation, you know. It hurts just watching you."

"Uh-huh," Tom said absently as he rose. "Now if I only had a pull-up bar. Maybe a tree with a low branch...."

"Ugh," said Percy, and his head vanished again into his sleeping bag.

Tom grinned. He gathered a handful of clean clothes and walked into the bathroom. His naked torso in the mirror was flushed after his exercise, and his eyes traced over his hard shoulders and solid chest to the four-inch vertical scar down the right side of his abdomen. He heard again the roar of the crowd on that early winter evening five years ago; saw the haze of lights as he hurtled toward the end zone, football clutched tight in both arms. He'd twisted deftly, evading one defender, then another, and another—fought his way down the entire length of the field, until—*pow!* The flying tackle had nailed him from behind, and he'd gone down, holding the ball for dear life. Somehow the defender's cleats had gotten tangled up in Tom's shirt, and one of the points had ripped that jagged line down his flank.

Tom winced at the memory, then smiled. It had been worth it, in the end—he'd scored the touchdown. After picking himself up off the muddy snow, he had hurried to the stands, to Doc Phillips in the first row. Borrowing that worthy gentleman's half-empty flask of medicinal brandy, he'd slathered the burning stuff all over his wound, stuck a gauze patch over it, and been back on the field in time for the next possession. He never had gotten the laceration stitched up properly, and because the kicker had gone and missed the extra point after the touchdown, Tom always called the resulting scar his Six-Pointer.

He shook his head. Those were the days. Now it was just a lot of studying—memorizing engineering formulas, working endless calculations, wondering what to do with life once school was done. He enjoyed pushing his brain to the limit, but he'd always tried to balance academics with sports and hard physical activity. Lately, it hadn't been possible. The mind-work was eating up all his time, at least during the school year, and his neglected thirst for adventure had been crying out inside him till he thought he might burst. He hoped he could last out his final year at school without going crazy. That yearning to push his body hard, to demand it to function once again at its peak, had been one of his main reasons for coming to Glacier—that, and his life-long love of the outdoors.

Oh well. He pushed the thoughts from his mind. This was a vacation, not a time to worry about the future. He turned the shower on and washed for ten minutes under the hissing water. Stepping out of the steaming white cabinet, he toweled briskly, shaved, and dressed in khaki trousers and a long-sleeved black cotton sport shirt—as close to formalwear as he would ever allow himself to get in the mountains. When he returned to the main room, he noticed the empty bed for the first time, and couldn't remember whether it had been occupied or not when he'd first woken up.

As he pulled on his well-worn leather hiking boots, Tom contemplated various ways of getting a firsthand look at Villerot, whom Katherine had portrayed as exceedingly sinister, and who had, Tom admitted, unnerved him by his dark appearance at the window the night before. He decided the most direct solution would be to call for Katherine at her room, rather than waiting in the atrium. He would go up a little before nine, apologize for being early, then ask to meet Dr. Stamford Zimmerlee, the noted author of one of his textbooks—and in this way he might also encounter Villerot.

The professor's textbook, Tom recalled as he laced his shoes, had been a real page-turner: so dense and unreadable, a product of the professor's rarefied stratum of thinking, not the student's, that one turned the pages very quickly indeed.

At half past eight Tom put the scout knife and weatherproof butane lighter he invariably carried into his pocket, and stepped again over Percy's sleeping bag. He opened the door and a grumble rose from the floor. "Not again...I'm going to nail that door shut."

"What time did Nick go out?" Tom slung a black windbreaker over his shoulder.

One large hand pulled the lip of the bag over the fair head. "Don't know," Percy muttered. "Daytime. While you were showering. Go away, eat breakfast. Eat a big breakfast for me."

"You saw him go?" Tom asked.

An affirmative grunt rumbled from the bag. Tom walked out of the room, pulled the door closed behind him, and stood at the railing, looking down on the atrium. He couldn't see

Nick anywhere, so he went downstairs and looked through the windows of the gift shop and the restaurant without success.

Walking outside, he scanned the gardens. There were plenty of people enjoying the early summer day—playing croquet, tossing sticks to a lean black dog, tapping golf balls over the sculpted lawn surrounding the lodge, or simply strolling—but no sign of Nick.

Tom went back into the lodge, and looked at his watch. Ten to nine. Close enough. He climbed the stairs to the top and walked down the long balcony to the wooden door near the end. He rapped his knuckles on it and took a deep breath.

After a short pause, the chain on the other side rattled. The deadbolt clicked and the door swung inward, opened by a short man of perhaps sixty. He had a lined, friendly face with a full beard and thinning white hair, combed straight back. He wore long white trousers and a white pullover sweater with a light blue collar peeking out from the neckline. His eyebrows arched and he said, "Yes, young man?"

Tom said, "Good morning, sir. My name is Tom Connor. I'm here to meet Katherine. We've planned to take a ride on one of the tour buses today."

"Ah, yes, she mentioned something quite hurriedly about that, before dashing into her room to prepare." The man nodded toward the connecting door. His blue eyes, the same shade as Katherine's, twinkled in amusement. "That was fifty-three minutes ago. I believe she said she was to meet you downstairs in the lobby at nine o'clock."

"Yes," Tom shifted uncomfortably. "Am I correct in assuming you are Dr. Zimmerlee?"

The man nodded.

"Well, sir," Tom said, "Katherine told me last night that you're a professor of Mechanical Engineering, and I realized you had written a textbook I used in thermodynamics class. I wanted to meet you."

"I used to be a professor, Mr. Connor," the elderly man said gruffly. "I hold a doctorate, but am not currently employed." He stepped back and his voice relaxed. "However, you may come in if you wish."

"Thank you." Tom smiled and walked into the room. It was larger than his own, with two beds, both of them rumpled. Between the beds stood a bureau with a lamp on top, a traveler's alarm clock, and, seemingly out of place, a miniature replica of Michelangelo's Pieta with a string of rosary beads draped over it.

The room appeared to be empty, except for the professor. The bathroom door was open, its interior darkened. Tom's eyes settled on the window and his mouth tightened as he remembered again the dark head that had stared down on him through it. The door connecting with the next room was closed. Tom heard muffled rustling beyond it.

Zimmerlee said in a relaxed voice, "I am confident Katherine will be along soon. Sit down, if you like." He placed himself on the bed nearest the door. "So, you are a student of Mechanical Engineering?"

Tom sat on the opposite bed. "Yes, sir. Just finished my third year. I used your book through most of it." His eyes took in the room as he spoke. The white closet doors were closed. Two suitcases and a solid-looking black briefcase were lying on the floor. A table and chair stood in the corner of the room by the bathroom entrance.

"What did you think of my textbook?" the professor asked, raising his eyebrows.

Tom searched for the right words. "It seemed very thorough." His attention was still focused on the table. He saw several untidy piles of paper on it, plus a folded sheet that looked like a blueprint with a single black object on top. The object looked like a camera.

The professor said, "You may be direct with me, young man."

"I wasn't lying, sir. It was thorough, perhaps too much so for an undergraduate class."

"Well," Zimmerlee tossed his hands up as if the point was self-evident. "The book was never intended for undergraduates. Others worked on it, after me, revising it—butchering it, in fact, though I doubt that you care greatly one way or the other. It does not matter, as I am no longer associated with the academic world."

"Oh?" Tom looked at him. "Why not?"

The professor frowned. "Many reasons. I found a position more rewarding in every way, for a time. Other things have happened since then, which frankly are not your concern."

"Of course." Tom held up a placating hand. "I'm sorry."

Zimmerlee shrugged and looked at the little clock on the bureau. "I see it is nine. I shall hurry my niece along. I'm sure you would prefer to get away from my company, and into hers." He smiled suddenly and stood up with a wink. Crossing the room, he knocked on the connecting door. A girl's voice answered indistinctly, and the professor inched his head through. "Katherine, a handsome young man is waiting for you...." His voice filtered away as he disappeared through the opening, closing the door behind him.

Tom walked to the table. The camera had caught his attention as soon as he had noticed it. It was more square than most, and Tom grew more interested as he saw the lack of any trademark name or manufacturers label. The top half of the folded blueprint beside it was hand-drawn, and appeared to detail the device's construction.

Next door, the voices of the girl and the professor were steady in some sort of conversation. They weren't moving toward the connecting door, so Tom picked up the camera and flipped it around in his hands. It felt solid and was heavier than he'd expected. He looked through the sight and saw pale green lines forming a rectangle in front of the scene beyond, with a red crosshair at the center.

Something dark sprang up in the foreground, filling the viewfinder. A hand like a bear trap closed around Tom's forearm, and a rasping voice hissed, "Replace that on the table, immediately."

Tom tipped the camera and stared into the most disconcerting eyes he had ever seen. They were horribly bloodshot—black irises on a red backdrop with no white showing at all—and they were set in a long, narrow, hairless head. It was unquestionably the head Tom had seen at the window the previous evening.

The man could only have been forty-five or fifty years of age, but his face was weathered like an old sailor who'd lived a life of harsh wind and salt spray. He was well over six feet tall, ascetically thin, but the hold on Tom's wrist told of great power. His shoulders were broad, and his body was wrapped in a slippery-looking kimono of crimson silk, with a single gold dragon snaking around from front to back, its head snarling out at the world over the man's right breast.

The movements of the narrow body, and the pressure of the hand on Tom's arm, were precise and economical. Tom thought, this is a man who has led a hard, tough life. He's been knocked around, and probably knocked a lot of other people around, too. Katherine had been right; it was a sinister face, with cruelty and cunning etched in every line. The man had been waiting silently in the bathroom—hoping to remain unobserved, or lying in wait?

The man's thin lips parted, and the accented voice rasped again. "I don't believe we have met before. This is hardly an auspicious introduction."

"We met, in a way, last night," Tom said stoutly. "You watched me for some time, Mr. Villerot."

"Ah, then." The man nodded with dawning understanding. "It was you, walking with Stamford's niece. And you know my name, which means she spoke of me."

Uh-oh, Tom thought. He tried to divert the subject. "I'm sorry for disturbing your property. I have an engineering background, and I saw the camera and the prints. They looked technical and I was interested. I let my curiosity get the better of my discretion."

"Typical American," Villerot said coldly. "Intruding yourself where you have no right to be." He shook his head and his bony fingers bored with crushing pressure into Tom's wrist. Tom's hand opened. The camera shook free and fell, banging down onto the tabletop.

Click.

The shutter release button depressed, and the black box leapt as though at the end of a snapping rubber band. Villerot cursed and lunged to one side. Tom watched in astonishment as the camera bobbed six inches into the air and toppled back down onto the blueprint. There had been no noise, no flash of light, no precursor to the unexpected action. He said, "There has to be one powerful spring in that winding mechanism—" and broke off as his arm was wrenched to the side, pulling him in line with Villerot.

The man's deeply tanned face drew close and he said, "Understand this, meddler. In the future, keep your eyes to your own things, or you may find your eyes cut out."

"What?" Tom asked disbelievingly.

Villerot's lips twisted into a cunning leer. "You heard correctly. If I catch you intruding again, then law or no law, I will take it upon myself to remove the instruments of your intrusion."

Tom said, "I know I may be wrong here. Even so, that's a rotten thing to say." His eyes narrowed and his voice hardened. "Now take your hand off me."

The man frowned again and his grip tightened. "Young one, if you only knew to whom you spoke, you would fall to your knees and beg forgiveness for your insolence."

Enough of this, thought Tom as the anger swelled inside him. He said, "I just told you to let go. I won't say it again." Villerot started to laugh, but Tom jerked his right hand up suddenly, clapping it over Villerot's eyes. The man's head pulled back in surprise and the force on Tom's left wrist vanished. Tom pulled his forearm free and brought his hand up, shoving hard, thrusting Villerot six feet back into the wall with a slam that shook the room.

The man's crimson eyes, briefly vacant, regained their focus and settled on Tom as he rebounded with a swift step forward. Tom lifted the chair off the floor behind him and brought it into view. His eyes threatened. He said softly, "Stay where you are."

Villerot halted with a guttural snarl. The voices next door grew louder. Tom moved the chair back into place, shot a warning glance at Villerot, and turned as Zimmerlee entered.

The professor saw the fury smoldering on his associate's face. His lips pursed. He said to Tom, "I see you have met Villerot."

"Yes," Tom said.

Zimmerlee's eyes darkened as he read something in Villerot's expression, but he shook his head and looked toward the connecting door with a smile. "Well, here she is."

Katherine came through the door and was to Tom, after the previous moments, a true feast for the eyes. She wore a white cotton blouse, a tan skirt with a broad black belt, and had a small backpack slung over her shoulder. Her brown moccasin-style shoes looked functional while complementing the outfit perfectly. The long golden hair was brushed back behind her ears, and a warm smile lit her face.

Tom smiled back. "All set?"

"Oh yes." Katherine looked at Villerot. "Definitely."

Tom released his hold on the chair and walked over to stand beside the girl. He said in his Shakespearean best, "Then let us away...," and stopped as she frowned. Her eyes were focused on the far wall. She said in a voice thick with hesitant shock, "What happened to the window?"

Tom, the professor, and Villerot all turned to look at the bright square of glass. Its single pane was deeply cracked, a hundred tendrils snaking through a series of radiating circles.

From the periphery of his vision, Tom saw Villerot's narrowed eyes flash a message to the professor's before the angular man's voice said calmly, "The window? Ah, yes. You were next door. You would not have heard. A bird struck it this morning at full speed. We must inquire with the staff about having the glass replaced, don't you think, Stamford?"

"What?" Zimmerlee sounded troubled. "Oh...of course. I'll see to it later."

Katherine was on the edge of saying more, and Tom interjected, "Well, that's settled then. We'll be on our way." He looked at Zimmerlee. "Good-bye Professor. I enjoyed meeting you."

"As I did you, young engineer." The man's inset eyes were briefly sorrowful. "Take care of my niece. She is the one joy in my life." He reached out and touched the side of the girl's face. "Have a pleasant time, Katherine."

"I will, Uncle Stam. See you later." She leaned across and kissed the elderly man on the cheek. Then she looked at Tom.

He nodded gallantly toward the door. "After you."

As Tom followed the girl into the hall, he heard the shrill burr of the telephone. It cut off in mid-ring and Villerot said, "Yes?" followed by a more attentive "Oh?" and then the door clicked shut.

They walked down the hall in silence. Katherine looked at Tom uncertainly and reached out to poke his shoulder. "Hey. Why so quiet? What's the matter?"

Tom shook his head. "Nothing."

Katherine smiled tentatively, "That's a pretty intense look on your face for nothing."

"I was trying to figure something out. Remind me, and I'll tell you later." Tom cast his thoughts to the side. "Right now, the sun is shining, and we have a date I'm excited about. I just realized I'm looking forward to spending the rest of the day away from anybody who lives life in a perpetual bad mood."

The girl's eyes twinkled. "How do you know I'm not in a bad mood?"

"You might be, but you disguise it well behind that big smile."

"Oh, dear," she said. "I'll have to work on that."

"Don't," Tom replied. "It's a lovely smile."

Katherine blushed.

They descended to the main floor. "First things first," Tom said brightly. "Breakfast. I hope you brought your appetite."

"Of course. I'll need all the fortitude I can get before a day of adventuring with you."

"I'll take that as a compliment." Tom nodded emphatically.

They stopped outside the restaurant. A deep aroma of French toast, bacon, and fragrant coffee wafted through the open doors. The menu was posted on a stand in front of the entrance, and Tom's jaw dropped as he scanned the prices. "This is worse than the textbooks—" he caught himself. "Well, breakfast is breakfast." Cheerfully outside, resignedly inside, he gestured toward the half-full room.

Katherine chuckled. "Please don't think that you have to spend your fortune on me."

Tom lowered his arm. "It's kind of you to assume I have a fortune. All right, we'll walk into town. There'll be something more reasonable there, and just as good." He shrugged apologetically at the maitre d' who had materialized from the depths of the restaurant, and who took on an air of offended dignity as they departed.

Outside, they walked down the path through the gardens and followed the intersecting road up to the main highway. They waited as two trucks thundered past, and crossed over to the row of shops and eateries.

Rejecting one restaurant as too touristy, and another as too dirty, they settled on a quiet mid-sized diner. An elderly but capable-looking waitress smiled and led them to a table in the corner by the window, promising a hasty return. She made good her word, bringing with her two menus and glasses of water. Ice tinkled as she set the glasses on the table. "Back in a minute," she said, and swished away.

Tom smiled and lifted the glass of water. "Here's looking at you—" he broke off. The uncertain expression he had seen on Katherine's face as they'd taken leave of Zimmerlee and Villerot was back. The girl seemed to be making up her mind about something.

At last, she took a sip of water and said, "You're very nonchalant, Tom, but I think something's wrong. What happened upstairs in the lodge? You said you'd tell me later, but tell me now. And don't say 'nothing.' I heard an awful noise when I was in the other room. I know Uncle Stam heard it too, though he didn't say anything. It was like someone dropped a bowling ball from the ceiling to the floor."

Tom swirled his glass slowly. "That was your favorite menace, making friends," he said, watching the ice circle round and round. "I don't like him any better than you do." He looked up at the girl and related the morning's events. As he reached the culmination of his encounter with Villerot, Katherine's eyes widened.

"Tom, you shouldn't have. He is dangerous, I just know it. He's not the kind of person to take lightly being thrown against a wall. Please don't do anything like that again."

Tom shrugged. "I hope I won't have the chance. I plan to avoid him. Maybe I had it coming, sticking my nose where it didn't belong. But I don't like being threatened. Surely he can let me know I've overstepped my bounds without threatening to cut my eyes out." He looked thoughtful. "Why *does* your uncle hang around him?"

Katherine was interrupted by the return of the waitress to take their orders. When she had bustled away again, the girl answered: "We need money, very badly. They're working on some kind of invention. Uncle Stam is—" she corrected herself, "—was, a professor of engineering. I know he's absolutely brilliant. He must be doing a lot of the brainwork. I have no idea what Villerot is, besides evil, but I'm sure he's clever, too."

"How does that camera tie into it?" Tom asked. "And what are you all doing out here, in the park?" He smiled. "Not that I'm sorry, at least as far as you're concerned."

"I don't know about the camera," Katherine answered. "Uncle Stam won't tell me anything about the project—says they're under contract not to reveal any information, so that competitors can't find out and steal their idea. We came here because he says it's a place where they can work but also get away from it all. I don't mind. I've always loved being in places like this."

"How often has that been?" Tom asked.

"Oh, often," Katherine smiled. "Many times we've lived near wildernesses of some sort, Uncle Stam and I—except in Europe—and if I wasn't studying, I would be outside exploring.

I'd find the most remarkable plants and animals. I thought I would grow up to be a botanist and zoologist *extraordinaire.*"

Katherine, eyes aglow, started to tell of one venture into the hills in Colorado in search of wildflowers for her collection, and was describing how she had stumbled onto a particularly aggressive western rattlesnake, when the food arrived. She paused as the waitress set steaming plates before them, and went on:

"It seemed to leap right up from the ground. Fastened its fangs onto the handle of my pail and just about scared me to death."

"I'd think so," said Tom. He drank a swallow of fresh-squeezed orange juice. "What did you do?"

"Scream." Katherine shrugged meekly. "And drop the pail on the ground. Spilled those poor blue columbines all over. Then I took the trowel I was carrying for digging flowers, and cut its head off."

Tom blinked. "What?"

The girl's voice was innocent. "I cut the snake's head off." Her hand made a chopping motion. "With the edge. I was so frightened that the trowel went all the way into the ground and I twisted my wrist." She smiled sheepishly. "And then I sat there in the middle of all those spilled flowers and cried for an hour. Absolutely bawled. It was three weeks before I'd go into the hills again."

"Wow," Tom looked at the girl with new respect.

The story failed to dampen his appetite, and he turned to his food, devouring a simple, delicious breakfast of sizzling scrambled eggs, seasoned and dripping with melted cheese, followed by a hearty stack of honey buckwheat pancakes. He topped the first off the stack with real maple syrup, and the remainder with what was proclaimed to be a house specialty, homemade huckleberry syrup. It was similar to blueberry, and extremely good. At last he sat back and grinned. "This place was a good choice."

"I'll say," Katherine observed. "You sure can eat."

Tom waved his hand. "*I* need all the fortitude I can get before I go adventuring with me." He pushed his plate away and signaled the waitress for the check.

Katherine's mouth twisted wryly. "With that much fortitude, this promises to be quite a day."

Tom paid at the register near the door, and they exited the diner. He rubbed his hands together. "Now for a little bus ride." As they crossed back over the highway, he asked, "When were you in Europe?"

"From when I was fourteen until about three years ago. Uncle Stam had work over there—it was what he gave up teaching to do. It was classified work and he could never say anything about it, but I know it got shut down, and that's when we moved back to America. We lived off his savings while he was looking for another position, but he didn't look very enthusiastically—I think he was quite hurt when the European project was cancelled. I took a few little jobs to help out: pet store, library, anything I could find; but he never came up with anything. We just scraped by until a year and a half ago, when Villerot appeared. Things haven't been the same since."

"Doesn't sound like they've ever been the same, for you," Tom said. "You've certainly lived a life out of the ordinary."

What a girl, he thought. She's seen much more of the world than I have. Probably never felt like she's had a permanent home. An outcast, by circumstance, not by choice, with no family but her uncle. She's taught herself more than a lot of people ever learn, and she's learned to love travel and the wilderness, looking continually for something new to stave off the loneliness and boredom that would be knocking constantly at her door. On top of it all, she's incredibly beautiful.

Tom found himself completely attracted to, and fascinated by her.

They reached the lodge. Katherine looked at the cracked window, three floors up, and said, "That poor bird. I wish I knew where it was, whether it was still alive or not. Can we look for it?"

"No," said Tom.

"Why not?" she asked with a hint of belligerence.

"Because there was no bird."

Katherine looked dubious. "How do you know?"

Tom said levelly, "That window wasn't broken before your uncle went into your room to get you. I remember looking right at it as soon as I entered the room. It was fine, then. Something shattered it between that time and when we left, and it wasn't any bird."

"What, then?"

"I'm sure nothing hit it from outside. I would have noticed. Villerot would have noticed. It must have cracked when I shoved him into the wall—but I didn't think I shoved that hard.... " Tom shrugged. He glanced over Katherine's shoulder, and his eyes widened. "Whoa, we're late. Back in a minute!"

The next bus tour was in the process of loading, and Tom ran into the lodge to buy two tickets. Re-emerging, he hurried with Katherine down to the line of buses. They reached the nearest, and found there was just space remaining in its second row. The front seat was reserved for the driver, and the third, fourth, and fifth rows were filled to capacity. Tom climbed in first, giving Katherine the window seat. The top was open to the outside air, mountain-cool, but not cold—a perfect complement to the sun on their heads. A gentle breeze rustled the surrounding trees, and as Tom looked at Katherine sitting next to him, he felt suddenly that it was a perfect day.

They settled into their seats as the driver climbed aboard, a stocky dark-haired man with a clean-shaven, good-natured face. "Morning, folks," he said as he pulled himself in behind the large wheel. He pressed a switch on the microphone that hung beside him and his voice was amplified: "Ready to drive the most spectacular road in the world?"

A chorus of enthusiastic cheers filled Tom's ears.

"Those of you who haven't been down it may think I'm being melodramatic. I'm not. There's nothing anywhere to touch it." The driver raised a fist dramatically. "So let's go."

The engine fired, and the driver made a few preparatory checks. Some impulse made Tom turn and look back at the big lodge. His eyes found the cracked window, motionless, empty. He felt a tug on his sleeve.

"Look," Katherine whispered. "By the totem pole."

She's still looking for that bird, Tom thought. He leaned around the girl to peer through the window. His eyes traced up the path to the lodge's entrance, and he saw a tall figure outside it, unmoving in the continual trickle of people through the open doors. A tingle danced up his spine.

It was Villerot. The man was staring down the path toward their bus. He was dressed now in a heavy black pullover shirt and green cargo pants, and his bearing contained the same watchful stillness Tom had found so unsettling the previous night. The prickling in Tom's back changed to an uncomfortable warmth, as though an ultraviolet light had been turned full on him. Seconds ticked by and then, abruptly, the tall man turned and strode down the hill in front of them. Villerot reached the parking lot at the foot of the hill, unslung a leather case from his shoulder, and climbed into a small red Volkswagen. He backed the car out, slammed it into gear, and roared past the bus with a final scything glance inside.

"Maniac," the driver muttered, thumb off the microphone switch. "Better to have him in front of us." He looked both ways and shifted the transmission into drive.

"That's odd," Katherine said.

"What?" Tom asked.

"Villerot. He never goes out. Not when he doesn't have to. He always gets Uncle Stam to do his errands."

Tom waved a hand. "This morning it must have been his turn."

The girl looked thoughtful. "What would he want that he couldn't get Uncle Stam to do...?" She sat up straight. "Tom, we're going to be all right, aren't we?"

Tom smiled. "Of course. We're on a bus full of people, about to travel through the heart of a national park full of hundreds more. What could he do, even if he wanted to? Follow along and give us dirty looks, maybe."

Katherine looked down at hands that were slightly trembling. "I wish I had your confidence," she said. "I hope you're right."

The engine rumbled; the bus pulled forward. It turned into the cloud of dust raised by the Volkswagen in its passing, and accelerated away, trailing in the little car's wake.

CHAPTER 4

The asphalt of the road was in decent condition, and the ride in the ancient red vehicle was smooth. As the bus emerged from the outskirts of East Glacier, the driver began to talk about the Blackfoot Indians who had inhabited the park's land and its surrounding regions, and whose land still bordered it today. He spoke of the mountains in the park that the Indians still regarded as sacred. He gave a concise history of development in the park, of the string of Swiss-style chalets built throughout, of the advertisements proclaiming Glacier to be the Switzerland of America, and the well-to-do travelers who had once traversed the park from one end to the other on horseback, stopping to rest each night at yet another spectacular lodge.

He described the entrance of the government, the work of the Civilian Conservation Corps during the Great Depression, constructing the buildings and trails still in use today, always clear and concise, speaking in a low, clipped voice. He knew his history, could present it well, and Tom found it completely fascinating.

With his mind on the ongoing spiel, Tom glanced around. To the right, low green and brown hills rolled away to the horizon. On his left, the same range of hills gave way to towering granite peaks shrouding the rest of the park: ominous and forbidding, majestic and beautiful, and still, at this time of year, magnificently crowned in deep white snow. Tom breathed deeply of the fresh cold air streaming over the open top of the bus and through the open windows.

The driver was now discussing the method and controversy involved in deciding which mountain pass would best serve construction of the Going-to-the-Sun Road—and the marvel of that construction: how it remained to this day an engineering feat, using throughout its length only a single switchback—the name for points in mountain roads where they double back on themselves while climbing or descending, to avoid becoming too steep. Most similar roads used dozens.

Tom nudged Katherine. "You see—engineering triumphs again."

Her reply of, "Yes, score one for the *civil* engineers," failed to blot his tinge of pride.

They had covered many miles with no sign of the little red Volkswagen, and Katherine had relaxed again. In due time they reached a little collection of motels, restaurants, and filling stations. The bus slowed, and turned left onto a road leading toward the mountains.

"This is Saint Mary," called the driver. "Park entrance, and beginning of the Going-to-the-Sun Road. If you haven't been looking around, shame on you, and now it's really time to open your eyes."

There was an entrance station a little ways down the road. The bus slowed to a crawl and the driver waved a hand at the bored female ranger inside the booth. She waved back, and they were through and into the park itself.

To his left, among the low hills, Tom saw a sliver of blue, and then the driver pointed it out.

"Saint Mary's Lake, folks. You'll get a good look at it later on." They drove on, the driver naming various tree and brush types and talking about the geologic formation of the mountains. He told his audience about the crushed powder, "rock flour" produced by glacial activity, which is suspended in many mountain lakes. This glacial sediment refracts the surrounding light a certain way, giving the water a permanent blue tint even under a gray sky.

Once his interesting but level commentary gave way to an excited "Moose, middle range on your right!" and everyone's head craned right just in time to see a four-legged muscular brown body disappear into a cluster of trees extending down from a patch of woods on a hillside. Several camera shutters clicked, too late.

"People and animals co-inhabit this park—always keep your eyes open," said the driver.

Good advice at any time, Tom reflected. He examined his fellow passengers. They were a typical bunch of tourists. Several couples, some young, some very old. A handful of families on vacation, frazzled parents looking anything but rested as they tried to control antsy children. A small group of smartly dressed Japanese tourists sat toward the back, their outfits ranging from business casual to near formal. One of them appeared to be interpreting the driver's talk for the rest of the party. Tom found their fancy clothes a little out of sync with the surroundings, but had to admit that they seemed to be having the best time of all—smiling, chattering and snapping photos incessantly with expensive cameras.

The driver's discourse had ceased for the moment. Tom looked at Katherine. "What do you think?"

She smiled. "It's beautiful. And it looks like it only gets better. I hope this bus stops sometimes and lets us out—" She broke off and pointed out the window to the right, her eyes alive with excitement. "There—another moose." She looked pleased. "The driver didn't see that one."

Tom grinned. "I'll have to add 'sharp eyes' to your list of admirable qualities." He reached over and patted her hand.

She looked at his hand and shook her index finger. "And 'sharp yell'—and 'sharp teeth'—if anyone steps out of line." The twinkle in her eyes stole the bite from the words.

Now on the right they passed a cluster of wooden buildings. "Rising Sun," proclaimed the driver. "Campground, small motor inn. Picnic ground and boat launch across the road by the lake."

And the inevitable gift shop, Tom thought cynically.

As they progressed beyond this settlement, the open countryside surrounding the road began to be spotted with trees. The mountainsides, sloping steeply up, were nearer now out the side window. The road, which had been fairly level, began to rise and fall. The driver glanced ahead, grinned, and looked into the mirror.

"Hey folks, you know what? Several weeks ago a young Blackfoot named Falling Rock was lost in this area. Extensive searches by both rangers and Indian tracking teams have failed to locate him, so they're requesting help from all of you." He had the story timed perfectly, pointing out the window at a sign passing by. It said, in plain black letters against a yellow background, "Watch for falling rock." A light chuckle reverberated through the bus.

Tom could tell that Katherine was getting more excited, pointing out species of trees and varieties of little colored wildflowers flashing by with the same elation she had shown relating the snake story in the diner. She was in her element, flushed and exuberant. Seeing her happy made Tom feel good. He also thrilled to the sight of mountains, trees, and lakes, but Katherine's years of wandering and observation enabled her to appreciate the variety and beauty of the surroundings in a way that was beyond him.

The bus came around a bend. Tom saw through a thin veil of trees the sparkling water of the lake, very blue. A small rocky island covered with pine trees stood close to shore.

66

"Goose Island," said the driver.

From the island, the lake stretched away for miles, ringed spectacularly with jutting mountains. The road dipped and the view was lost behind a thickening wall of trees. There was no longer a stretch of plains leading to the mountains on either side—just upward, rocky slopes, with high peaks jutting above.

The driver's voice came authoritatively through the speakers: "Folks, up ahead is Sun Point. Best view of the lake and the mountains this side of the Pass. We'll stop there and you can get out and treat your eyes for a few minutes."

There were hikers among the trees now, whipping past. The bus slowed, and Tom saw a parking area ahead to the left, three-quarters full. His gaze halted at the side of the lot reserved for longer vehicles. Another of the antique buses, a duplicate of their own, was parked there.

The driver turned into the parking lot and headed toward the other bus. He peered ahead and said, "Looks like our fellow sojourners are in difficulty." A cluster of people blocked the left front quarter of the other bus from view.

They pulled up broadside and stopped. The driver opened his door and jumped to the ground. Tom and Katherine rose from their seats, as did most of the other passengers, and as they climbed through the doors they heard their driver say, "Hey Stu, what's wrong?"

"Nothing to break a sweat about," replied the other driver, a short, brown-haired man in his forties, crouching beside his left front tire. "Tire busted. Must have hit a loose rock or something on the road a quarter-mile back. This was the first place to stop."

"That it is," said the driver of Tom and Katherine's bus knowingly. "Need a hand?"

"No. Got all the help I need right here." Stu waved his hand at the crowd. "Too much, in fact."

The driver nodded and turned to face his own party. "All right gang, about twenty minutes, then meet up back here. It's a long walk home, so don't be late or you'll miss your supper."

Everyone dispersed, heading for the trails leading away from the end of the parking lot. Tom pointed to one marked, "Sun Point Outlook," and said to Katherine, "Let's go this way."

She stood tall and saluted. "Whatever you say, bwana."

They started down the trail through the trees. It dipped for a short distance, then rose steeply up the side of a large outcropping of rock.

"Race you up," Tom challenged, and he broke into a sprint up the hill. To his amazement, Katherine quickly drew alongside him and, as they neared the top, was about to pass him when her left moccasin slipped. As she struggled to keep her balance, Tom reached out and caught her outflung arm. She steadied herself with her other hand against his chest.

Tom smiled into her widened pale eyes. Katherine smiled back and they looked at each other with an ever-deepening gaze. Then, perhaps to express gratitude for being spared a skinned knee, but more definitely to break the tension filling the air around them, she said awkwardly, "Thank you, Tom," and glanced down at his hand on her arm, then back up at his face.

Tom found it hard to withdraw his hand but willed himself to do so. "All right," he said, his voice thick. "Let's go up."

They climbed the last few yards at a reasonable pace, and stood and looked out at what Tom knew was the most beautiful view he had ever seen.

The point of land they were on sloped down to the lake surrounding them on three sides. Stretching to the west lay a square mile of water over which brisk wind swept, covering the water's surface with small white-crested waves. Forested hillsides arched up toward the sky, ending in a succession of

SNAPSHOT

massive, uniquely crested peaks that formed a ring around the end of Saint Mary's Lake. Far out in the water, a gleaming white boat inched its way toward them. Tom could just make out the figures of tourists swarming the deck, straining for the perfect photograph angle, undoubtedly finding the surroundings too huge to be captured by a single shot.

He looked at Katherine. "It's not bad?"

Shaking her head, she said "Not bad," and smiled. "I've seen a lot of places, but never one quite like this." Her blue eyes grew introspective. "Just think how little it's changed in hundreds or thousands of years. People, generations, come and go, we live our lives, struggle and worry, love and hate, die... the mountains remain. Silent and beautiful. Standing watch."

"So," Tom said, "you're a philosopher, too."

The wind, already strong and cool, had increased its intensity. Blowing toward them off the lake, it whipped at the hem of Katherine's skirt and sent most of her hair streaming behind her, bright in the sun, a few isolated strands across her face. She turned sideways, cheeks flushed, and lifted a hand to brush the straggling locks away.

"Cold?" Tom asked as he started to take off his jacket. Katherine had left her bag, and the sweater inside it, on the bus.

"No," she said, shivering as a fresh gust of wind swept up the point.

"Good." Tom ignored the half-hearted shake of the girl's head as he placed his jacket over her shoulders. For an instant she leaned against his arm, then she stood upright.

They looked at the water a while longer. Tom didn't want to say it, but he was also beginning to chill, more so now with only one layer of clothing protecting his skin from the wind. At last, three blasts of a horn sounded from the distant parking lot.

Katherine took Tom's arm as they picked their way cautiously down the steep trail. A short walk brought them back to the parking area and the bus, where they found most of their party already assembled. It was warmer there, away from the lake, sheltered by the trees.

The driver of the other bus was just rolling his spare tire around to the front of his vehicle. Tom and Katherine's driver walked over, pushed his way gently through the ranks of people, and said, "Stu, you all right?"

"Yeah," the other man said. "No problem. Lug nuts were stuck pretty good—I think the last time they were off was before the Civil War—but I got them now. Should be on the road in no time."

"You sure?" the driver asked. "Looks like these people want to get moving." The expressions on the faces of the other bus's passengers were far from patient. One little boy began to cry, and his mother's attempts to stop the outburst succeeded only in intensifying it.

Stu looked at them over his shoulder.

"Sure, I'm sure. Get going." He grinned and cocked his thumb in the direction of the road. "Don't need two busloads of people mad at me for keeping 'em waiting."

Tom and Katherine's driver, with a final resigned look at his counterpart, rejoined his party as the last of the group walked up. He gestured toward the bus. "Okay folks, all aboard. Next stop, Logan Pass."

The menagerie of tourists clambered aboard, a moment of chaos resolving as they all found their seats, and the engine fired up. The driver shifted out of park, and they pulled away. Tom glanced again at the crippled bus. Its driver had the wheel on the axle now, and he was just reaching for the first of the lug nuts.

They reached the junction with the main thoroughfare and turned left. The road climbed rapidly, hugging the mountainsides. Here and there, small waterfalls trickled down from the slopes to their right, coursing under the road to fall into the drop-off on their left. A knee-high stone wall stood between the road and the deepening valley. Tom looked up. The bus was nearing the tree line. Above it lay bare ground, brown and rocky, the stones ranging in size from pebbles to massive boulders. Above that were remnants of a snow line. Tom knew from his reading that before they reached Logan Pass, they would pass between snow banks piled many feet high.

Looking left, he felt his stomach knot. The bus was very high now, a thousand feet above the trees at ground level. Across the valley one bulky mountain stood detached from the rest, alone and proud. It was breathtaking. Tom turned to nudge Katherine, but there was no need. She was taking it all in through live and alert eyes.

"Heavy Runner Mountain, on your left," intoned the driver. "The little molehill we are ascending currently is Going-to-the-Sun Mountain. You can see the peak above us, now. That is the highest point along the Going-to-the-Sun Road."

Tom craned his neck and saw a tall, cone-shaped apex of black rock.

"Look up in the mountains," the driver said, "and you may notice little moving flecks of white. Take a closer look if you have the proper equipment. Those are mountain goats. They live up there, and climb up and down footholds so tiny you wouldn't believe it. Any one of us would probably fall from sheer vertigo. They never do."

"I see them," called one man, eyes glued to black binoculars.

The bus curved around the mountain to the right, and Tom looked behind. The magnificent view of the deep valley and the lake was passing out of sight. Far below he saw a little moving flash of red. The other bus was mobile again. Ahead, the mountains seemed to be closing in on the road.

Turning toward Katherine, Tom said, "Take your last look at—"

The girl's expression was not at all what he had expected, and he stopped short.

"Hey!" said the man with the binoculars, his voice full of wonder. "The goats are running—this way, all of them. They've gone mad! What the...?"

Katherine was staring behind the bus, and the skin on her face was drawn tightly down to her pursed mouth. Her eyes were wide and watchful. If she had been a cat, Tom thought, her ears would have been standing straight up on her head. He said, "What is it?"

The girl's eyes narrowed and a quick emphatic shake of her head silenced him. He turned to look out the aft window, but his gaze was arrested by one of the Japanese, an older man in the rear seat. The man raised his arm as he leaned back, extracting himself from his huddled group of happily chattering countrymen. His hand cupped his ear as he directed it out the rear of the bus. He waved his other hand back and forth. The talking stopped.

Now Tom could hear something, just barely, over the growl of the engine. Thunder. A distant, menacing rumble that might be the herald of an approaching cloudburst on an overcast day. He glanced upwards. Not a wisp of cloud in the sky. Senses confused, he realized the thunder was not dissipating. On the contrary, it was getting louder—slowly, to be sure—but without a doubt, increasing in intensity.

What, besides thunder, made that kind of noise? Tom's mind raced as he considered the possibilities, and then, in a snap of realization, he knew. He looked anxiously up the slope, but failed to see anything out of the ordinary, which, if anything, worried him more than if he had seen what he had expected. He turned to Katherine and spoke, his voice unexpectedly strained.

"Rockslide."

She nodded. Her face was pale as she said, "I think it's behind us."

Tom looked rearward again. The whole bus had fallen silent, even the children. He saw only the backs of fourteen heads, but it was no stretch of the imagination to guess that their faces would be strained and gray. Was the ground shaking now, or was he imagining it?

The rumble was very loud now, rolling, a physical noise with a quality more solid than thunder; unearthly, but very much of the Earth, ripping the calm of the majestic vistas around them, drowning the now-pathetically insignificant roar of the engine, and reaching into the depths of all who heard it, shaking them to the core.

From over the edge of the cliff shielding their view of the road behind, a plume of gray smoke puffed into the open air. The noise of the rumbling remained constant for a moment, then began to diminish as the patch of sooty cloud spread and darkened in stark contrast to the brilliant sky behind it, until all that remained in their ears was the steady pounding of the engine and the echoing memory of the clamor of hundreds of tons of rock crashing into the valley below.

"I hope no one was under that," Tom said to no one in particular, his voice thin and far away. He shook his head to get free of the shock he felt, and leaned over the front seat to address the driver. "Did you see what just—"

"Yes," the man said.

Tom waited for him to continue, and when he didn't, said heatedly, "Don't you think we should go back and see if anyone was down there?"

The driver's voice was restrained. "Of course. Soon as you see a place where I can turn this crate around, speak up. But I'll save you the trouble—there isn't one—not till Logan Pass."

His brows were knit, his mouth grim, and he looked straight ahead.

Tom nodded. He should have thought of that. "Sorry," he said, dropping back into his seat. He looked at Katherine's face and wondered whether his own was also that white. He put his hand on hers, and she did not pull away.

The remainder of the climb passed in silence. The great snow banks now present along the side of the road held no interest for any of the passengers. Tom's mind was filled with turmoil—he could not release the sense of disaster that seemed to give the surroundings a surreal aura, or the forlorn hopelessness he felt for anyone caught under that devastating fall. Nor could he ignore the warm, damp hand under his own....

They were turning left. Minutes had passed, and Tom hadn't paid attention. The scream of sirens snapped him back to reality. He looked out in time to see a park ranger patrol car roar by, lights flashing, its sandy-haired driver hunched tensely over the steering wheel.

The bus entered a parking area, much larger than the one at Sun Point. Another vehicle screamed past. At one end of the parking lot, up a snow-covered hill, stood a large, official-looking structure of wood and stone. The driver braked, and they stopped. He twisted around in his seat.

"Folks," he said, his voice brusque, "this is Logan Pass—that up on the hill is the visitor center. Wait here. I'm going to see if there's anything we can do about what happened back there."

He jumped through the doorway and raced along the path, up the stairs, and into the visitor center.

The passengers waited five minutes, after which the door swung open and the driver emerged. He walked slowly, tiredly, down the steps back to the bus, and leaned through the front side window. His face was somber.

"There aren't many details," he said. "There has been a rock fall of some magnitude. That is a real danger at this time of year—at any time, really, but especially now, in the warming period after winter when thermal expansions and contractions loosen the rock. The news was radioed up here from below—apparently the rangers saw the cloud of smoke from the Saint Mary Station. Fire trucks and ambulances are on the way. We're supposed to stay clear and let the emergency people do their job."

The driver gestured toward the road where several overall-clad men were putting up signs and bright orange barriers. "It's likely the road is blocked off. We'll know soon enough. If so, we'll descend the other side of the mountains as planned, but instead of returning the same way, we'll swing around the southern end of the park to get back to Glacier Park Lodge. It's going to be a long day."

There was a resigned murmur from the passengers as the driver continued, "Meantime, we can all use a break. Hop out, look around. We'll get underway in about half an hour."

He turned, paused, and swung back, his face haggard. "One more thing. You might pray for the people under that heap." The low, steady voice cracked. "They're saying the bus we passed on the way up—Stu's bus—was at ground zero. They can just see its red tail end sticking out of the pile on the other side." The driver turned and walked slowly up into the visitor center.

Tom thought back to the crowd of jostling passengers milling around the good-natured, ornery driver replacing his wheel in the Sun Point parking lot. *Why,* Tom asked himself? This sort of thing wasn't supposed to happen to innocent people who had saved and strained to come spend their cherished time in a place of such beauty. The weight of it hit him hard, and he knew he had to get moving again.

Several people had already climbed out through the open doors. "Come on," Tom said shortly, "let's get out of this."

Katherine nodded. They disembarked and walked up the stairs to the visitor center, not looking back as another wave of banshee screaming wailed in their ears, a fire engine and a string of ambulances rushing by.

Tom glanced up at the same blue sky he had admired before they'd left the lodge this morning, the same soaring snowcapped mountains. The sun warmed his face, the breeze cooled it, but the day was no longer beautiful. He turned, Katherine beside him, and they entered the visitor center.

It was a typical park building—official but welcoming, bright and crowded. To one side was the information desk, the rangers behind it looking anything but informative as they huddled around a crackling radio. The bus driver was leaning on the counter, chin in hand, staring moodily at a point on the wall.

Opposite this was a gift area full of mineral rocks, playing cards, figurines, patches, cups, and several rows of bookshelves. Katherine murmured something about the books, and they moved off in that direction.

They looked over the assorted volumes, scanning the names without comprehension. Tom put his hand on Katherine's shoulder and shook it consolingly. She spoke, her voice hushed. "That could have been us, back there."

"I know," he replied—inadequate, but all he could come up with to say. They turned to gaze out large windows to the parking lot below, and the mountains beyond.

A car pulled up at the foot of the stairs leading to the center. Three people clambered out and came up the stairs, a man, a woman, and a young girl. They pushed through the doors. The girl was crying, and all three were pale. They looked around for a moment, saw what they were looking for, and walked toward the center of the building.

Tom looked after them. Their destination was the drinking fountain protruding from the wall. The man pointed to it and said something, and the little girl shook her head, tears pouring down from reddened, puffy eyes. The woman knelt beside her and the girl buried her head in her shoulder. The man stooped, drank thirstily, then wet his hand and wiped it over his face.

A crowd gathered around them, and a general murmur of "What happened?" and "Did you see it?" reached Tom's ears. The man looked up and responded in low tones that Tom could not distinguish. He moved closer.

"—in front of them when we heard it. I was driving and my wife screamed. Right in my ear." The man attempted a chuckle, but the laugh mirrored his weary face. "I think I nearly drove off the road."

He looked at the woman, eyes somber. "I never heard her scream like that, not in fifteen years. 'Faster!' she yelled." The man shook his head. "Next thing I know, rocks are banging off the top of the car. Go check it out—looks like Swiss cheese. Then, *crash*, goes the back window. Miracle we weren't killed, especially my girl in the back seat."

The girl began whimpering again, her tiny hand covering her face.

Tom could see that the man was looking inwards, though his eyes never stopped scanning the crowd. The man's voice grew hushed.

"Then—I'll never forget it. One second, I see that red bus on the road behind me in the mirror. Next, all I see in the mirror is pitch black—one gigantic boulder. Slammed into the ground like nothing I've ever seen before, and I was in the Army." The color drained from his face. "We lifted clear off the pavement. Then we were back down, and still going. I didn't know what I was doing. Finally my head cleared, and I stopped to take a look. Thick cloud of smoke behind us, and I couldn't see that bus at all." Tom saw the driver of his and Katherine's bus lower his head.

The man continued, "After a minute, I knew it was over, and I put the car in reverse and headed back down. Shouldn't have, I suppose, but—well, never mind. We couldn't get through. The road is blocked real bad—the big boulder, and a ton of smaller stuff around it."

He was quite pale now. "And the screaming. At least a couple of people alive under there." He looked down. "Nothing I could do... I looked for a way to climb past it, but there wasn't one. A bunch of other people arrived, all come down from this side. We milled around. Then the rangers got there, told us to pack it up, and that was it. We drove up here."

For some moments no one said anything until a woman in the crowd looked at the information desk and called out, "Is there any blasting going on around here?"

One of the rangers shook his head emphatically. "Absolutely not."

"What about all this smoke?" she pressed.

"Ma'am, a boulder of that size would generate an incredible cloud of dust and dirt on the way down."

The woman seemed unconvinced. She said to the man, "Did you hear anything beforehand?"

He scratched his head. "Like an explosion? No, just a rumbling that got louder and louder."

There were a few more questions, but the man had no further information. Small discussions broke out among the crowd, and the people dispersed slowly.

Tom had been thinking hard throughout the man's story. There was one question he knew he must ask the family. He left Katherine by the books and approached the three forlorn figures, sitting now on a bench near the drinking fountain. Tom stopped in front of the father and said, "Sir?"

The man looked up, spent.

Tom tried to sound nonchalant: "Did you notice in the crowd of people at the scene, a very tall man, a man with a lined face and very red eyes?"

The father appeared too shaken by his experience to wonder what would be the point of this question. He shrugged and said, "Not that I can recall. I didn't look at anyone very closely. Had other things on my mind, but no, I don't think there was."

The little girl's steady, quiet whimpering had broken off. Tom looked down and saw her staring at him. She had big blue eyes that would be pretty without the puffed red circles around them, and long streaming blond hair. She looked a lot like a young Katherine. Tom knelt in front of her, ignoring the mother's questioning look.

"Did you see him?" he asked. "A tall man with red eyes?"

Her little head bobbed up and down twice and her voice quavered. "He looked at me mean." Her body was trembling, a fact not lost on her mother, who leaned over and asked, "What's this all about?"

Tom thought for a moment. "Someone I'm worried about." It was true, obliquely. He shook his head as the woman started to speak, and then his face softened. "I'm sorry for bothering you. I was on another bus a little ahead of the rock fall. Scared the daylights out of me, too." He smiled at the three harried people. "I'm glad you weren't caught in it." Without waiting for comment, he moved away.

Katherine was standing by the window where he had left her. He wondered whether he should tell her his suspicions. It probably hadn't been Villerot at all. The whole thing was likely just a bad, tragic, accident. A little girl who had just seen things no one should ever have to see was not the most reliable witness—and yet she had reacted, strongly, to his description of Villerot, without being asked directly. Was the tall man connected with it?

No, Tom thought stubbornly. *No.* It had to have been an accident. There was no reason for Villerot to do such a thing— but then, he realized with a shiver, yes, there might be, and if so, it meant that suddenly everything had turned very bad on him.

Tom walked to Katherine's side and smiled reassuringly, but his heart drummed a much faster rhythm than normal as his eyes swept through the visitor center and down across the busy parking lot, settling on the orange roadblock. He thought back over the previous twenty-four hours, working to extract from his mind every detail of what it had seen. He knew that somehow, upon returning to East Glacier, he had to find—and he *would* find—a means of investigating the nondescript room with the Pieta next to the bed on the upper floor of the great lodge.

CHAPTER
5

"All right, folks, we're moving on." The driver climbed back into the bus and surveyed its rows, counting heads to make sure everyone was present. He had nothing new to add to what little information the passengers already had of the rockslide, and he started the engine. After a quick check of the area surrounding the bus, he notched the shift lever beside the steering column into drive and pulled out. He turned left at the parking lot exit, his only option with the orange blockade on the right, and the bus accelerated onto the Going-to-the-Sun Road.

Almost immediately, the road took on a downward grade. Clearly in no mood for commenting on the scenery, the driver sat very still, peering grimly through the windshield, his hands administering slight adjustments to the steering wheel, his foot gently plying the pedals. He reached up and shifted the transmission to a lower gear. The bus quivered, and its speed slackened.

Tom took a quick look back at the visitor center and shifted his gaze to Katherine on his right. He had decided to tell her his suspicions. Lowering his voice to keep the other passengers from hearing, he spoke in urgent tones.

At the end of his explanation, Katherine shook her head and said, "But why? Of course, I've said there was something sinister about Villerot, and I don't like him, and we did see him race off ahead of us this morning—but what reason could he have for doing something so horrible? And how could he do it?"

Tom waved a hand at the boulder-ridden slopes passing by their window. "There's no shortage of rock around here. The driver said plenty of it is loose, especially at this time of year. *How* may not present much of a problem. Villerot was right there on the scene afterwards."

"If that little girl truly saw him," Katherine said pointedly.

"She must have." Tom braced a hand on the back of the driver's seat in front of them as they angled around a sharp turn. "When she heard my description, she sat bolt upright—she recognized it. There can't be that many tall, thin, red-eyed men running around."

"Well, why would he do such a thing?"

"It's obvious."

Katherine's expression said that it wasn't obvious at all.

Tom said, "He wanted to kill us."

"What?" Katherine looked at him in horror.

"It has to be that. At least," Tom said quietly, "he wanted to kill me. It's established that he doesn't like me."

The girl's voice was thick with disbelief. "So he causes a rockslide on a different bus?"

"He must have got it mixed up. Thought it was our bus...." Tom's voice trailed away for a moment. "And it should have been ours. I'll bet he counted up how many buses he passed on the road ahead of ours, and rushed on to find his boulder. Somehow he dislodged it, and got it onto the bus in the correct place in line all right—but unfortunately for his plans, and for all the innocent people on that other bus, they had blown a tire and were held up. We passed them. Waiting up on a mountainside somewhere, Villerot couldn't have known we'd switched places with them. They ended up in our position and got crushed for it."

Tom looked out the window somberly. They were still weaving through the series of snow-clad peaks that formed the pass. Katherine touched his arm and said, "You don't know that, Tom. It's a dreadful accusation to make."

He sighed. "I know. But I've got a nagging feeling about it—it's too big for coincidence after this morning's events at the lodge, and the little girl's reaction."

Katherine pursed her lips for a moment, then said in an unconvinced tone, "Why this method at all? Why go to so much trouble?"

Tom shrugged. "I believe he thinks I saw something back there in the room at the lodge. Which, I may have. He might have thought he had to act fast, before I could tell anyone— meaning, while I was still on this bus. And he might have thought this sort of 'accident' would arouse less suspicion against himself than any other way of getting rid of me. Foul play, a knife sticking out of my back or something, would have the authorities asking all kinds of questions—questions he would want to avoid. I really don't know, which is why we need to take a look around that room when we get back. If we can figure out what this project is he's working on, maybe we'll understand why he'd go to such lengths to protect it."

Tom looked at Katherine. "We've got no evidence, so we can't go to the authorities about it. But I'm worried about you. If Villerot is involved as I'm saying, then he's obviously willing to get rid of you—he doesn't care enough about keeping you alive to make sure you're safe before coming after me. If I'm right, you'll be in danger if you stay in that room, so close to him."

"He couldn't get away with killing me in my room—it would lead to all that investigation you said he wants to avoid," Katherine said.

Tom shook his head. "I wouldn't be comfortable if I knew there was a ravenous lion unchained in the room next to me.

Accidents happen, both the genuine ones and the other kind. Let's try to get Villerot and your uncle out of there as soon as we get back, so we can look the place over."

"How do you propose to do that?"

"I'm working on it. Don't worry."

Katherine's face relaxed slightly. Tom smiled into her eyes, and she smiled back. So beautifully, he thought. He took a deep breath, wanting to tell her so, not sure how to phrase it. As he prepared to speak, a high-pitched horn honked from behind.

Now what? As Tom turned his head he saw their driver's weary eyes glancing backward, reflected in the mirror.

There were several cars in line behind them, stretched up the narrow stretch of black road clinging to the mountainside. From the driver's window of the nearest car, a narrow arm gestured with frantic urgency, alternately waving back and forth and bobbing the index finger up and down, pointing at the ground.

"They want to tell us something," Tom said to the driver.

"Have to wait till we reach a turnout," came the short reply.

A head poked out the passenger side window of the sedan. It was a middle-aged woman. Her mouth was open, her hands cupped on either side. Tom strained, but could hear nothing. The elderly Japanese man at the rear leaned out the window for a moment, then pulled his head back in. He shrugged his shoulders. The man beside him, the translator, stood up. The proceedings had attracted the attention of the other passengers, and for the second time that day, Tom looked at rows of strained necks and backs of heads.

The translator was the image of pure concentration as he extended his head out the top of the bus, hand cupped to his ear, lips pursed, brows furrowed. His black hair, caught by the wind, blew straight out. The woman spoke again. The translator shook his head and gave a shrug, exaggerated to convey his meaning to the woman. Her mouth opened a further time.

He can't hear her, thought Tom. *Or, he doesn't know English well enough to pick out the words. Either way—*

"Look out," he said. People leaned to either side as Tom climbed up and pulled himself over the rows of seats toward the rear of the bus, half expecting to hear, and preparing himself to ignore, an authoritative "sit down" from the front. He glanced back. Katherine was looking at him in open-mouthed surprise, but also with a twinkle in her eye. Tom wasn't sure whether the twinkle was admiration or a stifled chuckle at his bravado. The driver's eyes were flickering between the road and the mirror.

Then Tom had to pause, his gaze transfixed despite the circumstances. The tall peaks on their left had receded a great distance, opening into a tremendous valley that stretched for miles ahead. Thousands of feet below, the valley floor was lined with pines, and its sides sloped steeply up, verdant and green. At the level of the road, the green gave way to hard, gray rock, and above this, extending as far as the eye could see, stood peak after snow-capped peak.

Directly across from them, streaming down from a glacial bowl carved deeply into the mountainside, a cascading waterfall painted twisted patterns in the rock face. The magnitude of the surroundings rendered the waterfall artificially small to the initial glance, but a comparison with the heights of the peaks, and with familiar references such as the odd tree scattered over the face of the rock at that height, showed it to be hundreds of feet high.

As the view from Sun Point had been the most beautiful of Tom's life, so now he realized that this was the most awe-inspiring, overwhelmingly spectacular panorama he had ever set eyes on. It dwarfed the impressive road, this brilliant marvel of engineering, into insignificance.

For a moment, perched on top of the seats halfway down the length of the bus, Tom was completely enraptured by the beauty and power of the setting. Then the high-pitched horn interrupted his reverie, and he turned again toward the rear of the bus.

The translator slid over obligingly, and Tom planted a foot on the rear seat and pulled himself up until his head was above the top of the bus. The sudden blast of roaring air was shockingly cold, and he turned his collar up to shield his neck. The wind caught it and pressed it firmly into place. He waved his hand until the woman looked at him. "What's wrong?" he called.

She opened her mouth again. Tom could just make out the sound of her voice, but could not understand what she was saying. He waved his hand to stop her, pointed at his ear, and jerked his thumb upwards twice. The woman stretched a little further out the window and cupped her hands to her mouth. Her face, exposed now for some time to the rush of cold air, was brutally flushed. She drew a very deep breath, and when she yelled, Tom could just barely catch the words before the howling wind snatched them away.

"*You're...,*" a pause for a gargantuan intake of air, "*... leaking...,*" another breath and a gesture at the road below them, "*...oil!*"

She followed this with an emphatic gesture downward. Tom pulled himself a few inches higher, as the edge of the roof bit into his fingers. He stretched over the back of the bus.

At first he saw nothing, just gray-black asphalt racing past his line of vision. Then he saw it, a quick dull black patch in line with the inside of their right wheels, immediately carried out of sight by their forward motion. A moment later there was another patch, followed a few seconds later by one on the left.

Tom climbed down into the bus. He pulled himself across the seats to the front, not so careful this time of the assorted heads in his path, and dropped into his seat. Katherine looked at him, her eyes still twinkling. "You look like Woody Woodpecker," she said. "Your hair's a flaming mess."

Tom grinned. "You should see my nose after a day in the forest." Katherine rolled her eyes as he leaned forward and tapped the driver's shoulder. "We're losing oil. That's what they wanted to say."

The driver frowned and cocked his head. "Engine sounds okay." His eyes swept the dashboard. "Gauges look good." He motioned ahead. "We'll pull into that turnout and check her out." Tom looked up. A small, elongated semicircle of gravel and dirt, perhaps eight car-lengths from front to back, was nestled into a cleft in the mountainside about fifty yards ahead. It was empty except for one small blue hatchback at the forward end. When they had covered half the distance, the driver put his turn signal on and stepped on the brake.

He gave a snort of surprise and jerked the wheel reflexively a couple of millimeters as he encountered an unexpected lack of resistance in the pedal. The bus swerved. The driver corrected quickly, then stamped hard on the pedal. Tom leaned backwards instinctively. He felt Katherine stiffen next to him. There was a muted thump as the back of the pedal struck the floor. The doubling of Tom's heart rate and the powerful surge of adrenaline coursing into his veins were simultaneous with the soft curse that forced its way from the driver's mouth.

They hadn't slowed at all.

Tom's palms were suddenly moist. Their speed, quite comfortable a moment before, now seemed to verge on out-of-control. He half-stood, looking out at the cavernous gorge grinning hungrily at them from across the pitiful stone barrier, and he swallowed, hard. It was a long, long way down.

Not oil, he thought. Brake fluid, the viscous liquid in the pipes running from the brake pedal to the wheels that transmits pressure from the foot to the brake calipers. Without that force-carrying medium, the calipers wouldn't clamp on the rotors, and the wheels wouldn't stop. The bus could only roll down the road, its speed on the downhill grade building steadily to the point of blinding uncontrollability. And then....

Ahead, the little hatchback, oblivious to the bus's undiminished speed and noting the blinking turn signal, edged forwards, its front end protruding into the road.

"Get out of the way," growled the driver as he snapped the turn signal off and moved his hand to the horn. The klaxon sounded two imperative blasts, and the hatchback's brake lights flashed. Its nose dipped as it skidded to a halt, and its occupant gave one long blast on his own horn in return, emphasizing his wrath with an obscene gesture as the bus swept past, barely a foot from his bouncing hood.

The driver cursed again. His brows were tightly knit, and the line of his mouth in the rear-view mirror was straight and narrow. His shoulders hunched as he leaned forwards over the wheel. He shifted the transmission into its lowest gear. The bus shuddered, the engine roared in protest, but its speed dropped slightly, beginning immediately to increase again. Without taking his eyes from the road, the driver said, "If I were you son, I'd take my seat." He called in a loud voice, "Folks, everyone stay down. Protect your heads."

Tom nodded as someone behind started to cry. His hands were slippery on the guard in front of him as he lowered himself into the seat. Katherine, pale beside him, asked, "What is it?"

Tom shook his head, his jaw clenched in anger. "He got us. I didn't honestly think that—" He looked at her. "I'm sorry, Katherine. We should never have gotten back on this bus."

"Tom?" There was real fear in the girl's voice.

"It's Villerot," Tom said fiercely. "Has to be. He cut the brake lines. I should have realized it wasn't oil when I saw the streaks just inside the wheels on either side, instead of down the middle."

The taut nerves of the passengers, in no fair shape as it was after the morning's events, were now stretched beyond the breaking point. Two calls to slow down, tinged with hysteria, rang in Tom's ears. These gave way to whimpers from the children, and pleading calls for divine intervention from the adults. A tremulous stream of Japanese from the back of the bus undoubtedly carried the same sentiments.

The air screaming in through the open roof whipped at their heads. Ahead, the yellow lines down the center of the dark road flashed by at ever-increasing rates. Tom couldn't see the speedometer, but he thought they must be doing in excess of forty miles an hour now. The road ahead was clear, but that could not last forever on this, the showpiece of the park.

A tight bend to the right loomed ahead. Pain in Tom's hand burst through his tension, and he looked down to see the knuckles ghastly white on his left hand, clenching the guard ahead of the seat. He couldn't bring himself to release the hold.

They bore down on the turn, the nose of the bus devouring the distance rapidly. Then they were into it, and the driver swung the wheel. Tom held his breath as they arced right. The wheels lost traction and the bus dry-skidded across the center lane, wrenching a tortured gasp from the overwrought passengers as the left rear quarter of the bus slammed into the knee-high barrier and grated along the stone. Tom sensed the wheels on the right side trying to pull up from the asphalt below.

Across the long seat, the elderly woman at the window gave in to irresistible temptation and looked through the glass, beyond the barrier and straight down 3,000 feet. She collapsed backwards into her husband's arms in a dead faint. He held her gently to his shoulder, his own face white. His eyes widened as he looked ahead.

Scarcely thirty yards away, an ancient black pickup truck lumbered up the road toward them, filling the lane in which they were now trespassing. A low horn rumbled ineffectually.

The bus driver worked the wheel grimly and the grating against the stone wall ceased. Somehow he tore his hand away from the wheel and flicked up the turn signal lever to signal his intentions and prevent the other truck from inadvertently mirroring their actions. He edged the bus over, delicately holding it in balance against the downhill momentum, back into the right lane as the truck flashed past and was behind them.

Tom released his breath, too soon. Already they were bearing down on the tail of a dark green sedan directly ahead. Fifty yards beyond, in the opposite lane, a long white motor home climbed exhaustedly toward them.

There was no choice. Muttering softly and incessantly, the driver touched the wheel around to the left, moving them into the path of the motor home. Even this was almost too much. The bus veered hard over. Someone screamed. Several of the children were crying loudly now.

The little yellow road stripes were only a dancing blur. Slowly—too slowly—the green sedan moved backwards and behind them as the camper ahead grew larger in the windshield.

No, thought Tom—we're going to hit. Look out!

Katherine's hand clutched his arm. A horn crackled; they were very close, and Tom shut his eyes and opened them as the bus jerked violently to the right and the motor home flashed by, a wild-eyed old man hanging on to the steering wheel scant inches from their flank—and the road ahead was clear.

Tom felt as though his pounding heart would burst from his chest. Glancing back, he saw the green sedan, still so close that he could not see its front wheels. But they were beyond it, and he grinned weakly at the passing of immediate danger, a short-lived relief. They were quickly round a shallow turn, and another small car lay twenty yards ahead of them. They would be onto it in no time, and beyond that lay a hard bend to the left. At their current speed, there was no chance they could hold the curve.

The driver set his jaw grimly and edged the wheel over. The bus swerved, control virtually gone. Again it scraped the barrier as the small car flew behind and passengers screamed. There was no one immediately ahead and the driver made no attempt to guide the bus back across to the right side. He wanted to save every inch of room for that turn.

Fifty yards. Forty. There's no way he can make it, Tom thought. Thirty yards—but he's going to try. Twenty yards, and now the barrier on the left was snaking away into the turn; ten yards—the driver twisted the wheel, there came the dry scrape as they skidded, and then, *yes*, Tom thought, they were coming around—but the turn was too sharp.

The left side wheels lifted off the road. The gray serrated cliff loomed in the right-hand windows as they tilted drunkenly to meet it, and Tom flung his arm around Katherine as they slammed into the rock face side-on with all the momentum of three tons at runaway speed.

There was an incredible jolt and a sharp crash. Glass shattered, and agonizing pain lanced through Tom's wrist as Katherine's shoulder pinned it at an acute angle to the window frame. His head snapped forward and sparks danced before his eyes as whiplash seared his neck. His body was crushed against Katherine's and he was vaguely conscious of frenzied screaming behind him, mixed with a deep gravelly rumbling as they scraped along the cliff wall, everything blurring as his senses overloaded...his breath gone, fire in his neck, light disappearing, screams fading, all sound muted but the heavy staccato of his own heart, *thump-thump, thump-thump, thump-thump*. Tom slipped toward the welcome grip of unconsciousness....

Cold water falling on his head through the open top cleared his vision and started his mind moving again. Tom shook his head. He could hear again, the crying and the whimpering, and there was a clunking in the engine that sounded bad. The pressure on his hand lessened, and he pulled it free. Katherine looked at him dizzily.

The right flank of the bus was scraping against a long section of relatively flat rock over which cascaded a light veil of water. Tom had seen this on the map. The Wailing Wall? No, that was in Jerusalem. They called this the Weeping Wall. He shook his head blearily and looked around. All four wheels were on the ground again, and they were moving slowly—not more than fifteen miles an hour.

The bus broke free from the rock, its nose swinging out to the left, speed increasing, heading for the little barrier across the road. Some thirty yards ahead, in the opposite lane, a midsize car was coming straight at them.

Turn. The thought flared in Tom's mind as the car's horn sounded in the distance. Dazed, his eyes settled on the driver for the first time, and he knew they would not turn. His throat had been dry, but that was positively lush compared to the way it parched now.

The driver was bent over the wheel, body huddled and motionless. His head lolled far to the right, swaying loosely to and fro behind the shattered left half of the windshield. A thick crimson streak dripped down from the tangled center of lines and circles.

No time to waste. Without thinking, ignoring the pain in his right hand, Tom threw himself over the seat, sprawling over the driver, reaching around the man's thick shoulders to find the wheel. He applied pressure, but it stuck fast. He pulled the driver back, and the wheel moved. They were almost onto the barrier. Tom turned the wheel hard, and the bus pulled around. As its front end cleared the barrier, lining parallel with the road and nosing toward the right lane, Tom saw the car ahead swerve into that lane. He yanked the wheel back, level on, and the two vehicles passed, each in the respective wrong lane.

Tom glanced down. The speedometer read twenty-five, and the needle was creeping upwards. There was no longer any braking effect from the engine—the transmission must have separated during the impact. Hysterical screaming and irrational cries from behind started again, but there was no time to look. Unable to afford delicacy, Tom pried himself up from the wheel, reached down, and hauled the driver to the side.

"Katherine..." he started to say, but she was already up and reaching. As Tom dropped into the driver's seat, Katherine lowered the motionless body of the driver to the side, placing her bag between his bloodied head and the sidewall. The edge of a deep cut protruded from above the man's hairline. She cradled his head in both her hands.

"You've got no protection like that if we crash," Tom called over his shoulder. "Get back in the seat."

If we crash, he thought grimly. *When* we crash. What's the alternative? If not into another car on the road, then for certain into the mountains on the right or the valley floor on the left.

He pressed down on the brake pedal—a useless but instinctive motion. The lack of any change in their speed was an unsettling sensation, strange, something beyond the tension he already felt. He realized that feeling the vehicle slow when applying the brake was a phenomenon he'd always taken for granted.

The needle crept past thirty. Tom couldn't see a thing through the shattered glass in front of his eyes. Carefully, but wasting no time, he raised his left foot and twisted sideways in the seat. His foot lashed out twice, knocking a jagged hole in the cracked web. He squinted, as a portion of glass, dangling by a corner, broke loose in the gusting wind and flew up, past his face and out the top of the bus.

Sitting on the left side of the bus in the left lane, Tom had an excellent view of the drop-off beside them. His stomach quailed. He edged the wheel over and the bus traversed the road back to the right lane. Some way, any way, he had to stop this downward plunge. Risking a glance in the mirror, he saw row upon row of ashen, stricken faces, open mouths, puffed, reddened eyes. People expecting death, a sickening, gut-wrenching plummet into that vast expanse, the green trees and black rocks rushing up to meet them in a flash of oblivion.

Thirty-five miles per hour now. All those people, depending on him. They would crash—how could they not? But whether they lived or died, whether others in their path lived or died, was up to him. Their only hope was a long stretch of level road or even an uphill slant—commodities in short supply here. No runaway truck lane would appear magically to save them.

The wheel was slippery in Tom's grip. How big it felt! Big, awkward, and imprecise. He reached one hand down, and then the other, wiping them on his trousers. When he returned them to the wheel, they were as slick as before.

Forty. Anxiously, he scanned ahead for any possible means of stopping. All he could see was yard upon yard of cliff on the right hand, and the low barrier and hair-raising drop on the left; in front, the little narrow road, always downhill, the thin yellow lines down the middle racing under the nose of the bus ever faster.

Then he squinted. Could it be? A hundred yards ahead the road curved around to the left, and the sheer, towering walls that lined it on the right receded from the corner of the turn, leaving a large shallow bowl in the ground behind a turnout— and a gentle upward slope beyond. All in a nearly direct line with the road.

It would be perfect. He would hardly have to turn the wheel. A jolting, careening exit from the road, a short bouncing run upwards, then roll back to a jarring halt in the bowl, and wait for the emergency teams. He had already seen evidence that day of their excellent response capabilities.

It would have been perfect, except for the long station wagon parked in the turnout, its four occupants temporarily stretching their legs in and around the bowl, gazing out at the vistas before them.

Nonetheless, a spark of hope ignited inside Tom; his heart leapt, and as he flipped on the right turn signal and pressed urgently down on the horn, he thought, maybe we'll make it, if only—

He jerked the wheel convulsively and then twisted it back as the nose swung too far left. They roared past a bicyclist, hunched low over his handlebars, enjoying his coast down the road—the reward for the long climb he had made up the other side. Tom, fully engrossed in the geography ahead, had not noticed him until the bus had pulled to within fifteen feet of the bicycle's rear wheel. Tom had a fleeting glimpse of a face registering pure bewilderment, and then the cyclist was out of his thoughts.

Come on, move, *move*, he begged the station wagon in the turnout, as he bore down on the horn again. He reached up through the open roof into the cold stream of air and jerked his index finger repeatedly left.

The four people in the turnout had realized finally that something was amiss, and had clustered in front of their vehicle, staring dumbly at the bus hurtling down upon them. It was obvious they could never move in time now. Tom scanned the spaces on either side of the wagon desperately.

No chance, he thought. The bus would either get pinched between the wagon's rear bumper and the cliff edge to the right, or run straight into the mountain face as it curved back around the bowl, on the left.

The needle was above fifty. Could they hold the turn? Again Tom glanced in the mirror. Most of the passengers were in extreme hysteria: shrieking, holding hands in front of their mouths, clutching children, weeping tears that gushed from red eyes down over pale faces. Katherine looked like she was keeping herself under fragile control, but her face was tightly drawn.

The mathematics of the situation thrust unbidden into Tom's mind. Seventeen of you, they said. Seventeen of you, and only four of them by the station wagon. Go on, crash through their tail end and the half-space behind them—the rear end of the wagon will help to slow you down, too. It's criminal not to. It's the only chance you'll have. Seventeen lives versus four. They'll probably jump at the last moment.

Fifty-five miles per hour, and only ten yards to go. Tom gritted his teeth. *Do it.* Seventeen to four, seventeen to four. They'll jump.

He couldn't. He tore the wheel around to the left and the bus skidded into the turn as he cast a last despairing glance into the bowl. The people didn't jump; they hardly even moved as the bus's rear wheels scraped around the curve, throwing pebbles into the recess, grazing the faded brown paint and shattering one of the headlights, miraculously missing the four of them huddled together, arms over their heads.

Tom fought with the wheel, turned it against the sweeping arc of the rear axle, then back again as they lined up with the cliff face. Several times more he turned the wheel this way and that, holding the bus in a razor-sharp balance he knew he would never have been capable of under normal circumstances.

Sixty miles per hour. Perspiration poured from his brow; the salt stung his eyes. He hardly noticed. The bus was in a long series of slight curves, back and forth, its steering almost gone, every nudge of the wheel sending them veering one way or the other.

Tom's heart shot to his throat as they whipped around another of the interminable bends and he saw the caravan. Unconsciously he counted them. Five. All in a line. Five motor homes, inching their way delicately down the road, no problems with their brakes. The bus was on them in a moment, its speedometer hastening past sixty-five.

There was only one option other than plowing end-on into the rearmost motor home, undoubtedly fatal for both vehicles. Sounding the horn, Tom turned the steering wheel a fraction. The bus shot into the left lane, and they were past the first motor home and flashing by the second. The bus's horn boomed in his ears. Why weren't the drivers of the motor homes hearing it and slowing down so he could get by them faster?

Tom was looking every way and doing everything at once: eyes flickering from the road to the motor homes and the barrier and the road; hands slick while nudging the wheel back and forth, holding the bus's position between the stone wall and the motor homes; all the while sweat dripping off his brow into his eyes, rolling down his nose.

They barreled past the third motor home and Tom looked ahead and felt an ice-cold knot of fear welling in his stomach. The hairs crawled on his scalp. A little compact car, directly below them some sixty yards ahead, had just passed the nose of the leading motor home. The bus hurtled toward it, midway along the caravan and trapped between the motor homes and the barrier. A crash was unavoidable.

Knowing it was useless, Tom tried to open up space between the bus and the barrier, but with the little needle now passing seventy, control was virtually non-existent. They had drawn even with the fourth motor home as he edged the wheel to the right. The bus swerved and struck the motor home broadside. The motor home's horn blared and its brakes squealed painfully.

There was a great rending crash as it disappeared behind them, its front fender snagged on an outcropping of rock. Tom heard the noise of more crashing from behind as the trailing motor homes, unable to stop in time, rammed their jackknifed fellow.

What have I done, thought Tom, his heart thumping in his chest as the howl of the terrified passengers intensified in his ears, and then there was no more time to think. The little compact car was yards away, its instinctive slamming of the brakes and desperate pumping of the horn postponing the inevitable for only a fleeting moment. Its driver edged the car over till it scraped the barrier—and it was not enough.

Tom watched in agonized horror as the left front quarter of the bus ripped into the car's fender and lifted the vehicle around like a cardboard box. A section of barrier shattered as the car's tail slammed into it, and another three yards crumbled as the front of the car spun free of the bus and smashed through the stone. The little car spiraled over the edge and disappeared into the ghastly abyss, the receding wail of its horn punctuating its descent.

Tom's breathing was quick and shallow as his composure neared the breaking point. *What have I done,* he thought? A distant crash and explosion reached his ears and the horn was gone. He shook his head, back teeth grinding painfully in his jaw. *What have I done; what have I done?* He wanted badly to look into the mirror behind them but he could not tear his eyes from the road as, trance-like, he fought to keep the bus on course.

There was a hand at his upper arm. A soft hand, and a quiet, pleading voice in his ear. Katherine.

"Hang on, Tom, stay with us. Please stay with us. You couldn't have avoided that. No one could. Don't let go. I know you can make it. Please."

Could he? Tom's mind climbed painfully away from the questing tentacles of hysteria, and the view ahead cleared fractionally. Now, when it was too late, the remaining motor home slackened its pace, and the bus pulled clear, its needle passing eighty.

The road ahead was empty for the moment, and Tom held the bus evenly over it, straddling the center yellow blur. He looked further along and his heart plummeted: this time they were finished for sure. The road seemed to end, but as he looked again, he saw that it curved hard left, doubling back on itself.

The switchback. The loop. The one point along the way where the Going-to-the-Sun Road completely reversed its course. There appeared to be some sort of parking area at the bend; several cars were stopped, and people were milling around. A few had paused—glancing away, then looking back in astonishment as the bus bore down on them. Its speed was beyond belief. No sane man would think of driving any vehicle down this road like that. Tom knew that no amount of dexterity could get the bus around that hairpin turn, knew it better than anyone on the bus or in the parking lot.

Again his hand found the horn. People scattered. Tom cast about desperately. The crash was imminent. Across the hairpin, curving around from the edge of the mountains on the right, was a little stone barrier, very much like the one that had paralleled their descent on the left. Beyond it, green forest stretched away and down—a slope, but not a pure drop.

Could they take it, he wondered? He knew the answer: they would have to.

Forty yards... thirty... twenty. The little barrier grew larger through the broken windshield. Then in the last fleeting moment Tom saw a little dirt walking trail leading away from the bend, up and to the right. It was worth a try, infinitely better than plunging straight off into the forest. He sounded the horn, on, off, on, off. His hand reached over, and for what seemed like the hundredth time, for the final time, snapped the turn signal lever up.

A couple of hikers dove for cover as the bus shot past the remaining twenty yards in less than a second. Tom twisted the wheel and the bus veered, thrusting everyone on board hard left. They went through the barrier like a cannonball through plywood as the wheels on the right lifted. The bus flew up the trail, balancing on two wheels, and then the path was gone, twisting above them—and they were in open air.

Tom's stomach plunged, but even as realization hit that they had left the ground, the bus banged down again onto a forty-five degree slope. The outer wheels stuck and the top of the bus pivoted over them and down. Tom saw the ground rushing toward him; there was a loud crash and the shattering of glass, and the next thing he knew was the cold window frame crashing into his cheek with a bright flash, and a sharp pain stabbing into his skull. He had a dull impression of blue sky and dark earth tumbling through his dazed line of sight; of cries of terror and pain; of the tortured screaming of twisted metal and wood piercing his ears; of a pinching in his arm, a sudden blow to his head, crushing pressure on his torso; all blurred into a violent symphonic assault on his senses as the broken shell of the bus rolled over and over down the slope, caroming off trees, skewering dirt, smoke billowing from the gasping engine in its death throes, down, down, down....

CHAPTER
6

"Wake up!"

Tom Connor choked and opened his eyes. Bright light stabbed into them painfully and they flushed with tears. He had an impression of a girl's face, blurred, and then he squeezed his eyes shut again. He hurt all over.

Something was pulling at his chest. Tom opened his eyes again. Through a great deal of haze, the girl's face became clearer. She was very beautiful with long, blond hair and a tightly drawn face. Without quite realizing who she was, he felt a wave of affection.

She was shaking him by the front of the shirt. "Tom! Wake up—we have to get out of here!"

It was all he could do at the moment to smile. "Hello," he said. He looked on stupidly, his brain registering events in slow motion, as she drew her hand back to slap him.

"I'm sorry," she said in a tentative voice, and she whipped her hand down and across.

The sting in Tom's cheek and the noise of the slap were two dissociated events in his mind, but some of the haze disappeared. The girl held her hand clenched in front of her mouth, her face pale. Her other hand continued to shake him.

Tom sniffed the air, coughed as he breathed in smoke, and chuckled weakly. "Hey, you're singeing my shirt."

The shock and crack of a second slap jarred him back into focus, and he remembered who the girl was and where they were. This time her fingers did not ball up at her mouth. Both hands were down, shaking him, and not gently.

"Katherine..." he said thickly, "I lost control and we fell. How far—?"

"A long way. We have to get out of here! Can't you smell the smoke?" The girl shook him again. "*Hurry.*"

Tom tried to sit up, and the pain in his stomach was back. He looked down and saw the steering wheel bent over, pinning him to the seat. He tried to twist around it and grimaced as his muscles screamed in protest. His head and lungs felt like he had inhaled a pint of molasses, and all he wanted was to tumble into bed—a concrete floor would do as well—and sleep for a week. A thick wave of smoke poured over him and the immediate jolt of adrenaline and fear imparted new life to his shuddering body. He squeezed around the edge of the wheel, reached for the top of the seat sagging brokenly above him. With Katherine's supporting arm around his waist, he hoisted himself up.

The bus had landed upright—more or less. Its underbody and frame were badly twisted; "upright" was a slant of severe angle. As Tom's legs straightened, and his head poked above the open roof, a new wave of smoke burst into the bus. The dirty brown haze rendered the scene unearthly and grotesque, as though a depiction of Judgment Day crafted by some medieval artist: the crumpled metal frame and torn fabric; the bodies strewn over the seats, the limbs dangling; the macabre pall hanging over it all; everything added to the impression of divine wrath descended to earth.

Some of the limbs were moving. In the back, the Japanese translator sat up, grasping his elbow, his face knotted in pain.

"We have to get these people out of here," Tom said to Katherine. "That smoke means this thing could explode any minute."

"Can you support yourself?" Her voice held genuine concern.

Tom straightened, pulling away from her. "Do I look that bad?"

The girl disengaged her arm from around his waist. Tom moved across the seat toward the door. He winced as his full weight came down on his right foot. The pain wasn't the numbness of a sprain or the sharp lance of a break, but he must have twisted the ankle pretty badly in the crash. He gritted his teeth and sank into the twisted seat, reaching for the door handle. He caught it and pushed.

Nothing happened. The door stuck, held fast by the twisted frame.

"I hope they're not all jammed. We'd have an awful time trying to get everyone over the top." Tom ran his eyes around the perimeter of the door, estimating the severity of the deformation. It didn't look that bad. He bent his back and pushed with all his strength. The handle bit into his palm. Sweat beaded on his forehead, and the muscles in his back rippled and groaned. The door refused to budge. Another wave of filthy smoke swept over him, wringing a fit of coughing from his lungs.

Then Katherine's arms were around his torso, lending her strength to his effort, unwittingly intensifying the pain stabbing into his side from the crash. Tom's breath rasped through clenched teeth, his tortured body cried out, and his head began to go light. Suddenly all resistance vanished and he was flying through the doorway. He overcompensated, flinging himself back, landing with a thump against Katherine. The girl gave a muffled cry of pain as she struck the battered steering wheel.

103

Tom ignored the throbbing in his flank and twisted around. "Are you all right?"

Katherine nodded and managed a shaky smile as she rubbed her back. "I'll collapse in a heap later."

Feeble groaning from the passengers reached their ears. The smoke was thicker and Tom pulled himself to his knees and reached for the supine body of the driver. "We'll try all the doors, but we can't waste much time. The others may all have to come through the front, and we'll have a tough time with anyone else till we move him. Then we start on the women and children, right?"

"Yes, boss," Katherine's drawn face broke into a tense grin. Tom grinned back, and turned to the driver.

Grasping the man's shirt at the shoulders, Tom pulled the hard, massive body to the edge of the seat, raised it to sitting position, and half-carried, half-dragged it out the door. The clean fresh air was a blessed relief on the lungs, but the driver was heavier than he looked, and Tom panted at the exertion as he set the man down behind some trees about fifteen yards from the bus. He glanced up the hill. A dozen people were scrambling down toward them. The nearest had covered about a fourth of the distance.

Fighting the urge to turn and run as hard as he could, Tom returned to the smoking bus. As he reached it, Katherine climbed out with one of the children cradled in her arms. Tom gave her a quick encouraging smile, more reassuring than he felt inside. He had no way of knowing the situation in the engine compartment, and no time to check. If the heat causing this smoke ignited the oil or the gasoline....

Tom stooped to the second door down the bus's right face, grabbed the handle in both hands, and got a foot up against the frame. He twisted and pulled with all his might. The door scraped loudly and then, with a pop, swung free into the air at an odd angle as Tom tumbled to the ground. He picked himself up and climbed inside. This was the seat where he and Katherine had sat during the trip, the one where the old woman had fainted into her husband's arms after looking at the yawning valley as they'd plunged down the mountain.

The man was leaned far to one side, crumpled with his arms still wrapped around his placid wife. She was breathing loudly, regularly, and looked pristine—not surprising, as she had been relaxed throughout the crash, supported by her husband. He did not appear to be breathing at all, and the acute angle of his neck suggested that he would never do so again.

Tom felt angst at the pitiable scene as he reached over and touched the woman's arm. She sat up straight and screamed. Tom recoiled instinctively, then got his left hand on her other shoulder and shook her. She looked at him with uncomprehending eyes. Her protracted scream showed no signs of letting up, and with no other recourse, Tom slapped her once, hard, across the face. The scream broke off and she looked at him, dazed.

"Where—"

"Please, we have to get moving," Tom said. Sympathy and explanations had to wait. "This bus could literally blow up any moment."

The woman jerked back as Tom attempted to pull her upwards. She gasped as she saw her husband for the first time. "Harry!" She leaned toward the man, her eyes wide. Tom knew he must stop her before full realization hit and the floodgates opened.

"*Get out of that seat.*" His voice was harsh.

She looked back at him, eyes moist but unflinching. "Not without Harry."

There was no time for arguments. "All right," Tom said with an apprehensive glance at the engine. "Can you walk?"

"Yes, yes."

Tom wrapped one arm around the motionless shoulders of the man and got his other under the knees, and lifted. There was no resistance. Katherine was back, and stepped aside as Tom hastened through the door, the aged woman at his heels. In an instant he was across the grass. He set the body down beside the others and spun around, making again for the twisted bus. He glanced behind as he went, and wished he hadn't. The first tears streaked the woman's lined face as her hands reached for her husband's prone body. Tom wanted to go back, wrap a consoling arm around her shoulders, and hold on tight as the forlorn sobbing racked her frail body. But there were almost a dozen people still inside the wreckage, a ticking bomb with no visible timer.

He paused outside the wreckage for Katherine to pull one of the older children to the ground, heels dragging. Then he plunged again into the dark cloud. It was thicker, and visibility was down to a few feet. He plucked up two children, one under each arm, and carried them into open air. The pain in his body, still present, had subsided to a tolerable level and some of his strength was back, to be sapped again by the repeated transitions from dirty air to clean and back again. His stomach was getting nauseous. Locking out the sensations, Tom set the children down in the grove and retraced his steps.

Katherine was far inside the second row, struggling to heft a moaning, heavyset woman from the third row over the back of the seat between them. Tom climbed in as Katherine looked up and said, "I couldn't get her door open, and I can't move her alone. She's too big, and I think her leg is broken."

Tom's stomach knotted at the unnatural bend in the woman's right leg. He shook his head in frustration. "Hold on a second." He poked his head outside and glanced at the third-row door. The twisted frame overlapped its latched edge by a good two inches. Tom pulled back inside. "There's no way that door is opening without a blowtorch and crowbar. We don't have time for a splint. I'll get her around the shoulders and take the bad leg. You carry her good leg."

Katherine nodded and bent to one side as Tom clambered over the seat past the woman. The woman's face was screwed into a tight knot and her sobs came in staccato bursts. Tom pulled her right arm around his neck and passed his arm around her back and under her left arm as Katherine lifted the left leg fractionally. Tom set his other hand gingerly under the woman's soft right thigh. A shudder passed through her body and her eyes flicked open.

Tom looked at Katherine with his eyebrows arched and she nodded. He tensed his muscles and said, "All right. One, two, three, *up*."

His legs throbbed as he straightened them, and the strain in his arms was almost unbearable, but the woman lifted off the seat.

"*Go*," he grunted. He knew the dull ache igniting in his back would become intolerable quickly.

Tom's eyes clenched in pain as the woman's fingers clawed his shoulder, simultaneous with her scream, millimeters from his ear. The foot dangling below her broken leg had hooked on the seat as they'd lifted. They inched her back down, and Tom guided the leg into the open, precious seconds lost as his strength drained. The woman screamed again as her bad leg touched the other.

"Move," said Tom desperately. His arms and his back were on fire now. *Don't let go*, he told himself. *Don't drop her....*

Some of the burning left his arms. The Japanese translator was leaning in over the second row with his unbroken arm around the woman's back, right below Tom's. The sleeve of his other arm, hanging limply at his side, was moist and red. Tom could not fathom how the man had managed to climb up from the fifth row with such a handicap.

The translator nodded once. He eased his body over the intervening seat back and squeezed down beside Tom. "I am with you," he said.

Tom smiled in return. You are that, he thought, and never more welcome—but the ache in his back was returning. He jerked his head toward the door. They all bent to the task, and the woman's body lifted through the smoggy haze.

Twice more she screamed, but they maneuvered her over and down into the second row, then through the open door and out to the bright grass and clean air. Tom choked fiercely as nausea clutched at him. His eyes cleared again, and they hurried to the shelter of the trees, setting the woman down beside the others.

How many remained? Tom remembered counting fourteen besides himself, Katherine, and the driver, which made seventeen. He ran his eyes over the clearing. Eight figures lay there. That, plus himself, Katherine, and the translator, was eleven. There should be six left.

As they cleared the line of trees on their way back to the bus, Tom glanced up the slope. The climbers had covered about three-quarters of the distance to the bottom. He hoped at least one would be a doctor.

The translator was abreast of him.

"Stay back," Tom said. "Take care of your arm." It looked bad.

"When we are finished," the man's voice was clipped, riddled with pain, but decisive.

They climbed back into the smoke-ridden interior. It was very hard to see now, and Tom squinted as he peered into the remaining seats. All the children were off. There were two women left. He gestured the first, petite and awake, huddled against the door of the fourth row. "You two take her." He climbed into the row and lifted the woman without difficulty over the seat and into the arms of Katherine and the translator.

As they pulled her into the second row, Tom reached for the final woman, one of the Japanese, slumped in the fifth row. He caught her up in both arms and hefted her into the fourth seat. No one had tried the door here, and he turned the handle and kicked for all he was worth. The hinges cracked and the door fell to the ground. Tom counted three more bodies in the gloom, and then he was out the door and into the sunlight with the woman in his arms. He felt sick again, but pressed on and set her down with the others behind the trees.

Wait a minute, he thought...three more? He had expected six, and they had just taken two. Shouldn't that leave four...?

The translator started back, weaving as he walked. Katherine was leaning against a tree, head down, coughing. Tom put a hand on her shoulder and she looked up. Her pale face and golden hair were streaked gray from the smoke, but the eyes were as clear and blue as ever.

"Stay here," Tom said. Smoke poured from the door of the bus, through the broken windows and out the open top.

Katherine shook her head, still coughing, but with a firm gaze fixed on him. "Not while I can still stand."

"Katherine—" he began.

"I'm fine." She stifled another cough and pushed his arm away.

They ran side by side back to the bus. The translator had already disappeared inside. Tom plunged inside the black cloud and up into the fourth row. He choked as the pungent smoke met his nostrils, then stumbled full force into the translator. Even directly in front of him, Tom could only just make out the man's form in the gloom.

The translator was struggling with his one good arm to hoist up the man at the far end of the seat. That man was awake, and choking furiously.

Katherine touched Tom's shoulder. "I'll help." Then she was coughing too. Tom climbed into the back seat. He threw all his weight against the door, and it didn't budge. He wasted no more time with it, bending toward the man closest to him, the elderly Japanese.

Jagged shards of bone poked through the sleeve of the man's left arm, showing faintly white in the smoke that was slightly thinner here than at the front. Tom barely stopped his churning stomach from retching. He pushed the compound fracture out of his mind as he reached down. The man was heavy, and either unconscious or dead, for he made no sound as Tom jerked him up and over the seat back in front of them, impelled by desperation. Tom climbed across and tried to hold the man's broken arm steady against his side as he shuffled him to the edge of the seat. He managed to keep the arm from brushing any obstructions.

Katherine and the translator had already left the bus with their charge. As Tom stepped to the ground, another cloud of smoke disgorged from the engine compartment and surrounded him, plunging him into hot acrid darkness. His eyes watered and he staggered against the sidewall until some subconscious impulse got his arms and legs moving again, and he seized the man's limp body and staggered into the sunlight.

The bright light on his stinging wet eyes and the shock of clean air on his sooty lungs was too much, and Tom took two faltering steps and dropped. It was all he could do to keep the man in his arms from slamming into the ground unchecked, and then he was rackingly sick. As the spasms eased, the urge to keep moving fought its way to the surface, and he shoved away the desire to collapse into blissful oblivion. The job wasn't finished yet. Tom summoned all his strength and pulled the man upwards.

Then they were both on their feet, as Katherine and the translator wrapped their arms around them and heaved. They made it to the trees, and crashed in a heap on the earth.

The world was wavering before his eyes, but Tom knew he had to get back, just once more. One man left...he struggled up to a sitting position, when the man he had just carried began to murmur softly. Old trembling fingers closed on Tom's arm and the man's eyes opened. The translator put a hand on him and said something but the man showed no sign of understanding.

"He says, 'black sun falls.' I think it is nothing," the translator said to Tom. "Poetry he once read, perhaps."

Then the man was babbling incoherently, his whole body shaking.

Tom looked over. "Katherine...."

She wasn't there. Tom's eyes shifted from the empty spot where she had been kneeling, through the trees to the raging black cloud. Oh no, he thought, tearing his arm free of the fingers gripping it. She'll never do it alone. Tom stumbled around the edge of the trees. Got to help her.

The first rescuers reached the bottom of the hill and were running toward them, shouting vigorously. Tom was almost gone—the last powerful burst of smoke had all but finished him—and he spared them no more than a quick unseeing glance. His legs betrayed him and he slipped to the ground. *Get up. Go help her.* He tottered back to his feet, lurching forwards—and then he stopped in amazement.

Ten yards away, Katherine emerged from the dark haze obscuring the bus from view, coughing painfully but eyes alight, moving in slow motion as if dragging her feet through new-poured concrete. Behind her she hauled the last survivor from the bus.

Tom couldn't understand how she had found the strength to do this, for the man must have been twice her size. But she was moving far too slowly, and he started forward to help.

Katherine looked up, saw him coming, and smiled. It was a perfect smile, in which the beauty of the girl inside shone through the tired, dirty, disheveled exterior and etched itself into Tom's mind, not to be forgotten, frozen for all time—for in the next instant there came a muffled boom from the smoking wreckage behind her, and even as the smile extinguished from her face and her head and body began to turn, a brilliant white light flashed from the depths of the billowing haze and a cloud of yellow and orange flame exploded outward with pent-up fury, engulfing Katherine and hurling her and the man she had retrieved toward Tom.

An impossibly loud thunderclap detonated in Tom's eardrums. He roared in futile helplessness, surging forward, determined to snatch the girl from the grip of the flame. But even as he moved, a gigantic oven opened before him, the shocking blast of burning air picking him bodily off his feet and thrusting him backwards. Tom had a fleeting glimpse of would-be rescuers diving for cover as he twisted in the air, and then his flight ended as his back slammed against a tall pine. Agony ripped through his body and his head snapped backwards. It struck with ringing impact, and as Tom dropped to the ground, darkness rushed in, mercifully extinguishing the pain and drowning his senses to the chaos of the raging inferno creeping slowly, steadily toward him.

CHAPTER

7

First, there was nothing. Then, though he could not say when it changed, there was everything: turmoil, thunder, and fierce agitation. Then there was only something. Time passed; the turbulent waves quietened.

He tried to fight his way through them to the surface. Desperately flailing, twisting, but he was not moving.

He gave up and took a breath. Strange that he did not choke. Could he breathe? What was this? Through the darkness he made out a line dividing the black below him from the deeper black beyond. He was hovering at the edge of a precipice, weightless. He could see nothing after it, but what lay beyond called to him, tempting him to roll off, to plunge into the murky depths below, twisting away, descending into peace. He knew that if he went, the dull ache that filled his body would leave.

It called to him, enticing, seductive, and his resolve dissipated. Why not? So easy to let go....

A figure took shape dimly in the gloom swirling before him. A girl. It was her—then another shape took form behind her, a vaporous kaleidoscope of angry and churning, puffing, billowing clouds of thick black smoke.

The girl looked at him. She smiled. He knew that smile. He had seen it before.

He began to fight again, harder, trying to move, straining to find some surface to push off of, some way to move toward her. There were only moments. He could save her. He had to save her.

Straining....

Through the gloom, an incandescent burst of flame erupted from the churning black cloud, reached hungrily for her.

Must save her....

The tongue of flame caught her, surrounded her, lifted her. No....

She was flying at him, hair scorched, clothes afire. He tried to reach out to her.

No movement in his arms.

All at once he was moving, rolling through air. Dark sky spun above him, then, below, the inferno with the twisted hulk at its center. It passed out of sight. Beyond it, the would-be rescuers dove for cover. From the shifting scene, one of them, tall and gaunt, twisted around and looked straight through him with an angry, narrowed gaze, eyes shining bright red in the darkness.

What...?

Everything flashed brilliant white.

Tom Connor woke with a start. His eyes opened, and he saw a hand at his shoulder. He jerked his arm, chopping the hand away, and twisted up, ignoring the pain in his head as he drew his fist back to deliver a solid blow. He heard a girl's scream.

Tom's hand stopped in midair and the fury drained from his face, though his heart thumped wildly. A cringing nurse was bent over in front of him, her eyes wide with terror. Behind her a door jerked open and light streamed into the dark room. A man in a dark green U.S. Park Ranger's uniform burst through.

Tom opened his fist and raised his other hand. The ranger stopped, uncertainly.

"I'm sorry," Tom said, smiling gently at the nurse. "I won't hurt you. I was having a bit of a nightmare; woke up too fast. Thought you might have been someone else." His head hurt terribly and he dropped back down on the bed.

"You can say that again." The nurse lowered her hand from her mouth and rubbed the one he had struck gingerly.

"Ma'am?" the ranger said.

She nodded. "It's all right. He's fully awake now." The man shrugged and stalked out, and the nurse looked at Tom. "You certainly have fierce reactions. You were tossing and turning, and mumbling to yourself. I thought you were about to wake up."

"You were right," Tom said dryly. "If you knew what I'd been through, perhaps you'd forgive me for reacting badly."

Compassion and curiosity mixed in the girl's face. "I do forgive you. I know what you've been through. It's incredible." She hesitated, then continued, "It's all over the papers: 'Death Run Down Going-to-the-Sun Highway,' and such. And then, you rescuing all those people afterwards—why, it's nothing short of heroic."

Tom looked at the girl—black-haired and young, about his age, with more in her smile than professional medical concern. "I'm no hero," he said. "I don't feel like one. I did what I could, and it wasn't enough."

"No, you're wrong. If you hadn't done what you did, everyone on board would have died." The girl put a hand on his arm, a warm hand. Tom hardly noticed as his thoughts turned inwards, as he saw the little compact car spinning into the gorge; as he saw the driver of the bus and the old husband, both with their heads akimbo on their necks; as he saw again the brilliant flame reaching out for Katherine.

"They didn't all live," he said somberly. "I know that."

"No one could have done more." The girl patted his arm. "It was just horrible bad luck for you to be caught on an old bus when it broke down."

"What?" Tom looked up at her.

"Well, that's it, isn't it?" the nurse said. "The paper says so: old vehicles combined with poor inspection schedules— what with the park budgetary cuts and all—they're calling for grounding the other buses until they're checked out. This might even finish them off forever." She continued excitedly, "Did you know there was another bus accident earlier in the day? A rockslide, no less; can you believe it?"

Tom's head throbbed so that he could hardly think, and the girl was patting his arm again, which did nothing to settle his thoughts. She said, "You talked a lot while you were unconscious, and—"

"Knock that off." Tom pulled his arm away. "How long have I been out? And where am I?"

The girl withdrew her hand, abashed. "I'm sorry." Her face flushed and she looked down. "I'm not being very professional. Forgive me."

"It's all right," said Tom. "Forget it. How long was I out? Where am I?"

The girl cleared her throat. "You're in the Kalispell Regional Medical Center. You've been here one night." Her voice regained its bubbly tone. "Anyway, you were talking a lot. I couldn't make out most of it, just a little here and there." She tilted her head coquettishly. "Who is Katherine?"

Tom flinched. "The girl I was traveling with on the bus. She was caught in the explosion. Didn't they bring her here?"

The nurse's expression showed sympathy and embarrassment. "I don't know."

Tom stared at her. "You don't know?"

"No...yes...I don't know." The girl lowered her eyes. "I'm monitoring the patients in this wing. I'm not sure how many casualties—uh, how many survivors there are. The most seriously injured people are across the building."

Tom sat up and gritted his teeth as new pain lashed his head. "Who's in charge here?"

"Dr. Greenwell, but—"

"I want to see him."

"I don't know—" the nurse bit her lip.

"Now," Tom said. His voice softened as he added, "Please."

The girl hesitated before giving in. "All right. But you stay here. You're not fit to move." Finding Tom's expression less than encouraging, she said, "I'll get the doctor, and I'll find out where Katherine is. What's her last name?"

"Lancaster." Tom sat back and managed a smile. "Thank you."

"Susan," the nurse offered.

Of all the crazy.... Tom sighed, and nodded fractionally, "Thank you, Susan."

With a flushed smile, the girl swept through the door and banged it shut behind her. Tom rolled his eyes, and grimaced as the results of the action hammered his skull. He looked down to see himself dressed in a ridiculously effeminate blue gown. Where were his clothes? Why couldn't they give you something decent to wear in a hospital? And what was this nonsense about being unfit to move? Silly, hero-struck girl. He would move, all right.

Tom swung his legs off the side of the bed. Intense dizziness blasted him, and the room receded behind a light mist. The fit passed and he eased himself to his feet. His head protested fiercely, but he found he could stand without support—though only gingerly on his right foot—and he looked around.

It was a typical hospital room: the railed bed, its metallic rungs folded down; a television set hanging in one corner of the ceiling; incomprehensible pieces of equipment scattered here and there, riddled with screens, dials, and levers—their full operation known only to members of the medical profession and those patients who had been unfortunate enough to require connection to them.

A strong antiseptic scent filled the air, mixed with a subtle nauseating odor of decay, and Tom recoiled at the whole thing. This place was for the sick, the injured, the dying, and the dead. He felt a powerful impulse to run, hard and fast.

He thought dismally about Katherine. Could she have survived the explosion? The flames had reached her, but the blast had thrown her away from the bus, as it had him. He felt a burst of hope mixed with determination. If she was anywhere inside the hospital he would find her, even if he had to raid every room himself.

The door swung open, and a man wearing a long white jacket over turquoise hospital fatigues entered the room. He looked to be about forty-five years old, with graying hair and a salt-and-pepper beard.

"And just what are you doing out of bed?" he asked in a level, good-natured tone as he reached for the switch by the door.

The overhead light clicked on.

"Looking for my clothes," Tom said.

The bright light cast shadows in the crevices of the doctor's brow—lines of concentration and stress, contrasting with those at the edges of his brown eyes, which Tom suspected were etched by the dry sense of humor found so often in practitioners of technical fields.

"Ah," the doctor said. "Your clothes. You won't find them."

"Why not?" Tom asked with a hint of impatience.

"They're being cleaned. Quite dirty you know."

"I believe it." Tom looked at the plain white clock hanging on the wall. "When will they be finished?"

The man's eyes twinkled as the lines ringing them deepened. "I expect about the time your discharge from the hospital is issued."

"Come on," Tom exploded, "I've been in this place long enough for you to wash a load of laundry. I'm ready to leave. I'm ready to get out of this gown."

"I say," the doctor's mouth opened in mock surprise. "Please restrain yourself on that count, for the nurses' sake, if not my own. I believe we are better able to judge your physical condition than you are. How does your head feel, for instance?"

After a pause, Tom said, "A little sore."

The doctor snorted. "An understatement which suggests a certain natural modesty, despite your instincts with the gown. As you have suffered a mild concussion, I presume your head is more than slightly sore. And the more you talk, the more you move around, the worse it will feel."

Tom looked at him sourly. "What else is wrong with me?"

"I suspect the pain in your head is the only distraction keeping you from focusing on the rest of your body. You are a walking mass of abrasions and contusions."

"Huh?"

"Scrapes and bruises. Concentrated primarily in your abdomen, both fore and aft, and your right hand, but there are many more scattered over your body." The doctor peered downward. "And from the way you favor your right foot, I daresay your ankle is also tender."

"You don't miss much, do you?" Tom said, "Even if you do take the long way around saying it. Dr. Greenwell, I presume?"

"Indeed, yes. The one and only. I do like to think I know my profession. For instance, I know that you should be in that bed right now, not standing in front of it—and I believe you know that, too, if you are honest with yourself."

Tom grunted noncommittally, and the doctor sighed. "My boy, you should consider yourself lucky. You would be attached to a catheter and assorted other bits of wiring and tubing if the hospital was not so entirely overwhelmed with patients at this moment. But I could possibly be convinced that we have made a mistake prioritizing our allocations," Greenwell motioned toward the bed, "if you grasp my meaning."

Tom scowled and sat down. The pressure in his head eased a little, and it did feel good to take the weight off his foot. He said, "Doctor, I was traveling on that bus with a girl—"

"Yes," the man nodded. "Susan told me. She has gone to investigate. But you needn't worry. The deceased are all male."

Tom's heart leapt. She was alive then! He sobered as the import of Greenwell's words struck him. "How many dead, doctor?"

The twinkle left Greenwell's eye. "Four, I'm afraid. All pronounced dead on arrival." He clasped his hands and paced slowly across the room.

Tom nodded quietly. "The driver, the other man with the broken neck—"

The doctor waved a hand as he turned to face Tom, "No, no. The driver is alive—a bull of a man. Neck fractured; a great deal of blood lost from his scalp laceration, but he has survived an operation and transfusion, and I feel he is out of danger."

Tom said with surprise. "Who else, then?"

"'The other man with the broken neck,' as you eloquently phrase it; a second Caucasian, apparently thrown from the bus as it rolled down the slope; a third, nearest the bus and caught in the explosion; and one of the Japanese."

"The one thrown from the bus coming down explains why I thought I'd miscounted when we rescued the others. The Caucasian in the explosion must have been the one Katherine was carrying off the bus when it blew. But you said she was not killed."

Greenwell hesitated. "I said that the deceased brought to this hospital were all male."

Tom shook his head, "A technicality, assuming everyone was brought here."

The doctor shrugged, and Tom said, "You mentioned one of the Japanese? None of them appeared to be fatally wounded to me." The I-know-my-profession look was back in Greenwell's eyes, and Tom added hastily, "Not that I'm an expert."

"Of course, of course." Greenwell smiled placatingly. "As you say, none of the Japanese was fatally wounded, until a six-inch shard of steel chanced to protrude itself through one man's forehead during the explosion, piercing the brain. A freak occurrence, and a tragic one."

"Which man?"

The doctor shook his head. "I understand Greek, Latin, French, and, occasionally, English. Japanese eludes me entirely. I couldn't begin to tell you the name. Would you recognize it if you heard it?"

"No," said Tom. "I never had a chance to ask. What did the man look like?"

"Young, black haired, a squarish face, though his appearance has, er, altered since you saw him last. One badly wounded arm."

"The translator," Tom said sadly. "He should have stayed put when I told him to. I'll bet he went and followed me when I got up that last time." He looked into the corner of the room and his mouth twisted. "The man deserved better." His eyes focused on the bare olive green wall, and the room was silent, except for a mechanical hum and some occasional digital twittering.

After a time, his thoughts ordered again, Tom said, "What about those motor homes I hit, halfway up the road? I know what happened to the car I rammed."

Greenwell lowered himself into a steel-frame chair. "No deaths aboard the motor homes, an extremely fortunate result. Smaller injuries, a broken bone or two, but nothing major—more than can be said for the vehicles themselves. Put it this way—" he succeeded in a smile, "—all the motor home owners are in sound enough shape to want to lay their hands on the madman driving that bus."

"That's something, anyway. How about the rock fall earlier in the day?"

Greenwell seemed uneasy. "Those survivors weren't brought here. We are on the west side of the park. They were taken to a facility on the east side. You'll have to ask Ranger Hollis for more information. As a matter of fact, I understand he is most eager to speak with you—when I 'give the okay,' as he put it."

Tom searched the man's face. "You know more than you're saying."

"Do I?" The doctor seemed tired suddenly.

"Come on, doc," Tom said.

Greenwell looked him in the eye. "The report is fourteen dead."

Tom nodded moodily. After the tale told by the man with his wife and little daughter at Logan Pass Visitor Center, he had expected no less.

There was a knock at the door. The handle turned, and Susan entered. Behind her, the ranger looked in with eyebrows raised, and then she closed the door.

"Well?" Tom said.

The girl shook her head, with a curious expression in her eyes. "You did say her name was Katherine?"

Tom frowned and said edgily, "You know I did—you asked me who she was."

She raised her hands helplessly. "I know. I can't understand it. The only girl in the hospital with that name—woman, rather—was admitted three weeks ago with a stroke. I checked the computer, and there are no unidentified patients on the premises, living or deceased."

"Katherine with a K, not a C?"

The nurse nodded, "I checked both."

Tom was on his feet again. Forget his pounding head and twisted ankle—what was going on? "She's a little younger than me, blonde and," he winced, "probably burnt pretty badly." Tom turned to Greenwell. "If the dead are all men, then she must be here, and alive."

Susan stood motionless, looking confused. Greenwell stood up and shook his head. "Our staff would not make an error of that magnitude. Neither would the rangers." He shook his index finger. "Which begs the obvious conclusion that there was no girl of that description, either on the bus or brought here later, a fact you yourself should know best as you are the one who carried the other passengers away from the bus."

Tom stared in disbelief. "She was there with me the entire time—she helped me carry them. I want to see the other survivors, all twelve of them."

Greenwell looked perplexed. "Twelve?"

Tom sighed. "Even if you don't know Japanese, you're smart enough for a little math. Four dead and myself is five. That leaves twelve other survivors out of seventeen people who rode that bus. Twelve survivors, and one of them is a slim, blonde-headed girl. You take me to them and I'll soon—"

Greenwell was shaking his head, as color flushed his face. "I assure you that I had mastered both basic and advanced mathematics before you had mastered the removal of your thumb from your mouth." He took a moment to regain his composure and said, "Forgive me, it has been a long day. But it is your math that is in question: Four dead and yourself is five, truly. Eleven others were rescued, making sixteen in all."

Tom opened his mouth in prelude to an angry reply, but stopped. Despite Greenwell's air of occasional buffoonery, the doctor would not have achieved his position through incompetence. Tom's voice was tense but controlled as he said, "You're quite sure? Sixteen people recovered, and no girl like I've described?"

"Absolutely," Greenwell said. "I do—"

"Yes, you do know your profession. I know." Tom allowed a brief smile, and said mildly, "But I'm telling you that seventeen people boarded that bus when it left East Glacier. I counted them." It was a statement of fact, and his quiet, level tone left no latitude for argument. The doctor and Susan looked at each other, puzzled. Tom nodded at the door. "I think it's time to talk with the ranger. Unless you feel my head needs more rest." He would go open the door himself if Greenwell opposed him.

But Greenwell did not. "No," he said, "I believe this is a good time to permit the official's official entrance."

A moment later, ushered in by the doctor's outstretched arm, the ranger walked through the white door into the hospital room, holding his wide-brimmed Smokey-the-Bear hat loosely in one hand. He nodded, and an easy-going smile broke on his lean face. "Steve Hollis," he said.

Tom shook the proffered right hand. The grip was warm, dry, with coiled force behind it.

"Tom Connor."

"Glad to know you, kid," Hollis said. "That was a nice job you did yesterday on the bus."

Tom frowned. "Not nice enough, I'm afraid. Listen, sir, we've got a problem." He talked for one minute, at the end of which the ranger was also frowning deeply.

"You saying we missed somebody back there?"

"Yes," Tom said, "though I don't know how you could have. Katherine was right in the middle of everything."

Hollis looked at Greenwell and back to Tom. He thought for a moment. "I hate to bring it up, but the doctor says you've got a concussion. We went over that scene with a fine-tooth comb. You absolutely sure about this?"

Tom's fists clenched and relaxed. "Of course I am. She's the one who woke me up after we fell. She helped carry some of the people off the bus. Why don't you ask them? Someone should remember a beautiful girl with long blond hair."

The ranger placed his hat over his sandy-brown hair. "I believe I will. Doctor, who's awake?"

Greenwell, regarding Tom with evident concern, said to Hollis, "May I speak with you a moment?"

"Certainly." The ranger nodded at the door.

The two of them left the room, leaving Tom, smoldering and feeling completely foolish in the feathery blue gown, alone with Susan.

"Doc thinks I'm crazy," he said. "I see it in his face."

Susan looked startled. "No, not at all. But," she hesitated. "He knows you've suffered an injury which could have affected your memory." She took a step toward him, holding her hands clasped and lowered before her. "If it helps, I heard you speaking out loud while you were unconscious, and I believe you. You seemed very troubled." Bafflement crossed her face. "I don't know what on earth could have happened."

"Could Katherine have been taken to a different hospital?" Tom asked. "One better able to cope with burns, for instance?"

"No," she said, "we're well-equipped to handle burns. All the reports say that sixteen people were recovered from the crash site, and all of them brought here."

Tom sat on the bed and rested his brow on his hand, thinking hard. He remembered the images swirling in his mind before his dramatic reawakening. Were they more than a dream? He had read once that the mind records everything entering it through the senses, trivia as minute as the lettering on a pencil,

125

lying on a desk in an office visited once, many years in the past; that these memories can be drawn out if the brain is properly stimulated and freed from conscious restraint. Perhaps, during those fleeting seconds when he had flown through the air, senses overtaxed and unable to distinguish any individual's features, his brain had recorded the presence of the red-eyed Villerot among the rescuers below. If the rangers and medics had not found Katherine at the site, and knew nothing about her, then someone must have carried her away. Who could that someone be, logically, besides Villerot?

Assuming the man had been present, and had removed Katherine, where would he have taken her? The lodge? Was she being medically attended? Tom's heart was pounding again—too many unanswered questions. He thought of Katherine, of her beauty and bravery. If she was being maltreated...there had to be a way out of this hospital. He looked at the door. Greenwell wouldn't believe him, but Hollis might.

He hesitated. If the ranger didn't accept his story, the doctors might pack him away for a good long time—time in which everything could be lost. On the other hand, if Hollis believed him, but investigated clumsily, the situation could also be worsened. The pulsing in Tom's head intensified.

The door opened. Greenwell entered, looked back, and tossed a parting comment to Hollis, who made to move off down the hall.

"Ranger!" Tom called out, shoving his doubts aside. Susan jumped beside him, and Greenwell looked on in surprise as Hollis poked his head through the door.

"Yes, son?" The ranger lifted his brows.

"Can I have a word with you, sir?" Tom asked urgently. "Alone? It's important," he added as Hollis glanced at the doctor.

"All right." The ranger walked through the door. Tom looked steadily at Greenwell, who shrugged and exited the room followed docilely by Susan.

Tom waited till the door clicked shut, then turned to Hollis. Without preamble he explained the circumstances of his meeting Katherine, of her feelings regarding Villerot, of the encounter he had had with the sinister man before the bus ride, and the details of the disastrous trip itself. He held nothing back.

As his words poured out, the ranger's face grew more and more serious. When Tom finished, Hollis sank into the chair next to the bed, lost in thought for several minutes.

Finally, he frowned. "These are serious accusations, or suggestions of guilt, rather. You realize I have only your word for them?"

Tom nodded and the ranger continued, "I'll be frank: I don't know if I should believe you or not. In the hall just now, the doctor dished out a compelling list of the effects a concussion can have. I don't think he missed one, and he didn't pull any punches, either."

Tom said nothing. Hollis reflected further, and said, "You do seem fairly lucid." He sighed. "I already have more than enough to do, but that's another story. What you've told me is too outrageous to be ignored. But, get this—" his green eyes fixed on Tom's. "We're not playing games here. There will be consequences if I find out you're lying."

Tom nodded. "Yes, sir."

"All right, then." The ranger stood up. "Which room in the lodge are these folks staying in?"

"Upper floor," Tom answered immediately. "Right-hand front section as you face the lodge entrance from outside."

Hollis nodded. "Greenwell says you're going to survive, despite your own best efforts to the contrary, and that he can't do more for you by way of treatment, only give you a place to rest." The ranger smiled grimly. "As if I didn't know the answer, but do you feel well enough to travel? This Zimmerlee should identify you readily enough, if what you say is true."

Tom shot to his feet. "The sooner I'm out of this, the better." He stifled a grimace as the room swayed around him.

Hollis chuckled. "You remind me of...well, never mind. I don't like hospitals any more than you do. Been in a couple times, myself." He grew serious. "I'll tell Greenwell to find your clothes—I take it you don't mind if they're dirty. You get dressed, and stay here till I get back: before we go, I still plan to speak with any survivor who happens to be awake. Then we'll find a back door. There are a dozen journalists milling around the front lobby, and more arriving every hour, all of whom I would rather avoid—a more wretched flock of vultures I've never seen; they'd take a corpse over a survivor any day, if only the corpse could talk. They're jockeying for position right now to sink their claws into whoever wakes up first. So far, officially, no one has."

The ranger's lean face hardened. "The Going-to-the-Sun Road is closed for at least a week, so we'll drive around the south rim of the park back to East Glacier, pay a call on your friends, and try to discover what mischief is afoot here in the Backbone of the World." He turned, opened the door, and strode into the hall.

As the man departed, Tom felt the surge of the racehorse when at last the gate is thrown open before its itching hooves—this, coupled closely with the bristle of danger in his spine at the prospect of standing once more before the red-eyed man he believed responsible for calling the clouds of death and destruction down onto the pristine park.

CHAPTER
8

The green and white patrol vehicle sped down the highway, its engine pulsing rhythmically in the late afternoon stillness. Ranger Hollis drove with a precision borne of natural instinct, thorough training in mountain vehicle operation, and an intimate familiarity with every inch of the road. He read each rise, fall, and bend quickly and accurately, holding the car always at the speed limits—values which in some uneven regions placed entirely too much confidence in the ability of the average driver—with a relaxed competence that left his passenger completely at ease.

Tom looked out the window and wondered how the sandy-haired ranger would have reacted to the tour bus's loss of brakes on the Going-to-the-Sun Road. Probably wouldn't have sweated a drop, he concluded.

He asked about the aftermath of the rock fall which so shortly preceded that event.

Hollis was grim. "It took all the equipment we could muster to pull the boulders off that bus. Twelve people were crushed—died instantly. Two others were barely alive but died before reaching the hospital. Lucky, that way, really. The funny thing is," he laughed humorlessly, "two more walked away with only minor scratches after the wreckage was opened. Strange how it goes."

"I saw it happen from a distance," Tom said. "Shook the ground, even where we were."

"If this Villerot of yours is involved, he has a lot to answer for. Eighteen deaths. Possibly nineteen," Hollis added pointedly. "Plus the financial burden of getting the Going-to-the-Sun road reopened. It's littered with rocks and craters now—you'd think you were walking on the moon. Probably cost us half a million to clean it up."

They drove on for a time, snaking through the forested hills lining the southern end of the national park, listening to the engine's growl and the rumble of the road under the tires. The heavy air was broken occasionally by static laden bursts from the radio. "Want to listen in on a ranger's life?" Hollis asked, turning up the volume.

Tom found himself engrossed in intermittent reports of an ongoing rescue of two climbers stranded in a remote region of the park.

Hollis shook his head. "You climb?"

"No," Tom said. "I'd like to, someday."

"Well, if you do, the first thing is to learn your own limitations. Every year, it's the same thing: climbers get into predicaments beyond their control—either scared or hurt, and then it's up to us to bail them out. Complete waste of time and money. Someday our budget will get cut just a little too much, and then it'll be too bad. We may even have to prohibit climbing in the park altogether."

"Are you in charge of emergency rescues?" Tom asked.

Hollis laughed. "Not often. I do lots of things, more every year, but mainly security related jobs. Right now I'm in charge of preparations for the president's visit."

Tom's mind flashed back to the train, and Percy's newspaper.

"I'd heard about that," he said. "How do you end up investigating bus accidents, then?"

SNAPSHOT

"Simple enough," Hollis answered. "The president was due to travel the Going-to-the-Sun Road—won't now, of course—and make a speech at Logan Pass. I was up at the pass, tying off some loose ends, when word of the rockslide came in. Being so close, I headed over, but there was nothing I could do except keep order till the rescue teams arrived. I no sooner got back to Logan Pass when I heard about a second incident involving a park bus, down the road the other direction. So, off I went again."

Tom regarded him carefully. "Coincidental, don't you think?"

Hollis's eyes narrowed. "Disturbing, more like. I figured I'd better keep tabs on the hospitals; see if anyone had something to say when they woke up. Anything that smacks of trouble needs to be put down, hard, before the president arrives. He's determined to come out here for his vacation, and you can guess that there's no talking him out of anything he sets his mind on."

"It's one of the things I like about him," Tom said.

"Sure, me too—there are too many pansies and not enough real men running around nowadays. But suddenly the last day or so, I'm sweating an awful lot because of his visit." Hollis pursed his lips. "I admit that his trip is one of the reasons I'm paying more attention to your story than I might otherwise."

Tom looked at him sharply. "You believe Greenwell, then?"

Hollis thought for a moment and said delicately, "I believe you're a young man who acted with courage in a desperate situation—and suffered a head injury in the process. I'm making a determined effort to think nothing more until I've looked into what you have to say."

Tom nodded in resignation. "When does the president arrive?" he asked.

131

"Two days," Hollis said. "The afternoon of July third—at which time Montana becomes the center of the known universe." The ranger laughed. "The president thought he could make a quiet visit. Yeah, right. The governor decided to rent an orchestra and throw a real live ball his first night here." He drew his thumb and forefinger in a mock headline across the dashboard. "'Crown of the Continent Honors Crown of the Nation During Independence Day Celebration.' What a mouthful. It's been in the works for months. I'm sure all the president really wants is to hit the trails and disappear for a few days."

"He could use a rest after duking it out with Congress and the world the last couple of years."

Hollis nodded. "I admire him, but I don't envy him. One man, against the political machinery of our country, and all the others, too. But he seems to come out on top more often than not."

Tom smiled. "That's him. He dominates. Keeps the peace through strength; earns respect by his integrity. Nobody I know would fault his character, even if they hate his guts."

The radio crackled again and a woman's voice reported a grizzly bear sighting without incident near Bowman Lake in the northwest corner of the park.

The car slowed. They passed through a sparse settlement consisting of a few small buildings and several signs advertising vacation cottages and cabins.

"This is Walton," Hollis said. "Named after the famous fisherman."

In moments they were accelerating again, flying down the twisting road. Both of them grunted with relief as the report came through that the climbers, one of whom had fallen sixty feet and broken a leg, had been safely evacuated.

"Nice to hear some good news," Tom said.

The radio rattled again and a man's voice spoke about poaching in the southeastern section of the park, several squirrels shot with nine-millimeter rounds.

Hollis frowned. "Probably some kids coming in off the Blackfoot reservation, or up from one of the towns to the south. Having fun blasting away where no one's watching. Usually shoot twenty-twos, though. One more item for the list." He shook his head. "Ordinarily I'd jump on it, but it's nothing at all right now."

The conversation petered out until Hollis said, "Tell me more about this girl of yours." He turned the radio down in the middle of a report of a partially decomposed elk carcass whose distinguishing feature was a severely shattered skull.

Tom reflected over the day or so preceding the bus crash. "She's not like anyone else I've ever met. Beautiful and fascinating inside. Sort of a girl lone wolf." He paraphrased what he knew of her background, and went on, "She knows a lot and she's capable—showed that when we were pulling those people off the bus—and she doesn't seem focused on all the glitz and glamour most girls get wrapped up in. The fashion model stuff, the faces full of makeup, the flirting; you know—the girls you can't have a real conversation with because they're too busy stringing you along."

Hollis said mildly, "Some people think the fun and games make it more interesting."

"Well," Tom said, "I'd like to find a normal woman."

The ranger chuckled. "You may have just insulted my wife, but we'll skip that. I know what you're saying. Tell me though, if ninety-nine percent of women like to doll it up and play yo-yo with their men just because they can, and one percent doesn't, is the one percent normal?"

"Normal for me," Tom answered. "I don't care what the rest of you think."

Hollis laughed again. "What does this paragon look like?"

Tom described Katherine.

"And she educated herself?" the ranger asked.

"Mostly."

Hollis swerved to avoid a gigantic pothole without missing a beat. "She in college now?"

"No," Tom said.

"Applied? Thinking about it?"

Something rustled in the back of Tom's brain. There was an edge in the ranger's voice. Tom realized that Hollis was measuring his every remark for weakness and discontinuity. He said carefully, "Not that I know of. We didn't talk about it."

Hollis was quiet for several moments. Then he said, "Okay, listen. When we get to the lodge, we'll go straight up and see these people. I want you to come along. No names of survivors from either bus have been released, and I want to see the expression on the men's faces when I put you in front of them. But leave the talking to me, got that?"

Tom nodded, realized the ranger's eyes were on the road and not him, and said, "Yes."

They lapsed into grim silence. Tom's mind turned introspective, sifting through the assorted problems and potential dangers ahead.

Five minutes later they arrived at the turnoff from the main road to the lodge.

Full circle, thought Tom. I'm lucky to be back. He looked up the serpentine road leading to the wooden structure reposing before the mountains. The sky was violet, and yellow lights were appearing in the lodge windows. Tom shook his head. Had it really been fewer than two days since he was here last? It seemed like a century, and the placid scene in front of him had an unnervingly surreal quality. What was Percy doing right now? Worrying about him? And Nick? Not worrying about him, probably.

Tom's eyes moved along the brown edifice to the window that stirred so many emotions inside him. It was illuminated, and his palms moistened. Just one more out of so many other windows, not worthy of another glance from any of the several dozen people ambling over the lodge grounds, but for Tom, it was the whole focus of his being. There was nowhere else to look—they had to find something here.

Hollis drove up the winding path and pulled into a parking stall reserved for official vehicles. He looked at Tom. "Remember what I said. Stay calm; keep your head. We have nothing tangible against these people. They may be quite innocent."

Tom shook his head. "How else could you explain Katherine's disappearance?"

The ranger thought about it and said, "She could have been knocked silly in the blast, but still been able to move, and crawled away without knowing what she was doing."

"Surely there would be some sign," Tom protested. "You said you guys scoured the area thoroughly."

"We did."

"Well then?" Tom's mouth turned down. "My concussion, right?"

Hollis said slowly, "Before we left the hospital, I went to talk with all the survivors who had regained consciousness. I found four, and none of them remembered a blond girl on the bus. You'd think someone would, if she were the corker you've described."

"We sat in front," Tom said. "The others probably never got a good look at her. Nobody pays attention to incidental people when they're in a place like this. Besides," he added, "once things went wrong, they had other things on their minds. The disasters, being injured and knocked out, might have crowded her out of their minds."

"If you admit that being knocked unconscious could have such an effect," Hollis said, "you should acknowledge that your concussion may have done a similar thing to you."

"Oh, come on," Tom said. "It's easier to forget a glimpse of someone you've barely seen than to manufacture someone as being there with you the whole time, who never was."

"Seems so, intuitively" Hollis admitted. "Still, Greenwell makes a good argument. How is your head, by the way?"

"Fine," said Tom, annoyed.

"Good," Hollis smiled. "Well, no point delaying—let's go do this."

Tom swung the door open and climbed out into the brisk evening. He squeezed his eyes as the movement made his head spin, then opened them quickly, inching the door shut and using it as a support until everything focused. Glancing across the top of the car at Hollis, he was glad to see the ranger looking the other way.

They walked up the short path, replying tersely to greetings from the passers by, and reached the lodge. Tom inhaled the woodsy smell of the fire in the stone hearth. The snapping and popping of the logs was drowned by the mix of people's voices, coming from every direction. One group on the side appeared to be a father and three children, gathered in a circle, playing cards. A few sat alone, eyes buried in paperback novels or staring vacantly into the dancing flame. The grand piano stood silently in its corner.

"See either of them down here?" Hollis asked.

"No," Tom said, "but the light was on in their room."

The ranger nodded. "Lead the way."

Tom strode to the staircase, Hollis at his heels. They climbed quickly, their stark faces drawing a wide berth from people coming the other way. Reaching the top, they turned the corner and moved down the long balcony. At last they stood outside the well-remembered door, and Tom steeled himself.

He thought of the rock fall on the other bus, and his own deadly plummet, and willed himself to show no emotion. Let the two men in the room make the slip, if one existed to be made.

Hollis motioned the door and arched his eyebrows. Tom nodded. The ranger squared his shoulders and rapped on the door. There was silence, and after several moments passed, Tom decided the occupants must be absent after all, but then he heard a rustling inside. The deadbolt clicked, the handle twisted, and the door swung inward. Stamford Zimmerlee's stocky figure filled the entrance. Tom looked at him twice. The man's eyes, widening as they saw Tom, seemed sunken. His face was worn and haggard, and its wrinkles seemed deeper. His brown sweater and tan pants were rumpled, and the overall impression of strain was heightened by the tired voice that said, "Yes, gentlemen?"

"Professor, you look awful," said Tom. "What's—"

Hollis gave him a stern look and said, "Good evening, sir. My name is Steve Hollis, and I'm a ranger with the national park. Are you Doctor Stamford Zimmerlee?"

"I am," the professor replied.

"Do you know this young man?" the ranger asked, pointing at Tom.

"Why, yes," Zimmerlee said. "We have spoken briefly. Mr. Connor, isn't it?"

Good, thought Tom. He said, "Yes, we—" and Hollis cut him off, asking Zimmerlee, "Are you alone?"

After a brief pause, the professor said, "No, my associate is with me."

The gaunt figure of Villerot appeared behind him, clad again in the crimson and gold kimono. Tom fought to keep the scowl off his face. The tall man's piercing red eyes betrayed nothing of the thoughts behind them. They rested on Tom for three seconds and then moved to the ranger. Hollis, official to

the core, remained impassive. "You are Mr. Villerot?" he asked
in a steady tone.

"Yes, Ranger." Villerot's voice was carefully neutral. "What
can I do for you?"

"You could start by letting us in." Hollis was looking at
Zimmerlee. "We have something to talk over that may concern
you." The ranger seemed more interested in gauging the
professor's reactions than Villerot's, and Tom reflected that
if the two men had concocted a story, Zimmerlee was the one
more likely to slip when telling it. Hollis had a good head on
his shoulders.

"Certainly," Zimmerlee stretched his hand into the room.

The low-wattage lamp on the bureau was switched on,
casting the room into a mixture of warm illumination and
shadow. Glancing about as he entered, Tom saw that the table
near the bathroom was bare. The two beds were made, but
rumpled. A thick open book lay face down on the far bed, and
Tom could just make out the title: *The Summa Theologiae of
St. Thomas Aquinas.* The pillow of the near bed was pulled out
from under the blankets and deeply indented. The door
connecting with the next room was tightly closed. Was
Katherine behind it? Tom envisioned dropping all pretences,
rushing to the door, jerking it open...but no, that wouldn't be
wise, not yet. He looked back to the center of the room.

Hollis, next to him, took a quick look around and then said
to Zimmerlee, "Do you have anyone else in your party?"

Tom watched the professor. The man's hooded eyes flickered
toward him and back to the ranger as he said, "No."

"Just the two of you?" the ranger pressed.

"That's right," Zimmerlee replied, a slight tremor in his
voice.

The indignation in Tom cried out, but he held it back as
Hollis said, "Where were the two of you yesterday?"

Zimmerlee motioned the chamber. "Right here."

"In your room, all day?"

"Mostly," the professor said. "In and around the lodge."

Hollis glanced at Tom, then back to Zimmerlee. "Have you heard anything about two incidents which took place yesterday involving Glacier Park tour buses?"

"Something, yes," the professor nodded. "Quite a lot of talk down in the lobby. Vastly differing accounts, I'm afraid. A rockslide was a common theme."

Hollis pursed his lips. "There was a rockslide on this side of the park. It severely damaged one of the buses. A second bus lost control going down the mountains on the other side. Brake failure, it seems. It crashed in the end. This young man was on it."

"How dreadful," the professor said. "I'm delighted he has survived." There was compassion in his voice, and Tom, despite his rising frustration, began to feel that whatever had transpired, Zimmerlee had not been a willing party to it.

"In fact," said Hollis, "Mr. Connor is the primary reason that anyone survived on that bus. Unfortunately, there were several who did not survive." Hollis took a long look at Villerot for the first time since entering the room, and the ranger's eyes were not friendly. Villerot remained quietly unmoving, his face a blank mask.

Hollis turned back to Zimmerlee. "There is also one passenger unaccounted for. Mr. Connor says he was accompanied on the bus by a girl. Your niece, to be precise."

"My niece?" The professor looked acutely uncomfortable.

"Does that surprise you?"

"Yes—well, no, not exactly." The old man rubbed the side of his neck. "It simply isn't possible."

"Why not?" Hollis asked.

"My niece departed for home yesterday afternoon, and without having been on any bus ride, I assure you." The professor's hands had begun to shake and his frail voice was badly strained now. Tom looked at Hollis impatiently. It was obvious that the professor was under duress—but then, Hollis had never spoken with Zimmerlee before. He wouldn't know that this was different from the man's normal tone, would he?

"She had been staying here, with you?" Hollis asked.

"Yes, of course," Zimmerlee said. "We arranged for her to occupy the connecting room. I wondered if you were referring to her when you asked about our traveling party, but as she had already departed, I answered as I did."

Hollis took a long look at the connecting door, and turned back. "What's her name?"

"Katherine Lancaster. I am her mother's brother, hence the difference in surname."

Hollis pointed at Tom. "Mr. Connor asserts that a girl of that name was on the bus with him, and that she was badly burned in the ensuing explosion. This is at great odds with your story. Can you suggest an explanation?"

Zimmerlee shook his head. "I cannot, frankly. It sounds as if he has survived a horrific experience, and I commend him for his—for what sounds like his heroic actions. He must have met my niece during the time she was staying here, if he knows her name. Perhaps the trauma of the accident has caused him to confuse certain facts."

"Perhaps," Hollis said levelly, "but I must investigate his claim as a matter of policy."

"Of course."

Hollis turned suddenly to Villerot and asked, "Have you ever seen Mr. Connor before?"

Say no, Tom thought, and we've got you. I described your looks and your voice very accurately to Hollis back at the hospital.

But Villerot's narrow face showed no signs of being caught off guard. The thin mouth opened and his voice was cold and precise. "Why, yes. Stamford told you he had spoken with this young man briefly. That was yesterday morning, when he came up here and introduced himself as a student who had used one of Stamford's books in his engineering classes. I was also present at that time."

The ranger turned back to Zimmerlee. "How did Mr. Connor know that you, the author of one of his textbooks, was visiting the park and staying in the lodge?"

"I haven't the slightest idea." Zimmerlee looked at Tom. "I never asked. If he met my niece over the course of the last few days, my identity might well have emerged during their conversation."

Hollis nodded. "Was your niece present when Mr. Connor spoke with you yesterday?"

"No," the professor said as he lowered himself heavily onto the bed nearest the door, twisting away from the ranger's steady gaze. "I believe she was wandering about the lodge and its environs during Tom's visit."

Hollis walked around to face the professor squarely again. "Do you know where she is now?"

Zimmerlee turned his head. "On her way to Breckenridge, Colorado. I maintain a small house near there. I must tell you, however, that she has quite the taste for camping and wandering, and may not arrive home for several days."

Hollis took a couple of steps, again lining himself up with the professor's pale face. "You're not concerned about a young girl traveling through the wilderness alone?"

Zimmerlee looked down at the floor. "She is of age, Mr. Hollis, and, unfortunately, very independent."

Tom wondered dryly whether the ranger would crouch now to bring himself again into the professor's line of vision, but the official stood where he was and said, "May I have the address and phone number of your home in Breckenridge?"

Zimmerlee looked up. "Of course. I am anxious that this be resolved." He stood up quickly and walked to the dresser between the beds. Villerot coughed, his first action in some time. Hollis looked at him, but Tom's eyes stayed on Zimmerlee as the professor pulled the top drawer open. Inside it, Tom saw what appeared to be the same stack of technical papers he had seen in the room the last time—shoved in the drawer when the ranger had knocked on the door several moments ago?

Zimmerlee pulled out a pad of paper and a pencil. He wrote several lines of neat cursive, tore the top sheet off the pad, replaced the pad and pencil in the drawer, and closed it. He handed the sheet to Hollis and smiled.

"Thank you," said the ranger. "One more thing."

"Yes?" asked the professor.

"Do you carry a picture of your niece?"

"I do. She is one of the few bright spots in my life." Zimmerlee dug into his pocket and took out a fat black wallet. He opened it and handed it to Hollis.

Tom peered over the ranger's shoulder at the portrait of a girl—fit, undeniably beautiful, with many qualities of strength and character showing in her face—but the dark hair, hazel eyes, and round face were not Katherine's. Hollis, without asking, extracted the picture from its plastic cover and turned it over. Three short lines of flourishing script were written on the back: "Uncle Stam—love always, Katherine."

Tom was near the breaking point. This sham had to end. He growled, "Professor, you know that—"

"Tom!" Hollis's voice cracked. He handed the photograph and wallet back to Zimmerlee and said, "I'm sorry to have bothered you, gentlemen. Thank you." He looked at Tom. "Let's go."

Tom stiffened. "But—"

"Now," the ranger said, his voice soft but commanding. He motioned his head toward the door.

Glowering, Tom fell in step, and Zimmelee drew up beside them as they walked away. The professor said, "If we can be of further assistance, Ranger, please don't hesitate to ask."

"Thank you, Professor," the ranger smiled. "I may take you up on that. Good night."

"And, young man," Zimmerlee said, "whatever's happened, I do hope you manage to straighten it all out."

Tom looked at the professor. Villerot was still behind them, and Zimmerlee's eyes widened and he opened his mouth as if to say something—but Villerot came up quickly, and all emotion vanished from the professor's worn face. Then Tom and the ranger were out on the balcony, and the door clicked shut behind them. Tom turned to Hollis in anger. "Ranger—" he began, but Hollis cut him off swiftly.

"Come on."

They strode back down the hall toward the stairway. Tom said, "You didn't probe. You didn't even ask Villerot directly what he's been doing the last couple of days."

"How dumb do you think he is? What's he going to say? 'Well, Mr. Hollis, you bet I caused the rockslide. Clipped the other bus's brakes, too.'" The ranger shook his head. "I never saw such an expressionless face in my life. If their story was a fabrication, they had it down pat. No loose ends—they're protected, no matter what we come up with. And they've left me with only your word to keep investigating on."

"Well, you do have that." Bitterness hung in Tom's voice. "You'd think someone on the bus would have remembered Katherine. How could Villerot know for sure that no one would?"

"Think about that a minute. The story those two handed us—if it was just a story—stands up. The picture Zimmerlee pulled from his wallet didn't look anything like your description. So what if someone saw you on the bus with a blond hair blue eyed girl? It wasn't their girl. We'd still have no reason to investigate the two of them. And, since their girl happens to be this big-time wanderer, we have no reason to worry at her current absence. We also can't expect to track her down for questioning, at least for a while."

"Doesn't look to me as if you'll track her down, ever," Tom said testily.

Hollis bit his tongue and said nothing. They reached the stairs and started downwards. The ranger stopped, and asked Tom, "Did either of your friends see this girl?"

"Yes," Tom said. "We all saw her."

"Let's have a word with them."

They walked halfway around the second level. The murmur of dozens of voices rose from the lobby below. The air was warm, carrying just a trace of the smell of the fire burning in the stone hearth. They reached the door of Tom's room and Tom knocked on it.

After a moment, it swung inwards and Percy gaped at them from the other side. "Tom!" he said. "We heard that—"

Tom waved him to silence as Nick's scowling face poked around the corner.

"This is Ranger Steve Hollis," Tom said.

Percy and Nick nodded at the ranger as he walked past Tom into the room. Hollis noticed the jumble of sleeping bags and hiking gear. "Indoor camping, eh?" His green eyes looked amused. "Seeing this is a single room, would it be prudent of me to ask if all three of you are registered and paying your extra-person fees?"

"Absolutely not," replied Percy, grinning.

"All right, then." Hollis gave a brief explanation of the situation.

Percy said, "We all saw her, a cute blond girl, and later on, Tom told us he was going on a bus ride with her."

"Did you see them go?" the ranger asked.

"No," Percy said. "I was sacked out—about where you're standing, in fact. Vacations are for resting, you know." He chuckled weakly. "Ranger, if Tom says she was there, then I'm sure she was, beyond any doubt."

Hollis gave a dismissive shake of his head. "I'm sure his word is good for what he thinks happened, but maybe he isn't firing on all cylinders."

"Tom's not the kind of guy who hallucinates or gets mixed up about things," Percy said belligerently.

The ranger stared at him. "If he'd been shot through the heart, would you say he wasn't the kind of guy to die as a result? It doesn't matter how good he is normally—anyone who gets whacked on the head can have problems. *Anyone.* Did you talk to this girl?"

"No," Percy said, abashed, "but Nick did."

"Well?" The ranger looked at Nick.

Nick shrugged. "Maybe, yeah, I saw a blond girl the first night when we were all downstairs. We talked, but not for long." He looked at Tom pointedly.

"Hey," Percy said. "She played piano with Tom. A lot of people should remember that."

Hollis thought about it, and shook his head. "It doesn't matter who remembers that. What's important is whether anyone saw them get on the bus together the next day. One doesn't imply the other. Tom, do you remember anyone noticing the two of you immediately before you left on the trip?"

Tom shook his head. "Villerot," he said. It seemed hopeless.

Hollis tossed his hands up. "I don't have time or the legal footing to cross-examine everyone in the lodge. There's one more thing we can check, but frankly, Tom, you're out of luck. All I have is your story, which has been completely shot down by the professor—the one man who, above all others, should have corroborated it." He walked to the door and said to Tom, "Come on downstairs with me."

Nick made a mock snicker. Tom scowled at him and followed the ranger out of the room.

They walked down to the ground floor, past the stuffed goat in the glass case and toward the front desk. The lobby was still full of people. Hollis asked Tom, "She was in the room next door to theirs, right?"

"Yes," Tom said. He looked up to the two rooms on the top floor. Both doors were tightly closed.

They reached the desk and the ranger gave the room number to the young dark-haired clerk and asked, "Is a Miss Katherine Lancaster registered here?"

The clerk glanced at Hollis's badge and uniform, and consulted his computer. "No, sir," he said, slightly awe-struck in the presence of the official. "That room has been vacant since yesterday."

"Were you on duty when she checked out?" The ranger kept his voice easygoing, friendly.

"According to the time log, it would have been my shift," the clerk answered.

Hollis asked, "Do you remember what the young lady looked like?"

"A lot of people come through here." The clerk looked at his screen again. "But, yes." He riffled through a stack of receipts. "Uh, I mean, no. I'm sorry, sir. I don't remember what she looked like. The room was charged to Mr. Stamford Zimmerlee, in the room next door. He closed the balance on this room."

"So you never saw Miss Lancaster?"

"Not that I recall."

Hollis nodded and touched the brim of his hat. "Thank you."

They walked away, and Hollis said to Tom, "That ends it, for now. Doc Greenwell will let me know when the other survivors wake up. I'll put a call in to the Breckenridge police, ask them to check Zimmerlee's address. Tomorrow, when it opens, I'll check with the tour office to see if they kept records on how many bus tickets were sold. At best, that will only turn up a question no one can answer. Who's to say an extra person bought a ticket and then decided not to go? Or even got stuck in the bathroom? Whatever the records show, there still won't be a connection to Zimmerlee or Villerot. And I'm up to my ears in work right now, important work that has to take precedence." The ranger tapped Tom on the chest. "Let me know if you see anything, or come up with an angle we haven't thought of, but in the meantime, keep out of trouble." His voice became stern. "Don't harass Zimmerlee and Villerot. They're innocent till proven guilty. The only thing we know for sure is that you've had a bang on the head—so get some rest." His tone relaxed. "All right?"

He handed Tom a card with his name and telephone number inscribed, and extended his hand. "Whatever else, you did a fantastic job with that bus, both driving it and getting those people off afterward."

Tom shook the hand and smiled farewell. He was tired, his head was sore, his back ached, and climbing up and down the stairs had inflamed his twisted ankle.

"Okay, Ranger," he said. "Sorry you've been put out of your way. Good luck with your preparations."

"Take care, son." Hollis tapped his hat brim again, turned, and headed for the large doorway.

Standing there in the lobby, surrounded by all these people coming and going, all of them smiling and chattering and laughing, Tom had never felt more alone. The doctors' evaluations were against him. The law, such as it was, had no evidence of crimes committed, and believed the doctors.

Well, Tom thought as he watched Hollis depart, his head did hurt, but he knew what he had been through. Katherine had been with him, certainly. And, upstairs, just now, Zimmerlee had been frightened out of his wits.

Tom thought back to what Hollis had said: "Nor can we expect to track her down for questioning, at least for a while." Perhaps that was it. Eventually, when no girl showed up at the Breckenridge address, the seams in Villerot and Zimmerlee's story would show. Investigation would turn up pictures, records; *something* to prove the photograph in Zimmerlee's wallet was false. The tour bus records, if they existed, would show the additional ticket sold. Searches would be conducted, and requests for the holder of that ticket to step forward would be issued and remain unanswered, provoking more investigation.

But it would take time. The truth could be unraveled, but it would take days—maybe weeks. Assuming then that a few days were all that mattered to Villerot, it followed that whatever he was planning was coming quickly. Tom shivered. The single, obvious event looming in the near future was the visit of the President of the United States. Tom didn't know what goal a combination of the sinister Villerot and the technologically brilliant Zimmerlee would seek in connection with the president's visit, but whatever it was, it wouldn't be good.

The camera and the papers, he mused...the answer was there. When he had been caught looking at the camera and technical documents, Villerot had warned him off. The murderous attacks had quickly followed. What did those papers contain? What lay beneath the camera's quiet black shell?

And, what of Katherine? Tom knew he had already formed the beginnings of real feelings for her. Alive or dead, he must know what had become of her.

His mind turned rapidly. The answers, if they could be found anywhere, lay in the room on the top floor. If they were there, it was up to him to find them. Hollis had told him not to bother Zimmerlee and Villerot, but Hollis hadn't seen all the things that Tom had.

He looked up. There must be a way to get inside.... As his eyes swept through the atrium and the succeeding levels ringing it one above the other, he began to see how it might be done. It would be tricky, and there was no one he could confide in or ask to stand as lookout besides Percy or Nick. Percy might. Nick might or might not. Tom wasn't sure he should ask Nick, but one way or the other, he would get into that room tomorrow. If either of them assisted him, so much the better.

If not, he would do it alone.

CHAPTER 9

"Wow."

Tom had never in his life seen anyone who actually fitted the expression "eyes bulging out of their head," but, as he finished telling his story to his two companions, he thought that Percy's face was as close as anyone could ever come.

Percy said, "Don't take this the wrong way, Tom, but I can't believe this happened to someone I know."

All three were sitting in their room, Tom still in his stained clothes from the bus trip. He and Percy sat in stiff wooden chairs, while Nick sat on the bed, swinging his feet and staring at the floor.

"It's not finished yet," Tom said. "We need to figure out what's going on, what happened to Katherine, where—"

"She's dead, and you know it," Nick muttered from the bed.

Tom and Percy turned to look at him. Nick's voice was sullen. "They didn't find her 'cause she's blown to bits. You should have asked at the hospital if they had any unclaimed arms or legs. Then you might have got somewhere."

Tom's jaw tightened as Nick continued, "Some hero you are. First you steal her away from me, then you take her out and get her killed."

"Come on, Nick," Percy said. "We're all friends here."

150

"*Come on, Nick,*" his friend's abrasive voice mimicked. "*Be nice now, Nick. We're all friends here.* Yeah, sure. I don't know where your head's been stuck the last three days."

Tom said, "I was never out to steal her away. And I think she's alive. Nobody was blown to pieces. There would have been traces found."

Nick sneered, "Hey, Tom, you sound different. You talk all slurred now, you know that?"

"No. I'm pretty tired," Tom admitted. "That might explain—"

"Ha. You know what?" Nick's voice was high. "I like you better with a concussion. You talk funny, and make less sense, and you're more tired but no less tiresome. Why don't you lie down and go to sleep? Sleep forever if you like, it's all right with me. You won't be able to stab anyone else in the back."

Tom's fists clenched.

"Ooh, look at him get mad. My friend." Nick's words trembled. "My friend, and her friend. You stole her away and got her killed, and maybe now you'd like to get rid of me too, Tom? You probably would. I wouldn't put it past you." His chest heaved. "I know you're out to get me, Tom. You've been trying ever since we started this trip. You think you're better than me. You do; everyone does—all of you, you all hate me. You— *you*—" His face contorted, and he hurled a stream of profanity at Tom, fluent, venomous, edged with fury.

Finally the tirade ceased, and for some reason, Tom found himself calmer after the verbal battering. He said quietly, "Nick, you have no reason to be this angry."

Nick leapt off the bed. "I hate you, Tom, like you hate me. You're just like every other person I've ever known. You pretend you're my friends—and when I turn around, you screw me over." The voice was almost a scream. "I wish you hadn't survived, Tom. *I hate you.*"

Nick spat on the floor, missing Tom's feet by three inches. He was shaking all over now. To Tom, he appeared dangerously unbalanced. There could be no reasonable discussion, and Tom didn't want to start a fight, so he did the only thing he could think of: raising both hands, he backed to the door, opened it, and walked out. He leaned against the banister overlooking the lobby and took a deep breath.

The door opened again and Percy joined him at the railing.

"Tom—"

"I'm all right, Percy."

"He's lying on the bed sobbing right now."

"What do you want me to do?" Tom asked. "Go back in and give him a hug? I don't know what makes him so unstable. Why the anger all the time?"

"He doesn't mean it, Tom. I told you before he has a compulsive need for winning, but that's not the whole story, not by a long shot." Percy lowered his voice. "The way I understand it, Nick's earliest memories, pretty much his only early memories, are of a drunk father who liked to beat him and his mom once a day—whether they needed it or not. That went on for a long time. One day, his father decided simple beatings weren't doing the job, and he got himself a pistol. That evening Nick lost his mom, and his father landed in jail for life—should have fried the guy, but the state didn't allow it. For the next ten-odd years, Nick bounced around from one orphanage to another. I was his only friend in high school. When he was eighteen, the state turned him out cold into the street. My parents and I tried to help him—we put him up for a while, helped him find scholarships for college, things like that. It was never easy."

Percy's eyes were solemn. "No matter how mad he makes me, and sometimes he sure does, I'll never believe I could do better in his place. He's had it beat into his skull his whole life that he's worthless and unlovable. What does that do to a person? You and I know the difference a solid family makes."

Tom thought about it and nodded. "I suppose after what you've said, he makes a little more sense. I have to say this, though: you said on the train he needs friends. He needs more than that. He needs therapy, lots of it, and soon. He's on the edge."

"Of what?" Percy asked.

"A breakdown," Tom said. "A big one. Look at him; he's all over the map. He's falling apart. He's like a volcano—about to explode, and more pressure building up inside all the time. If he can't find a way to let go...well, it'll be bad for him and bad for everyone caught in the blast."

Percy's eyes were now as sad as Tom had ever seen them; they were getting a full workout this evening. Tom shook his friend by the arm. "We'll do what we can. We'll get him some help. I want that. But in all honesty, we have other things to worry about right now. Nick and his problems hardly seem like anything at all."

"Oh?" Percy looked at Tom uncertainly.

Tom frowned. "We're in the middle of a nightmare. It's a mess; you heard some of it from Hollis. I have an idea that may help straighten it out, but it'll be hard to do alone. I could use your help."

Percy attempted a smile. "That sounds like trouble."

"It is trouble," Tom said. "There's a lot of trouble brewing. I told you before about Villerot and Zimmerlee. Tomorrow, I hope to get into their room without them knowing. That means we have to get them out for a while. Then, I'll need a lookout to keep an eye out in case they come back early."

Percy coughed. "Tom, you're nuts. Can you pick locks or something?"

"It'd be handy—I wish I could."

"Then how will you get in?"

"So easily you won't believe you didn't think of it yourself," Tom tapped his skull.

Percy shook his head. "I'm not up to breaking and entering. You shouldn't be, either."

"I won't do any breaking. The door will be wide open when I enter. And I don't want you to go in at all." Tom smiled at Percy's relief. "I had a hunch you'd rather not."

"I don't want anything to do with this Villerot," Percy declared.

Tom nodded, "I'll keep you as far away from him as I can."

Percy breathed a heavy sigh, "Well, what do you want me to do?"

"A little talking and a little watching," Tom said. "Come downstairs and I'll explain what I've got in mind."

Although they passed the time in silence, none of the room's three occupants slept that night. Nick glared in silence at Tom and Percy when they returned from their reconnaissance, before he rolled over in the small bed. Through the night they heard him tossing and turning, and at first light he threw back the covers, spent ten minutes in the bathroom, and stalked out through the door.

Some vacation, Tom thought. One for the history books, if we live to write them.

After hearing Tom's plan the night before, Percy had agreed, reluctantly, to participate. They had agreed Nick was best left out of it, and with no other subject to talk about and their minds swimming in the details of what was to be done, neither said a word until Nick's departure.

Now Tom sat up. His body was tired, but his mind was alert. His back still hurt from slamming into the tree, but the few hours off his feet had reduced the throbbing in his head to a mild ache. He wanted to get up and get going.

"You awake, Percy?" he asked.

Percy rolled over in his sleeping bag. "Hard to sleep with all this talking going on," he smiled wearily.

"What talking?" Tom threw the lip of his own bag back and started to climb out.

"The talking in my head," Percy said. "I've been arguing with myself all night—why your plan won't work, why I'm stupid to go through with it."

Tom smiled. "You don't have to, you know."

"I know. Do I have to be the one on the phone?"

Tom stood up and winced as he put his full weight on his bad ankle. "They've never heard your voice," he said. "They'll know mine. But don't do it if you don't want to."

"I want to." Percy sat up and stretched his fat arms out to either side.

Tom flexed his foot, trying to work the stiffness out of the ankle. "Do you?"

"No," his friend answered.

"Well, then—"

"But I will," Percy interrupted. "You're my pal, after all. I believe your story, and I won't be in the middle of it, anyway."

"You sure?" Tom limped to his backpack and pulled out a clean pair of khaki trousers and a long-sleeved green and white checked button-down shirt.

"Yes." Percy lurched out of his sleeping bag. "Besides, if I don't watch out for you, you'll just get your skull cracked again."

"Thanks, Percy."

"You're welcome. But I expect a major dinner in reward for my services."

Tom grinned. "You got it."

In twenty minutes they were ready to go, haggard but excited. Percy, dressed in tan pants and a short-sleeved light-blue shirt, shifted apprehensively from one foot to the other.

"It won't be for a while yet," said Tom. "Come on, we'll walk around."

They left the room, went downstairs, and across the deserted lobby. Every few steps, Percy cast little surreptitious glances at the row of telephones by the restaurant, or up to the closed doorway of their target on the top floor. Tom clapped him on the arm and said, "Hey, big felon, don't act so guilty. It'll be fine."

They walked outside and breathed in the crisp, early-morning air. Apart from the sun shining into their eyes over the long train station across the gardens, the sky was empty. It was another perfect day.

The pain in Tom's ankle had begun to ease, and they strolled over the sloping grounds, discussing the upcoming action several times over until he looked at his watch and said, "We'd better get back."

"Time for breakfast?" Percy asked.

"No."

Percy's voice was hopeful. "Do you think the two of them might leave on their own, beforehand?"

"We'll know for sure when we put through the phone call," Tom said.

They walked back into the lodge and sat in two chairs by the stone hearth. No fire burned in its mouth at this time of day, and Tom's eyes swept lazily, casually, over the layered walkways ringing the atrium.

None of them was out yet. Where would they begin? It was the one random element in his plan.

Well, he corrected himself, that and the response of Zimmerlee and Villerot. He thought he could count on the professor's response, though.

They sat for another twenty minutes—Percy, upright as a pole, his hands wiping continually down his trousers; and

Tom, outwardly relaxed. Inside he felt more like Percy than he wanted to admit. What if it all went wrong? He checked his watch again, looked around, and straightened. There they were.

A cleaning attendant, a young college-aged man, had come out on the second level, languidly pushing a cart loaded with cleaning supplies and toilet articles. Moments later, a uniformed girl moved out onto the third floor balcony. She pushed her cart into the walkway diagonally across the atrium from Villerot's room, stopping at the first door.

Tom watched her knock and tilt her head in anticipation of a response, which did not come. She unlocked the door with a key from a full ring on the chain at her belt, detached a vacuum cleaner from the cart, and disappeared inside.

Tom checked his watch and looked up again at the little postage stamp-sized open doorway on the third floor. The time was 9:53. The young attendant reappeared in the hall several times to pull various items from the cart. At last she closed the door and pushed her cart along to the next room. Tom's watch read 9:59. At six minutes to a room...he counted doors around the balcony, calculating rapidly in his mind.

His thoughts were wiped clean as his eyes landed on a second attendant, a young man of about eighteen, who had appeared on the third floor and was making his way along the segment opposite the one Tom had been watching—the one leading to Villerot's room. The boy was pushing his cart toward that room. He stopped three doors away.

Noting haphazardly that several attendants had now appeared on each floor, Tom shot to his feet, heart pounding.

"Let's go, Percy," he said excitedly.

He couldn't make out Percy's mutterings as they hastened to the bank of telephones, all vacant. A few people strolled through the lobby, but it was still empty and quiet in comparison with the bustle of the evenings.

They reached the first phone and stopped. Tom fished some change from his pocket, lifted the receiver, and dropped two coins into the slot. He dialed the number of the front desk, which he had copied from a card beside the phone in their room earlier that morning.

The desk clerk's eyes dropped. There was a click as the man picked up a receiver. A courteous voice said in Tom's ear, "Good morning, Glacier Park Lodge, front desk."

Tom gave the number of Villerot's room and asked to be connected.

"One moment, please," the voice said. The line went hollow.

Tom handed the receiver to Percy, bringing his own head close to the earpiece. He heard one ring. Two. He glanced up again at the cart three doors from his goal, then to the closed room in which the phone beside the Pieta would now be ringing. Had the two men gone out for the day? That would simplify things.

Three rings, and the fourth was cut off. A guttural voice answered, "Yes?"

Okay, Percy, thought Tom. Showtime. You can do it—just relax.

Percy hesitated for a heart-stopping second. Then he spoke, sweat beading on his forehead.

"Good morning, sir. This is Ranger Bill Edwards at the Saint Mary Visitor Center. May I speak with Mr. Stamford Zimmerlee please?"

Tom felt relief. Percy looked like a wreck, but his voice was steady, even conveying a hint of authority.

"What is the nature of your business, Ranger?" asked Villerot's harsh voice.

"That depends," Percy said. "Are you Mr. Zimmerlee?"

Now Villerot would be mulling it over, Tom guessed. Trying to decide whether to hand the phone to the old man, or play the professor himself. Tom begged him silently to turn it over. Zimmerlee would be the more pliable target, less likely to see through the ploy. And, if Tom had read Zimmerlee's pleading expression correctly the night before, the professor might play along even if he did realize the deception.

After a moment, Villerot replied, "No. I am his associate. May I take a message please?"

"I'm sorry, sir," Percy answered immediately. "This business is urgent, and personal. I must speak with Mr. Zimmerlee as soon as possible."

There was another lengthy pause. Finally the rasping voice said, "Very well. I shall fetch him."

Percy wiped a hand across his brow and shook his head unhappily at Tom.

After a moment, a new voice, soft and haggard, echoed in the earpiece. "Hello, this is Stamford Zimmerlee."

Percy stiffened again. "Good morning. This is Ranger Bill Edwards at the Saint Mary Visitor Center. One of our men—Steve Hollis, whom I believe you spoke with last evening—asked me to give you a call. He would have done so himself except he had urgent matters to attend to."

"Yes, Ranger," the professor said. "How may I help?"

Percy's voice took on a somber tone. "This is a difficult thing to have to relate," he said, "but earlier this morning a girl in her late teens or early twenties was badly injured in an automobile accident driving south of the park on Highway 89. No driver's license or other identification was found either on the girl or in the vehicle, and a bulletin with her photo was circulated. Mr. Hollis believes he recognizes the girl as your niece, and is asking that you and your associate, Mr. Villerot, please drive to the station as soon as possible to identify the picture—if it is your niece—and also to answer a few more questions."

"Both of us?" Zimmerlee asked.

"Yes, please," said Percy. "Mr. Hollis asked specifically for both of you to come."

In spite of his pounding heart, Tom had to grin. His friend was doing an admirable job of remembering his lines, and of keeping the trembling and perspiration out of his voice.

It had been the best story Tom could cook up. If Villerot and Zimmerlee wanted to maintain their line from the previous night, they would have to appear concerned at the news. For that, they would have to leave for the ranger station at once. Tom, remembering the route from the bus trip, reckoned that Saint Mary was far enough away to give him the time he needed, but not so far that the two men would risk damaging their story's credibility by choosing not to make the effort.

Tom heard muted discussion between Zimmerlee and Villerot, too low to make out. His head turned as the strident call of a familiar horn filtered through the doorway: the Empire Builder, making the first of its two daily calls at East Glacier. Not long ago, Tom reflected, it had been him and his friends stepping off the train. How many people had climbed down onto that platform over the years? So many come and gone, alone, or with family and friends, for a few days or weeks in this spectacular place—resting, re-energizing their minds and bodies. But not him. He had stepped into a whirlwind.

Zimmerlee spoke again. "Ranger Edwards, we will leave at once. But, where—if it is truly her—is my niece now?"

Percy squeezed his eyes shut. His face tensed, and then relaxed as he remembered. "Kalispell Regional Medical Center. If you do identify the young lady as your niece, we'll find a way to get you to her as quickly as possible. When you arrive at the Visitor Center, just ask for Steve Hollis or Bill Edwards."

"Thank you, Ranger," said the professor's studious voice. "We will be there shortly."

Tom heard a soft *click*. He looked up to the third floor as excitement flooded his veins. It had worked! The room

160

attendant was two doors away. Now, if Zimmerlee and Villerot would just get moving....

Percy replaced the receiver on its cradle and released his breath in a slow gust. Tom grinned at him. "You earned your dinner, pal. Great job."

"Do I look smaller?" Percy patted his sides. "I think I've melted all over the floor. Must be just a wisp, now. Toughest phone call I ever made."

"You're still there," Tom answered, "and in all your glory. Now all you have to do is watch the entrances."

"Right. And buzz the room if they come back before you're done. What if the desk clerk is busy when I try to call?"

Tom glanced toward the front desk. There was only one man on duty. "He should answer at least, and try to put you on hold," Tom said. "Don't let him—tell him it's urgent. Same story: niece involved in car accident. He'll put you through. It's the best we can do. Remember also, I'll need to know when they're in a stairwell or something, so I can leave the room without them seeing me."

"I've got it," Percy said.

"Don't get involved," Tom warned. "Keep a low profile. And relax, I'm the one in the hot seat now. If things go wrong, anything that happens will be to me."

Percy looked worried. "Then be careful, Tom."

"I intend to." Tom thought of the pain in his head, in his back, in his foot, and smiled. A little caution wouldn't go amiss.

Minutes ticked past slowly as the two of them gazed up at the third floor. Tom grew restless. The attendant reappeared in the hall and pushed his cart to the next door, the last before Villerot and Zimmerlee's. He unlocked it and passed inside.

Suddenly the next door swung open. Zimmerlee came out, followed by Villerot, who pulled the door closed and gave the

161

handle a solid rattle. Tom identified each in turn to Percy as they reached the stairwell and began to descend.

"Here goes." He punched his friend on the arm lightly and stepped behind a pillar, leaving Percy by the phone. The two men reached the ground floor and crossed the atrium to the main entrance. Villerot gave a last glance up at the room, and then both were through the massive doors and out of sight.

Tom forced himself to walk at a leisurely pace to the stairwell around the corner from the bank of phones. He knew there was time before the attendant got to the next room, and that hurrying would only draw attention, so he climbed slowly, trying not to limp. Adrenaline heightened his senses and cast everything around into extreme focus. The success of his plan up to now filled him with cautious optimism.

He stopped at the second level and walked onto the balcony. Making a show of taking in the whole vast lobby, he glanced upwards.

The attendant was out of the room, fiddling with something on his cart. After a moment, he went back inside.

Tom climbed up to the final level. He turned the opposite direction from the cart and started walking around the gigantic rectangle of the walkway, pausing before several of the massive oil paintings, appearing to admire each one. Always his attention was focused on the worker.

When Tom was directly across the atrium and parallel with the cart, the attendant emerged, closing the door behind him. He pushed his cart to Villerot and Zimmerlee's room, stooped to the handle, and unlocked the door.

I'm in, Tom thought.

He glanced down to where Percy, only as big as his thumb from this distance, stood looking up at him. *Don't watch me,* he thought, looking away emphatically. *Keep your eyes on those entrances.*

SNAPSHOT

Tom kept going and turned the corner, passing door after door until he reached the cart and open doorway. He slowed to a lazy amble. Inside, the attendant was bending over the half-made bed nearest the open door, obviously under no motivation to hurry through the task. Tom could only wait, restraining his rising impatience behind feigned indifference.

At last the boy moved to the second of the two beds. His ministrations here were no more inspired than with the first. Chafing at the sluggish progress, willing the boy to get moving, Tom began a second forced stroll around the balcony. He noticed more people coming into the lobby. Another phone was now occupied in the bank at which Percy kept his vigil. Percy was glancing upwards far too often.

Tom came around and approached the cart again. The boy stepped through the open doorway, and Tom turned away. Ashamed of the reaction, he reminded himself that to everyone else he was just one more faceless guest, an insignificant part of the grand surroundings.

Then the boy was back in the room, and Tom heard the whine of a vacuum cleaner. He glanced at his watch, surprised to find that it was only five minutes since Villerot and Zimmerlee had departed. He could have sworn it had been half an hour.

He passed the cart. The boy's back was turned as he swept the droning cleaner over the floor between the two beds. Tom rounded the corner and walked ten paces. He knelt, facing away from the room, fumbling with his shoelaces as from the corner of his eye he peered through the open doorway.

The cleaner switched off, and Tom felt a tingling sensation that this was it. The boy unplugged the cord and coiled it. He walked into the bathroom.

Not yet, Tom thought, eyes narrowed: he's only taking stock.

The boy emerged from the bathroom, walked past the beds and through the doorway. He picked two bleached towels off the cart and piled two tiny bars of soap on top of them. Tom's eyes flickered over the three levels of the atrium in a final check. Nothing was different. No one was paying him any notice. He set himself like a runner before the gunshot.

Completing his stack with a roll of toilet paper, the boy turned from the cart to re-enter the room.

Now.

The boy crossed the room, and as his back disappeared through the bathroom doorway, Tom rose. Restraining himself with an iron will to normal pace, he slipped past the cart into the room.

Without a glance at the bathroom, he walked straight to the closet, reached for the handle, pulled the door open, and passed inside, ducking under several garments as he eased the door toward the frame.

He stumbled on something, lost his balance, and let himself go down softly, not risking the noise of a frenzied thrashing. The pain in his back sharpened as his body bent. His face buried itself in the prickly folds of a woolen overcoat, and he landed on something smooth and flat about a foot off the floor. It shifted, and he gritted his teeth, expecting a loud clatter, but the motion ceased. Tom reached up, felt blindly for the door handle, got it, and pulled the door through the last inch. The latch clicked.

Lowering his body cautiously from its out-flung position to whatever lay between him and the floor, Tom pulled his face from the scratchy fabric and took several quiet breaths. He wondered whether it was possible for his thumping heart to make enough racket for the worker outside to hear.

Footsteps passed. Then there was no sound, and when almost a minute had ticked by, Tom wondered if the coast was clear. He reached for the door handle. As he did so, the outside door banged shut, and then he knew he was safe. The attendants left the doors open while they worked.

Tom let out a measured exhalation and opened the closet door. Light streamed in and he looked to see what he had fallen onto. It was a stack of books. Closer examination revealed them to be high-level engineering textbooks, most of them on vibration theory and heat flow.

He untangled himself from the row of clothing and stepped into the room. The little bureau with the lamp and alabaster Pieta on top and its two closed drawers underneath stood innocently against the wall between the beds.

CHAPTER
10

Downstairs in the lobby, Percy wiped his hands together. The flow of people up and down the stairs and through the various doors and passageways around him had increased from a trickle to a steady stream.

He had taken a good look at both Villerot and Zimmerlee, and was confident he would recognize them again, even in a crowd—particularly Villerot. A person couldn't mistake that combination of height and bloodshot eyes, or the prowling stride that made the man so disconcertingly panther-esque. Percy had listened to Tom's suspicions, and seen nothing in Villerot's demeanor to contradict them. The man had none of the bumbling, wide-eyed innocence of the normal tourist.

Percy looked around the lobby again, from the passage beside the fireplace leading to another wing of the building, to the gift shop and the main entrance, and then over to the front desk and the restaurant. His eyes landed again on the portly man in the Hawaiian shirt who had been staring at him for two minutes now, scowling and tapping his foot. Percy averted his gaze, glancing back at the row of telephones, all of which were now in use—except the one in front of him.

Percy pleaded silently with the man: be patient. The other phones will open up. It won't be long. We're on vacation here just wait a bit. Only a few...oh, no. Please don't walk this way—

As though hearing the unspoken entreaties, the man strode up to Percy, who put on a smile as the man stopped in front of him. There were no polite formalities.

"Are you using this phone or not?" the man asked stridently.

Percy said in an apologetic tone, "I'm waiting for a call, sir. An important call."

"Well, I need to make an important call," the man said. "Only take a minute, so get out of the way."

Percy gulped. "I can't do that."

"Sure you can. It's easy. Just step to the side," the man placed his palm on Percy's shoulder.

Percy planted his feet and said, "Take your hand off me!" as his face reddened.

The woman on the phone next to them glanced up, and several people passing by halted. The man stepped back, raising both hands.

"Look, fella, my son isn't feeling well, so I want to take him to the doctor." The man pointed out a small boy huddled in one of the armchairs by the fireplace. "I want to call his mother at Lake MacDonald Lodge, across the park, so she knows what's going on, why we won't be back for lunch. Okay?"

Percy looked away. He thought of Tom upstairs, sifting through Villerot's lair, counting on him to be his eyes down here. Could he abandon his post, even for the moment it would take to let the man make his call? He hadn't thought about having to explain why he was waiting here. Neither he nor Tom had anticipated every other phone's being taken. How brief would the man be? If his son wasn't feeling well, he wouldn't want to be too long....

Everyone was watching. The man's explanation had clearly shifted their sympathies to his side. Percy's shoulders slumped, and he nodded dolefully. He would stay close, though. When the man was finished, he would reclaim the phone, ensuring

167

its retention by picking up the receiver and carrying on a mock conversation until his job was done.

"All right, all right," he said. "Please be quick, though."

The man moved in. Percy stepped away from the phone and looked at the main entrance pensively.

Tom Connor pulled the top drawer of the little bureau open and frowned. He lifted out the hardbound Gideon's Bible and riffled its tissue-paper pages.

Nothing. Apart from the book, the drawer was empty. The bottom drawer held only various pieces of park literature and a phone book.

He turned away from the bureau and scanned the room. The table by the bathroom was bare. Dropping to his hands and knees, he looked under each bed. Except for dust, the space beneath the bed nearest the wall was empty—but a small suitcase lay under the bed by the door.

Tom pulled out the battered brown case. The tag in the leather holder tied to the handle read "Stamford Zimmerlee," and listed a Breckenridge address. The case's rusty clasps sprang open as he slid the catches to the side. He opened the lid, but his heart sank as he poked through the bits of clothing and toiletries. Nothing of interest here. He thought hard as he replaced the suitcase under the bed. Neither man had been carrying a camera, bag, briefcase, or backpack of any kind when they had departed—he had watched for that. The camera and papers should still be in the room, somewhere.

He went into the bathroom and flicked the wall switch. The light and whirring fan clicked on simultaneously. Less than a minute's searching satisfied him that what he sought lay elsewhere. He closed the cabinets, turned off the light, and walked back into the main room. There appeared to be no loose floorboards, and the white plaster ceiling offered no prospect of a hiding place.

That left the closet. Tom opened its door wide for maximum illumination. Immediately he saw what he had not noticed before: a small black case in the corner, concealed behind the low-hanging overcoats and two stacks of textbooks. Reaching for the case, Tom paused, noting that every textbook contained several markers. He pulled the nearest stack into the light.

Each book in the pile dealt with vibration theory. The marked portions related to vibration suppression, shock, acoustics, wave amplification and absorption. Tom had taken a course in vibration engineering, which barely enabled him to recognize that the exposition and innumerable equations strewn over the pages before him occupied a far loftier plateau than anything he had ever encountered.

He pushed the pile back into place and pulled out the other stack. The top two books were on heat flow and internal combustion engines. Under them were three handbooks of material properties, their marked pages focusing on plastics and synthetic rubbers. There was also one book on mechanism design, and, lastly, a civil engineering textbook on explosives for construction purposes.

Tom shook his head. Were they going to blow something up? The lodge? A bridge? Why so much interest in vibration theory?

He shoved the books back into the closet and reached for the black case. Placing it on the floor, he tried the catches and was unsurprised to find them locked. The combination wheels were randomly set. With little hope, he clicked them around till they showed zeros and tried again.

No luck. Tom shook the case. It was heavy, and something bulky thumped inside. Drawing his scout knife from his pocket, he opened the screwdriver blade and looked thoughtfully at the clasps. Was it worth giving away to the enemy the certain knowledge he had been here? It would be tantamount to a declaration of war. He thought of Katherine, of the disastrous events he had lived through, which had culminated in her mysterious disappearance and signified great danger looming now, and decided that yes, absolutely, it was worth it.

But when Villerot found the latches broken, would he suspect the young cleaning attendant who had made up the room? To let harm come on an unsuspecting bystander...Tom hesitated, then rejected the thought. The identity of the person audacious enough to snoop so openly would be more than obvious to Villerot—and Tom would just have to watch his back.

If he came up with something concrete, something pointing to evil plots or revealing Katherine's fate, he could go to Hollis and the law would draw the net around Villerot. Hollis might not be happy about the method, might even prosecute Tom on a couple of wrist-slap charges, but that didn't matter. The basic, unalterable reality was that if he was ever going to find out what was going on, then this, now, was the one chance to do it.

Tom bent to the case again and fitted the blade under the left latch, wedging it in as far as it would go. A vicious jerk of his arm snapped the little clasp and sent it clattering across the floor. He moved to the second latch, and in a moment the case lay open.

Tom's eyes glistened. *Bull's-eye.* The black camera rested on top of several folded technical documents. He picked it up gingerly—if it was a weapon or transmitter of some kind, the last thing he wanted was to set it off. He decided it would be wise to look at the papers first. Setting the camera on the bed, he pulled out the sheaf of papers and unfolded the top one, spreading it on the floor. It was a cutaway view of the camera, divided into two segments: the main body, and the lens extending from it.

The main body was separated by a divider into front and rear chambers. A rectangular cartridge was drawn outside the back chamber, and an arrow pointed from it into the chamber. The diagram indicated that the cartridge attached to the wall dividing the rear from the front. Mechanical linkages extended upward from this wall to the buttons and knobs on top of the camera.

The second, larger chamber at the front of the main body had a cylindrical cavity in its center, stretching from the cartridge attachment at the rear to the lens attachment at the front. Small tubes radiated out from this cavity, feeding maze-like through solid material into a peripheral opening just below the surface of the camera's shell. Mechanical and electronic gadgetry lay at both ends of the central cavity. Tom identified what looked like gearing below the lens attachment, but had no idea what the rest of it was.

The lens was solid, except for a needle-like shaft cut through its center, running all the way along its length. At the far end of the lens, a data table pointed to the shaft's opening and indicated that its diameter was adjustable.

Tom thought furiously, wishing he knew more about cameras. Many had variable lenses, he knew, but surely they required larger openings to capture images than the tiny shaft indicated here. Also, in the rear chamber, where the rectangular cartridge attached, there were no spools for winding film.

Before reaching for the next drawing, Tom folded up the first one. If the phone rang, Percy announcing that Villerot and Zimmerlee had come through the main entrance, Tom wanted to be ready to go instantly, without having to fold up and stow away several sheets of paper.

The second diagram showed several electrical schematics. They weren't labeled by function, and Tom didn't understand them. He refolded it and reached for the next.

His eyes narrowed. This was better. It was a copy of the first diagram, but with several annotations in black ink, written in a neat hand. Next to the lens were tabulated two columns of numbers, the left running from f/4 to f/22, typical aperture settings, and the right from 0 to 30. This second column was labeled "Hz."

Hertz. The technical unit for "cycles per second." It applied to any kind of vibration or periodic motion: a clock pendulum swinging back and forth; an alternating current feeding an electrical outlet; anything with repeating, cyclic behavior.

Most importantly, it could be applied acoustically. Tom scratched his head, thinking of the stack of books, of how many of the marked passages had related to sound. He knew that people hear sounds when vibrating air strikes their eardrums. Higher frequency vibration means higher-pitched sound. Tom checked the diagram again. If the long lens was properly designed, and air was forced through the channel down its center, sound might be produced, like a person whistling by blowing air through pursed lips. The frequency of that sound might be changed by adjusting the aperture opening.

The other major notation on the diagram, a data table, pointed to the rectangular cartridge that went into the back of the camera. The table had three columns: first, a list of colors; second, a range of energy values in foot-pounds; third, corresponding values in decibels, ranging from 120 to 200 dB.

Energy and decibels, Tom reflected. Decibels...sound intensity. 200 dB was extreme: he recalled from one of his classes that rock bands during concerts and heavy-duty aircraft engines only put out 100 dB or so. Just what did that little cartridge do?

The rest of the notes scattered across the page were made up of chemical symbols and long strings of letters, mostly C, H, and O. Tom guessed that they were plastics used in constructing the camera.

Explosives, heat transfer, acoustics, varying sound pitch and intensity. Energy and decibels...energy translated into decibels? Tom's jaw dropped; his hazy incomprehension burned away in the glare of horrible understanding. The device functioned by setting off a controlled explosion within its main body—its source, the cartridge in the rear of the camera where film should have been placed—hence, the tabulated energy values next to the cartridge and all those books on explosives, heat transfer, and combustion.

This explosion would provide an intense expansion of air whose only means of escape was through the narrow passage in the lens. A tremendous wave, forced through a tiny opening—a mechanical version of whistling, but on a devastating scale, judging by the tabulated sound intensities.

And then there were the material properties: much thought would have to have gone into the materials used in the camera, to absorb the generated heat without the body rupturing or becoming too hot to handle.

What was it for, Tom wondered? Shocking people with unbelievably loud noise? Breaking their eardrums? No...not people, in general. Tom had inferred the night before that Villerot's purpose was sinister and near-term, meaning almost certainly a connection with the president's visit. The purpose was now crystallizing.

He remembered back to the morning of the bus trip, and the final piece dropped into the puzzle. Zimmerlee had gone to collect Katherine next door, leaving Tom alone in the room. Tom had picked up the camera, and been confronted immediately by Villerot. The camera had fallen to the table, and shot into the air again with an unexpected rebound. There had been no sound.

Later, everyone had seen the window, broken with terrific force. Villerot had said it was a bird. Tom had thought it was the result of shoving the man into the wall. He had missed the truth by a thousand miles: the camera was not only immensely powerful; it was completely silent. It had gone off, shattered the window, and Tom hadn't understood—even after watching Villerot dodge to the side to get out of its path. But Villerot had thought he'd understood....

Unable to keep a slight tremble from his hands, Tom glanced at the door, then his watch. He closed the print and replaced it. His lips tightened as he unfolded the final document in the stack. His heart raced.

It was a printed map, showing the park and the Blackfoot Indian reservation to the east. Tom checked the scale, and looked back at the diagram. About seven miles east of the park, deep inside the reservation, a red line had been drawn in by hand. It extended north from the east-west line of Highway 2, and ended in a slashing letter "X". If the line had been accurately rendered, "X" was about five miles from the highway.

Tom frowned. All one could expect to find on the reservation—besides Blackfoot Indians—was wide-ranging spaces, cattle, horses, dogs, sporadic shacks and the occasional small town. Because the printed map showed no road where the red line had been drawn, any road that was there would likely be dirt or gravel, probably quite secluded. So what did the "X" signify?

Was it the place where Katherine had been taken? That made sense to Tom—a lot of sense. She was not at the lodge. She was not at the hospital, and Tom decided his goal now was to follow the map to its destination as soon as possible. If he could find Katherine—if by some miracle she was still alive—he would have everything he needed to take to Hollis.

Smiling grimly as he folded the map, tingling with fresh hope, Tom knew his reconnaissance had been a full success.

He put the map back in the case and turned again to the camera. It looked normal, except for the lack of a brand name. The f-stop numbers ringing the lens barrel matched those he had seen listed in the documentation opposite the frequency values. He picked it up and searched for a way to open the rear of the casing. The flap was hinged on the right, so the locking catch would be on the opposite side, making the lever on the top left a likely candidate.

As he reached for the lever, the phone on the bureau burred, shattering his thoughts and setting his nerves on edge.

Rising swiftly, Tom set the camera on the papers in the black case and hastened to the phone. Relax, he told himself, keep your head; work with Percy. He picked up the receiver on the second ring and said urgently, "Yes?"

Percy's voice was flushed with excitement, which Tom had expected. "Tom, they're at the door now."

"Good," Tom said. "Watch them and tell me when they get to the bottom of the stairs—"

"No, Tom," Percy said feverishly, "the hotel room. Your door! They're right outside you and about to—"

Oh, no, thought Tom as he slammed the receiver down, remembering in the last millisecond to ease it onto the cradle. Sweat dripped from his forehead as he raced to the black case, closed it, and swept it into his arms. It could not be locked with both clasps shattered.

A key scraped against the lock outside. Tom scrambled to the closet, ignoring the pain in his foot, thrust the case in behind the stack of books, whisked the door shut and twisted, leaping for the far bed. Everything blurred; he heard the handle turn on the door as he flung himself through the air, hurtling over the bed to catch himself with one hand on the mattress and one on the floor below. He lowered himself into the space between the bed and the far wall as the edge of the door separated from the frame and swung into the room.

Desperately restricting his breaths to short, silent gasps, Tom eased edgewise into the dusty gap under the bed, focusing his attention on preventing the blanket hanging over the side of the bed from shifting, signaling his presence to the returning men.

He watched two sets of feet come through the open doorway. The door banged shut and Zimmerlee's voice said, "Well?"

"Wait, my friend," Villerot's voice rasped. "You will see."

Something had gone wrong, Tom thought as his body slid completely under the bed. He felt a throbbing in the back of his head. Hadn't Percy been paying attention? Of course he had—he would have been sweating and watching like a hawk the whole time. Maybe it had taken too long to make the connection through the front desk.

Everything under the bed was shrouded in dust. A few particles entered Tom's nose and he drew his shirt across the lower half of his face. To sneeze now!

Villerot's feet moved toward the closet. Tom knew that his break-in would be discovered any moment. Would the two men suspect he was still in the room? He was thankful his instincts had been to hide under the bed and not in the closet.

Zimmerlee said, "You're certain you heard the train's horn outside the lodge, and on the phone at the same moment?"

The closet door swung open and Villerot's head and torso bent into view as he pulled the black case out. He rose again and spoke, his voice triumphant: "Of course. A most distinctive sound. I should have realized it instantly, not eleven winding miles up the road. Judge for yourself. The phone call was a ruse, to give us a compelling reason to leave the room, and my case, unguarded."

The professor's voice was mild: "It has been forced, obviously. Couldn't it have been the maids, looking for something valuable?"

"So brazenly, knowing they must be the obvious suspects?" Villerot paused. "Even to the extent of leaving the latch pieces in the middle of the floor?"

Tom's eyes darted across the floor, and he clenched his fists. The jagged brass clasps lay three feet from his face. Villerot's feet moved toward the bed and stopped. Tom shrank back into the claustrophobic space. His shirt caught on one of the wires in the steel lattice above him. Villerot's legs bent and one knee came down. A long gloved hand collected the two pieces of jagged metal.

"What will you do now?" Zimmerlee asked.

"This young man has been a thorn in our flesh," Villerot said. "A poor analogy—I would not call him sharp. But he is persistent. He should be dead twice over, but has survived. It is now awkward to kill him, seeing he has acquired some celebrity with the authorities. Fortunately, they do not accept everything he has told them, as witnessed by our encounter with the man Hollis last night. It does not matter. We can dispose of him by turning him over to those authorities on a charge of breaking and entering."

"Can we?" Zimmerlee asked dubiously. "On what evidence?"

"My dear Stamford, I have just stated that I do not find him particularly gifted—more a blunt object than a finely-honed blade. A statement at which he would no doubt be bristling," Villerot chuckled, "*if* he could hear me speak, that is."

Tom closed his eyes.

"Given what we know of his patterns of thought and action," Villerot continued, "I would wager much that he did not wear gloves when handling this case—unlike myself. His fingerprints, which we mustn't blot, will be on it."

"He was here with the ranger last night," Zimmerlee said. "He could say he touched it then."

"The ranger was intelligent," Villerot said. "He observed all of us closely, including our young friend, and he will know that the boy touched nothing during their visit. I will state solemnly that my case has never been in his hands with my approval."

"I still wonder," said the professor.

Villerot's tone was assured: "You will see. He has made an additional blunder of the grossest proportion."

"That being?"

Villerot laughed outright. "Go down to the front desk and tell them we have experienced a break-in. Tell them I have trapped the culprit in the room, but do not know how long I can hold him—that they would do well to hasten their security people."

"*What?*" the professor asked incredulously.

Villerot moved to the center of the room and said, "Young man, if you wish to live, you and those you care about, show yourself immediately."

Tom's heart leapt to his throat. His stomach crawled.

"Look," Zimmerlee interjected. "If—"

Villerot cut him off harshly. "You know the penalty if you interfere with my plans in any way."

There was a pause, and the professor said, "You are an evil man for that."

"It is the ace card I hold against you in our little game. Perhaps I should say, my queen." Humor, briefly present, left the man's voice. "Young one," he said. "Come out. I will not say it again, and you know well that I will act on what I say."

Tom could not allow Percy or Nick to come under this man's wrath. He doubted Villerot was bluffing, and refused to take the chance.

He pulled himself out from under the bed and rose to his feet, dust-covered and grim-faced.

Zimmerlee stared at him, aghast. "How did you get in here?"

Villerot spoke wryly. "Not through any finesse with the door. He has demonstrated his lock picking proficiency with my attaché case. I should say rather that he rode in on the shadow of the housekeeper." He bowed. "Ranger Bill Edwards, I presume?"

"Yes," said Tom without hesitation.

"Hmm. You are very skillful at disguising your voice." The red eyes looked probingly into Tom's.

"You are also clever at hiding your true self," Tom said.

"I wonder," Villerot mused. "Who are you hiding?"

Tom shrugged, "I don't know what you're talking about."

Villerot's eyes narrowed. "Surely you do not so completely lack sense as to sneak into this room without engaging an available second to act as lookout. You are rooming with friends. It was not your voice on the telephone this morning—do not lie to me that it was; I know it was not."

Tom shook his head. "They know nothing about who you are, or what you're doing here."

"And so it shall remain," Villerot said.

Zimmerlee coughed and looked at Villerot. "How did you know he was still in the room?"

Villerot watched Tom as he said, "I was certain he could not have finished with the materials in the case before our return. I do blame myself that he has seen them at all." The tall man smiled a smile that did not touch his eyes, "I should add, perhaps, that I heard him speaking on our telephone before I unlocked the door. Also his subsequent scurry for cover. Faintly, to be sure, but you must learn to be alert to such things, Stamford. Tell me," he said pleasantly, his eyes boring into Tom's, "who was on the other end of that call?"

Tom shook his head. He said through his teeth, "Jump off a bridge."

Villerot reached his gloved hand inside his coat and drew a long, narrow-bladed knife. All warmth vanished from his face. His dark eyes were a tomb: empty, cold, waiting. The weapon shifted loosely back and forth in his hand.

"Your life or death means nothing to me," he said. "I have you, and can kill you within the bounds of the law by asserting that you attacked me in the course of your very obvious break-in. Stamford will make any statement to the authorities I direct. He has no choice. If you do not tell me everything I want to know, truthfully and the first time—"

"Please," Zimmerlee said.

"Stamford, *go*," Villerot barked. "Do as I said. *Now*."

The professor turned to the door with the air of a whipped puppy and twisted the handle. Villerot advanced toward Tom.

Zimmerlee opened the door and turned back again. His eyes found Tom's and narrowed. The professor made a motion with his hand, squaring his shoulders. Tom didn't know what the man was up to, but he tensed, ready for something.

Zimmerlee hooked his foot on the door with a loud thump and dropped to the ground, giving the appearance of stumbling as he let out his worthiest imitation of a surprised gasp. The attempted deception would not fool a five-year-old child, and Tom feared for the professor's future, but as a distraction it was perfect. Villerot's head turned, and Tom lunged as if a switch had been thrown. He snatched up the wooden chair next to the table by its back and swung with all his strength. The hard seat slammed into Villerot's flank, a crashing blow that splintered the wood and knocked the man sprawling onto the bed. Tom tossed the chair on top of the struggling figure, took two running steps toward the door and jumped, clearing the fallen Zimmerlee who remained in a balled-up huddle on the floor.

In a fleeting glance over his shoulder, Tom saw Villerot shake the chair to one side and push himself off the bed. The man retrieved his fallen knife and veered toward the entrance as Zimmerlee shrank back. Then, raging adrenaline imparting wings to his feet, Tom was away and racing down the balcony toward the stairwell as three startled elderly people scattered like ducks in his wake.

CHAPTER
11

Heart racing, Tom stopped on the landing of the second level, prepared either to continue down the stairwell or to dash out onto the balcony. He looked up, but there was no sign of pursuit, so he walked cautiously onto the balcony, watching the open doorway across and above.

He saw nothing, and hoped fervently that the professor could convince Villerot he had taken an innocent fall due to age, physical ineptitude, or the stress of the situation. If Zimmerlee hadn't intervened as he had, things would have gone badly: Tom had been convinced by the relish in Villerot's eyes that the man had intended to kill him as soon as the professor had gone, and then spin a tale of self-defense to the authorities.

Tom glanced down to the lobby. All the phones in the bank at the wall were taken, and none of the callers was Percy. Motion in the corner of his eye attracted his attention. Percy was at the front desk, waving his arms vigorously. Tom waved back in acknowledgement and looked back to the upper level. He still saw nothing, though the door remained open. He inched rearward to gain a better angle of sight, and his back brushed the wall.

At that moment Villerot stepped through the doorway, with the camera in his hand. Tom jumped for the stairwell a few feet away, but it was too late. Villerot had seen him.

Racing downwards, feet hardly brushing the steps, Tom's mind worked feverishly. How could a person defend against a weapon of sound? What materials might absorb a sonic wave? The wave would be highly directional—it would have to be, if the device's handler was not to be injured by his own weapon. Assuming it was tuned to attack some part of the human body, the effects would likely be absorbed in large measure by the first person struck by the wave—which meant that if Tom could keep another person between himself and his assailant, he might be protected.

But whether an innocent human shield would prevent Villerot from firing was unknowable. If the camera's effects were such as would draw attention, an assault might be restrained except at a clear target in a secluded setting. If the effects were invisible, then the weapon could be used any time, anywhere, with no fear of discovery.

Tom reached ground level, panting, and ran into the lobby, looking for a way of escape.

"Tom!" Percy hurried up. "What happened?"

"No time now," Tom said. "Go back to our room and stay there. Don't let him see you."

"Who?" Percy asked. "Did you—"

Villerot emerged from the stairwell, camera poised before him, eyes sweeping in search of his prey.

"I'll explain later." Tom turned and spoke without looking back as he moved away. "Get away from me."

A group of tourists entered through the main door, chattering excitedly in German. Glancing across, Tom saw Villerot still scanning the atrium, his scrutiny focused on the opposite side.

The tourists gathered in the center of the atrium. Taking a deep breath, Tom hurried over to the group and stopped, positioning one particularly tall and big-boned man between himself and Villerot. Several people in the group looked at him as he asked as casually as he could manage, "Does anyone have the time?"

"Ah, yes." The big man looked at his watch for a moment and then up again, smiling good-naturedly. "German time. It is seven twenty-six in the evening. Time for dinner, hey?" The group laughed, and made to move on. Tom's mind raced to keep the conversation going.

"What part of Germany are you from?"

"Bavaria. A village called Füssen. It is a beautiful place, much like here." The man raised his bushy eyebrows.

"Is it?" Tom asked.

The man looked at the group and chuckled. "I see you do not know it. Have you heard of Castle Neuschwanstein? Our mad former king Ludwig's contribution to the tourist trade." His head moved, and in the distance Tom saw Villerot's eyes moving over the group. They swept past, stopped, and returned. They looked directly into his.

Tom swallowed. "Uh, no. I haven't. What does it look like?"

Villerot took two steps to his left, and Tom matched them, keeping the burly German between them.

"It is the most photographed castle in Germany," the man said proudly. "I am told it was the model for your Mr. Disney's Cinderella Castle. But I am keeping you from something?"

"No," Tom smiled, "not at all. Please continue."

"No, no, it is all right. I see you wish to move along. And we must find our room. Perhaps we will meet again in the evening." The man raised his hand. "*Auf wiedersehen.*"

The group moved away. Tom knew he could not follow without raising awkward questions.

Villerot lifted the camera, and Tom cast about for any obstruction. Spying the historical display boards behind the piano, he slipped behind them and got down, pretending to tie his shoes. He edged around the side and saw Villerot advancing. The man was fifty feet away.

A ranger entered through the main door and paused, looking about with some urgency. Tom saw the opportunity and took it. "Ranger!" He jumped to his feet and ran toward the man, waving his arm, wincing as the dull pain woke again in his ankle.

The official looked at him uncertainly as he drew up. "Are you the one who called?" he asked.

"What?" Tom frowned, caught off-guard by the question.

"About the breaking and entering," the ranger said.

"No," Tom said, "but I—"

Coming up the lobby behind Tom, Villerot roared, "Thief! Hold him—he's the one!"

Now Tom understood Villerot's delay in leaving the room. The tall man must have paused to phone a break-in report to the rangers, and it didn't take a mastermind to guess how things would go if the ranger detained Tom for investigation.

Tom said, "That's not true," and took a step toward the door.

The ranger stepped back, placing his body squarely in the entrance. "Hold it there, sonny. Stay cool and let's sort this out."

Villerot approached rapidly. The ranger stayed in the doorway, and Tom knew he couldn't attack the man, even under these circumstances. Not while there was any alternative.

He bolted abruptly, doubling back into the lobby, shearing away from Villerot, past the gift shop, gaining several steps on the startled ranger, who paused for an instant in confusion before collecting himself and starting forward in pursuit.

Tom didn't look back to see how close either man was, or whether the camera was being lifted and aimed. He tore headlong into the corridor by the fireplace connecting the lodge to its large wing. Windows and chairs whipped past, startled people looking up from books and card games. Heavy muffled footsteps pounded against the carpeted floor behind him and Tom expected every moment the crashing impact of an all-out dive into his back. That fear propelled him on despite his protesting ankle, despite the pain worsening in the back of his head with each desperate step.

He emerged from the corridor into the wing and saw a red exit sign over a door to his right. He slammed through it as the ranger came out of the corridor.

It was a stairway. Tom took it downwards and came out into a small open area with armchairs and a fireplace. Beyond was an open door leading to a porch.

Crisp air filled his lungs as he jumped the porch steps to the rocky ground. He grunted as his weight came down on his weak foot, but quickly gathered his bearings and broke into a run along the side of the lodge. He had come out at the rear of the building. Down a short hill to his right was a pool, closed at this time of year as the water was still too cold for swimming.

A thump followed by hasty scraping came from behind, the ranger leaping from the doorway. Crunching staccato footfalls pressed in on Tom, and he strained to increase his pace, reaching the end of the building and bearing left.

Now he was on grass, passing the front of the lodge and heading into the fields between it and the highway. Tom stumbled on something and regained his balance, glancing down. It was a thin metal wicket. Several people shouted at him as he trampled through their croquet game, their cries switching to expressions of surprise as they saw the ranger barreling along several yards behind.

The flower gardens flew by on the left, and Tom was at the road leading to the highway. He took it, knowing it led to town and a better chance of evading his pursuer. As best he could tell, there was only one set of footsteps behind him. Where was

Villerot? He dared not look around; glancing away would slow his pace.

Up ahead loomed the squatting bridge over which the trains passed each day. The road dipped under it, rising on the other side to join the main highway. The strain of the sprint began to register; fire ignited and extinguished in Tom's lungs with each breath. He heard every heartbeat in his ears, in time to the thumping in his chest. Behind him the urgent footfalls snapped at his heels like an angry mastiff.

A gasping voice called, "Stop, boy," but Tom kept going, under the bridge and up the other side to the edge of the highway, halting frantically as a trailer-truck roared by, inches away. Cars swept past from each direction, and panic welled up inside Tom as he saw the ranger burst out from under the bridge. There was no opening in the stream of traffic, but Tom ran. Brakes squealed nearby on the left, and a horn bellowed on his right as he saw the dark hood of a blue sedan nearly on top of him and still coming.

Tom jumped, throwing his legs to the side as the sedan's brakes screamed. He sprawled on the hood, rolling up as the car continued forward. An astonished face swept by beneath him as he tumbled up the windshield, and then the car stopped moving and his slide ended.

Tom swung his feet down to the hood and leapt to the sidewalk, grimacing as he landed. Every step on his right foot sent pain shooting up his calf, and his head throbbed mightily, but he had gained several steps on the ranger who was momentarily hemmed in by the stopped cars.

Tom turned left into a narrow street and ran, straining to wring the last drop of speed from his legs, pressing his advantage to the limit, gritting his teeth on every other step. Each breath was a tortured rasp. He reached an alley and turned into it, passing two dogs that sniffed at him curiously.

The alley was lined on one side by the backs of stores and restaurants, and on the other by houses, garages, and fenced yards. Tom had run about three-quarters of its length when he realized he could hear no sound behind him. The ranger was not following.

He stopped. The opening from the alley to the street ahead was clear, with no sounds of pursuit coming from that direction, either. Where was the man? A ranger wouldn't give up that easily.

Behind there was still nothing. Tom tried to get his breath under control, to clear the rushing from his ears. He knew the worst thing would be to stand there indecisively, and he jogged the short distance to the other side of the alley and up a driveway leading to a low garage. He pressed around the corner and advanced through the narrow passage between a chain link fence and the garage's drab tiled wall.

Ducking beneath several low-hanging branches of a tree whose trunk was on the other side of the fence, he reached the far end of the garage. Here the passage opened onto a lawn stretching down to a quiet cross street.

Tom's breath cut off and he stumbled mid-stride before turning to plunge back into the slim passage through which he had come.

Villerot stood in the lawn in front of the garage, still holding the black camera.

Tom ducked under the tree again and raced for the alley. His mind calculated frantically. Villerot must have paralleled his flight, watching him from some distance off, then done an end run to catch him from behind. Tom glanced back as he neared the corner of the house and saw Villerot dart under the tree, dropping into the classic pose of the rifleman, one knee down, elbow planted on the raised knee, the camera to his eye.

Tom cleared the end of the garage and leapt sideways, grunting with surprise as he ran full-force into an unexpected obstruction. A strong hand closed on his wrist and another slammed into his back, thrusting him into the fence. The top row of chain links dug painfully into his stomach and the ranger's voice bellowed, "Got you!"

Tom said, "No, listen—" and suddenly the pressure on his wrist slackened, replaced with a burst of pain and a churning nausea inside. Wrenching his forearm against the ranger's thumb, breaking loose, Tom twisted out from under the man, grimacing at the torment that racked his own body. He hadn't heard anything, but knew that Villerot must have fired the weapon. Then he froze, as he came around and saw the ranger in front of him.

Pure agony contorted the official's face, and labored gasps hissed through his clenched teeth and bared lips. The man's body had been between Tom and Villerot, and must have taken the brunt of the weapon's effect: there was no sign of external injury, but the man's hands clawed at his stomach as if trying to tear through the wall of flesh. His trembling knees buckled.

Villerot lowered the camera from his eye, reaching quickly for a lever on the top. He snarled as the ranger dropped writhing to the ground, boots scrabbling on the concrete driveway. The ranger gave a dry, retching gasp and choked as a trail of blood with little bubbles in it smeared down across his chin from the side of his mouth.

The back panel of the camera popped open. Villerot extracted a small cartridge as a cloud of dark smoke disgorged into the air. He placed the cartridge in his pocket and withdrew a second which appeared identical, starting forward as he inserted it into the rear of the camera.

Horrified, Tom broke into a run in spite of the upset to his own body, down the short driveway and into the alley, turning right, knowing the street was closer on that side. He stumbled on loose gravel and recovered. Reaching the street, he turned left, placing a building between him and his enemy.

How long did it take to reload the device? Tom had never seen anything like it. If it was only a matter of inserting the cartridge, then it was operational already.

Now Tom heard racing steps behind him and he looked. Villerot bore down on him, the camera halfway to his face. The man stopped and brought the weapon fully up.

Tom shifted hard left, and immediately back again. He kept running, weaving, anticipating the clutches of excruciating force, unblocked this time.

The racking pain did not come, and Tom did not look back again. He passed several children who yelled something he didn't hear as he swept by.

Now he was coming up on the main highway. He turned left and found himself racing down the long row of shops and restaurants. He reached the little diner in which he and Katherine had eaten before their bus trip. The front door swung open, directly in his path. Tom swerved, nearly colliding with the exiting patrons. Then, on impulse, he sprang through the doorway.

"Oh, hello," an aged feminine voice said, "where's your friend today?"

Tom stopped. His eyes were acclimated to the brilliant sunshine and the room was dim, but he recognized the elderly woman who had been their waitress.

"What did you say?" he demanded.

"I said, where's your friend? The young lady you came in with the other day. You made a lovely couple."

"You remember her?" Tom asked. "A beautiful blond girl?"

The woman looked confused. "Well, of course. Like I said—"

Tom waved his hand to stop her, "Do you remember the specific day that we ate here?"

"Well," the woman squinted as she thought about it. "I—"

Villerot appeared at the window outside, peering into the restaurant's interior. He spotted Tom, and leapt for the entrance.

Tom pointed at the door. "That man is a murderer. Call the police!" He remembered where the door to the kitchen had been, and ran for it. He heard jingling of bells over the main entrance, and the hated voice: "Someone stop that boy—thief!"

A man reached out a half-hearted hand which Tom twisted to avoid. Then he was at the kitchen door. He banged it open. Two chefs looked up from their work with indifference that turned quickly to consternation.

Stovetops and ovens lined the two side walls. In the corner stood a massive refrigerator. A large gray sink had been attached to the far wall beside an open door, and a long table stretched through the center of the room. Tom saw several smoking pans and cauldrons on it as he entered, along with a bevy of dishes and utensils.

The door swung open again, and Villerot surged through. Tom dashed for the table, catching up the first pan within reach. He pivoted and flung the contents at Villerot, who ducked and bellowed as steaming soup seared his face.

Tom got around the side of the table and heaved a second smoking pot at the man. Without pause he gathered up a fistful of knives. He hurled them, one after the other, as he retreated down the length of the table, watching his tall malefactor cradle the camera behind him as a mother with her baby. The two chefs had withdrawn to corners of the kitchen, regarding the proceedings with horror. They left Tom unmolested as he reached the far end of the table.

The door behind Villerot burst open, and two men who had been eating in the restaurant came through in response to the racket. For a moment they stood, temporarily blocked by Villerot, crouched in the entryway, and Tom didn't wait. He bent to the end of the long table and pushed with all his strength, angling it as it scraped along the linoleum floor, directing its opposite edge into the cluster of men. More dishes fell off its sides at the impact, and all three men staggered back. The two newcomers disappeared through the doorway. Tom whipped around and ran for the open door beside the sink. He passed through and slammed it behind him.

Finding himself in a dim, narrow hallway, Tom saw a door at the far end. Bright light streamed through the slit at its lower edge. To his right, a door opened into a dingy bathroom.

There were only moments. Tom ran to the end of the corridor and pulled the exit open. He took a quick look around the parking area beyond, then dashed back to the bathroom, slipping inside as the kitchen door was thrown open. A stream of fluorescent light flooded the corridor.

Tom inched quietly behind the bathroom door, not daring to release his breath though his lungs hurt. Multiple sets of footsteps clattered by. He counted three people passing by in the space between the hinged side of the bathroom door and the frame—Villerot and his two unwitting assistants. The outer door creaked, and voices filtered through the passage. Tom moved around the door to the bathroom entrance, listening intently.

Villerot said, "You, check the garbage dumpster, then go that way. You, the opposite way."

Tom looked down the corridor, temporarily empty, guessing that Villerot would return. His pursuer had probably noticed the bathroom door. Tom started for the kitchen, then changed his mind. Making sure he was still unobserved from either end of the hall, he hurried to the open exit door and stepped into the narrow space between it and the wall.

He was not a moment too soon. Villerot strode through, and Tom pressed back into the narrow recess, prepared either to fight or run, as warranted.

Villerot walked straight to the bathroom, reared his foot back, and kicked the door, a jolting blow that would have stunned anyone behind it. Then he jerked it back and plunged inside.

Tom crept around the exit into the sunlight. The other men were gone. He spotted the dumpster and raced for it as soundlessly as his limping stride would allow. He hoped Villerot had watched the man he'd instructed to look inside it complete his task. Tom got around the far side, planted his good foot on a metal protrusion, and vaulted over the edge onto the refuse below. Thankful to find most of it wrapped in black plastic bags, Tom burrowed beneath the top layer, pulling the bags out and placing them over his body, worming his way down as far as he could go.

A large bee flew up before his face. Instinctively, he clapped his hands on it and swept it off his palm before the incapacitated insect could deliver its sting. A moment later, a sharp prick in his lower leg followed by prolonged burning told him that a second bee had been disturbed. Tom gnashed his teeth at the fire spreading under his skin around the sting, and met further discomfort as his elbow ripped through one of the bags, plunging into something soft and clammy. His nose wrinkled at the odor.

All these distractions vanished from his mind as crunching footsteps approached. Tom kept absolutely silent, not daring to breathe or move as the steps circled round the dumpster. Had Villerot seen him racing toward it? Had the noise of his entrance and shifting of bags carried back to the building? He remembered his scout knife, and eased it out of his pocket. The walking stopped, and a second later he heard a metallic clang near his head. There came a tearing noise as one of the bags at the top was roughly shoved aside. Then more rustling, and Tom felt pressure in the bags closest to his body as those above were moved back and forth. He worked the longest blade up from the handle of the knife and clicked it into position.

A spot of light shone onto his chest, then another just behind his head. Villerot had worked through to the layer just above. Discovery was imminent.

Tom saw movement through the gap over his head. A narrow hand thrust through the gap and grasped the bag covering Tom's head, inches from his face. The fingers dug in, and a hole appeared as the black plastic separated. A stream of cold liquid dripped onto Tom's face and ran inside his collar. His shaking hand gripped the knife tightly as he tensed to strike.

Unexpectedly, a little black and yellow spot flashed from the bag, landing on the sinewy hand. Villerot gasped in pain as the insect's stinger drove home. His bony hand darted upward. Tom heard a sharp rapping on the side of the dumpster, and the crushed bee dropped back through the gap, bouncing off the bag by Tom's head and landing on his right cheek, soft, warm, and furry.

There came a muffled thump, Villerot descending to the ground once more. Tom quietly thanked the improbable intercessor that had stopped the man's investigation at cost of its own life.

There was no sound at all for thirty seconds. Then Tom heard the soft footsteps again, circling back around the dumpster. After a further pause, the crunching tread resumed, moving away, growing fainter and fainter until it had gone.

CHAPTER
12

Tom lay still for some time, surrounded by the trash bags, taking stock of his injuries and continuing to listen for any hint of danger outside the dumpster. His right leg throbbed, both at the ankle and halfway up the calf where the bee had stung him. The queasiness in his stomach, the peripheral effect of Villerot's weapon, was only beginning to dissipate. His head was pounding away, and his back still ached. In spite of his pain, and his desire to do nothing more than lie in one place for several hours, Tom knew he had to move again, and soon.

It would be only prudent to keep out of sight until nightfall—but not here: If Villerot elected to go to the rangers or the tribal police to file a report on the morning's events, then the ensuing dragnet would undoubtedly cover the spot where Tom lay. After the authorities heard Villerot's tale and the stories of the eyewitnesses in the lodge who had seen Tom run from the ranger—and, particularly, once they had found the stricken man—it was only too easy to imagine their hostility. They would shoot first and *not* ask questions later.

But where to go? Tom thought about it for a moment. If he could get across the road and past the grounds of the lodge, he would find all the concealment a fugitive could hope for in the depths of the forests beyond. It seemed the only possibility; there was little chance of concealment inside the town itself or on the open plains. He knew that unless he could produce some sort of evidence against Villerot, he could not come out of hiding—he was in hot water with the law now. And, beyond his desire to clear himself, producing such evidence was also the only way he could see of averting possible disaster on a national scale.

Tom resolved again to trace the location of the red letter "X" he had seen on Villerot's map. He would hide out in the forest until night fell and he could move unseen; then he would contact Percy to arrange some supplies before setting out.

Tom's thoughts died as a new realization hit: He'd never had a chance to explain the latest developments to his friend. Percy would not know the extent of Villerot's malevolence or if the man knew of his acting in cooperation with Tom. If Percy or Nick left the room to look for Tom, or just out of boredom, wanting something to do, they would be open to attack. Tom had told Percy to stay in the room, but with no further explanation given, and no sign of Tom as the day wore on, his friend would venture out at some point.

As quietly as possible, Tom shook the plastic bags above him to the side. Brushing the dead bee from his face with a tinge of pity, he clambered up on top of the pile and peered warily over the dumpster's rim. All was quiet. He folded his knife and put it back in his pocket.

Planting two hands on the metal edge away from the row of buildings behind him, he leapt over the top and dropped to the ground, landing on his good foot. He remained exactly where he was, questing with all senses in every direction.

He saw and heard nothing unusual. A few birds chirping; the steady muted hum of traffic from the highway beyond the buildings. No sirens, no urgent voices. No rangers, and no Villerot.

At last, Tom stepped out from his shelter. He felt like an old man. With his pursuers gone, his mind was acutely aware of every creak and grumble from his tired body. He marshaled his old football resolve, and moved across the dusty parking lot to the line of brick walls, creeping slowly along it to the street.

Now, he wondered, where to find the nearest telephone from which to place a call unobserved? Tom yearned to avoid entering the lodge where the greatest concentration of rangers would be—though if it came to it, he would risk discovery for the sake of alerting his companions. But surely there would be a phone in one of the shops or restaurants lining the highway. Smiling thinly, recalling his dash through the diner's kitchen, Tom knew which establishment not to check.

As a token attempt at disguise, he unbuttoned his dirty green shirt and removed it, leaving only his white undershirt. He folded the green shirt under his arm and tried to hide his limp as he walked along the side of the buildings to the main sidewalk.

No one looked at him with more than a passing glance until two older women strolling by rolled their noses, moving quickly on. The odor of garbage had thoroughly infested his clothes, but there was nothing he could do about that right now. Ducking into the first entrance, a tiny drugstore, Tom saw a pay phone hanging on the right hand wall. He lifted the receiver and dug into his pocket, glad he had stocked his pockets with plenty of extra change before the morning's work. He checked the scrap of paper on which he'd scribbled the lodge's number, dropped coins into the narrow slot and dialed.

There were three rings and the fourth was answered with a soft click and the sudden background murmur of voices and activity.

"Glacier Park Lodge, front desk."

"Hello." Tom gave the number of his room and asked to be connected.

"One moment, sir."

Tapping his foot on the hardwood floor, Tom looked through the window in the direction of the lodge. An eternity passed, then the murmuring voices were gone, replaced by a hollow emptiness as the connection was transferred. At last he heard the intermittent tones of the phone ringing.

Once, twice, three times it rang, and with each recurrence Tom grew more anxious. At the sixth he had reached the limit of his patience and was wondering where to go look for his friend, when the ring cut off and a tense voice answered, "Hello?"

"Percy! Were you sleeping?" Tom lowered his voice. "Things have blown up—I'm okay for now, but I won't be back till tonight, so listen: You and Nick have to stay where you are until I get back. Do you understand? Don't go out, not for anything. Is Nick there? I know it may be hard to convince him—"

"Tom," Percy said quietly, "he's here."

"Well, tell him—"

"No, Tom, *him*."

Tom heard the quavering in his friend's voice. His stomach tightened with a fear he had not known through all the morning's exertions. The tingle of adrenaline was back in his system. "Villerot," he said softly.

Of course, the man had known which room they were staying in from the beginning—he had watched Tom enter it from across the atrium the night Tom had met Katherine.

"He's here," Percy said. "Sitting on the bed. He—he says he'll kill me unless you come back right away. If you come, he promises we'll both stay alive. I'm sorry, Tom. He came up a minute ago and knocked, and I didn't know what to do."

Tom wiped a forearm over his brow. "Has he hurt you?"

"No. Not yet. Tom—"

"Has he got a camera with him?" Tom interrupted.

"A camera?" Percy's voice was rivetingly urgent. "He's got a knife! Please come back. He says he just wants to talk to us."

Tom thought desperately, but the frantic scraps of plans flashing through his mind were dominated by the knowledge that everything had gone wrong, and the fault was only his. Percy was in a worse spot than he could begin to know.

"Percy," Tom said. "Villerot's up to something a lot bigger than any of us. He has no scruples at all. If I just come walking on in, he'll turn us both over to the police at the very least— more likely he'll kill us and assume no one will come looking for a few days."

Tom heard Percy's sharp intake of breath, a prelude to further impassioned entreaties, and said; "Don't worry. I'll come back. I wouldn't run out on you. But we have to fight him, all right?" There was no reply and he said again, "All right?"

Finally Percy said, "No. Please, Tom."

"Percy," Tom whispered fiercely, "he wants to kill the president. Do you hear me? He's got some newfangled weapon, and there's no reason for him to be here with it other than to use it on the president."

"But—"

"And we're the only ones who know about it. Do you really think he just wants to talk to us? He'll kill us with less heartache than you'd have stepping on an ant. If he gets us, no one will stop him. We have to fight."

Percy pleaded, "I just want to live. I want to go home. Please, Tom. Come back."

Tension rose inside Tom. This was taking too long. Villerot would guess what was going on under his nose. Tom shrugged into his outer shirt and started buttoning it.

"Percy," he said, "watch your answers. Whatever we do next won't decide whether he tries to kill us or not, only whether we stand up to him or go down without a fight. Understand me? You've *got* to be brave. Look around and find the chair by the desk. See it?"

After a long pause, Percy said, "Yes."

Tom said swiftly, "Tell him I'm coming. When I get there, I'll knock as loud as I can. When he looks away, take the chair

and smash him, hard. Don't think about it, just act. Then open
the door and get out of the way. I'll take care of the rest. I'll get
him."

The receiver was slippery in Tom's grip. "If he attacks
before I get there, use the chair to hold him off. Sacrifice your
arms to save your body. Retreat, block, kick him low: knees,
shins, groin. Just hold him off till I get there. I won't be long."

"Please, Tom," Percy's words were trembling and without
hope. He said agonizingly, "I don't want to die."

Tom closed his eyes. He opened them and said, "I'll be
there. I'm a minute away. Tell him I'm coming. And hold on,
pal, just hold on."

"I—" Percy squealed and Tom heard a tremendous crash.
The line cracked in Tom's ear as the receiver on the other
end banged into something—not its cradle, for the connection
remained open—and a clamor issued from the earpiece as
though the mythic gates of the underworld had been flung open:
desperate tortured cries, sounds of bodies thrashing about and
objects shifting, falling, more crashing, then, from under it all,
distant and smothered, an anguished yell: "Help, Tom! Nick,
help me! Somebody—"

Tom dropped the receiver and left it swinging on its coiled
cord. He slammed through the drugstore door and raced into
the highway, heart thumping, legs driving like pistons despite
his injuries. Angry cries sounded over screeching brakes, but
no one hit him and he reached the far side and kept running,
down under the bridge and up the other side into the grounds
of the lodge. The lawns flew by, the trees, the croquet players,
the picnickers. The pain was back in his right ankle, but
he pounded along despite the repeated jabs of agony, eyes
narrowed, jaw set, breath rasping in explosive bursts.

He was beyond the gardens and flowers, and the lodge
was there. Then he was inside the double doors of the main
entrance and past bewildered tourists and porters darting

out of the way of the human maelstrom as it crossed to the staircase. Tom bounded upward, three steps at a time, and sprinted onto the second-floor balcony. Sections of wooden banister whipped past, and he rounded the corner, reached the door of his room and drove heavily into it, shoulder lowered. The door flew open easily and he stumbled forward. His foot slid beneath him, and he nearly fell. The room was dim, but he saw that the side containing the table, lamp, chair, and phone was an utter shambles.

Blood roaring in his veins, hands cocked before him, ready to strike or grapple with the enemy, Tom spun around in a circle, but there was no sign of Villerot. As he came around, his foot slipped again. He pressed his finger to the floor and flinched as it touched something warm and sticky. Sick within, he knew what it was.

His eyes adjusted to the faint light, and he saw a huddled mass of blankets on the bed. A dark, uneven stain descended from this onto exposed sheets, trailing down to the floor, across it to his feet.

All else was forgotten. Tom advanced, eyes riveted on the shapeless rolled-up mound, fearing to look, yet drawn to the heap as if by a magnet. His breathing was strained and shallow as he peeled the top of the stained blanket away from what lay below, revealing a tuft of short blond hair. The pale forehead followed, and the blue eyes. When Tom saw the eyes, he knew that his friend would not be seeing through them again. They were open and unwavering and quite empty.

The blanket dropped from the nose and mouth. Tom had to roll the body to continue, and it offered no resistance. At the neck he recoiled. A dark line stretched under the fat chin from one ear to the other. He smelled it now, but ignored the odor and leaned in close.

The line was jagged—obviously Percy had struggled to the end—but the arteries on either side of the neck had been slashed through, and the blood had poured down, draining with it the sight from the eyes and the breath from the lungs, leaving behind it this mindless, lifeless shell.

Tom stared in shock. The image focused unsought in his mind of the chubby old woman in the little house three states away, ignorant as yet that her only son had traveled to the mountains to die—to die because of him, Tom Connor, who had totally underestimated the dangers, the deadly cunning of the enemy. The skin of Tom's upper face began to burn. His eyes stung with tears that would not come, and he sank to the bed and closed them, bowing his head.

A single creak behind him set his senses alert, but for a moment he did not care. Then the rage boiled up inside him, and his face contorted as he turned.

Villerot, advancing from the bathroom doorway with a stained dagger in his gloved hand, was taken aback by the livid fury before him. He spoke with a calm voice, however.

"You are late. It was evident by the length of your phone conversation that you were attempting to regain the initiative." He sniffed the air and his nose wrinkled. "I see I allowed myself to be discouraged too quickly when seeking you behind the restaurant. I should have known you could not have gone far. It does not matter. All is well, now."

"All is well?" Tom's voice choked with wrath and sorrow. "You killed my friend. You ripped him open, and he didn't know anything."

"Fortunes of war." The voice was pitiless and without remorse—it could have been that of a man sitting on his porch, drinking lemonade and discussing the weather. "A sheep has no business running with wolves."

"There is only one wolf here, and it ought to be hunted down and killed. Slowly, with as much pain as possible."

Villerot shook his head. "You are as much a wolf as I. Yes, young one. A man is one or the other, and though most are sheep, you are not. I am not."

"I am nothing like you," Tom said coldly.

"Incorrect. We both persevere to achieve our ends, execute our plots with guile and ruthlessness, and are comfortable defying laws that hamper our goals."

"If I trespass," Tom growled, "it is only with good reason. You, only for evil."

Villerot smiled. "A matter of perspective."

Tom straightened. "You just killed someone who meant no harm toward anyone. Young, with his whole life waiting to be lived, and now it never will be. And, you're planning to kill the president." Villerot raised his eyebrows but said nothing as Tom went on: "You've caused the deaths of many others in your attacks on me. You're the worst man I've ever known; you deserve to die."

"And you intend to be the agent of my demise?"

Tom spoke quietly. "I've never killed anyone in my life. If this were a dark alley, or out there in the forest—" he motioned toward the window, "—I almost believe I could. But, no. I'm going to beat the daylights out of you, and then turn you over to the law. You're in my room without being invited, now. That ought to offset the trespassing charge you were going to level at me. And I'll expose what you're doing with that weapon of yours. Once the authorities understand it, and realize what you've already done, you'll end up in the electric chair, if not shot outright."

Villerot bared his teeth in a chiding grin. "You are afraid. You would kill me yourself, right now, if you were not. In your place, I assure you that I would."

Tom felt his control slipping. "Don't tempt me, mister."

"Bah," Villerot flung a hand in the air. "Your whole generation is timid. Your friend died screaming your name, and you sit there on the bed, unable to rouse yourself to avenge him."

Tom rose from the bed, cold and hollow, snarling but saying nothing.

Villerot continued, "Your friend died begging and squealing, and I spoke in error concerning him: He was not a sheep. He was a fat swine useful only for the butcher's block." He laughed. "I have simply done my part in restoring the balance of nature."

Enraged, Tom flung himself at the man. Villerot made a curiously halfhearted thrust with the knife which Tom evaded, stepping inside and turning in a half-circle as he parried the lunge with both hands gripping the man's forearm. Immediately the arm pushed upwards and Tom strained with all his power to keep the dancing steel tip away from his chest. This left Villerot with one hand free, which he clenched and drove into Tom's side.

Tom's knees buckled as a second blow reined in. He let go of Villerot's arm with his right and whipped that elbow up, aiming for the man's lower jaw. Villerot jerked back and Tom's elbow slapped into the man's raised palm. There was a clatter and Tom glanced down.

The knife had slipped from Villerot's grasp and tumbled to the floor. The odds were unexpectedly evened.

Tom opened his other hand, releasing Villerot's forearm, and aimed a lancing strike with the tips of his fingers at the man's eye. Even as Tom's arm came up, Villerot's freed arm followed it, parrying the thrust as his head shunted sideways.

Tom had put all his strength into the blow, and Villerot used the momentum to spin Tom around until his back faced Villerot. The man pinned Tom's right arm behind his back, and his forearm pressed across Tom's throat, digging in, cutting off the air to his gasping lungs. Tom's chest started to burn as his body, seeking heightened oxygen intake, found itself completely deprived.

His left hand was still free and he thrust it up and back at Villerot's face, but the man dodged repeated blows and pressed with both arms. Ripping agony seared Tom's wrist and elbow behind his back. The room began to waver as he tried in vain to breathe. He ceased his futile jabs and grabbed hold of the man's wrist at his jaw, straining to lever its iron weight from his neck.

The force reduced, but not nearly enough, and the room before his eyes began to look like a static laced television screen. He focused through the haze on Percy's huddled corpse, and a final wave of angry energy surged through him. He remembered the knife on the floor, almost at his feet.

Tom stomped hard against Villerot's instep. The man grunted and the strength of his hold on Tom's arms slackened. Tom brought his foot up and drove it back into Villerot's shin. He released his frantic grip on the man's wrist, driving his elbow back into the man's solar plexus. He had not been able to put any force into the strike, but Villerot bent and his hold relaxed again.

With a last burst of strength, Tom hooked one foot around Villerot's and, driving off his other foot, pitched them both to the floor. He scoured the floor blindly with his left hand and his fingers brushed the blade of the knife. The muscled forearm under his chin strained, pulling Tom's head back. Tom flicked the knife, spinning it about its handle. The rotating shaft struck his palm. His fingers closed on it.

Suddenly he was released and thrown forward with great force, sprawling full on the ground. He choked at the sudden rush of air into his lungs but sat up quickly, fighting away the burst of dizziness as he pushed himself to his knees, astonished to see Villerot in fast retreat. His opponent ran to the door, opened it, and vanished into the walkway beyond.

Tom stumbled to his feet, determined to give chase. He shook his head to clear it as he moved toward the door, but the effort intensified his dizziness.

Not quite over the concussion, he thought.... He had to halt until the room stabilized around him. When he moved onto the balcony, Villerot was gone, but a family halfway down the passage was pressed to either side of the walkway, regrouping after the man's flight. The father saw Tom, and the knife in his hand. "What—" he said, moving to shield his wife and children.

Tom shook his head and tried to smile reassuringly despite his grief and rage. He stepped back into the room, knowing he had missed his chance. No one would interpret correctly the spectacle of him chasing Villerot through the lodge with a knife. Tom pushed the door closed and cast the knife to the side.

Percy's body lay desolately on the bed. Tom, feeling as empty inside as his friend was devoid of life, forced himself to concentrate. He had to move quickly, and though he could not go to the police in person, he could not leave his friend there to rot. The authorities must be notified. He decided to take some supplies and leave the lodge quietly. Back in town, he would phone a message to Hollis and explain what had happened—though whether the story was believed or not was unknown—and then he would strike out for the location marked on Villerot's map. He groaned inwardly at the thought of the long hike. His body hurt all over, and he felt more tired than he'd ever have thought possible a week ago.

Tap.

Tom jumped, and spun around. From somewhere in the room had come the faintest sound. Tom looked at the knife lying against the wall by the desk, and left it there. Villerot was gone—this was something else.

There was another sound, and it came from the closet. Tom pulled the door open, and heard a muffled sob. He reached in, and his fingers closed around a sleeve. He pulled. Nick Brenner sprawled out of the dark interior and landed on the floor.

Tom turned on the room light, illuminating the ghastly red stain on the carpet. Nick stared vacantly at the bed, waving his head softly from side to side. He moaned to himself, "No, no, no, no, no, no—"

"Stop it," Tom said.

The moaning stopped, and Nick said slowly, "He's dead."

"Yes."

The green eyes looked up at Tom, puffed with fear and hysteria. "You, you—"

"I didn't do it." Tom looked down and saw blood on his hands from the blanket and Villerot's knife.

"You know who did it, Tom?"

Nick's voice was high and strained. Tom didn't like it. He said, "Villerot."

Nick cackled harshly, his head lolled to the side, and he rocked back and forth on his haunches. "No. You're wrong, Tom. Wrong again. Always wrong. It was me." He sprawled on the floor and sobbed again, "I did it, I did it."

It's happened, thought Tom. He's over the edge. "It was Villerot," he said.

"No!" The tear-streaked face looked up at Tom. "It was me. I started it."

Tom stared at him. "What are you saying?"

High-pitched laughs cut through Nick's sobs. "I called him on the phone. Villerot. The morning you went on the bus. I wanted to get you, Tom. Oh, I wanted to get you. I couldn't wait. So I called him, as you left their room. When I had talked to that girl our first night here—when I had talked to her, first—" the tremors heightened in Nick's voice, "—she told me she was here with her uncle and his friend, and they were

SNAPSHOT

working on some engineering thing. So I called Villerot and said you were an engineer, and you were all excited because you'd found out from her what they were working on. I said you were a scheming opportunist using her to move in on the project. She'd said the guy was a creep. I thought maybe he'd do something to scare you."

Tom shook his head in disbelief. "Why? How could you?"

"Hah. To hurt you; the way you'd hurt me, Tom. I couldn't have her. I knew I had no chance once you moved in. So you weren't going to get her, either. Now, no one can have her." Nick bared his teeth. "You think you're better than me, Tom. Everybody does. Everyone but Percy." More tears dripped from his eyes. "I didn't think he'd—I only thought he'd scare you off. Maybe beat you up, if I was lucky. But he didn't. He came after you, and now he's come after Percy. You shouldn't have done it, Tom. You shouldn't have started this. The last night on the train. The first night at the lodge. You shouldn't have messed with me. I sat here and listened to Percy die," Nick snarled, "because of you."

Tom's eyes narrowed. "How long have you been here?"

Nick was rocking back and forth again, humming lowly. Tom repeated, "How long have you been here?"

Nick murmured, "I went in the closet when Villerot knocked on the door. Percy said it was him, and went to open it. I hid in the closet. I knew...I knew he would...."

Tom said angrily, "And you never thought to help Percy?"

"I—I was scared, Tom. I'm not like you. I couldn't. I knew what Villerot had done to you. I couldn't move."

Tom's fists clenched. "And Percy never said a word to give away that you were in the closet, did he? You just sat there while Villerot cut him up...." He advanced toward the hunched figure.

"Stay away!" Nick shrieked. Tom stopped. Nick began to shake as mixed sobs and laughter racked his body again. He sank to the floor. "We killed him, Tom, you and me and Villerot. We killed Percy. We should die, too, all of us. We should die. Let's go die, Tom."

Nick eyed the fallen knife and Tom placed his foot on it. Nick sat up. The tremors were gone from his body and his cackling stopped. He said, "We killed him. I killed him." Fresh tears dripped from his swollen eyes onto reddened cheeks. "I killed him, and he was the only friend I ever had." He rose slowly to his feet. "We should die with him, Tom."

Tom watched, alert for anything. "What are you saying?"

Nick laughed emptily. "I'm going to beat you, Tom. For once in my life, I'm going to win." His eyes were wide, his breathing shallow. "I'm going to beat you, and you'll never beat me again." He made a sudden half jump and Tom tensed, ready to meet him.

Then Nick leapt for the door. He pulled it open and flew into the corridor, banging it shut behind him, howling loudly as his voice echoed through the atrium.

Tom called "No, Nick, wait!" and lunged forward. Wrenching the door open, he dashed into the hall. Immediately his arms were seized from behind by a powerful grip. He turned his head and looked straight into the hard eyes of Ranger Steve Hollis.

CHAPTER
13

Tom struggled against the ranger's grasp as Nick emerged on the ground floor, running at an all-out sprint toward the main entrance.

"Nick!" Tom called again. "Nick!" But his erstwhile companion was out the door without a glance behind.

"Ranger, listen to me," Tom said. "He's about to—"

"You listen to me," Hollis said. "Get back in that room."

"He's about to kill himself," Tom said angrily. "Let me go!"

The ranger gripped him by the shoulders and looked him in the eye. "You're not going anywhere. Get back in that room. I'll send someone after him."

Tom stopped struggling and backed through the open door. Hollis, at the railing, called down, "Elroy, go after that kid. He may be suicidal—restrain him if you have to. *Go!*"

The ranger entered the hotel room and looked around with artificial carelessness. "Why do you think he wants to kill himself?" he asked.

Tom said, "He blames himself for what happened here."

Hollis saw the knife on the floor. He walked to it and looked down, careful not to disturb it. "Tell me what happened here." As he moved to the bed, he unfastened the leather strap looping the handle of the revolver on his belt. Still taking pains not to touch anything, he surveyed the pile on the bed as Tom began his account.

Tom told Hollis everything that had happened from his phone call to Percy at the drugstore, to Nick's frenzied exit. As he spoke, the ranger stood very still, listening and contemplating the scene silently.

When Tom had finished, Hollis asked, "What possible reason could Villerot have for murdering your friend?"

"The same reason he would have for attacking one of those tour buses and sabotaging another," Tom said. "To silence those who suspect his game."

Hollis poked at the edge of the blanket hanging down over the bed with his toe. "His game being...?"

"To kill the president," Tom said.

Hollis looked up sharply. "That is a dangerous accusation, son. Don't forget I act in an official capacity. You better have an excellent reason for making a statement like that."

Tom hesitated, thinking. Finally he said, "I haven't told you everything that's happened today."

"I know," said Hollis.

Tom frowned, and the ranger said, "Go on."

Tom described the events of the morning: his entrance into Villerot's room, his assessment of the camera-weapon, his confrontation in the room with Villerot and subsequent escape.

"You admit breaking into that room this morning?" Hollis asked.

"There was no forced entry," Tom said.

Hollis sighed. "Don't play word games with me. You admit going in without the knowledge or approval of the room's occupants?"

"Yes," Tom answered.

"To find out what happened to the girl."

"Yes."

"And in the process, you stumbled onto this weapon." Hollis folded his arms.

210

"Not exactly," Tom said. "I'd seen it before; I thought I might find out more about it. I did."

Hollis shook his head. "This notion of an acoustic weapon sounds far-fetched, no pun intended. I don't like Villerot's looks, but you can't produce a single shred of evidence against him beyond what you claim to have seen. That doesn't count for anything legally; not enough even to force him in for questioning. Meanwhile, you've practically built a gallows underneath yourself."

"Evidence? Good grief," Tom said. "Talk to the ranger who chased me today."

"I can't," Hollis said soberly.

Tom saw grief in the ranger's blue eyes, and he looked down. "I'm sorry."

"You will be," Hollis retorted.

"What do you mean?" Tom asked.

"I mean *this*." Authority was back in the ranger's voice. "The state police are on their way here now. The tribal police are giving them temporary jurisdiction at the lodge because of the president's arrival tomorrow. Maybe I'm cynical, but that way, if anything blows up, it's not the tribe's problem. At any rate, two complaints have been received from Villerot against you today: one, declaring a break-in to his room this morning. The second, just now, stating that you lured him up to your room, at which time, having already killed your friend, you attacked him with a knife. I was down in the basement and heard the report on the radio," Hollis tapped the walkie-talkie on his belt, across from the revolver. "So I came straight up. You admit the earlier break-in. Were you wearing gloves then?"

"No," Tom said.

The ranger nodded. "Then your fingerprints will be all over his things. And you're not wearing gloves now, either. A few minutes ago you were spotted by a man and his family—who went straight to the front desk to file their own report, by the way—leaving your room, brandishing a knife, moments after they'd seen Villerot racing away in apparent fear for his life. Your friend is dead inside, and your fingerprints will be on the knife." Hollis looked keenly at Tom. "Will Villerot's?"

The cunning behind Percy's murder and the ensuing fight hit Tom with staggering force and left him dazed. What had seemed to be a life-and-death battle had been nothing more than a tactical gambit on Villerot's chessboard, and Tom had played right into it. Of course Villerot had been wearing gloves, and as Tom thought back to those moments of desperate struggle, he realized that the man's knife had slipped far too easily from what would have been a sweatless grip. When Tom had gotten hold of the dagger, Villerot had fled instantly—not at all in keeping with his previous fearlessness.

It had been a set-up, a masterstroke on the tall man's part, crafted to take Tom out of the way once and for all while leaving Villerot in the clear. To kill all the room's occupants would leave the chance that a cleaning attendant might discover the bodies before the ultimate plan was executed—in which case, because of Tom's previous statements to Hollis, Villerot would become a prime suspect. But to kill Percy, and then frame Tom as his murderer, took both out of the way neatly and robbed all credence from any future story Tom would tell.

Tom answered the ranger's question hoarsely: "No, Villerot's fingerprints won't be on the knife."

If only that ranger Hollis had dispatched would catch up with Nick, he thought. Villerot's scheme might yet be foiled if Nick talked.

Hollis had more to say: "In the middle of all this, you fled from a ranger who died during the ensuing chase. The body is going for autopsy, but even if your story about this weapon is true, do you really think the coroner will conclude independently that he was killed by a *sound wave*?"

Tom shook his head disconsolately.

Hollis said, "The only thing the law will see is a ranger dead, with all signs pointing at you—the prime suspect in another brutal killing the same day. Even if the doctors decide the ranger's death was due to natural causes, it's still going to be blamed on the fact that he was chasing you at the time. The death of a law enforcement official in the course of his duty colors a case in the authorities' minds so completely that all they'll want will be to nail you to the wall."

"It sounds hopeless," Tom said. His eyes flickered to the door.

"Don't even think about it," Hollis warned. "General orders are to find you and keep you in custody until the police arrive." He tapped the butt of his revolver. "At all costs."

"Would you?" Tom asked.

Hollis nodded stonily. "My concern for the security of the country is greater than my compassion for any individual."

Tom said, "So is mine. That's why I've done everything I've done. You've got to believe me."

Hollis looked at him a long while before saying, "I'd like to, son. I've dealt with hard cases before, and despite everything you've done, despite your virtually having the word 'guilty' carved across your forehead in blood, I can't convince myself you're one of them. It's possible you're a raving lunatic, but I can't believe that, either. That's why I intend to give your story one chance. If," he added as Tom straightened, "you don't give me any trouble by trying to resist arrest."

Here at least was a glimmer of hope, and Tom said, "I understand."

"The police will be here soon," Hollis said. "They will investigate both this room and Villerot's for evidence against you. When they go up to Villerot's room, I'll go, too. After they hustle him and the professor out, I'll look for a camera and papers. If I find anything, I'll follow up on it."

Tom's heart dropped. "You don't expect them to leave those things sitting around now, waiting to be discovered, do you?"

"We'll give them no warning before we go up," Hollis said.

Tom made no reply. It was a minimal chance, but as one of only three possible ways his story could be shown to be true prior to a devastating attack on the president—after which event, any personal redemption would be all too empty—he did not want to discourage Hollis from trying.

The ranger finished his grim inspection of the room and said, "Let's go."

"Where?" Tom asked.

"Downstairs. There's an empty room I'm going to keep you in. This is a crime scene now."

They walked along the balcony to the staircase, Hollis keeping Tom always a watchful step ahead. On the ground floor, the ranger motioned Tom toward an open door at the back of the atrium. As he lowered his arm, there were urgent footsteps and a breathless call from behind. "Ranger Hollis, Ranger Hollis, sir!"

Tom and Hollis swung around as the young ranger Hollis had sent after Nick stumbled to a halt before them, his tilted hat and disheveled clothes testifying to a long sprint. His face was flushed and his chest heaved as he sucked great lungfuls of air.

Hollis frowned. "Elroy, I told you to get that kid."

Elroy shook his head. "I—I wasn't in time. You were right about him. He ran like he knew he wouldn't have to run again. Too fast. I almost got him." Still gasping, the young ranger paused, bending over with his hands on his knees.

"Well," Hollis said impatiently. "What happened?"

"Sorry, sir," Elroy straightened up. "He turned around, saw me coming, and took off like I was red-hot lava pouring out the door behind him. I nearly caught him under the bridge, and I thought for sure he'd stop at the road."

"But he didn't," Tom said heavily, as Elroy pulled the brown hat from his head and flung it to the floor in anger.

"No," he said. "He didn't go into the road at all. He swung right; ran out onto the trestle crossing Midvale Creek. It's a train track, but he ran like it was flat pavement." His eyes dropped. "I couldn't do it that fast. I didn't want to fall."

Hollis laid a hand on the young ranger's shoulder. "I know you did your best."

"He looked up at me and smiled," Elroy said. "A great big sweet smile like he was the happiest guy in the world. And then he jumped. He *jumped*. He—I couldn't—" Elroy stopped as the trauma overwhelmed him.

Hollis squeezed his shoulder and said, "Don't blame yourself."

"No, sir. But to watch him go like he was enjoying it...he's down there now, belly-up in the creek with the water washing over him..." the ranger's shaken voice trailed away.

"Go and sit down," Hollis said kindly, and he guided the young man to one of the chairs. "I'd better see about the body."

"The state police are there now, sir," Elroy said, voice suddenly empty of emotion, eyes focused on the far wall. "They arrived as I was finishing, and took charge. I figured I'd better get in and tell you."

Hollis nodded approval. Then he said, "Listen, boy, I know you're worked up, but when the police come in, just tell them to come find me in the back room, okay?"

"Yes, sir, I will." Elroy sat up.

"Good." Hollis turned to Tom. "Come on." As they moved out of earshot he added quietly, "Better for him to have a tangible duty to focus on."

Tom felt hollow inside. Only two possibilities left now, he reflected morosely. If he had just seen it coming. They didn't have to die. They shouldn't have died. If Nick had just held on.

Villerot, for all his cunning, had not anticipated the presence of an observer in the closet. It was the one element that could have foiled him and set everything right. Why did Nick have to crack up now? If he had just held on.... With Percy and Nick dead, and Katherine vanished, Tom had no allies. Hollis, despite sympathizing tendencies, was a ranger first, with his loyalties to his duty. The state police would be against Tom outright. He was completely alone.

Hollis directed Tom through the open door. It was a room much like the one they had left upstairs, only reversed. The single bed was on the other side, but there was an identical chair and desk. The painting hanging behind the bed was different, more of a pattern than a picture.

Tom lowered himself onto the bed and lay still, staring up at the white ceiling, glad to be off his aching right foot, glad to put his throbbing head onto something soft for even a few moments. Hollis spun the chair around backwards and sat down, watching both Tom and the entrance. Neither spoke. As Tom's body calmed for the first time in hours, he realized he was exhausted and ravenously hungry.

Some time later there came a solid tap on the wall beside the open doorway. A burly man with a florid, pockmarked face and thinning black hair stood in the entrance. He wore the brown uniform of the state patrol.

"Ranger Hollis?" he said.

Hollis's eyes briefly glanced over the official's insignia. "Yes, Captain."

The man nodded and came into the room without offering his hand. He looked narrowly at Tom, then back to Hollis. "Captain Charles Hanleigh. This the suspect?"

"This is Tom Connor," Hollis said.

"Fill me in."

Hollis spoke for five minutes, after which Hanleigh went to the door and called over a group of men, some in uniform, the rest in plain clothes. One of the uniformed officers came up to Tom with a small ink kit. He asked politely if he could take Tom's fingerprints, and Tom nodded wearily and sat up. The officer knelt, and pressed Tom's prints onto a beige card while Hanleigh spoke to the rest of the group in low tones. The officer rejoined the others outside, and the captain returned to point Hollis toward the group as Tom lay back down again.

"Officers and forensic guys," Hanleigh said. "Two teams, one for each room. Will you show them the way?" That this was a statement and not a request was abundantly clear in his tone. "The suspect and I will have a chat while you're gone."

Tom looked the captain over and thought, this is a man bred in the world of ranches and dirt and guns. He's going to have about as much patience with, or understanding for, the things happening here as he would a problem in physics or a badly operating computer.

Steve Hollis went to the door. He looked back at Tom. His face was expressionless, but Tom knew by the mere fact of the glance that the ranger would keep his promise to search the room on the top floor. Hollis motioned to the gathered men beyond. They joined him, and the group walked into the bustling lobby and out of sight. Several people glanced after them, and then into the room at Tom with curious expressions. Hanleigh waved them off with an impatient sweep of his arm, and sat down in the vacant chair. He looked at Tom with unwavering eyes. "You have anything to add to what the ranger said?"

"No, sir." Tom heard the tiredness in his voice.

"Okay," the captain's lips pursed. "Did you enter these folks' room this morning?"

"Yes," Tom said. "Hollis told you why."

"Hollis told me what you said was why," the captain corrected. "For the record, did you kill this friend of yours?"

Tom bristled. *"No."*

Hanleigh stifled a smirk. "Naturally."

Tom propped himself up on one elbow. "You might at least consider the possibility that it's true."

"Sure," Hanleigh said. "A man is innocent till proven guilty. But it kind of sounds to me like you took care of all the proving." The captain tapped his skull. "Bumped your head on your bus ride, huh?"

"It's not bad now," Tom muttered as he dropped back onto the bed.

Hanleigh's voice cracked like thunder from a black sky: "That's not what I asked, boy. You'll pay attention if you want any chance at all."

Tom turned his head slowly and stared at the captain. "I *had* a mild concussion."

"Better," the captain said. His face leveled. "And you're accusing this Villerot guy of plotting to murder the president?"

"I believe he wants to," Tom nodded.

"Want to explain that?"

"Why else would he have done what he's done—?"

"What you say he's done," Hanleigh interrupted.

Frustration crept into Tom's voice. "Why else would he and the professor be working on what they're working on?"

"What you say they're working on. Yeah. The sound gun thing."

Tom sat up suddenly. Hanleigh stiffened and his hand dropped toward his pistol. The room seemed to reel before Tom's eyes; his head throbbed, but he clenched his teeth and said, "It's real, Captain. This is for real. That man killed a ranger today with his weapon, and then used a knife to murder my friend. He murdered a whole bunch of people two days ago." Tom's voice choked; his words were almost hoarse. "Why can't you see it?" he asked. "Why won't any of you see it? Why can't you believe me long enough to investigate him and see that I'm telling the truth?"

"Take it easy, " the captain said softly. "How about if you just lie back down and tell me how this thing works?"

Tom felt like sneering—or crying—at the captain's bored expression. He sank back on the bed and said lifelessly, "Why? What's the point?"

"Go ahead anyway, " the captain said.

"Fine." Tom stared at a point on the ceiling. "I believe the weapon uses a sound wave to destroy its targets through resonance."

"Resonance," the captain nodded solemnly. "Right."

Tom rolled his eyes without turning his head. Even that caused pain. "It's a well-documented phenomenon," he said. "Resonance has to be considered when you design almost any mechanical part or structure. There was a gigantic steel and concrete suspension bridge in Washington's Tacoma Narrows that collapsed back in 1940 because people didn't consider it."

"I never heard of it," Hanleigh said, smoothing a wrinkle in his uniform. "Keep going."

Tom tried to explain what he could of the science behind the device he had found in the room:

"Everything has a certain frequency where it vibrates naturally—like if you pull a child back on a playground swing and let go, he arcs back and forth without your doing anything else. Everything has a natural vibration, to different degrees and under different conditions—including your body and its organs.

"If you start pushing that child on the swing, and you time your pushes with his natural swinging motion—in other words, you always push when he's starting to go forward—the height of his arc increases. That's resonance. It amplifies the motion, builds it up."

Tom could see the captain beginning to pay attention, though it was obvious the man only dimly followed him. He found it gratifying to watch Hanleigh's befuddlement crowd the sneer from his face.

Tom continued, "You can do the same sort of thing with sound. I'm sure you've heard of wineglasses being shattered by sopranos singing high notes. It's the same thing. Sound is a wave, with a certain magnitude and frequency—more simply, a 'push,' and the repeated timing of that push. If you apply that wave at the correct frequency, the one the body's organs already want to vibrate at, then the wave could amplify that vibration, just like the child going higher and higher on the swing as you push him. It makes sense that if you make the organs vibrate too much, you could cause rupturing, bleeding—maybe even kill."

Hanleigh scratched the back of his scalp, then sat more upright in his chair. He said brusquely, "That's what you claim happened to the ranger chasing you yesterday?"

"I'm sure it is," Tom answered.

"After being fired upon by Mr. Villerot."

"Yes." Tom nodded emphatically.

"And this thing is disguised as a camera."

Tom nodded again.

"Must take a ton of power," the captain mused.

"I think he's using an explosive charge placed where you'd expect the film to go," Tom said, thinking back to the blueprints he'd found in Villerot's case.

Hanleigh looked doubtful. "Shouldn't that blow his hands off?"

"Your pistol doesn't blow yours off every time you fire it," Tom said. "Zimmerlee must have designed it to shield the blast, as well as to be totally silent."

Hanleigh's face grew more dubious. "You think two guys could have figured this thing out?"

Tom said confidently, "When one of those guys is a brilliant engineer, standing on the shoulders of maybe dozens or hundreds of previous researchers, and the other very likely has connections to shadowy resources of every kind, I could easily believe it."

Hanleigh stood up and shook his head. "We'll see, boy. We'll just see."

Tom lay still, glad for the respite, lost in thought as the captain paced the floor. Everything hung on the reports of Hollis and the teams scouring the upstairs rooms. If they brought back the wrong answer.... Tom asked himself again how certain he was of Villerot's purpose. Could there be another explanation for all that had happened?

That Villerot had carried out murderous attacks on Tom and his friends was a fact—unproved and perhaps un-provable to the law, but, for him, a fact. That there was a silent, lethal power concealed in the shell of a camera had been demonstrated unarguably to Tom and the unfortunate ranger. And the timing of it all—what would Villerot and his silent weapon be doing in a national park, of all places, at the same time as a visit by the president? That assassination was intended seemed plain. The president's upcoming visit to Glacier had been public knowledge for some time. With the inevitable high flow of tourists due to that visit, a man with a camera would be invisible to the security forces around the president.

Finally, the very magnitude of the attacks against Tom and the others spoke to the ambition of Villerot's plot. The man had spared nothing and no one in his attempts to squash Tom.

There were no doubts, no hesitations left in Tom's mind. Only a question remained: What was he prepared to do about it? If Hollis discovered any evidence, there would be hope for intervention from the legal sector. But if the ranger came up with nothing....

Time passed. As the captain paced watchfully, Tom remained still, conserving his energy and steeling his mind for the exertions ahead, watching the blue sky in the window fade to dusky indigo.

At last there was a knock at the door. "Captain?"

Hanleigh turned. A young sergeant stood rigidly in the doorway. "The teams are ready to report, sir."

The captain nodded. "I'll talk to them outside. Watch him." He jerked his thumb at Tom and strode out to join the group of men in the lobby. The sergeant took up position in the entrance, his eyes on Tom, his ears focused on the conversation outside.

One man detached himself from the huddled group. It was Hollis. He looked over the sergeant's left shoulder and his eyes found Tom's. For a moment he just stared, and then he shook his head. His eyes were sad and the corners of his mouth twisted downward. He walked back slowly to rejoin the group.

Tom closed his eyes at this second chance gone. Even expecting failure, he had still dared to hope. Now the crossroads were reached.

If he wished, he could cast his own life to the wind and make a final effort to set everything right. Should luck be with him and his strength hold out, he was the last factor against imminent tragedy. If anything went wrong, it was likely that, exhausted and hunted relentlessly by the forces of good and evil alike, he would die in the attempt.

The alternative was to let the police pack him off to jail. Within a day or two at most, they would release him with hushed apologies and averted gazes—after it was done, the president slain, the country plunged into turmoil, Katherine silenced, Percy and the others unavenged, Villerot, his work accomplished, gone.

In which case, Tom would live—but, he asked himself, would his life be worth living? To have the chance he had before him now, and let it go.... No. It was not a crossroads. For him, there was only one choice.

He sighed and closed his eyes as he focused on the future, envisioning the challenges, the potential hazards to be encountered and circumvented. The sergeant at the doorway watched him in bored silence. After a few minutes, Hanleigh pushed past the sergeant. The captain's face was ominous.

"Well, fella," he said triumphantly. "My teams have been over the rooms and guess what?"

Tom looked up, resigned. "You found nothing."

"Oh-ho, no," the man said brightly. "We found plenty, all with your name on it. Your prints, to be exact. We also have a couple of witnesses who saw you with a knife, chasing Mr. Villerot from your room this afternoon, as well as one old man who came forward to say he saw you fleeing from Mr. Villerot's room this morning."

Hanleigh unhooked a pair of gleaming handcuffs from his waist. "Thomas Connor, you are under arrest on suspicion of murdering Percival Norton this afternoon, and of breaking and entering the hotel room of Dr. Zimmerlee and Mr. Villerot earlier today. After we get our act together, you can also expect to get hit with attempting to elude a pursuing law enforcement officer, with possible complicity in his death. Sergeant, cover him," he snapped.

The sergeant drew a large pistol, stepped to the side and leveled it at Tom's midsection as the safety catch clicked off.

"Stand up," the captain ordered. He twisted Tom's arms behind him and clamped one cuff around each wrist. The steel jaws locked tight, and Tom grimaced.

"All right," Hanleigh said, "move it. For the record—" He proceeded with a memorized recounting of Tom's rights as he shoved him toward the doorway. The crowd of people outside parted. Tom blinked as he saw more than two hundred people watching him in the lobby and from the balconies above. An embarrassed silence hung in the air. Steve Hollis looked at him and then away.

They were at the door. *Now,* Tom thought, while the body of the captain was hemmed in by the doorframe and shielding him from the pistol-wielding sergeant's muzzle. Hanleigh in the way and the throng of people outside would discourage a careless shot. Tom would never have thought himself capable of assaulting an officer, but it was all or nothing now and he took one step forward and arched his leg...

His foot kicked backward, smashing with an audible crack against Hanleigh's calf, just below the knee. The handcuffs clinked as Tom twisted around, linking his hands behind his back. He rammed his right elbow into the captain's belly with a muffled thud. The captain gasped and his head rocked forward as he sagged against the door. The grip on Tom's biceps vanished.

A clamor erupted from the mass of people and suddenly everything was moving. The narrow corridor created when the crowd had split began to disintegrate, and Tom ran, not looking back. Hollis jumped and got one hand on Tom's shoulder, but Tom shook it off and plowed ahead.

Realizing that more police would be grouped near the front door, Tom bolted for the side corridor where he had been pursued by the ill-fated ranger that afternoon. He ran from the men who would be following, and from the swelling noise of the uproar. Startled faces in the long hallway looked at him for the second time that day, and then he was through the door on the right, down the stairs, jumping across the little porch to the ground, and away down the hill to the rear of the lodge. He tore past the closed pool, running hard toward the forest, forcing his bad ankle to push as hard off the ground as his good foot. The sky to the west was deep violet, and speckled with glimmering stars. The air was cold, and as Tom glanced back, he had a glimpse of the bottom edge of the full moon just clearing the roof of the lodge.

SNAPSHOT

As Tom reached the base of the hill, a pistol shot echoed behind him. The slug whizzed by his head and crashed into the tangled foliage. He broke left and plunged into the mass of trees. A second shot cracked and a splinter of bark spun away into the woods on his right. Then there were rushing footfalls as whoever was firing descended the hill in pursuit.

Tom ran on with a fury borne of life-and-death desperation. The moonlight filtered unevenly through the trees, casting the forest into eerie patches of light and shadow, allowing him to dodge the massive tree trunks. He pushed through sharp angulated branches decked with lancing needles that whipped his face and tore fragments from his clothing, leaving a sweet odor of pine. The pinioning of his arms behind him crippled his sense of balance, and he stumbled several times on rocks, roots, clods of earth, and dead branches littering the forest floor, but he never fell. The diminishing sounds of footsteps and snapping branches behind told him he was gaining distance on his pursuers—doubtless under less motivation to cut their faces and rip their clothes. Three more shots rang out, all going wide, and Tom bore on in his numbing sprint.

At last he stopped. The firing had ceased, and there were no more cracking branches or grunts coming from behind. Had they given up so soon?

No, there was no chance of that. They would be setting up the means to contain him. It was imperative that he get well away before the net could be drawn.

Tom's face stung. He needed his arms to shield him from the branches. He was in a small clearing, and he dropped to the cold ground and rolled onto his back. He raised his legs, got both hands past the seat of his pants, and pulled his right foot in, passing the chain of the handcuffs around it. He squeezed the left foot through and climbed back to his feet with his arms in front of him.

He moved softly. Still there was no sound of pursuit. He listened for any indication of what might be going on beyond the edge of the forest. As he listened, he concluded that his best bet was to make a wide arc around the grounds of the lodge, slip through the town of East Glacier, join the main road somewhere beyond, and make his way to the location indicated on Villerot's map. He shut his mind to the rigor of that ten- or twelve-mile hike over rough ground.

A new sound touched his ears, and he froze. His senses, heightened by danger, set on razor's edge by desperation, strained toward the source of the noise. What was it?

For a long moment there was nothing, then he heard it again, a low snarl, not human, far off and coming from the direction of the lodge. Tom shuddered and turned to flee. He heard nimble footsteps, fast and light, muffled by the intervening trees, and he knew what it was: The police were taking no chances, playing no games, and had unleashed a dog to track him and bring him down.

He did not run for long. The mad dash was tiring him uselessly. The animal was closing the distance rapidly and noisily, and Tom's best speed could only delay the encounter a few seconds.

He broke into another small clearing and stopped, mind racing, looking around in the pale rays of moonlight for something with which to fend off the approaching beast. He snatched up a thick bough. It was jagged at one end where it had broken off its supporting trunk, and it felt solid in his sweaty grip.

Tom kicked at a rock the size of a melon, and it rolled over lazily. Taking a stance over it, he shifted the branch in his cuffed hands so the jagged end was away from him like the point of a spear. He waited, teeth clenched, eyes fierce slits, marshalling his reserves for the attack and fighting down his instinctive, visceral fear.

The crashing noise and panting growl grew louder. A sleek brown body flashed in the trees and broke through the web of branches, exploding into the clearing, a lean, ferocious wolfhound, ears back and teeth bared. It snarled as its nose and then its eyes found Tom, and it sprang into the air toward him, jaws agape.

Tom rammed the branch forward, grunting at the shock in his arms as he thrust the splintered end down into the soft recesses of the dog's opened maw. A gurgling howl replaced its snarl, and Tom kept shoving against fleshy resistance, forcing several inches of branch down the muscled throat. As the wolfhound braced itself and got one paw up on the branch, Tom twisted downward, flipping the animal onto its side. He released the stick and threw himself on top of the beast, using his shoulder to pin it down as his fingers scrabbled at the earth for the rock.

Sharp claws tore at Tom's belly, quick painful slashes. Tom's fingertips touched the rock and he gripped it, but it slipped away. He got it on the second try and twisted up, bringing it over his head. With all his strength he slammed it down into the dog's skull.

There was a sharp crack, and the animal's howl took on a new, pitiable dimension. It continued to struggle, and Tom reared back with both hands and struck again and again. The paws scraping his stomach grew feeble, and the howl died to a whimper.

Tom got to his feet, hearing more crashing in the trees from the direction of the lodge. The men were coming on again, following the dog's wail. Tom looked down at the disfigured head and slender jerking limbs, and felt a wave of remorse at his own brutality—but he could not waste time he did not have. He tossed the rock away and slipped into the trees, pushing gently past the tangled branches, bringing his feet down noiselessly. The moan behind him diminished.

In the distance a group of flashlights converged on the clearing. A voice, heavy with grief, impeded by distance and the trees, called out, "Murderer! What have you done to my Jack? You dog killing..." A gust of wind carried away the rest. All Tom could hear was the agonized bestial howl. A gun cracked and the whimpering ended.

The man shouted again, but Tom stopped his ears to the epithets and melted into the cloak of the black forest, his heart leaden within him. His stomach burned where the dog's claws had torn through his shirt, but he hardly noticed. All his hopes hung on the only chance left him, one bound up in an enigmatically scrawled crimson "X."

CHAPTER
14

The full moon, its cold intensity softened by clouds intermittently blocking out the star-studded sky, cast the rolling plains into relief—bright patches of waving long grass alternating with regions of deepest shadow. The wind sifting through the grass was not strong, but its temperature had dropped steadily through the long hours of the night.

Tom paused and looked up. Knowing that a full moon rises at sunset and sets at sunrise, he reckoned by its perch high overhead that the time must be about midnight. He was grateful for the moon's presence, for his progress would have been much more difficult without it. As it was, he stumbled often, and the uneven surface exacted a steady toll on his battered right ankle.

Tom shook his head to clear it, groaned at the resulting pain, and resumed his journey, automatically picking up his step-count from where he had left off.

While running from his pursuers, and during the brief fight with the wolfhound, the cold fire of adrenaline had made him as alert as he had ever been. It had not diminished through the brief moments of naked exposure when he dashed from the cover of the forest over open fields to the highway, across it, and into the middle of slumbering East Glacier. It had spiked in his veins and constricted his heart at every insignificant sound while he picked his way through the little village.

Even for some time after, the chemical's lingering vestiges spurred him on as he left behind the town, the mountains, the sirens and flashing red and blue lights. Paralleling the road, he had put in a mile or more before fatigue had set in—as inevitably it must, as step after wearying step took him further from the excitement, as he dropped from the adrenaline heights while continuing to demand exertion from tired muscles that had not been rested adequately in days. Every so often he had to blink hard to clear blurry eyes, and his brain dulled as the hours wore on. The desire burned in him to lie down, to be engulfed in sweet sleep, to float away, to—

He shook his head. Don't listen to that, he thought. Allow even the possibility of weakness, open those gates, and you'll never get them closed again. Only an unrelenting focus on what you have to do will get you through. Think about Villerot. Think about Katherine.

And he did. He thought of the evil and of the good, of the sinister weapon and the red eyes, and of the beautiful face and the golden hair, as he put one foot before the other, one foot before the other, left, right, left, right, automatically tallying each step as it was taken.

It had been crucial from the outset of the trek that he have some idea of the distance covered, so that he would know when to look for the road leading away from the highway. It had been drawn by hand on Villerot's map, which meant it could not be a prominent feature. Roughly seven miles from East Glacier; seven miles, and then another five or so up that road. If he missed the path, or chose the wrong one and had to turn back, retrace his steps—well, his strength would not last forever.

So he had begun to count, estimating his pace at three feet. Five thousand two hundred eighty feet to a mile divided by three equaled 1,760 paces—roughly. It was laborious, repetitive, mind-numbingly boring, but he counted. At 1,760 steps, he had mentally filed 'one mile' and begun again.

Now he had reached three miles, plus a count of 1,300, which put him closer to four miles in reality.

Far to his right, on the highway, a pair of headlights appeared over the crest of a hill. Blearily, he watched them sweep by, turning his head to follow the taillights as they receded into the distance. He shivered, alone again with the endless desolate terrain, the silent moon, and the chill breeze that sucked the warmth from his body through his exposed neck and hands.

Hours ago, just starting out, Tom had walked along the very edge of the road, only to find himself dropping flat to the ground as the first car flashed by. Realizing the foolishness of this course, he had adjusted his position to a much safer one, a quarter of a mile north. From this distance through the undulating fields, he now paralleled the road.

So he walked, awkwardly climbing the occasional low fence with his bound hands. The long hours passed, and the miles turned with agonizing slowness in his brain like numbers on a dial, from three to four, then five, as the moon inched lower and lower behind him. Now and again his eyes traced the invisible line from the two stars at the end of the Big Dipper up to Polaris, the North Star, high on his left. To his beleaguered mind the North Star was an old friend. He had watched the stars nearest it sweep out a circle as the night wore on, while those farther away rose before him, passed overhead, and disappeared behind. Every other star shifted position. None of them was reliable. But Polaris was always there, right where it should be, faithful and true, never faltering. He smiled up at his trusty companion. Good old Polaris. He was not alone.

Something dim in his mind, obscured by the haze of exhaustion, told him he was being ridiculous. He shrugged, turning the collar of his battered shirt up. The breeze had gained intensity, and was bitter on his neck. He tried to draw his shivering hands into his shirtsleeves, but the metal cuffs connected by the clinking chain would not allow it, so he clenched his teeth and walked on. A rumble from the depths of his stomach signaled again the gnawing emptiness that had grown from merely a ravenous hunger several hours ago to an all-consuming scream for satiation. It was an insidious distraction that sapped the life from his legs as they marched toward his unknown destination.

The sixth mile passed, the gentle breeze long gone, replaced by brisk wind that raked cold air from the tops of the mountains down along the plains, lancing through his clothing and skin to scrape the bones. Thoroughly miserable, well beyond caring about patriotism, righteous indignation, vengeance, or any other ideal, Tom stayed on his feet only through stubborn obstinacy—the angry refusal to give in and be defeated by circumstances and the elements, a grim will not to lie down and quit like others would, but to forge on, take one more step, and one more after that, and then another and another, against the creeping hunger and crippling fatigue, all the while pressed on by the biting wind that whipped his clothes and set his teeth chattering.

Tom focused his mind on counting, on putting one leg ahead of the other, on taking another breath, on maintaining course by taking stock of the North Star above him and looking right to the dim line crossing the rolling hills that was the highway, on and on and on and....

He stumbled. Something had changed. What was it? The ground. He had stepped onto an even surface for the first time in hours. Peering down, Tom saw that he was on a dirt road, deeply rutted, with little particles swirling above its surface in the howling wind. His count stood at six miles and 923 paces.

Tom's eyes traced the line of the highway away to the east. As best he could tell in the brilliant moonlight, there were no other trails, paths, or roads breaking from it.

He had come just over six and a half miles by his reckoning, but the twists in his path, the unavoidable variations in the length of his step as he walked over the uneven ground, as well as his rough estimate of the length of his pace, meant he could have covered anywhere from five to eight miles. And his gauging of the distances involved had come from nothing more substantial than a quick measurement on Villerot's map.

There simply weren't that many roads in this empty landscape, and Tom decided this had to be the one. The resolution perked his spirits, and he started along it toward the north.

The road took on a downward gradient, and before long the highway was lost to sight behind a short hill. Sheltered now from the breeze, and counting his steps automatically with one corner of his brain, Tom turned his thoughts to what lay ahead. Assuming he found Katherine, what condition would she be in? He had seen her caught in the blast of the bus's explosion, only to disappear. But Villerot had hinted that she was alive. How badly injured was she? Had she received any kind of medical care? Could she walk? If not, how would he move her? Could she be moved safely? And yet she must be moved. Tom believed that Zimmerlee was telling the truth when he said his niece was the only bright thing in his life. If she could be pulled from Villerot's clutches, then the hold on the professor's tongue would be gone. Zimmerlee could tell the truth to the rangers and the police, and so could Katherine.

Tom knew that his only purpose now was to find the girl and get her back to the lodge, to the officials, before he himself collapsed, without harming her, and without Villerot catching them—and before the assassination attempt was carried out.

He saw light in the east. The president was due to arrive that afternoon. According to reports, he would stay two nights at the lodge, and then proceed into the backcountry, his trip up the Going-to-the-Sun road having been cancelled by the deadly rockslide.

Tom didn't know when the assassination was intended, but a hunch told him that today was the day. The event would have maximum visibility, and therefore deepest impact, at the lodge tonight, during the celebration when the president's arrival was fresh and all eyes were on him.

The road had been level for some time. Now it angled upwards, curving around another of the interminable low hills. Scattered trees dotted the surrounding fields. They thickened into a wooded region a mile ahead. Still counting, Tom estimated he had come a mile down this road.

Heavy gusts of wind hit him full force as he rose from the depression through which the road had been running. He winced. *Make it to the trees,* he thought. Repeating the directive over and over in his mind, he trudged along with head down and arms clutching his chest, his breath whistling through gritted teeth. All his thoughts turning inward, he remained oblivious to the surroundings as he plodded on to the dreary beat of his endless pace count, watching the brown streak of road under his feet growing more distinct in the intensifying pink light.

At last he reached the woods. Immediately, the force of the wind diminished, and with it, the haze in Tom's mind. He sagged against one of the trees. The ground below was so inviting. It called to him: *Sit down, just for a moment. Rest. You'll be on your way again soon.*

Tom drew his hands up and slapped a palm across his cheek with a startling crack. A tingle shot through his body and he stepped away from the tree. *Walk!* he thought angrily.

He walked. The trees went by, and the gnawing void in his stomach spread to meet the fatigue creeping up his limbs. His head lolled to and fro as he counted each trudging step that crunched in the hard dirt...two miles, three, four, each an agonized effort, each seemingly twice as long as the one before.

Tom glanced up wearily and saw the sun shining on him from the right. He realized that his count placed him at more than four and a half miles. His mind sharpened. He hurt all over; hurt from so many bumps, scrapes, twists, bee stings, cuts and concussions that he'd lost track of them all. And he was tired, incredibly tired, weary in a physically exhausted and mentally drained way he had never known before—and yet, suddenly, he felt he could go on, just a little farther. It was close. He could sense it.

The immediate area seemed as devoid of human habitation as that through which he had come during the long night. The trees sloped up on his right and the road plunged down a short distance and meandered out of sight through the forest. Tom walked carefully now, looking continually this way and that, eyes probing the foliage, the sky beyond, and the road ahead.

There was something new among the sounds of the forest. He stopped to listen, then walked a little farther and realized it was the noise of water bubbling in a nearby streambed. The road curved, and when Tom came around the bend he saw it, a little narrow water flow, tumbling down through the trees from green hills on the right. The road dipped to meet this brook, crossing it by means of a squat, tidily constructed bridge of thick wood beams and planks on short pillars.

But what captured Tom's attention and set his heart pounding was the little dirt path across the stream, snaking through the trees to a log cabin in a clearing halfway up the hill.

His eyes glittered. He had found it—this had to be the place. Resisting the urge to dash over the bridge and up, Tom knelt behind a tree and inspected the scene.

The cabin appeared to be of a two-room design. The entrance was through a door in the larger right-hand section. A smaller wing extended to the left, and a window of dusty glass was embedded in its wall. A gray stone chimney rose from the center of the roof, and to the right of the entrance stood a three-foot pyramid of chopped firewood.

No smoke rose from the chimney, and five minutes' surveillance revealed no signs of life. At last, Tom left his position and picked his way through the trees on the right, ignoring the road, paralleling the stream and angling up the hill toward the structure.

He stopped as he saw the front end of an automobile, parked behind the cabin. Crouching, he picked his way past more trees until he could see that the vehicle was an ancient brown station wagon. He reached the banks of the stream twenty yards above the cabin, where the water was low and the stream was shielded on either side by encroaching trees. Careful strides across two smooth boulders protruding from the water's surface brought him to the opposite side. He made his way through the trees to the edge of the clearing.

A glance revealed the station wagon's license plates to be issued in Montana. Tom would have expected Colorado plates on a vehicle owned by Zimmerlee. Villerot's car had been small and red. No rental agency of repute, with any regard for its professional image, would offer this relic. The worn tires and mud-spattered fenders seemed more suited to whomever had built the cabin than to those men who might have recently commandeered it.

Tom crawled around the vehicle to the corner of the cabin's walls and advanced along its side, stopping at the front corner for a final look. Everything was peaceful. Except for the car, the cabin, and the road, he could see nothing but trees, ground, water, and sky. He crept around the corner and reached the window in three long steps.

Tom's chest thumped mightily. He stayed down, just allowing his eyes to clear the boundary of the window pane.

The glass had gone a long time without a washing, and the accumulated layers of dirt blurred everything inside. Squinting, Tom thought he could make out a bed or couch in the corner near him on the right, and he caught his breath as he realized that something was lying on it. It was long and white, and Tom pressed his face in close to see a little more.

The white object moved.

This was too much. Tom could wait no longer, as a fresh burst of excitement drove the weariness from his body. He dashed to the front door and twisted the knob. It was unlocked and swung open easily, which would have made him pause at any other time, but now he burst through into some sort of combination living room and kitchen. A door on the left connected with the second room, and he was through it in an instant.

The object in the corner was a bed, and a whirlwind of emotion tore through Tom: joy, horror, love, and fear all intermingled in a gushing wave as he rushed to the edge of the bed—for Katherine lay on it, and she was alive! The entire left side of her body, face included, was swathed in a dirty tangle of bandages, and blistered patches of puckered red skin protruded from the wrappings where their edges had begun to come free. Her right half, in contrast, appeared untouched. Tom could see her again in his mind, turning away as the smile faded from her face, to look at the rumbling bus over her left shoulder as the inferno exploded outward. A plaid shirt, cut away on the left, had been draped around her bandages and buttoned loosely, and a white sheet was drawn halfway up her body.

Tom reached down with his manacled hands and touched her right palm. "Katherine," he said, seeming to hear his own voice from far away—faint, worried, strained. "Katherine," he repeated more urgently.

The girl's hand shifted under his and she sighed. Her eyes opened languidly. "Oh," she murmured, "hello, Tom. How are you?" Her airy voice was at odds with the evident trauma to her body.

Tom patted her hand and the chain connecting his handcuffs tinkled. Katherine heard the noise and looked down. Seeing the gleaming steel bands, she giggled and said with twinkling eyes, "Why, Tom, what *have* you been up to?"

"Getting into trouble. I'll tell you about it later." Tom picked up her hand and touched it to his face. "How are you feeling?"

The girl shifted a little. "I feel...wonderful."

"You're not in pain?" Tom asked.

"Hmm," Katherine smiled grandly. "Uncle Stam has been giving me injections of something or other. Dreamy stuff...." She sighed again.

Tom grimaced at the vacuous expression in her blue eyes. She was in bad shape if she'd been receiving morphine or some other narcotic.

"Katherine," he said, "can you walk? I need to get you out of here."

"You're sweet, Tom. Stay with me." Katherine's head nestled down against the pillow and her eyelids drooped.

Tom shook her gingerly. "Katherine, wake up. Try to focus. There's a car out back. Do you know anything about it?"

"Nope." Her head moved a little.

"Do you know where the owner of this place is?" Tom said urgently. "I think the car is his."

"You talk too much." Katherine giggled again and started humming.

Tom squeezed her hand. "I'm going to have a look around. See if I can find the keys. If I can't, I may have to leave you here while I scrounge up some transportation." He looked down at the girl and said, "It's wonderful to see you alive. I wasn't sure that you were."

That seemed to register. Katherine's eyes regained some of their old sharpness, and she smiled and shook the hand that he held, saying playfully, "Didn't I tell you once that you'd better not—"

The door in the next room creaked. Tom hushed the girl and stepped away from the bed, crossing to the other side of the connecting door. He looked around for a weapon but the room was quite bare. A patch of charred wood in the floor caught his attention, and he noticed shattered pieces of an oil lamp against the wall, but there was no time to investigate. He lifted his hands as his heart pumped faster. The hardened steel of his cuffs would deliver a solid blow.

There was a moment's pause, and a voice said, "Young man, this is Stamford Zimmerlee. Do not attack." It was the professor's voice beyond a doubt. "Villerot is at the lodge, being questioned by the rangers—but we have little time. I've brought a car. We must take Katherine to a hospital, and get to the police as quickly as possible."

Tom walked through the entrance to where the lone white-haired figure stood silhouetted in the doorway. He said exuberantly, "Now you're talking—" and stopped. There was a heavy bruise around Zimmerlee's left eye, and a welt on his cheek. "Professor—"

Something cold and hard ground into the side of Tom's head and a rasping voice said, "Turn around, carefully."

Tom obeyed. As his head came around, he saw that the object imprinting its outline into his skull was the muzzle of a long, double-barreled shotgun. At the far end of the gun were the bloodshot eyes and thin face he had come to despise so thoroughly.

Behind him Zimmerlee said, "I'm terribly, terribly sorry, young man."

"I, on the other hand, am not," said Villerot. "You are easily deceived, a quality I find delightful in others. It was necessary to move you away from the girl before making my presence known. She has her uses in securing the loyalty of noble Stamford, and a shotgun is an indiscriminate tool."

He read the bitter determination flashing in Tom's eyes and stepped back. "Unlike our last encounter, there will be no struggle over this weapon."

Tom fought to keep his anger in check. "I'm surprised to see you using it at all," he said, "when you have more refined options."

Villerot smiled. "My acoustic toy? My invisible dagger? That is to be used only when necessary. It is—how shall I say it? A prototype, still in development. It would be a pity if it ceased to operate before its official christening. It was necessary yesterday afternoon, given the crowds through which I was forced to pursue you, but seeing that no observer is remotely close enough to hear a firearm, the gun will restrain your violent instincts, or end them, if need be. Please have no doubt that I am quite competent with it."

"From three feet away with a shotgun you don't need to be competent at all," Tom said. "Have you been hauling that thing around with you? I missed it in your room."

"Not at all. It was a present from the owner of this residence. It remains here when I am absent."

Tom's eyes narrowed. "The owner is a friend of yours?"

"I know him better than he knows me," Villerot laughed. "A most accommodating man, nonetheless. I must introduce you. He is rather reclusive these days."

Tom shrugged. Villerot held the shotgun unwavering in his right hand as he gestured with his left to the door at the rear of the kitchen. "In there."

Tom walked across the room slowly, conscious of the twin barrels following him. A peculiar humming came from behind the closed door.

"Open it," said Villerot.

Tom saw a faded red stain on the wall next to the door. His heart beat faster as he reached forward, twisting the handle. A swath of dim light followed the opening door, illuminating the dark chamber. Tom stood for a moment in shock and then took a faltering step forward.

It was a large closet, with a few threadbare items of clothing swinging on a long bar in the gentle rush of air, two or three flies flitting among them. Beneath the clothes, sprawled on the dusty floor, was the body of a man, an Indian who had been perhaps forty or fifty years of age. That he had had black hair, dark brown eyes, and a large hooked nose was obvious, but beyond that, it was impossible to say what he had looked like in life. His whole face gave the impression of having been shifted, as though a child had put together a jigsaw puzzle and jammed in the pieces that didn't fit. The man's eyes were no longer in a straight line, the nose had moved to one side, the mouth was twisted and the jaw looked broken. An ugly bulge protruded from the left side of the head.

Tom felt sick.

"Turn him over," Villerot said behind him.

Zombie-like, Tom reached and pulled. The body rolled and its arms sprawled outward.

Tom recoiled. A cloud of flies swarming over a dark coagulated mass did not obscure the fact that the skull had been violently shattered and blown outwards in the rear. Strands of matted hair around the edges intertwined with jagged fragments of bone thrusting from the bloody crevasse. Several flies broke away at the movement and dove in again to resume their macabre feast.

"It's horrible," Tom whispered, sinking to his knees. "Horrible."

"You waste your pity," Villerot said. "He was nothing to look at before. Impressive results, though, one must admit."

Tom sensed something in the voice, or maybe it was the rustle of air, and he twisted around in time to see the butt of the shotgun descending toward him. He tried to move, too late. The heavy wood caught him squarely at the left temple, and everything vanished in black mist.

CHAPTER
15

Tom strained to climb through the murk back to consciousness. Gradually, through blurred vision, he became aware of a dim light in the distance. His ears were filled with hissing and he shook his head to clear them. Pain and nausea swept through him. From a distance he heard labored breathing. He realized dully that it was his own.

He clenched his eyes and opened them again, trying to lift a hand to wipe his brow, but he had no strength. Both hands seemed transfixed by a great weight.

The pain subsided slowly, and the mist cleared. Tom's brain still felt wreathed in fog, but the faraway light strengthened and grew smaller and smaller until it resolved to a point, and details of the surroundings emerged from the haze.

The light came from a lantern resting on a table about five feet in front of him. Its glass cylinder housed a single glowing mantle. A bronze pipe connected this to a regulator and screwed-in cylinder of propane.

A few feet beyond the table was a bed. Someone lay on it. Tom knew where he was now; in the cabin, in the side chamber and he was looking across at Katherine—but this was a different Katherine from the sedated girl he had found earlier. Her limbs twitched convulsively, her mouth was clenched, and her eyes were focused on his.

"Katherine, what's wrong?" Again Tom tried to move. Why couldn't he? His head still hurt and his stomach ached from hunger, but was he that weary? He looked down and saw that he was in a plain wooden chair, bound mid-forearm to its short arms with scratchy rope that chafed into his skin. The rings of the handcuffs still encircled each of his wrists, but the connecting chain had been chopped or sawed through while he was unconscious—presumably so he could be tied to the chair with his hands well separated. There was no play at all in the trusses on either side. A moment's inspection revealed his legs to be similarly bound. More rope crossed his chest and upper arms, passing around the back of the chair. He was completely helpless.

The door beside the bed opened and Stamford Zimmerlee entered, a look of extreme concern on his face. His eyes registered Tom's presence, but he said nothing as he moved to the bed. He had a cloth in his hand and he knelt to the bedside and touched it to Katherine's forehead. Tom heard a muffled sob, but the girl's twitching eased.

"Professor, what is it?" Tom's mouth was terribly dry, as if he'd licked a chalkboard.

The aged man did not turn around. "The effects of the drugs are wearing off. She must have another injection."

"Don't you have more?" Tom asked.

Zimmerlee hesitated. "Yes. Villerot has it. And he is withholding it."

Tom struggled against the ropes, but the effort was futile. "Untie me, Professor," he said. "We can jump him."

Zimmerlee shook his head. "I cannot, young man. He may return at any time."

Tom pulled uselessly at his bonds in frustration. "You helped me before. Help me again. Please, Professor Zimmerlee. If you love Katherine, take that chance."

"Do you love her, young man?" Zimmerlee's eyes looked directly into Tom's.

Tom hesitated, and said, "I think I might. Something's kept me going, trying to find her. I've never met anyone like her."

"Then understand why I cannot help you. She will die if I cross Villerot's path again in any way." Zimmerlee pointed to his black eye. "He has made that abundantly clear."

Tom started to protest, but saw the resignation in the man's bowed head and slumped shoulders. He said, "How did it happen, sir? You were a respected professor of engineering. How did you get mixed up with such a wretched man?"

Zimmerlee folded the cloth over and applied it to Katherine's forearm. He sighed. "I *was* a respected professor. I left that post for a position in a French laboratory doing more interesting and controversial research—controversial in some circles. I doubt that any layman was ever aware of it." His wizened shoulders stiffened. "One man who was aware, and who fervently opposed our work, is the man who now sits in the Oval Office. Such tools as we were developing should not exist in a civilized society, he said. We countered that they were essential for defense—because even if we did not develop these devices, our adversaries would. The difference was that we, the civilized nations, would never use them except as a deterrent or in self-preservation."

"I don't imagine he bought that," Tom said.

"No." The white head shook sadly. "Compromise has never been one of his traits. He wields more influence now, but even then his opinion carried much weight—much more than ours, though we worked with these projects day in and day out; we knew their power, their potential for securing good out of apparent evil."

Zimmerlee looked at the wall and continued. "To be brief, he undertook discussions with the French government and the European Community as a whole, and applied pressure so intense that funding for our researches was cut off, our group was disbanded, and all research results seized and sealed."

The man's voice cracked. "Years of work gone, and I had cast my future upon them. When I returned to this country, the government's disapproval, coupled with the stigma which still is wrongly attached to our research, resulted in my inability to be taken in again by my former university, or any research institution, anywhere. I wandered for a time, and rather foolishly expressed my discontent. There were some who listened, it seems. And, one afternoon...."

The professor's voice trailed away, but Tom knew the finish. He said, "You met Villerot."

Zimmerlee turned. The skin around his eyes was red. "Yes, young man. I met Villerot. And thus began the darkest days I have ever known. He also was disillusioned, he said. He spoke of crafting devices that would demonstrate the peaceful potential of alternative weapons. He was particularly fond of what could be done with acoustics. We would not kill anyone, only damage objects, structures, perhaps cause some few deserving persons to become ill. I was angry at the time—angry at the government, at the world." Zimmerlee looked regretful.

"It is dangerous to live and work too long in closed environments," he continued. "It directs your attention inward, focuses it on detached experiments and away from humanity and what it means to be alive. It leads you to regard other people as only objects or test cases. I went along with Villerot, and found that having begun, I could not go back. I realized very quickly that Villerot's first actions were to collect evidence behind my back that could place me in jail for the rest of my days. This became his means of assuring my loyalty, until he discovered that my affection for my niece was even more effective. I have been under his power for two years, and can tell you with certainty that he has no regard for life, at least not American life. He will succeed tonight, and no one can stop him."

"Professor," Tom said softly. "You can stop him, right here, right now. Look at Katherine, the condition he's left her in, and look at what will happen to the country tonight. Take the shotgun and shoot him down where he stands."

Defiance entered the professor's eyes. "Never!" he exclaimed. "I will not intentionally take a life, even his."

"*Shhh,*" Tom whispered, as rapid footsteps echoed beyond the door. The handle turned and Villerot entered.

"Ah," the tall man said, "returned to consciousness. I wondered if you were ever going to awaken." Villerot looked more pleased than Tom had ever seen him. "I fear you are antagonizing the professor. He rarely raises his voice."

Zimmerlee rose to his feet and pointed at the bed. "She must have another injection."

"Not now, Stamford," Villerot said soothingly. "You know the schedule."

"*No!*"

Villerot raised an eyebrow, but the professor continued, "The pain is too much. She must have a shot, or I will not go tonight."

Villerot's face darkened. He lashed out, striking the old man across the face. "You will go, Stamford, and you will do everything I tell you. Were I to leave you and the girl alone for even a short time, I would return to find both of you gone. In the interests of retaining my life and liberty long enough to achieve the objective tonight, I cannot let that happen. She will receive nothing more until our task is accomplished."

"You inhuman fiend." The professor ignored Villerot's raised hand threatening another blow. "She cannot take this. The agony—soon the drug's effects will be gone entirely. She could become unconscious, go into a coma, even die."

"Having witnessed similar cases," Villerot said, "I know that her chances for long-term survival are not great. With or without drugs, her only real chance is speedy medical care, and that will come when we have finished—successfully."

Zimmerlee saw the absence of pity, the total resolution in Villerot's red eyes. His voice dropped to a shaky whisper. "Then let us go now and get it over with."

"Soon," Villerot said, lowering his hand. "Remember a final consideration: Your presence tonight is also invaluable for me as you would make an admirable shield, should we be discovered. With that in mind, you will agree we should not carelessly invite defeat by exposing ourselves earlier than necessary."

He grinned malevolently at the professor's discomfort. "You concur? Well then, we wait."

Villerot moved to the center of the little room, his face golden in the glow of the hissing lantern. He looked down at Tom, at the tight ropes around Tom's arms and legs, and nodded in satisfaction. His voice was amiable. "And now we have time for a short dialogue. Are you aware that you have slept for eight hours?"

Tom glanced out the window. For the first time he noticed that the light, which had streamed through the glass the last time he had been in the room, was now feeble, dying.

"I haven't slept much, lately," he said.

Villerot pulled up a chair by the table, the twin to the one in which Tom was bound. "An unhealthy situation which will shortly be remedied," he said. "Not to your liking, perhaps, but very much to mine. You will sleep with your forefathers."

He drew a long dagger from inside his jacket and laid it on the table beside the lantern. "I have a question to ask you, a very simple one, and in exchange for your response, I offer to answer your queries."

"What?" Tom tried to fight down the anger, frustration and fear welling up inside him.

"Just this: The morning we encountered each other for the first time, did you have ulterior motives in visiting my room?"

"Ulterior motives?" Tom asked.

"Yes," Villerot said calmly. "Beyond meeting Stamford's niece for your excursion on the bus."

Tom thought back to that sunny morning. "No. Curiosity about you, perhaps after you watched me from your window the night before."

Villerot seemed surprised, but it was surprise mixed with understanding. "No notion of my plan for your president?" he asked.

Tom shook his head. "None at all."

The man leaned forward. "Then why did you investigate my camera?"

"Katherine had mentioned an engineering project," Tom answered, "and also said that she didn't like you. I'm an engineering student, I was curious, and I saw the camera and some technical drawings—and in them, a chance to find out what was bothering her about you. That's all."

Villerot appeared to be weighing Tom's answer in his mind. "This is the truth?" he asked.

"On my honor."

"You do possess that, to a degree." Villerot chuckled and said almost remorsefully, "This means I have brought my difficulties—meaning you—upon myself. With help from your friend."

"Percy?" Tom's voice was hostile. "The one you murdered?"

"No, the other one." Villerot leaned back again. "The one who disliked you, I believe. Immediately after my encounter with you, I received a phone call from him stating—"

"Nick told me what he saw. Right before he killed himself."

"Ah," Villerot paused. "Delightful. I was quite angry with you at the time, as you are aware, and his words rang true. I had assumed after the breaking of the window that you had seen enough to understand. Therefore I was compelled to follow and do what I did. I am almost moved to apologize, my young friend. Of those I have encountered in this country, you have shown the most purity of resolve. I regret having to end your life. You must realize that, at this late juncture, I have no choice."

Tom shuddered. Stalling for time, trying to think of something, anything to get out of this, he asked, "How did you cause the rock fall?"

"That?" Villerot said. "It was easy. When you have lived under conditions and carried on the activities that I have in the course of my life, you learn to identify weaknesses in the terrain which may be exploited. There is little difficulty with mountain ambushes. Certainly not in this place; the area is blessed with an abundance of rock projections, weakened by extreme temperature fluctuations during the passing of the seasons. I found a suitable boulder, climbed up and waited. Yours had been the third in a series of buses to depart. I counted three buses and set the rockslide—"

"There was no explosion," Tom interrupted.

Villerot looked perplexed. He thought about it, and smiled. "Yes. One would expect that. You do not consider the options. Resonance is not limited to human targets. I set my device to the proper frequency and fired, with gratifying results."

"Except you destroyed the wrong bus."

"True. I could not see clearly enough down to the road to distinguish this. I drove to Logan Pass, where I stopped to get the sense of the official reports, and found to my dismay I had made an error—for there I saw you and the girl leaving your bus."

"So you tried Plan B."

"Two occurrences on the same day of Plan A, in your vernacular, would be foolish. I waited until your bus was empty, parked my vehicle beside it, contrived to drop my keys beneath it in the process of leaving my car, and crawled below to retrieve them. With my knives, naturally. Sabotage of vehicles is well known to me. Considering the steep descent on which you were about to embark, it seemed a fitting means of disposal."

"Why didn't you kill me after we crashed?" Tom asked. "I know you were there."

"There was no time," Villerot said sadly. "The rescuers descended too quickly. I had to deal with the girl first—as the direct link to Stamford and myself, her removal was imperative. I brought her a safe distance through the trees, and returned to watch, in no small degree of rage, as you were carried up to the ambulances. Hours later, when the area was cleared, I carried the girl up and drove away, bringing her here. Then I returned to the lodge and instructed Stamford as to the proper responses if questioned."

Tom frowned. "And set about to destroy me."

"After seeing you would not end your opposition. I had hoped you would die in hospital or recover slowly—or, if released, let the matter drop. But you persisted, and your subsequent actions necessitated mine."

"You didn't have to kill my friend," Tom said bitterly.

"What little you claim he knew was still too much," Villerot retorted. "His removal also effectively removed you, as you will have surmised. I arranged to place your fingerprints on the killing weapon, and take you out of my way—I thought. Again I underestimated your persistence, and you escaped. But this time I have you, and no one knows where. No one will see or hear what will happen to you. This time there is no escape."

Tom nodded toward the table. "That?"

Villerot reached out to caress the dagger. "I have always preferred the knife. It kills without separating the user from the act. With the knife, you feel your enemy die. You know the power of what you have done when you watch the shock drain from his face, the life from his eyes; when you feel his blood warm on your hand and inhale his final breath. Guns, arrows, mines, even my acoustical toy—death by remote—they are for the squeamish. Unfortunately, they cannot always be avoided, as at the lodge tonight."

"Why?" Tom asked.

"As a practical consideration," Villerot said, "because I cannot gain the needed proximity to your president with the competent guard of the Secret Service. More importantly, because tonight I require a titanic spectacle. Tonight your president is in his element: the strong man, in the spotlight at the lodge in the mountains. Very big, very pompous, very American. He has emerged victorious over your Congress. He has succeeded in forcing many of your nation's allies to acquiesce to his policies, thereby making conditions intolerable for the rest of the world."

Villerot's mouth twisted angrily. "He stands at the peak of power, the pinnacle of adoration in the public eye. And there he will be cut down, in a way no one has ever seen a man destroyed before. All eyes will see, unbelieving, a thing they will never forget. And the world will know it need not fear your country for the lion it once was, but is no more."

"Until we strike back," Tom said belligerently.

"Against whom?" Villerot smiled. "Against what? The weapon is soundless. There is no flash. Zimmerlee designed it to perfection. What can be more natural than a man with a camera in a setting like tonight's grand ball at the lodge, with its magnificent guest? When I, one of a hundred or a thousand tourists, raise my camera and release the shutter, who will be alarmed?"

"I told the rangers everything I knew about you," Tom said. "They'll know after the fact that I was right."

"If they do not reach that understanding within one minute of the attack, it will not matter. Do you believe anyone will not be too stunned to act in that time? When the president's skull collapses before their eyes? When the back of his head is blown outward?" Villerot added feelingly, "I wish the front would go as spectacularly, but the skull has many cavities, some with acoustical frequencies that cancel each other out, according to Stamford. The effect as it is, however, is adequate. With the inevitable pandemonium ensuing, no one will act in the time it takes me to slip away. Once I am through the doors, I guarantee I shall not be seen in these parts again."

"And then what?" Tom asked.

"That, my friend, I do not know." The exuberance left Villerot's red eyes, replaced with a contemplative frown. The gaunt man said, "I am dying."

Tom raised his eyebrows.

Villerot seemed surprised. "You had not guessed that? Possibly you had wondered why I have no fear for my own existence? Or where we obtained narcotics to give the girl on such short notice? They are mine. I am wasting away from the inside, as is your nation. I feel some pain now, though I have not lost my vigor. The surgeons tell me it will grow worse, that I have a few years at best. I wonder," he mused. "It is true that I hate you for the trouble you have put me to. But I have also confessed a certain regret at the idea of your death. I wonder whether you could have pity for a man who will die more painfully and slowly than any he has ever killed in his life?"

"Sure," Tom said. "I pity you. I pity you that you haven't endured the same terror you've put others through. I pity that you'll receive an easy death tonight at the hands of the authorities instead of the slow, agonizing one nature would have given you. I pity your family, too, for the blight you are to their name. I pity the defects your parents must have had to produce you. They must have been awful people. Probably had syphilis, too. That would explain your looks."

Villerot's eyes grew wide. He snarled and rose to full height. Two strides brought him to Tom's chair, and he cocked his arm and backhanded Tom across the face. His eyes clouded, and he struck again, and again and again—stinging blows that left angry red weals. He continued, enraged, unthinking, pouring out his savage fury as Tom felt consciousness begin to slip, until, at last, the outburst subsided and the man collected himself once more.

"You have been a continual pain to me." Hands clenching and unclenching, Villerot returned to his seat by the table. His hands relaxed and he reached for the knife, turning it over until it caught the reflection of the lantern's glowing light.

Tom shook his head. His skull throbbed, and his cheeks were hot and puffed. He probed gingerly with his tongue and felt his lower left canine move. It had been a gamble, trying to antagonize the man, but Tom suspected that he had no chance at all of escape if he let the man go on with a clear mind. If he could rile the man's emotions, provoke the desire to fight....

Villerot rasped, "You will die tonight. Your president, whom you love so much, will die tonight. Your country, and others like you will die soon."

"Why?" Tom asked. His voice was a croak. "Why do you hate us so much?"

"Because," Villerot replied, leaning forwards and staring at Tom, "you are corrupt. All of you. You ingest sex and irreverence continually through your books, your television, your movie screens. It might be allowable if you contained it within your own borders. But your culture is pervasive. It consumes purer peoples like a tumor." His fingers closed around the knife.

Tom shook his head vehemently. "Many people in this country are appalled by things they see and read."

254

"Then let your leading citizens, your politicians, your celebrities proclaim that," Villerot said. "Let your media respond. The image you choose to present to the world says that you are all rotten to the core and do not care. So you must all go. Others have already acted. I will act. The world will know you can be toppled, and it will act." He glanced at an ancient clock ticking softly on the wall. "Your time grows short." Angling the knife, he said, "Femoral artery."

Tom looked down. The little reflected patch of yellow light hovered on his leg. It climbed across his abdomen, stopping over his chest. Villerot said, "Aorta, death instantaneous."

Tom's heart pounded. He said, "Where are you from? Who are you?"

"I am the man who will create the world every other man realizes he lives in when he awakens tomorrow morning. My father was a Frenchman. I was born and raised in the country of my mother, Algeria." Villerot angled the knife a little more. "Subclavian, death in three and a half seconds."

The little spot of light was at Tom's shoulder, and he shook his head, wishing desperately he could lift his arms off the chair to wipe the sweat from his brow. "You're just another zealot who thinks he has to destroy the world to please Allah?"

"Allah?" Villerot's nose crinkled. "You believe that only one faith sees the squalor of your country and acts on it? I learned in the country of my mother that war is effective at rendering change and peace is not, but I was my father's son. I am no Muslim."

"You mean...? I can't believe it." Tom remembered the little statue, the white Pieta in the room at the lodge. He had assumed it to be Zimmerlee's.

Villerot tapped the knife. "The world is forged under the flame of violence. It has always been so. The Crusades, the Inquisition. Consider the scope of the changes they wrought, contrasted with the minimal gains of today. I wield fire to fight fire. Others across the world, if properly stirred, will rise to the call. That is why they must see in living, horrific color, the symbol of your power fall. The confidence that gesture will inspire is priceless."

Villerot moved the knife again. Tom watched the reflection move up his shoulder toward his neck, and then it passed out of his area of vision. "Carotid," Villerot intoned. "Twelve seconds. The time it takes the blood to drain from your skull. As with your friend."

Tom clenched his teeth. "I don't think the Crusades or the Inquisition gained much in the end. Our scientists will work like mad. They'll find a way to counteract your weapon. I know if you get the frequencies right, you can make one sound wave cancel another. Once they have the means to stop your camera, you'll be powerless. And then the army will come and crush you and all your friends who love death and destruction."

"I do not fear your army." Villerot waved his hand. "Armies of men, and," he sneered, "women, who want to remain alive in combat cannot defeat armies of men who are pleased to die for the cause. Your military is made up of people who have been fed the same malnourishing diet of filth your country attempts to serve to the rest of the world—stripped of belief in anything as sacred or of value, nothing respected: God and country, the freedoms your ancestors cherished, they have become abstractions, things to be mocked on television. Your people cannot be prepared to fight to the death for things they take for granted, or don't believe at all."

He sneered again. "Your country is a superstructure, hollow within. The supports that made it strong have been burned out, beam by beam, pillar by pillar, and that destruction has been wrought by you, yourselves." His face tightened and his voice crescendoed. "You cannot survive. You *will* not survive. The world will learn that tonight."

The knife tilted again and the gleam was directly in Tom's eye. Villerot rose. "And now, your time has run out."

Behind him, Zimmerlee was very pale, and Tom saw that Katherine's eyes were on him. She was still twitching, but her eyes did not waver.

Tom looked at Villerot. There was nothing to lose now. "Coward," he said. "You're nothing at all, just a prating, gutless coward. Don't lecture me about willpower and integrity. All I've seen you do is kill unsuspecting tourists and a fat guy who knew nothing about how to defend himself. You'd be lost in a fair fight." He spat on the floor.

"Oh?" said Villerot.

"Untie me and fight me one-on-one, no weapons. I guarantee you won't win."

Villerot smiled. "I dealt with you easily in your room at the lodge. You would have no chance."

"Then prove it now," Tom raised his chin defiantly. "I was tired then, and shocked. Now I'm just angry, and I've slept for eight hours. You're the one with no chance. And you know what? If you tried a fair fight against the president instead of hiding behind your little coward's weapon, he'd rip your guts out with one hand and strangle you with them. You're afraid of him, of me, and of everyone else, and you know it. If you think you're not, then let's battle it out and see who the better man is. If you're as good as you say, you can take me out and still get to the lodge in time."

Villerot shook his head with admiration. "To the very end, you try. Most, like your fat friend, would be whimpering. I could wish for you to join my cause. You feel no fear." He advanced.

"*No!*" The voice was Katherine's, a hoarse crackle.

Tom looked Villerot in the eye, wishing fervently that he felt no fear. "I die then," he said, "certain that you will, too, confident you will not succeed tonight—but that if you do, the president dies a good man, a brave man, a hero. Others will rise to take his place. The people will pull together, not fall apart. Our spirit will not be crushed. Your spirit, yours and that of those like you, along with your lives, will be destroyed. I die knowing that."

Villerot stopped in front of him. He held the knife tip close to Tom's eye. Minutes passed. Tom stared unwaveringly into the man's red gaze, ignoring the threatening point.

At last Villerot said, "Next to the president, whose death is the culmination of all I have worked for, your death is the one thing left holding any meaning for me—but, not your death alone, which would be a hollow success, but the death of your ideals, a true victory."

He looked candidly into Tom's eyes. "To your young mind, your country will survive because it always has. You cannot imagine a world without America, though others can. You embody the spirit of which you spoke, and I desire that that spirit be crushed. I wish for you to die with the certain knowledge that you, your people, your entire country—everything you hold dear—are all lost."

Villerot mused softly, "And yet...I cannot allow you to leave this chair. No matter the rhetorical heights to which you ascend."

With a mischievous smile, Villerot dropped the knife into Tom's lap, scant inches from his bound hands. The man turned and walked into the kitchen.

"Professor," Tom pleaded, but Villerot was back almost immediately, carrying a rope, an empty plastic jug and a portable radio. He set the rope and the radio on the table and retrieved the knife. In a swift motion he cut away the top of the jug, then set the bottom portion on the floor below Tom's left arm.

He rolled back Tom's sleeve and said somberly, *"The just man is taken away from before the face of evil.* Brachial artery then, but carefully...."

Tom watched in horror as Villerot seized his left forearm and brought the knife up, fingers close to the blade. The man probed the wrist delicately with his forefinger. In a quick, lancing motion, he sliced. The sharp edge parted Tom's skin and cut into his arm with a sear of pain; then the underside of his forearm was warm and slick. He heard a plop in the bucket below.

Villerot watched the arterial spurts and rose to full height, satisfied. He placed his hand on Tom's head. "A full severance would leave you dead in under two minutes. Now you live a little longer. Do not fear; it is a relaxing form of death, hence its popularity with the suicidal. When approximately five pints are gone...endeavor to be calm, to control the pumping of your heart. Listen, and appreciate the grandeur of what will take place."

He leaned close and whispered, "Destiny awaits." Then he turned on his heel and walked to the table. He adjusted the radio's frequency dial and switched the set on. A flat voice, interrupted by a great deal of static, filled the room:

"...Where tonight's event is sure to be the highlight of what will be, for the President, a week of much-needed rest and relaxation. The motorcade is expected in the next half-hour, and the atmosphere inside the lodge is electric as the assembled visitors, staff, and foreign dignitaries await the big arrival..."

"Come, Stamford," Villerot barked as he plucked the rope off the table. Moving to the bed, he hauled the ashen-faced professor to his feet.

"Good-bye, Katherine," Zimmerlee stammered, and then Villerot shoved him to one side and leaned down. He looped the rope around Katherine's bandaged left wrist as she stifled a gasp. He passed the free end under the bed and up the far side, securing her other wrist. Then he turned the whole of the remainder around and around her body and the bed, tying the end to one of the short wooden legs. Convinced she was adequately trussed, he seized the professor by the arm and led him through the doorway.

The outer door banged shut. A few moments later, an engine fired and wheels skidded on dirt. The noise receded into the distance, and Tom knew that the two men were gone, and that time was running out. He strained to move in the little chair, alone with the sounds of the hissing lantern, crackling radio, whimpering girl, and the soft, rhythmic drops of his own blood streaming in little gushes down into the base of the container.

CHAPTER 16

Tom struggled for minutes against the taut ropes. At last he sat back, exhausted. His left arm was throbbing and very wet underneath, and he held still, willing his heart to slacken its pace, to slow the beat whose every pulse meant a little more life gone. Helpless, unable to act, he felt weariness set in, the weight of the trials he had faced and the unmovable obstacles he could not overcome crushing out his last embers of hope.

This is the end, he thought, knowing that despite his defiant words to Villerot, his enemy stood an excellent chance of success. The disaster would take place on schedule, and Villerot would vanish to spend the rest of his short life stirring up the radical factions of his world, gloating over the carnage that would transpire.

Tom admitted he had scored a mild victory simply by still being alive, but it didn't matter. He wouldn't live much longer, and neither would the president. The bitterness of his failure was overwhelming.

The radio announcer droned on, about the fabulous décor at the lodge, about the fascinating people who would be present, about the lights, and the orchestra that would occupy a portion of the main floor and provide patriotic songs as a background for dancing and socializing. A night to remember, he proclaimed.

A fresh sob startled Tom back to attention. It was Katherine. She was straining her left arm against the rope holding it fast.

"Katherine, no—what are you doing?" Tom said, wincing at the agony the girl must be experiencing as she twisted her burnt wrist back and forth.

"Must...do..." The words were forced out, and she said nothing else, despite his urgent pleading that she stop.

Slowly, a millimeter at a time, red blistered skin emerged from inside the bandages under the ropes. Then Tom understood what she had already figured out: The wrappings had provided a flexible buffer between her arms and the rope so that, in spite of Villerot's formidable strength, there remained sufficient slack to withdraw her arms—though at dreadful cost.

More discolored skin showed on Katherine's wrist as the tips of her fingers receded into the bandage. Tears dripped from her eyes, but she never paused. Knowing how much depended on their escape, Tom clamped his lips together and watched in silent distress as, sobbing, Katherine pulled her hand through. Her mottled fingers reached for the knot securing the end of the rope.

She found it and began to fumble awkwardly. The knot was tight, and Katherine tugged again and again, trying to loosen one of the strands. Minutes passed, each bringing both Villerot and the president closer to the lodge. Katherine continued to struggle.

Another minute ticked by, and the radio commentator's excited voice said, *"We've just received word the presidential motorcade is through the town of Browning, twelve miles away. Only a few minutes, and..."*

"Ha!"

Tom looked back at the bed. With the grunt of victory, a smile had broken through on Katherine's streaked face, and

Tom saw the knot visibly loosen. The girl's fingers pulled the intertwined segments apart.

She flicked the free end of the rope toward the wall, felt for the topmost loop wrapped about her, and pulled it around. She repeated the operation on the remaining turns, and was free. Ignoring the loop remaining on her right wrist, she tried to sit up, got three inches clear of the bed and slumped back down with a gasp. The spark of hope that had flared in Tom's heart died.

Then the girl's hands balled into fists and she drew a deep breath. Her eyes found his, and she smiled again. In one explosive action, she threw herself off the bed, landing with a stifled cry on the hard wooden floor. Tom watched unbelievingly as she directed the motion from her fall into a sideways roll, turning over and over, gasping every time her left side passed under her, coming toward him.

As she rolled, trying desperately to keep up her momentum, her foot hooked one of the thin legs of the table. The radio fell forwards and the lantern toppled onto its side. It spun the few inches to the table's edge and dropped to the floor, landing with a tinkling crash.

Tom held his breath, but there was no explosion. Katherine got her foot clear and laboriously shunted herself across the remaining few feet to Tom's chair. She pulled up under his right arm and reached for the knot.

"You're the most wonderful girl I've ever known," Tom said. It was all he could think of. Katherine smiled once and continued, working for some time, minutes in which Tom watched the floor beneath the still-burning lantern begin to smolder.

He looked down. Katherine was still working. A hasty check on Tom's left showed that the bottom of the plastic jug was now obscured by a dark layer of blood a quarter-inch deep.

A new glint of light showed amid the smoke surrounding the lantern. The floor had caught fire.

"Hurry," Tom said, and he regretted it almost immediately. Katherine could see as well as he what was taking place. The little strength she'd started with must be completely exhausted by now.

The tiny blaze began to spread outward as the surrounding wood heated and burst into flame. The drops fell faster into the plastic jug as Tom's heart thumped away. Sweat trickled into his eyes. If the fire engulfed the lantern's propane tank....

"Can you get over and kick that lantern away?" Tom asked. The girl made no reply and he said, "Katherine?"

"Never—get—back—again," she said heavily.

The patch of fire spread around the tank, creeping toward the walls, toward the bed, licking at the boards by Katherine's feet. A quarter of the floor was ablaze.

Suddenly Tom's right wrist was free, and he heard a *thump* as Katherine's arm dropped to the floor. She slumped over and sighed.

Tom pulled the ropes from around his chest and reached for his left wrist. His fingers worked at the knot. It stuck, and he fumbled some more as Katherine pulled her feet away from the consuming blaze. The room was filling up with smoke, and Tom coughed twice.

The knot came undone. Tom pulled his wounded forearm from the sticky arm of the chair and felt the warmth on his leg as fresh blood spurted on his trousers. He reached down and began untying the ropes securing his feet.

The fire reached the edge of the floor under the window and licked at the wall. The air on Tom's skin was hot.

There was a brightening across the room. The canister's blown, Tom thought, steeling himself for a blast of heat and shrapnel, but he was wrong. The sheet hanging down from the bed had caught fire. Then the entire bed was burning, and it was suddenly very bright and stiflingly hot in the little room. Acrid smoke filled Tom's chest and he choked again.

The fire crept to within a foot of his shoes. Katherine squirmed a few inches farther back.

Then his feet were free. The ropes dropped. Tom jumped up, and reeled with dizziness.

Blood loss, he thought. He shook his head, grasping the arms of the chair. *Move!* The room focused, and he got around the back of the chair and picked Katherine off the floor.

The girl's head lolled against Tom's chest. Despite the convulsive twitching of her limbs, she managed to murmur sardonically, "My hero." Then her fingers dug painfully into Tom's shirt as her face pressed against his shoulder. Her entire body sobbed and Tom felt tears soaking through his shirt to touch his skin.

He stumbled on the little makeshift bucket below the arm of the chair, spilling its gruesome contents across the floor, and he kept going. A searing blast of heat and light, and they were past the bed, through the door, and into the main room of the cabin. Tom kicked the front door open and got through into refreshingly cold air. He set Katherine down on the ground and rose to his feet.

"Where—you going?" she asked.

"We need a vehicle," Tom said. "The only one I know of is behind the cabin. I hope it works—it looks medieval. I've got to find the keys."

He didn't wait for a reply, turning to run back into the cabin. He felt weak and drained and knew he could not go much farther without stanching his blood loss.

The entrance to the bedroom was impassible. That was all right, there had been no place for keys there. But heavy smoke poured into the main room now, obscuring Tom's vision and breathing. He ran his eyes over the walls, table, and counters, seeing nothing.

Tom jerked the cupboard doors open, one after the next, finding no keys, but he stopped at the cupboard over the sink. Inside were several little unmarked bottles, and in front of them, a syringe three quarters full of liquid. He swept it up, dropped it into his shirt pocket, and moved on. The last cupboard was empty.

This left only the closet and Tom shuddered, remembering the hideous contents within, but there was no choice. He opened the door and plunged his hands into the pockets of the coats hanging on the bar, one by one, without looking at the floor. Every pocket was empty.

Swallowing once, Tom got on his knees and rolled the corpse onto its back. The stench was overpowering. He felt inside the right front pocket and his fingers closed around a bundle of keys. He withdrew it, and was on his feet in a moment. Then he remembered his blood-soaked arm—he wouldn't get far at the lodge looking the way he did now. Scanning the row of coats before him, he took the most inconspicuous, a plain green jacket, thrusting it under his good arm as he turned to head for the door.

Remarkably, the radio in the bedroom still functioned. Above the roar of the flames, the announcer's flat voice rose to a new note of excitement: *"...Ladies and gentlemen, the motorcade has just turned off the highway into the grounds, and you can feel the excitement sweeping through the crowd. The limousine is..."*

Tom waited no longer. He got outside and ran around to the rear of the cabin. Flames poked through the walls on the right, and as he bent to the driver's door of the ancient station wagon, there was a sharp crack and a shattering of glass. The propane canister, he thought, and went on with his work. In the dancing light, he selected the largest key and fitted it to the lock. It rotated with a click, and Tom wrenched the door open. He climbed in, tossed the jacket into the back, jammed the key into the ignition, and twisted. The motor ground protestingly, turning over and over. Tom pumped the gas pedal and the engine caught, roaring into life. He noted the half-full gas tank.

As he reached across and unlocked the passenger side, he had to pause to catch his breath. His deepest inhalations did not satiate him now, and he knew he must attend to his wound.

He unbuckled the belt around his waist and pulled it free. What had he learned so long ago in first aid class? The brachial artery, running down the inside of the arm, provided the conduit through which flowed the blood he had been losing. Pinch it off, and the spurts from the incision on his wrist should slow to a trickle, or stop altogether.

Tom wrapped the belt around his upper left arm, inserted the free end through the buckle, and pulled it tight until his arm felt like it would burst open on either side of the leather. There were no holes here to pass the pin through, so he forced the free end under the wrapped segment, back around, finally ramming it into the space inside the buckle. The arrangement held, and the staccato spouts of blood ceased.

A little fresh blood still dripped from the wound. Tom pulled a handkerchief from his back pocket and wrapped it around the cut. The white fabric darkened, soaked immediately. Tom shrugged. There was nothing more he could do now. They had to get going.

Grateful for the automatic transmission which meant he would not have to keep the hand of his bad arm on the wheel while his good hand shifted gears, Tom brought the station wagon up alongside the cabin, stopping next to Katherine. She tried in vain to sit up as Tom climbed out and hurried to her side. He scooped her up and maneuvered her through the passenger's door. In spite of his gentleness, she stiffened on contact with the seat. Tom closed the door, raced back, and threw himself in behind the wheel, reaching for the syringe in his shirt pocket.

"Katherine," he said, "I found this inside. I think it's the injection your uncle wanted to give you. I don't know for sure, but I'll give it to you if you want."

Katherine gave two emphatic nods without hesitation, and lifted her arm feebly.

Tom leaned forward. With no experience in giving shots, he searched till he found the little purple dot of a previous injection. The mark seemed to waver in the unsteady light of the flaming cabin. Tom gritted his teeth and pushed the needle through soft skin into the vein beneath.

He pressed the plunger and the level of liquid inside dropped slowly. He stopped when half remained, but Katherine shook her head. Reluctantly, he dispensed the remaining fluid, and withdrew the needle. He put it back in his shirt pocket and turned to the steering wheel.

Katherine leaned back and sighed. Her limbs still twitched, but as the car pulled away onto the dirt road, she was able to say coherently, "Thank you, Tom. You have no idea what the pain is like." She managed a laugh. "I...suppose I'm becoming an addict."

Tom glanced at her. "You think that's funny?"

"No." The humor left her voice. "Doesn't matter. I don't suppose I'll be one long."

"What do you mean?" Tom asked sharply.

Behind them, the blazing building vanished behind a screen of trees. The old car rumbled down the path, shot across the narrow bridge and up the hill on the other side.

"You heard Villerot...." the girl's every word was an effort. "...Won't last at this rate. I feel it...slipping."

"What?"

"Tired...ready for it."

"No you're not," Tom said irritably. "Katherine, don't talk that way. You're going to make it. I'm going to get you to a hospital."

They swerved around a bend, throwing dirt to one side. The rearward view was obscured by a cloud of dust.

Katherine sat up. The motion obviously caused her pain, though her speech was easier now. The drug was taking over, but her mind was not yet gone. "Tom, you have to save the president. I didn't go through everything back there just for me. The way I feel right now, I could just drift away.... You mustn't worry about me. Stop Villerot, and know that I'll be happy for it."

"Stopping him was all I had on my mind until a minute ago," Tom said. "I just realized how empty the victory could be. Assuming...."

"What?" Katherine looked at him.

"That I can find him in time. That I'm able to stop him. I can't go to anyone else for help—the whole world is after me."

"Tom," Katherine said softly. "It won't be a victory at all if you think only of me and let him go."

Tom drove for a time in silence. Finally he said, "I know." His voice caught, and he could say no more. With effort, Katherine raised her hand and squeezed his forearm softly. She eased herself into a more comfortable position between the seat and the door, and closed her eyes, leaving her hand on his arm. The convulsive jerks of her arms and legs slowed, and she breathed more evenly.

They drove in silence. The wagon cleared the trees and reached the end of the side road. Tom twisted the wheel right, and the car turned onto the highway. He reflected in passing that it took a lot less time to cover the distance by car than by foot. There was a dull glow way back in the woods, and he knew a substantial wildfire would soon be in full blaze. He hoped the firefighters weren't too far away. Then the wagon was over a hill and the light was gone.

Tom switched the headlights up to high and pressed the accelerator to the floor, determined to stop for nothing and no one. The president was at the lodge, and Tom could only hope against hope that Villerot would be cautious choosing his opportunity to strike.

The miles sped by, the desolate hills rolling past on either side as the road rose and fell, twisted, and leveled again. Ahead Tom could see the glare of East Glacier. It seemed an eternity, but at last they passed the first sporadic dwellings. Then the road turned right and they were up a short hill and into the town itself. Tom blinked at the transformation: Banners in red, white, and blue hung from every building front, and the town was abuzz. Its sidewalks teemed with people of all shapes and sizes, most of them headed for the lodge.

The car reached the turnoff to the lodge entrance. Tom braked hard and wrenched the wheel, turning left and cutting off a group of pedestrians who jumped back, yelling words that didn't make it through the wagon's windows. The car dipped under the rail bridge and roared around the long gardens toward the lodge. Tom glanced over at Katherine and saw her eyes open. She was smiling.

She read the quizzical expression in his eyes, and said, "I was just thinking...about our first walk. Through the flowers, after we played the piano."

Tom thought of how she had chided him on his lack of culture. "Seems like we had trouble finding anything in common to talk about," he said.

"You mean finding a subject you knew anything about." She smiled again. "Long ago. You know, Tom, being around you a few days is like being around anyone else for years."

"Thanks." Tom's heart was leaden as the wagon pulled into the parking lot at the side of the lodge, and the heaviness reached his voice. Katherine's face grew serious.

"Tom," she said, "don't think about me. Go do what you need to do. Don't hesitate." She paused, and finished quietly, "Just remember to come back for me when it's over."

There were no open spaces in the lot. Tom stopped the wagon directly in front of a line of parked cars. His face felt raw and swollen from Villerot's beating. His sustained physical and mental exertions, the lack of sleep and food, the loss of his blood had all devastated his reserves to the breaking point. He turned and looked at Katherine, at her pitiable face divided down the middle as if by a line, one half pristine, the other raw and swollen.

"I'll be as careful as I can," he said, "though if I lose you now, it won't matter much to me what happens. I care about you, more than any other girl, ever."

Katherine shook her head. "I wish there had been more time, I really do. Perhaps by a miracle there still will be. But..." she looked off into the distance. Her faraway voice cleared. "You have to go. The clock is ticking."

"I know." Tom drew a deep breath. "We've *got* to give you a chance, and it may provide a distraction so I can get inside unobserved." He motioned his blood-soaked arm. "I'll try to hide the arm with the jacket, but even so, I'd be lucky if I could get in on my own without anyone asking questions. So I want you to wait till I get away from the car. Then start hitting the horn, on-off, on-off, on-off, till people come. Tell them to get you to the hospital, no delays. On the way, tell them to contact the authorities—tell them what's happened to you. Call the rangers. Mention the name Steve Hollis. Stir up a commotion. And hang on. Can you do it?"

Katherine nodded languidly and smiled. "Of course. I will...just as long as I can." Her eyes were only half opened, and she looked far gone. "But if I can't, I'll just say: Tom, dear Tom, *forever and forever farewell*." She coughed. *"If we do meet again—"*

"—Why, we shall smile," Tom finished, the quotation from *Julius Caesar* popping from somewhere into his mind as his heart scraped the bottom of his soul.

Katherine's clear blue eyes opened fully. She glanced at the gardens again, then back to him with a speculative expression he had never seen before. She smiled, and said, "Why, Tom, you *do* know something, after all."

All Tom's emotions welled up as he reached across and lifted her head. The outside world and its problems evaporated for an instant as he touched his lips to the clear skin of her forehead, above the matted bandages on the left side of her face. Somewhere beneath the burnt odor in the golden hair, he smelled a lingering trace of sweet apples.

Then he drew away, and with a final long gaze into the girl's now-sparkling eyes, he turned and tugged at the door handle. The door opened and Tom stepped out of the car, instantly dizzy as he stood to full height. He sagged against the door as his brain struggled to draw oxygen. His left arm, numb below the tourniquet, felt as if it could fall off if a mosquito landed on it. He eased it through the sleeve of the dead Indian's jacket, then pulled the rest of the garment over his body.

Shaking his head, he staggered away toward the path to the lodge. He jumped as a car's horn shook the ground beneath him, shocking him into full alertness. Half turning, he remembered his instructions to Katherine, and he turned forward again. The intermittent blasts continued, on and off, on and off, and up ahead he saw door attendants and several other people looking past him down the path with curious faces.

Suddenly the horn was blaring, one long unbroken note that filled the air. The people were coming now, running hard, and Tom turned to find his apprehensions realized. Katherine was stretched over from the passenger's side, with the top of her golden head resting unmoving on the steering wheel. She had pinned her hand between her face and the button on the wheel, so that the horn continued to sound after she slipped into unconsciousness.

Several people were abreast of Tom, hurrying along and muttering in low tones. He kept going and held his breath as he passed a group of three men in tribal law enforcement uniforms running the other way.

Tom reached the doorman and took him aside. "That girl needs help," he said to the man, motioning toward the unmoving station wagon. "She's badly burned—call an ambulance, right now. Please."

The doorman hesitated, then nodded and hastened away. Tom watched him disappear into the lodge. The interior was filled with people, and the excited murmur of voices reached his ears, riding the sonorous wave of a waltz performed by a string section.

More people were moving toward the blaring station wagon. A state trooper came through the entrance and looked past Tom. Beside the car, one of the tribal policemen looked up the path and waved urgently.

Katherine's fate was beyond Tom's control now. He looked up, said a silent prayer, and strode through the massive doorway.

CHAPTER
17

The gala scene inside was one of joyful and patriotic festivity. Bright lights illuminated the lobby, its three staggered levels decked resplendently in red, white, and blue. Sweeping down on the left, a gigantic American flag hung from the second story banister, above the stone hearth in which a cheerful fire burned.

The orchestra, primarily a cello and violin section plus a handful of other pieces, was clustered to the right of the fireplace around the grand piano. The musicians were obviously the best that Montana had to offer. They played in tight coordination, making no mistakes as their instruments sparkled out with beautiful and breathtaking notes and chords, filling the atrium with warm sound.

Upwards of five hundred people filled the lobby, speaking in clustered groups or wandering about, admiring the lodge's sumptuous furnishings. Several couples danced to the music on a section of bare floor near the fireplace where the chairs had been cleared away. Hundreds more looked down from the levels of railed walkways surrounding the atrium above. With the exception of the ceiling and skylight, there was nowhere they could turn their eyes without seeing their fellow man. A relative few had dressed up in suits and dresses, but most wore everyday clothes despite this being the grandest event they had ever seen.

SNAPSHOT

The crowd was most dense around the cluster of armchairs, couches, and low tables in the center of the lobby, which on typical evenings provided a venue for reading, conversing, card playing, or even sleeping. Tom turned his attention here as he passed the front desk.

There was a continual motion of people through the area, and Tom's heart thrilled in relief as he caught a glimpse of that powerful man, very much alive, in whose honor the celebration had been arranged. Near the president, the long queues merged into a single line of people passing by for a handshake and a few words of hasty greeting from the leader.

Tom saw that tonight the president had forsaken his usual conservative suit for more traditional western attire: a short jacket and close-fitting trousers; a miniature silver antelope's head with hanging black strings replacing his standard striped necktie. He had even remembered the requisite white ten-gallon hat. It lay on the seat beside him. All he needed to complete the outfit, Tom reflected with a smile, was a pair of ivory-handled six-shooters.

Spread around the president, standing at each corner of the couch he reclined on, wearing plain black suits with no trace of western influence whatsoever, were four unsmiling agents of the Secret Service. They scanned the crowd continually, lifting their wrists to their mouths from time to time to speak into the transceivers beneath their cuffs.

Tom turned his right side as one pair of hard eyes swept over him. He melted back toward the wall, grateful for the number of people in casual clothes, which allowed him to blend in. A glance at his injured arm assured him that no blood showed yet through the sleeve. He raised he eyes again. Where were Villerot and Zimmerlee? Tom looked over the crowd with the same intensity as the dark-suited agents.

Careful scrutiny convinced him that neither man was present in the cluster around the president. Tom examined the dance floor and the orchestra, and moved on to the rest of the people milling about the spacious lobby.

He pulled back sharply. Steve Hollis was standing next to the glass box containing the stuffed mountain goat, also surveying the room quietly. The ranger had abandoned his uniform for plain clothing, and Tom might very well have walked right up to him, not realizing the man's identity until too late. The ranger's presence was no surprise. Even though the lodge was on tribal lands outside the national park, and therefore beyond the jurisdiction of the rangers, Tom was sure that nothing short of an all-out emergency would have kept Hollis away tonight.

On Tom's right, the state trooper he had passed outside re-entered the lodge. The doorman spoke with him, and they both began to search the faces in the crowd.

Affecting an air of relaxed nonchalance, Tom turned to walk past the glass-fronted gift shop. An elderly man blocked his way. He pointed to Tom's left arm. "You need help, young fellow."

Tom looked down. A single patch of red had soaked through the bottom of the sleeve. He gulped, and said, "I'm fine. It looks worse than it is—thanks, though." Time was running out fast. Once the Secret Service agents got a look at him with a bloody arm....

The man ignored the words as his gaze switched repeatedly from Tom's face to his arm. "You're fine, my foot," he said. "That there is blood. Say, aren't you the one who played that music the other night? Come on, we'll find you a doctor." He took Tom's good arm.

"No." Tom tried to shrug him off, but the man was determined, and Tom stopped and said, "All right. But I have to grab something from my room, first." The hand on his upper arm relaxed hesitantly. Tom smiled and brushed it clear.

Without waiting for further comment, he slipped away. The crowds closed in between him and his would-be benefactor.

The recessed stairway was just beyond the gift shop. Tom climbed to the second floor and walked cautiously onto the balcony. A mass of people lined the wooden rails. Tom wormed his way through and craned his head over a couple of acne-faced teenagers as he searched for the red-eyed assassin and his unwilling comrade. Tom couldn't see them, but his eyes landed again on Hollis. The ranger was looking at his watch.

Over on the couch, the president was still shaking hands and speaking to the people before him. The Secret Service men around him maintained their vigils, their eyes always on the crowd.

Tom glanced at the neon-blue wristwatch on the thin arm of the boy in front of him, and as he did so, the music filling the air ceased. The watch read eight o'clock.

The excited chatter all around diminished until absolute silence filled the atrium. Then, with great dignity, the orchestra, below and across from Tom, began *The Star Spangled Banner*.

Every head turned toward the music and the tremendous flag hanging above the musicians. The president was on his feet, as was every other person. Many began to sing, their voices brimming with patriotism. The lodge was filled with sound that could be felt.

Unexpectedly, Tom's knees began to shake, and he did not know whether it was due to the fervor of the moment, or the immense hunger and weariness oozing out of every pore in his body. His left arm was entirely numb, and he tried to shore up his feelings. Only a little longer, he thought. You don't get to quit till the job is done. Pull it together—keep going.

Under cover of the music, which distracted the crowd, Tom surveyed the people lining the top floor, seeing neither Villerot nor the professor. He twisted around and looked at the people above and behind him.

Nothing. He turned his gaze to his own level, checking the people near him, then looking down the rows stretching away on either side.

It was impossible to distinguish every person. Tom looked for the distinct figure of Villerot, whose hairless head would rise above most others. He knew that if he could not spot his prey from here, he would have to walk completely around each level before assuring himself that the man was not present.

The idea of further exertion caused his tired brain to wretch, but he steeled himself to it, when a new thought struck him. Perhaps the two men were not in the crowd at all, but waiting in their room upstairs until the precise moment of attack. Tom considered the idea, and rejected it. Villerot would not be able to resist being present with the crowd to inhale the sweetness of the moment, to savor the taste of victory before the assassination. There would be no time to celebrate as he made his getaway afterward.

Tom debated taking the direct approach to eliminate the possibility by going up and knocking on the door, as he looked idly across the vast openness before him to the crowd on the other side of the second level.

He froze. The roar of the singing voices melted into a distant murmur.

In all the mass of people, with all their heads facing the same way, every eye and nose pointed toward the flag and the music, two heads halfway down the railing stood out in sharp opposition. They were directed down and away, breaking the pattern, as incongruous as a branch floating upstream against a surging river.

Tom's heart thumped. Villerot's eyes were fixed intently on the unsuspecting president, and he held the camera loosely in his hands. Some instinct made Tom look toward the glass-enclosed mountain goat, and fear surged through him. He failed to notice as the national anthem ended, the final notes of music drowned by thunderous cheers and applause. Steve Hollis's eyes were looking up into his own. How long the ranger had been watching him was uncertain, but Tom grasped that the ranger must have spotted him the same way Tom had found Villerot and Zimmerlee: Tom's own movements as he scanned the crowd would have contrasted with the uniformly turned heads surrounding him—and the ranger, on the other side of the atrium, had noticed.

All chances for stealth were gone. Hollis and Tom moved in the same instant; Hollis toward the nearest Secret Service man, and Tom to the left, mustering his strength for a final assault.

The crowd had closed in behind Tom and a voice blared through powerful speakers. Tom strained to push his way clear against the crush of people throwing him back toward the rail.

There was no time for civility and Tom shoved hard. A path opened as several people resisted angrily, only to recoil as he raised his increasingly bloody left arm.

Tom glanced back. A man in a gray suit stood speaking at the podium below the flag. Hollis, in front of two stern-faced Secret Service men, had produced a little black wallet and Tom saw a flash of golden metal. The speaker's echoing voice said, "...proud to welcome to Glacier Park Lodge, the President of the United States of America."

A thunderous cheer erupted from the crowd as the orchestra began a vigorous rendition of *Hail to the Chief.* Hollis had his arm stretched toward Tom, and one of the agents lifted his cuff to his mouth. A second agent left the group, moving toward the stairway below Tom, even as the president stepped through a newly formed gap in the crowd and began to work his way up to the podium.

With newfound strength, Tom broke through the crowd massed at the stairs and started around the side of the atrium.

The flag hung down from the banister here, and he drew up short beside it as, from around the far corner, a third man in a black suit pushed the throng aside and launched into a powerful sprint.

Tom wheeled and dashed for the staircase. The agent coming up from ground level came around the bend in the stairs below him and Tom raced upwards, his head pounding furiously. The people he passed were murmuring, realizing that something strange was going on. A few reached out for him halfheartedly. Those on the ground floor seemed blissfully unaware of anything wrong, however, as the president reached the podium and faced the crowd.

He began to speak, but the words were an indistinct rumble in Tom's ears as he reached the top of the stairs and dashed around to the left. The crowds were thinner on the upper level, and he had space to run. The painful breaths he drew were already labored, but his purpose spurred him forward.

There was a shout behind. It made no difference. Nothing did, now. Tom was around the corner and barreling down the long segment above Villerot and Zimmerlee. He passed the piano two floors down, ran ten yards more and stopped, panting. He was directly above the two men. Villerot was raising the camera.

To Tom's right, the Secret Service man who had continued up the stairs behind him rounded the corner and stopped, legs astride, hand plunging beneath his left lapel.

Down below, the president's arms were extended to either side in a gigantic symbolic embrace as he finished an exclamation with the words "...this bastion of freedom!"

The crowd roared approval, and Villerot had the camera to his eye. An ugly black pistol appeared in the agent's hand, and Tom, not pausing, everything blurred in a haze of fear, adrenaline and noise, got his foot up on the railing and jumped into open space.

His hair whipped in the air and he heard screams. It was only a short plummet, but the fall sucked what little breath remained from his lungs as the scene twisted crazily and the figure of the unsuspecting man rushed to meet him.

Tom crashed heavily down on Villerot, sending both of them sprawling. A searing jolt of pain ripped Tom's left arm as it cracked on the hard floor. His tourniquet popped loose, and fresh blood streaked the sleeve of his coat. He felt it, warm on his flesh.

Tom got both hands around Villerot, pinning the man's arms to his torso. Villerot's legs flailed under his own, and the man's narrow head lanced backward. Tom jerked right, evading the blow, and twisted to look up at Zimmerlee.

The old professor looked down at him with eyes bulging in astonishment. "You—young man," he gasped.

Tom nodded, straining to hold the writhing monster trapped in his arms, and choked, "Get down there and tell the president what's happening. Tell him about Villerot. Get him out of here!" He grunted as Villerot's foot connected with his lower shin. "*Hurry.*"

Hope crowded the disbelief from the professor's face. "Then my niece—Katherine, she is—"

"Being attended to," Tom sputtered. "Go!"

Zimmerlee locked eyes briefly with Villerot. A smile of triumph broke through the old man's face, and he turned and hastened away, his wizened frame exuding an energy Tom hadn't seen before.

The professor was away and around the corner when a voice above Tom yelled, "Freeze!"

Tom turned, instinctively. The Secret Service agent leaned against the third floor rail with his pistol trained on Tom. Startled, Tom's hold on Villerot relaxed.

Villerot's forearm crashed through Tom's intertwined arms, and Tom was too late to stop the elbow swinging savagely into his jaw. The jarring impact knocked him backwards, and for a moment he could see nothing. Then he was face down on the floor with the bloody taste of iron and salt in his throbbing mouth.

He felt something hard inside his cheek as his tongue passed over the gap where he had expected to feel his previously loosened canine. With mixed pain and disgust, he spat the tooth out, and as he did, he heard a muffled grunt of surprise and agony from above. A woman's voice shrieked in terror.

Tom forced himself to roll over and look up. The agent at the rail had vanished from sight, and as Tom continued to roll around, he saw Villerot with the camera open and a black cloud surrounding it. Villerot dug a little cartridge out of his pocket and clicked it into the rear of the camera.

Tom struggled up. Villerot's eyes shifted past him just as Tom's arms were seized forcefully from behind. A rock-steady voice said, "Don't move an inch." Tom saw cuffs of a black suit behind the sinewy hands clutching his arms.

"Do you see that cloud of smoke?" Tom asked frantically. "This man just killed one of your agents. Look at my left arm. He did that to me. You have to take that camera from him, now. The president will die if you don't."

"What?" the voice said, unbelievingly.

"Please," Tom urged. "Ask questions later. *Just check that camera.*"

Villerot closed the device's back cover.

"Stop where you are," the agent said to Villerot. Tom grunted as his right arm was twisted up his back and held in place with a powerful grip. The agent thrust him against the thick wooden railing, and extended his free arm open-handed toward Villerot. "Give me that," he thundered.

"Of course." Villerot's voice dripped with awe-struck willingness to oblige. "It is an old foreign model. The smoke is from the flash." He held it out with his left hand and placed it in the agent's palm.

As the man's fingers closed around it, Villerot seized the agent's wrist. He jerked the man's arm, snapping his head backwards and pulling him close. Villerot's right hand flashed out and up, flicking a narrow blade from his left sleeve and plunging it almost to the hilt through the bottom of the agent's chin.

The man shivered once and sagged. Villerot pushed the body forward into Tom, pinning him to the banister. He wrenched the camera from the agent's fingers and propped his elbows on the man's slumped shoulders, bringing the camera up to his eye.

Tom strained to get clear of the weight above him as Villerot cocked a lever on top of the camera. Tom's wrist came free of the dead man's grip but it was too late. Above the lolling head, Villerot's lips clenched as his bony index finger depressed a button.

Horrified, Tom turned toward the podium. He saw, as a bitter snarl rasped from Villerot behind him, the president, crouched behind the podium, still alive—and before him, leapt in front at the last instant, the stout figure of Stamford Zimmerlee. The professor's limbs shook in frozen contortion. His lips twitched and his head quavered, but in the instant before the old man died, a fragmentary smile crossed the elderly face, and Tom knew the professor had finished life with the knowledge that the one person of value to him—Katherine—had escaped the enemy's clutches. Then the man's smile was gone and his lined face shifted violently, stretching and distorting. A crimson cloud burst from the rear of the silvery head, and the professor dropped to the floor in a shapeless heap.

Chaos erupted in the atrium, men and women screaming in terror, everyone moving.

Tom broke free of the agent's body and plowed forward. As he charged, he saw through blurred eyes that Villerot already had the rear of the camera open, venting a fresh cloud of smoke. Tom hit him and they crashed together against the railing.

Villerot held the camera in his left hand, and Tom grasped that wrist in his right and struggled to lift the arm. He got his nearly useless left hand onto the wrist, and with the combined strength of both hands, levered the arm upward.

Villerot's right hand crashed against Tom's neck, but Tom shrugged off the blow and slammed the man's forearm into the railing, once, twice. The long fingers popped open on the third impact, and the camera spun away to the lobby below.

Tom brought his left arm across, deflecting a second blow from Villerot. He jabbed his fingers at the crimson eyes, but Villerot seized his wrist, driving him backwards. They twisted around in a deadly dance to the death, inching along the railing toward the end of the atrium from which hung the giant flag.

All strength had vanished from Tom's left hand. It was going fast in his right. His gasping breaths were shallow. Blood spurted from the cut at his wrist, and everything around him, the pillars, the walls, the people, seemed a haze, with Villerot's savage face before it. Suddenly Tom's left wrist was twisted up, and pain ripped through his arm.

Villerot hooked his leg around Tom's and shoved. They toppled together to the floor, and Tom felt himself being rolled over onto his back. Villerot crouched above, his left hand straining to get free of Tom's right. Releasing Tom's injured left arm, Villerot plunged his hand into his shirt. He withdrew another knife. As Tom's left hand closed feebly on his wrist, Villerot's long fingers spun the blade around and angled it toward Tom's face.

Villerot pressed with all his might, driving the blade downwards. Tom's left elbow crashed into the floor, and he fought to keep the arm straight, letting its joints take the force of Villerot's weight. He felt as though the bones of his forearm would be driven through his elbow into the floor.

The rasping voice spoke, the man's breath hot on Tom's face. "At least...I will kill you before I die."

Villerot twisted to the left, directing his force in a new direction and before Tom could compensate, his arm was bent over, doubling back on itself. In seconds the knife, inches above his eye, would plunge home. Blue light flashed coldly on the blade.

A memory echoed in Tom's mind. He released his right hand from Villerot's wrist and grasped desperately for his shirt pocket. His enemy, losing the support of Tom's hand, caught himself with his free hand on the floor. Tom's scrabbling fingers caught the plunger of the empty needle and jerked the syringe from his pocket.

Villerot saw it coming and started to get his hand over to block, too late. Tom rammed the long point into the man's forearm. Villerot gasped and his knife halted against Tom's eyelid. Tom let go of the syringe and drove his palm with all the force he could muster into Villerot's jaw. His fingers clawed at the red eyeballs.

The man's head lifted. Tom folded his fingertips and jabbed his middle knuckles into the exposed throat. There was a rasping gurgle deep in the recesses of Villerot's mouth. The man drew back slightly and Tom didn't wait. He raised his knee and jerked his foot up hard, feeling it ram into the flesh of Villerot's lower abdomen.

The pressure on Tom's left arm eased. Tom struck his palm against the man's nose, reached over, and twisted Villerot's knife-hand around. He found the little finger and pried it away from the hilt, snapping the finger backwards with a crack that wrenched a scream from the man. The other fingers opened and the knife dropped. Tom leaned his head to the side and the blade clattered onto the floor next to his ear.

His knee was still up. Tom lifted Villerot's body with his shin, drew his foot back, and delivered a snapping kick to the man's face. Villerot tumbled backward as Tom rolled heavily to his feet, light-headed with exhaustion and rage. He drove forward with a head-butt to the man's stomach. His windmilling arms sent blow after slamming blow into the man's torso until Villerot crashed, reeling, against the banister.

Tom drew himself to full height as a succession of images whirled through his consciousness. He saw again the cloud from the rock fall, black against the clear blue sky. He saw the little compact car spinning over the edge of the Going-to-the-Sun Road, and the tangled bus exploding, catching Katherine in its blast. He saw the reddened heap of blankets enshrouding the corpse that had once been his best friend. And he saw Katherine, in bandages, her fair head resting motionless against the station wagon's steering wheel. Perhaps it lay there still.

Tom's fist clenched as his right arm dropped, and Villerot's eyes widened in realization of impending doom. Tom's fist shot out in a powerhouse uppercut, catching Villerot squarely on the chin. The crack of the man's jaw and Tom's knuckles was simultaneous, and Villerot flew up and back. He slammed against the wooden railing and jackknifed over it, plummeting down as a final terrified scream escaped his lips. Members of the orchestra scrambled frantically out of the way as the spinning body crashed through the cover of the grand piano with a jangling crack of splintered wood, twisted metal, and snapping strings that echoed back and forth in the cavernous atrium as the shattered hulk slammed to the floor.

Tom's mind seemed to close in on him as he watched the man's descent. The surroundings began to fade. He heard his heartbeat in his ears, loud and distinct. For the first time in an eternity, there was nothing left to be done, and he slumped against the railing, totally spent. His body felt as if it was dissolving into little particles of static and shooting away into space.

He sighed. Everything focused, then blurred again, a blur that deepened from white to gray as the labored breaths grated through his lips, and then, as consciousness departed, from gray to black.

His body slipped off the railing, dropped to the floor, and lay still.

The crowd parted and a man in a black suit stepped through. He looked down at the supine body with the crimson pool spreading beneath its left arm, raised his sleeve to his mouth, and spoke into his transmitter in strained, even tones.

In the lobby below, the president pushed through the ring of men shielding him, looking with sober eyes at the hunched and broken body of the old man at his feet. He took in the crushed mass of wood, metal, flesh and blood where the piano had stood, and looked up at the little throng forming behind the agent on the second level. He saw the crowd of onlookers around the lobby, all seeming to sense with him that the crisis was past; men, women, and children looking about uncertainly with faces pale and dazed. Ten yards away, the plain-clothed man he had seen flash a ranger's badge was moving toward him, peering at the camera cradled in his hands with a strange expression of understanding.

The last strains of the shattered piano's nerve-rending cacophony, the only sounds to be heard now throughout the hushed vastness of the lodge, diminished, and at last were silent.

CHAPTER
18

The mists were back, kaleidoscopic swirls of black and deeper black that formed and unformed in surreal patterns, holding him suspended everywhere and nowhere in their ethereal grip. Were they moving, or was he?

The black vagueness formed images. Things he knew, things from his life. They seemed far away, unreal.

The house he grew up in. A plain house in a plain neighborhood. The number on the door, 8092. A little wooden crib, seen from inside. Little dinosaurs dangling above, and there, on the side, where he had once scrawled his name, Tom, with a black crayon.

A school. Preschool. Wooden desks full of crumpled homework papers and pencils that stained the hand when sharpened. He smelled the shavings.

His parents. Dad's arm around Mom's shoulders. Was she crying? No. She looked up and she was smiling.

Rivers and trees. Nighttime in the woods they had camped in every summer. A million stars shimmering in a sky a million miles high.

Numbers. Letters. A big school—the images shifted, faster, swirling in and out of the haze. Men; women—people he'd known. Distant cousins seen once a year across a room full of relatives. Best friends come and gone. Places he'd been.

The train. The mountains. Percy. Nick.

Katherine.

Now he was moving, sliding through molasses. His body was empty, without mass, rolling.

Where was Katherine?

Through the shrouds he saw the dark line of the cliff and beyond that, dropping away, the black void. It was pulling him. Relax, it called. Drift over. You've earned it.

Over the edge the images and patterns would be gone, and, at long last, he could rest.

But she was nearby. He knew, though he did not know how he knew. Somewhere through the mists, she too was riding near the edge of the cliff, but she had not gone over, and he tried to call out to her. He strained but there was no sound at all.

Katherine.

He fought. Trying desperately to move, to penetrate the mists. Trying to stop his downward slide. Through the swirling haze, he saw a dim patch of light. Straining, struggling, anything to move—but there was nothing to get hold of, nothing to push off from. And yet, the gloom was fading, the light brightening....

Tom Connor opened his eyes. Everything was black. He tried to sit up, and a dozen places in his body signaled angry protest. He relaxed and the shooting pains subsided into a dull throb all over.

Turning his head gingerly, he saw on his right a bank of dimly glowing lights. He squinted. They were rectangular, with words written on them. One said, *Nurse.*

Tom lifted his arm cautiously. It felt unsteady, but he maneuvered it over and pressed the switch. Then he leaned back and waited.

The woman could not have been far away. In less than thirty seconds, a handle turned, and a crack of light appeared.

It expanded into a bright rectangle with a silhouette in the middle. A switch clicked, and light streamed into Tom's eyes. He clenched them shut.

"Glad to see you're with us again." The nurse bustled into the room with a stride that was all business. "Let's have a look at you."

She leaned down and lifted Tom's right eyelid, peering inside. Repeating the procedure on the left eye, she moved to the equipment by the bed, read several gauges, and wrote something on a clipboard. She smiled. "I think you're here to stay this time."

"This time?" Tom's voice was raspy and weak. His head felt clogged and his throat was dry.

The nurse nodded. "You've been conscious several times over the last few days. Not for long, and you weren't exactly coherent."

"Did you say days?"

"I did."

"Where's Katherine?" Tom asked softly.

The woman's eyes clouded, and she hesitated before saying, "I must tell the doctor you're awake. I'll ask him, he might know."

Tom seethed at the evasion, but said nothing as the woman left the room. He looked over the length of his body, astounded at the number of tubes and wires trailing away from beneath the plain white sheet. His right wrist was wrapped in a plaster cast, and he remembered the snap of his knuckles as his final blow had connected with Villerot's chin.

He nodded in satisfaction. It was worth a broken hand.

Then he sobered. I've killed a man, he thought; I've ended a life—and although he knew that if anyone had deserved to die, it had been Villerot, he knew also that the hollowness he felt inside would take a long time to heal.

He had seen enough death in one week to last a lifetime: the deaths of friends and of enemies. The deaths of people he had not known at all. Lives gone—most of them innocent. How many had been beloved parents? Treasured children? How many had had others depending on them? How many might have accomplished great things, but never would now because of one man so full of hate? Why was it that so many people could not simply live their own lives, possess their own bit of land, and raise their families in peace, allowing others to do the same? How much better could the world be?

The door opened and a man in a white coat with a stethoscope around his neck entered. Behind the man was Steve Hollis. The ranger nodded quietly but said nothing as the doctor walked up and stopped beside the bed.

"You're a very lucky young man," he said, reaching down to take Tom's pulse.

"I know," Tom said.

The doctor counted silently for a moment, then released Tom's wrist. "You lost a great deal of blood," he said. "I'm honestly not sure why you're still alive, but it seems the transfusion was a success." He gestured toward Tom's bandaged hand. "We patched the rest of your body up as best we could, and we've been feeding you intravenously. I was afraid you might leave us—your signs were weak—but it seems you've decided to pull through." He smiled.

"Where's Katherine?" Tom looked at the doctor, who blinked and looked at Hollis.

The ranger nodded, and the doctor turned back. "The girl has also walked a fine line. However..." he scratched his head. "A curious thing. She awoke at almost the same time as you. She is being checked now, as I am checking you."

"May I see her?" Tom asked.

The doctor shook his head. "You're hardly in a condition to be moved, and neither is she. Both of you have just emerged from one week in a near-comatose state. I think we'll keep the two of you under observation for a time, and if you both remain stable, then—we'll see."

"Doctor," Hollis spoke for the first time. "May I have a word with him? You know I've been waiting a long time." There was authority in his voice.

"I don't see why not, but please try not to excite him." The doctor read the screens on the bedside equipment approvingly and walked out of the room. The door clicked shut behind him.

Hollis sat down at the foot of the bed as Tom looked at him uncertainly. The ranger thought for a moment before speaking.

"I'm not sure what to say," Hollis cleared his throat. "I'm sorry, about a lot of things, for one. And, well done, for another."

Tom smiled. "I thought you might arrest me."

"No." The ranger grinned back. "Not this time. I ought to get the doc to implant a homing device, though, in case I need to one day." His face leveled. "Things are resolving fast. I picked the camera off the lobby floor after the dust settled. The government guys packed it off right away, no surprise—but I had a look at it first. Not like any camera I ever saw before, to say the least. Smelled inside of explosive, too.

"Forensics separated what was left of your friend Villerot from the piano, took some samples, got in touch with Interpol, CIA, various foreign agencies, and—to make a long story very short—nobody has any doubts now about who the bad guy was and who should get the Medal of Honor. Again, I'm sorry for doubting you. I hope you can understand that at the time—"

"I understand, sir. I probably wouldn't believe someone who said he'd gone through what I did, either." Tom shook his head. "I wish I could have done something differently, something to save all those lives."

The ranger punched Tom lightly on the side of the leg. "No one could have done better in your place," he said. "Incidentally, if you were worried, the president himself is preparing to issue a pardon on your behalf for any actions that, er, crossed the line—sort of a preemptive strike."

Tom shrugged.

"Actually," Hollis said brightly, "he's hoping you'll come out to Washington to receive it personally. Over lunch."

"Really?" Tom smiled and considered for a moment. "If you talk to him, tell him that I'd be delighted, but before I do, I have to pay a call on Mrs. Norton—Percy's mother. And all I care about right now is—"

"I know," Hollis said. "It looks like she'll make it, Tom. Don't worry."

Tom nodded, and sighed. Hollis said, "What?"

"I hate hospitals."

There was a knock at the door. The ranger stood up. "I'll be around. If there's anything you need, just ask."

Tom said hopefully, "Rip these tubes out of me and pin the doctor to the ground while I run?"

Hollis grinned. "I said anything you *need*. What you need right now is a thorough checkup." He went to the door and opened it, waving the doctor into the room. "All yours, doc."

"Very good." The doctor turned. "All right, my boy. Let's have a look at you."

"Please," Tom begged. "Tell me about Katherine."

The man laid a hand on Tom's shoulder. "She'll be fine. I looked in on her while you spoke with Mr. Hollis. She must remain in the hospital for a time. There is much tissue damage. But...actually, I shouldn't tell you this."

"What?" Frustration edged Tom's voice.

"Her first action was to ask about you," the doctor said. "I suppose it could help the recovery if the two of you were allowed to visit for short periods at a time...we'll see."

"Good," said Tom, but the doctor cut him short.

"Perhaps tomorrow morning, after you've both been examined and observed overnight."

"Tomorrow?" Tom exploded. "But—"

"That's the way it must be," the physician said with finality. "No arguing."

"Aw, doc," said Hollis. "He's strong as a bull ox. It won't kill him to move him from here to room two—"

"Hush," exclaimed the doctor, then, as Tom began to speak, "*No*. For the good of you both. Not another word, that's a medical order—" and he turned to his instruments.

Tom glanced helplessly at Steve Hollis.

The ranger's lips compressed for several seconds, and his lean jaw creased in a mischievous grin. He held up his hand and raised two fingers, then five, then four. He winked once and placed his hat over his sandy hair. "Like I said, Tom, anything you need. Be seeing you."

Hollis turned and ambled through the open door into the corridor, whistling a bright melody. Tom smiled at the retreating notes and sank back onto the bed.

Two interminable and uncomfortable hours passed, and at last the doctor was finished, and the tubes and sensors removed from Tom's body. With a promise that Tom could see Katherine soon, the doctor departed with strict instructions that for the time being he was "not to stray from this room."

"On pain of what?" Tom asked.

The doctor scowled at him. "A multitude of bad language." He shrugged. "I don't know that your influential friends would permit more. In all seriousness, though, lie back and rest. Your body needs it, badly." He closed his bag and departed with a kindly pat to Tom's shoulder.

Tom waited with crossed fingers, and released his breath in an audible sigh of relief when there was no click of a lock sliding home. He threw the sheet to the side, swinging his legs to the floor.

Dull pain racked his body and the room reeled. He grimaced, and stood up more carefully, plucking a robe from the chair next to the bed. Drawing its folds about him, he tied it off and limped to the door.

He stopped, spying his reflection in the rectangular mirror on the wall. He blinked once and leaned toward it. The face that looked back hardly seemed his, though he had trouble distinguishing what was different. He glanced over the line of the jaw. That was the same. There were no wrinkles. The brown hair was unchanged. Everything individually was the same as it had been before, and yet, somehow, he looked older, years older than the last time he had seen himself.

Then he knew: It was the eyes. Not the shape, or the color, but the quality. There was a maturity, and a sadness that was new—as if his father was inside him, looking out.

Tom gazed at the glass for some time, lost in thought. At last he smiled, and turned away.

He pressed his ear to the door. The corridor beyond was quiet. The clock on the wall across from his bed read eleven-nineteen. P.M., he guessed. Twisting the handle gently, he inched the door away from the frame. After a moment's scrutiny, he moved into the deserted hall. The number-plate outside his door read 243. The next down was 241. Tom walked the other way, crossing to the opposite side of the corridor as he went.

Two fifty-four was not far off. Tom stopped outside and listened, wondering whether to knock first. A murmur of voices sounded from one of the connecting corridors. It grew louder, making the decision for him. He turned the handle, slid the door open, and eased into the room. A light was on inside, and a soft chuckle touched his ears.

"That was as sneaky an entrance as I've ever seen. I deduce the doctor told you in no uncertain terms to stay where you were."

Tom moved into the room and smiled down at Katherine in the bed. "Brilliant, Holmes."

"Not at all." The girl tossed her head to the side happily. "They told me the same thing, although with me they don't have to worry. It'll be a while before I feel like standing. I am glad to see you up and around." Her voice softened. "I knew you were still alive, somehow." Her blue eyes looked candidly into Tom's, and suddenly he felt uncomfortable. He walked to the chair next to the bed and lowered his tired body into it.

Bandages still wrapped Katherine's left arm and part of her face, but there were fewer than before. Some of the red skin that had been covered was exposed now, and returning in places to normal color. Much of her hair on that side was blackened and partially cut away, but Tom saw bright golden roots at the bottom. The left side contrasted with her unblemished right half, yet it was not so disturbing to look at as he had expected. In fact, he hardly noticed it.

"Katherine," he said. "I know you only just woke up, but there's something I must tell you."

The girl read the darkness in his eyes. "I know what you're going to say," she said in a thick voice. "Uncle Stam. He knew it was coming. I heard it when he said good-bye at the cabin. He's...." Her reddening eyes turned away.

Tom nodded compassionately. "I know it's no comfort, Katherine, but he went like a hero. He saved the president's life. I'd swear his last conscious thoughts were happy. He knew you were out of harm's way, and that he'd won his own personal victory."

Katherine lowered her head into her hands. "Poor, dear old man. He could have—he didn't have to—oh..." her voice trailed off. Tom laid a hand consolingly on her uninjured shoulder.

After long moments of silence she looked up again, staring bleakly at the far wall. "That's it, then. I'm alone."

"Katherine—" Tom began.

"It's all right," she cut him off. "I'm used to it."

He squeezed her shoulder gently. "Maybe you're not as alone as you think."

The girl smiled dolefully. "Dear Tom, I appreciate that, but you hardly know me. I can be difficult to have around."

Tom waved his hand. "You said yourself that it seemed like years we'd been around each other. I've seen you in situations most people go through a lifetime and never see. I know how you react to the worst of times and, believe me, I think you're one of the rare ones."

Katherine's face was serious. "The doctor was straightforward with me about what to expect as far as recovering from my burns. It's going to be weeks, unpleasant weeks, maybe months before I'm out of here. You're walking now; you'll be out the door and back to your life in a few days. There's probably a hero's welcome waiting for you. And lots of pretty girls to swarm all over you." Tom heard the jealousy in her voice.

"I don't want them," he said. "Katherine, don't be silly. You're saying these things because you think somehow you'll be a burden, and—"

"I *will* be a burden," she said. "Time-wise, you'll be bored out of your mind waiting for me. Financially, I'm going to have bills, lots of bills to pay when I'm out. You think I have money? If you try to help, you'll be in debt forever, too. You have better things to do. School will be starting before long, if nothing else."

"Life seems a little different now than it did before," Tom said. "I know what's important and what isn't. And, I may be having lunch soon with someone who can help with the medical expenses. He'll probably be glad to, all things considered. Look—"

"Tom," Katherine said sharply. "You have an image of me in your mind, as I was. Look at me now. The scars will diminish, the doctor said, but it will take time, and a few lines will remain. He doubts they'll ever be completely gone. I don't want plastic surgery, and I don't intend to spend every day of the rest of my life covering them up with tons of makeup."

"Katherine—"

"Maybe I *was* beautiful, but I won't be again. You should move on, forget about me."

The words, and the pouting mouth, were more than Tom could take. He grasped Katherine's upper arm, leaned in, and kissed her hard on the lips, feeling her stiffen in shock. He expected at any moment a slap clocking ten on the Richter scale, but to his surprise she responded, pressing her mouth lightly against his. As her fingers closed on his forearm, he drew away, smiling, and said, "Will you stop interrupting me?"

Katherine looked at Tom with soft, coy eyes. She shook her finger in halfhearted reproach. "You...."

"Katherine," Tom said, "you're right, you were beautiful before. But you got one thing wrong: You're still beautiful, now. The right side of your face is untouched. The left side, the scars, they will fade until hardly a mark remains."

Katherine started to speak but Tom held up a finger of warning.

"Not this time. You're listening to my minute of philosophy: I may not be the brightest guy in the world, but I know that over time all the physical things we like about each other change—we get older, accidents happen, and so on." He pointed to his heart: "It's what's here, and," indicating his head, "here, that matters. Katherine, you shine in both. You have beautiful intelligence. You have incredible bravery. You know what the important things in life are, and you don't care about the meaningless things. You're a quality girl, a girl in a million, a diamond in a sea of charcoal."

Katherine shook her head, but her blue eyes glowed warmly.

Tom continued, "I have an aunt who lives a half-hour from school. She's all alone, and I know she'd love to take you in. I've only got a year left, and, well—I—" He broke off, and took a deep breath. Katherine was watching intently.

"Despite your protests," Tom said, "I believe that you like me, maybe even love me. And I know deep down that I love you. I realize it hasn't been long, but I also know how it felt when I thought you were gone forever. I'm not sure I could ever come to love anyone else after you."

"But, I don't know—I mean, we shouldn't—"

"I'm not asking you to do anything indecent; my aunt is a sweet old battle-axe. Nobody misbehaves on her watch. And I'm not asking either of us to make up our minds today about the rest of our lives. What I am asking is that you let me help you now, and that you give us the chance to spend some time together in the future."

Placing all the assurance he could muster into his voice, Tom said, "I'm not going anywhere until you're ready to go yourself. And when I do go, you're going with me."

He opened his hand and held it out to the girl, looking deeply, confidently, into her eyes.

For a long moment Katherine was silent, her eyes level, her face unmoving, and Tom wondered as his heart drummed furiously in his chest whether he had miscalculated somehow, had assumed too much and said the wrong thing.

Then the girl's lips broke into a wide smile. A single tear welled in the corner of her right eye, dropping down across her cheek as she stretched her hand across to place it gently, but firmly, into his.

Samuel Kalliman was born in Minneapolis, Minnesota. He holds an engineering degree from the University of Minnesota, and lives with his wife in southeast Michigan where he works for a major automotive firm. He enjoys reading and writing, as well as playing guitar, fencing epee, traveling the world, and much more. This is his first novel.